To Ms. Casini's class,
Thank you for inviting me to speak!

ADELLE YEUNG

Adelle Yeung

THE CYCLE OF THE SIX MOONS

BOOK ONE
THE STARRIEST SUMMER

Indigo Platinum Press

This is a work of fiction. Names, characters, places, events and incidents are products of the author's imagination or used in a fictitious manner and are not to be considered real. Any resemblance to actual events, locales, organizations, or persons, living or dead, is purely coincidental.

ISBN-13: 978-0-692-53988-0
ISBN-10: 0-692-53988-3

Indigo Platinum Press
First Edition October 2015
Second Edition April 2016

Visit Adelle Yeung's website at www.adelleyeung.com

Cover artwork by Brandon Lacey

For Linda McCarty

Contents

Part One
The Starriest World

Part Two
The Creator's Role

Part Three
The Quest for Tyme

Part One
The Starriest World

Chapter One
The Machine

My parents must've always had an inkling that my brother was a genius. Too bad they can't see the "evil" tacked onto the "genius" because they're now laughing their way down Tahitian docks.

"Now that Aaron's home from college," my mom told me, "your dad and I are going off on a trip!"

Yeah, because they're too cheap to take their kids with them. If I had a camera, I would've captured evidence of my brother hauling the electronics into the garage, then I would have proof that geek college turned my brother into a schizoid. If he paid attention to normal people's needs, I wouldn't have to survive off scraps.

My stomach rumbles like the center of an earthquake. I drag my feet downstairs and gaze at the dusty TV stand, where spotless shapes indicate the former resting places of the large flat screen and game consoles. My brother even swiped the DVD player, speakers, and all the lamps. Anything with a plug or battery, small enough to carry or push, he's abducted. Summer vacation is miserable without my video games.

I saved the world twice last week. Then my brother had to pull this crap.

I wobble into the kitchen, then the air conditioning clicks off and the house falls silent. For the thousandth time, I open the fridge door, hoping that it has magically refilled itself, or is growing some edible fungus. Mmm, mushrooms.

The smell of wet cardboard rolls out. Inventory of what might save me from keeling over: a damp, empty carton of eggs, red-tinged slimy lettuce, and enough condiments to stock a sandwich shop. Too bad it's not enough for an actual sandwich.

I look past the counter where the microwave should be, and glare at the door leading to the garage. Crookedly taped there is my brother's handwritten note, bold in red Sharpie: *Hey Michelle, I'm working DON'T BOTHER ME!!! K? Love you!*

My stomach growls again—the only sound in the house. For the first time in two weeks, I can't hear Aaron hammering away on his mad scientist experiment.

Not once has he even offered to drive me downtown in his car that he so affectionately calls Padmé, which now sits idly on the driveway to make room for his mystery science project in the garage. I'm a few months from the legal driving age, and have never put keys into an ignition, so unless I want to kill Padmé and myself, I'll have to disturb my brother's work.

I put my ear to the garage door. The silence chills me. I tap softly with my knuckles. He doesn't answer. Finally, I knock louder.

"Aaron? I know you said not to bother you, but I'm *really* hungry, so could you take me grocery shopping?"

No answer. I bang on the door so hard that it rattles, but still nothing. Is he even in there? I reach for the doorknob—

"Ow!" I scream, stumbling back and swinging my hand far from the zapping doorknob. My fingers continue to burn from the buzz, and I kick at the bottom of the door in frustration. What's he trying to hide from me, anyway? It's not as if moving the electronics was much of a secret.

"Fine! I'm stealing your car!" I wait for him to open the door, but even this threat does nothing.

I take a deep breath and back away to the window-side table, then snatch his keys from an open textbook with equations and insane diagrams that might as well be a recipe for wormholes. I grin at the LEGO Darth Vader keychain dangling from my fingertips. You and I are gonna be buddies, Mr. Skywalker.

My steps feel light as I realize I'm actually going to steal his car. I slip on my sandals, ready for the stifling heat and the oven that is his car. I'll bear the heat, because I'll finally get food!

Just as I reach for the front door, my brother screams. It's a drawn out, dramatic, "No!" Is he doing his Darth Vader impression again? At least he's not too late to save Padmé.

I hear several things clang and screech against the garage floor, and Aaron groans, "Idecia! Idecia!" I don't remember any Idecia from *Star Wars* or *Star Trek*…

He gasps when he storms through the kitchen door, and I scurry to the living room, tossing his keys on the couch before he can notice. I start back upstairs when he comes around the corner.

"Michelle?"

"Oh, hey!" I don't know what else to say. Did he hear me threaten to steal the car? At least he doesn't have his telescoping lightsaber to whack me with. He really needs a shower; his black hair is plastered to his face. In fact, it's been a while since I've even seen his forehead properly. He usually wears a red dealer's visor.

"Michelle!" he says again. He reaches toward me with both hands, like the Frankenstein monster. Uh-oh. Now he's definitely gone mad! I back up into the stair railing.

He leaps at me with a hug. The only time he hugs me is if I make him special spicy ramen with pickled radish, so what does he want this time?

"Yo," I say. "What's up?"

"I missed you!"

"It's not my problem you locked yourself in the garage."

"I'm sorry! I'm so sorry!" He pulls away so he can squash my cheeks and give me fish lips. I'm sure I look ridiculous, but he stares at me with the same look as when he hugs his Chewbacca toy. Then he releases my face and ruffles my hair. "How've you been?"

I flinch and narrow my eyes. He never asks me that. What did his experiment do to his brain this time?

I cross my arms and give him the most obvious answer. "Hungry. Take me grocery shopping."

"Yeah, of course!" He laughs nervously, and I tilt my head in confusion. "I'll get my keys!"

Alarm jolts through me. Before he realizes that his keys aren't where he left them, I say, "How about you go take a shower first? You're all sweaty and gross."

"A shower! A shower sounds amazing!" He leaps onto the stairs beside me and jumps up every other step. "I'll be just five minutes!"

"What happened to your visor?" I call after him as he bounds upstairs.

"Uh—I, uh—be right back!"

I let out a sigh of relief as he disappears into the upstairs hall. Wasting no time, I take his keys and wallet, then place them back on the table. That's when I notice that the door to the garage is ajar. Heat wafts into the air-conditioned kitchen, and I feel a sense of intrigue and danger, as if it's a mad scientist's lab with secrets of the universe.

I hear water running through the pipes into the upstairs bathroom; Aaron's in the middle of his shower, which gives me a few minutes to check out his top-secret, psycho science project. Cautiously looking over my shoulder, I reach for the door—avoiding the handle, which has bare wires taped to the other side—and I step into the blindingly bright garage.

When my eyes focus, I see light reflecting off three dusty old mirrors. All of the lamps from the house encircle a retro orange recliner, making it glow like something otherworldly. A grid sits on top of the garage door tracks, and attached to the grid are small appliances that create a halo over the recliner. Each appliance connects to another by their own cords and extensions; every few seconds, sparks shimmer across the grid.

The PlayStation 2 is attached to the microwave, and coiled around its turntable are the wires of my cell phone and DS charger. They're connected by sparking wires that cross over to my mom's sewing machine, which whirs away next to a buzzing generator. The door to the side yard is ajar to allow some air flow, and a floor fan oscillates over the setup, though it still smells like a gas station and burnt dust.

I stare wide-eyed at the setup. My brother has officially lost it. I shake my head at the order and placement of electronics, but it must mean something to him if he's been working so maniacally.

I wander into the center of the garage, next to the orange recliner. My dad's boombox from the seventies sits beside it, and on top of the metal box is an opened Twix; Aaron had only taken one bite out of a bar.

I suck in a loud, hideous gasp and immediately grab it. I rip off the plastic wrapper and shove the crunchy, semi-melted, chocolaty caramel goodness into my mouth. My stomach rumbles as the partly-chewed pieces descend into my stomach, and then I realize it's all gone before I could savor it. I lick my lips until I can no longer taste chocolate.

I crinkle the wrapper and replace it on the boombox. Twisted wires snake out of the speakers and into a cloth sack on the recliner's seat. I poke it—it must be full of metal BBs. Two souvenir pennies from Fisherman's Wharf are messily sewn onto the sack, about two eyeballs' distance apart. A black PS2 controller hangs from the armrest. I can feel the sugar coursing through my veins, and I become hyper with excitement as I realize what this contraption is.

"What are you doing?!" Aaron shouts from the kitchen door. His black hair drips all over his shoulders and striped tank top, but at least he washed up. Still no visor, though.

Instead of running away because he caught me in his lair, I hold up the PS2 controller. "Is this some kind of virtual reality game?"

"No! It's not a t—"

He freezes; his alarm at my discovering his experiment turns into something deranged. He doesn't seem to be looking at me, but at something far away.

Then he snaps out of it. "Yeah," he says. "I thought I could make you a better game than what you already have." He breaks into a bout of nervous laughter. "It's amazing! The graphics, and magic, and monsters. I think you'll have a lot of fun."

"Cool!"

"I only lasted twenty minutes, but you'll last longer! Maybe you'll even figure out how to end it…"

"End what?"

"The Cy… The game."

"Is it a puzzle game? I don't know if I wanna solve puzzles."

"No, no! It's… You'll see. T-take a seat."

I throw myself into the chair, and a puff of dust surrounds me. I swat it away with one hand and shield my eyes with the other, since the bright mirrors sit directly in front of me. I grab onto the PS2 controller—its shape perfect in my hands—and I dance in my seat, waiting for the mirrors to transform into a screen. Then Aaron takes the controller away from me.

"You won't need that," he says.

"But… Wait, do I actually get to swing around a sword?"

"Well, no. I mean, yes! Well, it depends. Do you really want to use a sword? 'Cause you can live a peaceful life—that's important. You don't always need a sword. You don't always need to fight. You don't have to get hurt. Should I even? But, yes…" He sighs, then shakes his head violently. "Aren't you hungry? Let's go get some food. Food's important. I can't let you die…from starvation."

"Dude, chill out! I was probably dying more of boredom than hunger." And I ate the rest of your Twix, so that'll keep me from dying for a little longer.

I bounce with excitement. "I can play for, like, twenty minutes, then I'll be ready for a big pig out session! Sushi, and Ben and Jerry's, and cake!"

"Someone will probably feed you before you're done."

"*You* will feed me, Aaron. So hurry up and start the game already!"

He groans uncertainly at himself. I crank the chair into a reclining position, and he hands me the sack of BBs. "Lie back and make sure the copper sits on top of your eyelids," he says.

I let out a mischievous giggle, anticipating the addicting world of gameplay ahead of me. I wiggle back into a reclining position and hold onto the sack while Aaron tweaks the radio. He sees my playful grin, watching me with concern before the lights flood the garage with white. That's when I place the sack over my eyes. The souvenir pennies are warm against my eyelids, and the heavy BBs mold to my face and block out the brightness. The heat from the lights and the air from the fan make me feel like I'm on a breezy beach. Better than a junky garage. Soon, I'll probably be somewhere even better than a breezy beach.

I hear the soft clicking of buttons on the boombox and PS2 controller. In unison, all of the electronics whir.

"Whatever you do, make sure the king doesn't reach the other worlds," Aaron mutters.

"*What?*" Is this some kinda chess game?

I hear him stumble over something and continue, "I hope I'm doing the right thing." He gasps. "No time to waste! Gotta do it now—can't regret this!"

"Aaron?"

"I love you, Michelle."

Now might be the time to panic.

He says, "Departing at 11:58 AM."

There's a strange feeling in my chest, as if my insides are emitting as much light as the lamps, and then—

Nothing.

Chapter Two
The Creator's Return

I don't think I've ever felt anything like this—not for so long, anyway. It's almost like that fleeting feeling right before falling asleep. I'm floating, relaxed, and I can't perceive anything but my own thoughts. I can't feel my body…if I even still have a body.

It's at this moment, when I'm lying in bed, that I wake up again and realize that I was just about to fall asleep, but this time I don't wake up. I don't know if I'm still alive.

Am I…dead?

Did Aaron just kill me?!

He might have, with his crazy experiment. I should've known that it wasn't safe! He came out of it even crazier than he was before, and it must've electrocuted me.

The phantom sensation of a heartbeat pounds at the core of what should be my chest, and a racing stream of something cool and relieving fills in the same area. Does this mean I still have a body? I hear a sharp gasp—at least I still have some working senses. I reach for my face, my fingers trembling. Before I can touch my cheeks, a gust blows past me, and flashes of scenery shoot by in my peripheral vision—white mountains, green fields, a red temple, a golden canyon... Something bubbles in my stomach, telling me that these are places I've visited before, even though I know I've never left California in my life. For a second, I can see my hands in front of me, and then the images are gone. What was that?

I can feel myself moving now. I'm floating, as if in outer space. I look around for the flash of light that just passed, but I can't see anything in the darkness.

On the bare skin of my upper back, I finally feel warmth. I spin around and there, not too far away from me, is a soft orb of pure white light. It glimmers with prismatic rays, which stretch out and soon blind me. I shield my eyes with my forearm, and clench my eyes shut.

Then I hear a voice. It's not coming from any particular direction—it sounds as if it connects directly to my mind. When the light fades, I see who the voice belongs to, and she's as beautiful as the light that surrounds her.

Just like me, she floats in nothing, but she's a lot more composed. Her hair is almost as black as the space that surrounds us, and it drifts in soft, shiny curls behind her, like wisps of smoke. Her white clothes are as radiant, and when she moves, they flutter like wings in slow motion. Wait, they actually are wings! I never gave much thought to the angels depicted in religious artwork, but she's the epitome of what I think an angel should look like. Her pale skin glows like moonlight, and her eyes twinkle with wisdom.

My small voice resounds, "You're here to take me to the afterlife, aren't you?"

I think she answers, but I can't understand a word that she says. I curl into a ball and turn away from her.

Am I dead, or is this the video game's epic introduction? Even with the warmth of her light, I find myself shivering. It literally chills me how real the sensation is. I feel even more helpless without anything to stand on.

I feel another blast of air, like the wind that passed me when I saw the flashing scenery. Whatever it is, something has changed, because now—

"Perhaps this will help you understand," says the angel.

I lift my head and look at her. She has large, golden eyes, and she looks at me with a certain expression. Is it sadness? Disappointment? Fear, even?

"Even if you are the Creator of the universes," she says, "you no longer have the privilege to manipulate the Cycle as you wish."

"Huh?"

She sighs. "Why have you returned?"

"Just tell me this, okay? I *am* playing a video game, right? Or did that machine really kill me?"

"Neither. The Cycle is not something you should take lightly, nor is it something you should toy with."

The bright light that once was the core of her being fades, and I'm not even sure if she's solid anymore. Our surroundings brighten, and she notices, because I hear more urgency in her voice.

"When all of this is over, you must destroy the device that brought you here. Meddling with the Cycle like this can throw it out of balance."

I feel the ends of my hair brush the base of my neck. I wave my arms in circles, the same way I'd try to regain balance if I stood on a beam.

"So what do I do?" I yell at her, reaching toward her, hoping that I can grasp her hand, or even her clothes or hair. The wind rushes into my ears, and she's disappearing into the midday sky.

"Live as Goddess." With the last echo of her whisper, she vanishes into the sky and takes with her all the surrounding nothingness.

Without anything to support me, I scream and flail my arms, reaching for the sky or the angel or something, anything to help me!

I can't twist around to see what's below me. I don't know if I'll crash into concrete, a glass building, or even an electric fence. All I see is the sky above me, and the wind is so deafening I can't hear my own shrieks.

With a back-breaking clap, I splash into water. At least I'm not dead yet, but I can't move at all! Electrocution, skydiving, now drowning? My brother's invention must really want to kill me!

My muscles tense up, wringing my lungs, and I choke out my last bubble of air, and desperately try to reach for the surface. I can see the sun shimmering in the sky, and a shadow on the surface of the water. I still can't move. Even if I could, I don't know if my feeble swimming skills could save me now.

The shadow darkens. This water is so warm, like a bath. So relaxing. I feel myself sinking deeper into the water. Yes. Darkness. Sleep.

A school of colorful fish spiral around me, and I find myself with sudden energy. I reach upward and kick my legs, and I'm certain that I'll make it to the surface—then as if the water itself is a net, it hurls me upward.

Moments later, I find myself lying on something solid. I spit out water and gasp for air, flicking away the fish flapping against me. Someone pats my back.

"Are you all right, Miss?"

He puts his hand on my shoulder, and I cough so hard I nearly retch. At least I can save this guy from cleaning up after me.

I think I'm okay. My lungs feel like they've been washed and wrung up to dry, but at least I can breathe. The warm air tastes both sweet and salty.

I glance upward but I don't get a full look at the man—I just see that he's wearing a lightweight but elaborate white cloak.

"Thanks buddy," I cough.

"I rowed over as soon as I could, but I feared I came too late. It seems that the fish have saved you, though." He chuckles and pulls one of them off my lap. "That was quite a fall you had there."

I cough again. "Yeah." I sweep aside the fish behind me so I won't squish them when I sit, then lean against the boat. The wood looks like it's melted onto itself, after years of maybe hundreds of people sitting and rowing for hours beneath this tropical sun. That's a nice touch.

Then I look at him.

I'm not the kind of person who would normally use the word "handsome," but I don't know how else I could describe him in a single word. "Attractive" seems inadequate, and "sexy" sounds too slutty for someone of his demeanor. He's about ten years older than me, and he has such a warm, welcoming smile that I can't help but smile back. His long dark hair is braided and drapes over one shoulder. His majestic clothes are still wet from when he pulled me out of the water.

"Oh, pardon me!" he says with a slight laugh. "Allow me to dry you."

But he doesn't have any towels. I'm about to tell him that it's okay, I'll just dry in the sun, but he raises his hands. With one graceful sweep, water droplets shoot from my body and then surround the flopping fish in a floating sphere, like iron dust sticking to a magnet. The fish calm down at once and swim happily around themselves. I look back at the man, but he's not holding any magnets or magic wands. The fluid movement of his fingers manipulates the water. It's magical.

That's right—I'm in a video game! This guy must be a water mage or something. He's wearing a blue vest, but nothing else could classify him with that rank, like blue hair, eyes, or skin.

Now that I'm in no immediate danger of dying, I think about my brother's invention and smile. He really is a genius after all. The graphics are flawless, the characters are gorgeous (from what I've seen with the angel and the water mage, anyway), and everything I had experienced since entering this game world was frighteningly realistic. Even though I know it will hurt a lot, I can't wait to get my hands on a weapon and start fighting!

"Excuse me, Miss?"

I jump and look back at him.

"Sorry, but I was wondering, where is your home? Would you like me to see you back?"

"Oh heck no! I just started playing—I can't go back yet."

Though he looks confused, he smiles. I guess he's not programmed to acknowledge that it's a game. He says, "I do need to return to Lereli and deliver these rush fish to the villagers. Would you like to accompany me, and perhaps then I can help you home?"

"I really don't want to go home at all, but sure, take me with you!"

"All right, then. To Lereli." He reaches over the side of the boat and stirs up the water to propel us forward. At first I'm afraid that the sphere of fish will fall off the side, but it stays in place.

"By the way, Miss, if you need to address me, my name is Gediyon."

Gediyon? Sounds like a name fitting enough for a game setting as beautiful as this.

"I'm Michelle," I tell him.

My first few moments in the game, and already I have my first party member! And he's a water mage, of all things. It's a good thing, because without Gediyon, I probably would've had a game over as soon as I landed.

I sit at the front of the boat near the colorful water sphere, containing what Gediyon called "rush fish." The water beneath us is so transparent that I can clearly see white sand yards below, but the water is tinged purple instead of green. Every now and then, flamboyant fish swim below, and sometimes we pass over bright coral. The colors ripple like a Van Gogh painting. I'm not sure what my parents are doing on their vacation now, but I think riding along in a boat with a handsome mage beats it.

The sea stretches to the hazy horizon all around, except straight ahead. Soft green mountains tower in the far distance, but before them are docks and a shadowy village. I hope that they're even more exotic than Tahiti, so I can one-up my parents. Even if the village isn't real, I can at least experience it as if it is.

I eventually hide under the sphere of water to shield myself from the sun. Gediyon offers me his white cloak for protection, but since I'm a lot tanner than he is, I refuse.

Sometime later, he asks, "Forgive me if I'm prying, but from where did you fall?"

"Gee, I dunno, space? There was an angel talking to me up there. She had a crazy amount of black hair."

"Goddess Saei?"

"She has a name?"

Gediyon laughs a little. "You've spoken with Her Serene Divinity Goddess Saei?"

"I guess? Doesn't everyone who plays this game?" I groan and stretch back, my view of the sky distorted through the water orb. "I guess that explains why she knew a lot, if she's like a goddess or whatever. And you don't know 'cause you're just my ally, right?"

"Michelle, could you be… Might you possibly…"

"Huh?"

He isn't even looking at me anymore. He's gazing at the sky from where I fell. "But how would that even be possible?"

While he's pondering, my stomach grumbles loudly. The satisfaction of my brother's Twix has diminished. I let out a long sigh and stare at the water sphere above me. I'm tempted to pull out one of the fish and bite its head off—talk about fresh sashimi—but Gediyon reaches for me with a fruit in his hands. Even inches from my face, its sweet smell is almost overwhelming. Its smooth skin is yellow near the stem, and darkens to purple.

I sit up and take it, curiously looking at Gediyon who smiles back at me. "I hope this will help. The rush fish are toxic unless properly prepared."

I give him a small smile and let out a tiny, "Thanks," then bring the fruit to my lips. If I die in this game, I want it to be in battle, not because of some stupid mistake, like eating poisonous fish because I'm so hungry. My teeth sink into the flesh of the fruit and I take a full, juicy bite. Sticky juice runs down my chin, and the meat bursts flavor into my mouth. I already feel some of the fibers getting stuck in my teeth as I chew. Whatever it is, it has the texture of mango, and tastes like plum and a hint of lemon.

"This food is godly!"

After a few bites, my hunger subsides.

"It's a pitrom," Gediyon says, probably sensing that I've never tasted anything like it before.

When I'm done eating, Gediyon takes the pit—which is about half the mass of the whole fruit—and places it into a leather pouch at his side. I wash my sticky hands in the sea water.

"Thank you *so* much!" I sigh with relief.

"You're very welcome," he says. "I do have more if you're still hungry."

I don't want to take all of his rations at once, so I'll ask again in a few more minutes.

Gediyon must think I'm an alien or something, because he's looking at me funny. He still smiles ever so slightly, but one of his eyebrows is a bit raised. The sunlight catches his irises, like a gem, and that's when I gasp and leap toward him, brushing the top of my head into the sphere. Water splashes over my hair, but the fish are still intact.

"Gediyon, your eyes are red!"

"Yes, Michelle. Yes they are." For a second, I think he frowns, but he covers it up quickly with that smile of his.

I crawl closer for a better look at his eyes. "Omigod, that's so cool! And they're real, too!"

I'm pretty sure he feels dead uncomfortable with me smiling in his face like this. His eyes are deep, blood red, and the light brightens his irises. They would be opaque if they were contacts. Out of direct sunlight, I could mistake them as brown.

"Geez, if you have eyes like these, I wonder what everyone else looks like."

He turns away bashfully. "Well, I'm glad you like them."

For the next few minutes, I sit on the other side of the boat, holding my knees close to my chest and rocking back and forth. At some point, I hope he can show me something else awesome, but he doesn't seem like the type of person—I mean, character to just show off.

I open my mouth to say something, but then a small black figure appears over the boat and I scream instead.

"Madam Manasa!" Gediyon exclaims, pulling his hand out of the water and allowing the boat to slow.

I look again and see that the black figure is actually a short woman wearing a dark, ornate, velvet robe. She hides her face well under her gray hair, but I can see that she has wrinkly cinnamon-colored skin and a nose the size of a slice of cake…and I'm definitely still hungry.

"How are you this afternoon?"

"I'm fine, Gediyon, thank you," she croaks. She swoops down on me, and I find myself pressed against the floor of the boat. Part of the woman's arm is inside the water sphere, and her sleeve drips. The water splatters beside my leg.

"It's *this* young lady I wanted to have a word with," she continues.

"M-me?"

"Yes, young Goddess, you!"

I hear Gediyon gasp, "So you *are*…!"

"Why have you returned?" the woman shrieks, inching closer to my face. Her breath smells like curry. "Starrs is not ready for your soul. You should have stayed in Tyme!"

"What are you talking about?" I start.

"She came from Tyme?" Gediyon asks.

She twirls around, and I can breathe. She says, "Yes, boy, and she should have stayed there."

"What about time?" I say. "I'm just playing a game!"

"No! No you are not! Starrs is as real as your '*Earth*,' and the Cycle is not a toy at your mercy. Your brother shouldn't have created that machine of his. He *knew* he'd be playing with the universe!"

I gape at her. "I… I don't understand."

"Of course you don't!" she spits. "The Creator should only enter Starrs when she is *born* here. She's raised and taught the ways of the Cycle. It's a lifestyle. A fifteen-year-old can't hope to learn how to be Goddess in six months. All because you and your brother wanted to play a game, you've awakened the dormant Cycle of the Six Moons, and all the universes are doomed."

She twists herself like thread on a spindle, then vanishes into nothing.

I'm not sure what she said, but I still want to believe that this is a video game.

"What was she talking about?" I ask Gediyon. When I look at him, he's bowing on one knee.

"You are the Goddess of Starrs after all! I should have known from simply looking at you. Please forgive me for my ignorance."

I shake my head. "I'm not a goddess. Don't bow to me like that. Please."

"But Goddess Michelle, I must—"

"No! No 'Goddess,' okay? Just Michelle. I'm nothing special." This is only a video game. I'm just the player.

Gediyon lifts his head. "If that's what you wish, then I shall address you as only Michelle, though I can't help but feel awfully—"

"No, no, no! None of this 'as you wish' crap. You don't need to be that formal to me." I'm not Goddess of any place, even in a video game.

"Very well." He sweeps his hand back into the water and propels the boat forward.

I look ahead at the village. It's not too far now. Funny, before I didn't notice the thick purple fog surrounding it.

Whatever this village has in store for me, it's my first task. As the player of this game, I will triumph over all obstacles.

Chapter Three
Ticking Toward Paralysis

Video games usually start out cheerful. You have an ordinary boy living a boring life on a sweet little island or in a cute fairy forest, when destiny calls and whisks him away on an adventure of a lifetime.

I guess this is the kind of game where I'm thrown into the frying pan from the start, which sucks because I was really looking forward to a stroll down Tahitian docks. I knew the peaceful boat ride with Gediyon was too good to be true…

As the boat approaches the village, the thick fog blocks out sunlight until it's as dark as night. A cool breeze swirls through the mist. Blazing torches illuminate the wooden docks, and I'm not even sure if they're grounded to anything. The docks and lower level huts must float directly on the surface. The boat ripples the water, and the docks make a hollow *clunk* against their posts. Above, the higher huts hang from the trunks and branches of massive trees that grow straight from the sea, and narrow walkways connect one tree to another.

"This place would be awesome if it were sunny," I mutter.

I look back at Gediyon. Apparently, the fog is affecting him too—his smile has faded. He pulls into a swaying dock, where the other boats are tied, and anchors his own.

"So, what happened here?" I ask.

"The dam has breached," Gediyon tells me, "contaminating the Crystal Lagoon with the toxins of the Tainted Sea. Even the purified drinking water has become poisonous."

"Is it deadly?"

"It can be, yes, but the effects are gradual. When enough poison has accumulated in the body, it renders a person immobile." He gestures toward the water sphere. "Normally, it's illegal to capture these fish, but I've permission from King Oresonn himself to cook these for the villagers." He smiles at me. "It's great luck that you had attracted them when you fell into the water. I might not have found them otherwise. When properly prepared, they produce an adrenaline rush that is otherwise fatal, but for these people, that's just what they need to recover. This fish can't sustain them for long, though, and that's why we must also repair the dam."

"So *that's* what I'm here for!"

"Everyone will appreciate it if you could do that for us, Michelle, but we should probably consult the mayor beforehand."

He manages to stand up without rocking the boat. I couldn't tell when he was sitting down, but he is *really* tall. Not like a professional basketball player, but still over six feet.

He steps onto the dock, then reaches toward me to help me out. I take his hands and—geez, how could anybody have hands that are so strong and gentle at the same time?

With a flick of his hand, the water sphere rises out of the boat and follows us down the dock. Looking around, I can't help but feel that something will jump out of the water and attack me, and I don't even have a weapon yet. At least Gediyon is with me; I walk closer beside him.

In the labyrinth of floating walkways around the corner, I catch the first glimpse of the villagers. They're more like statues, frozen mid-action, with a leg in front of another or an arm passing a basket from the left to right. Though their bodies are motionless, the wind flows through their hair and loose, colorful garments. They're like something from Medusa's art gallery, and I don't want to walk too close in case they jump to life, latch onto my neck and suck my life from behind.

Gediyon, however, walks right up to a particularly droopy living statue and says, "We've brought the rush fish. Hang in there. You'll be back to normal very soon." He waves his hand and says, "This way, Michelle."

"So this is what the poison did to them? They're not like zombified are they?"

He simply answers, "Yes," then adds, "I must hurry and cook this fish stew before their respiratory systems fail as well."

I giggle out of nerves when I pass one of the statues. I hope the same doesn't happen to me.

As he leads me into the heart of the village, more people come into view. Not all of them move as slow as the statues we had passed. Some of them only look like they're in slow motion, and others look normal. I see other men dressed similarly to Gediyon who also have water magic. Water forms at their fingertips, and they pass the fresh water around the villagers to drink. I smile when I see children thank the mages with hugs.

"*That* stuff is safe to drink, right?" I ask him.

"Fortunately, yes, otherwise the entire village would have succumbed to the poison."

He finally stops at the largest and probably most well-lit hut in the village. The main building is round and circular, built into a tree trunk that extends higher. Bird calls echo high in the treetops. Several windows, glowing orange with candlelight, are carved into the trunk, and fluttering from them are beautifully designed silk sheets. Pearly seashells frame the open doorway.

Inside, someone plays an instrument that looks like a lute. Everyone in here reclines on woven mats or snores against the curved walls. At least they aren't statues, though. The burning candles smell like sandalwood, but from somewhere else flows the scent of something delicious, like my mom's cooking before she became too lazy to cook from scratch. Whatever it is makes my mouth water and I'm almost afraid that I'll drool onto one of the sleeping villagers.

Gediyon starts inside. The villagers who are still awake reach for him and for a moment, he takes their hands and squeezes them, then gives them a smile for reassurance.

"Mayor Rayel!" Gediyon calls. "I've brought the fish, and a special guest."

From the other side of the hut walks a short, balding man of about sixty or so. He wears a blue, red, and orange square cap on top of his shiny head, tinted glasses, and a brown apron over his clothes, which resemble the other villagers'. He holds a spatula that appears to be carved out of a shell.

"Thank Goddess that you're back so early!" the mayor says. He greets Gediyon with a hug. "I've already chopped the vegetables for you, and the broth is in the pot. Thank you so much!"

"Thank *you*, Mayor. I'll begin right away." Gediyon pats the mayor on his shoulder, and leads the sphere of water around the hut into what I think is the kitchen. Poor fishies.

I follow him, when the mayor sees me and gasps, "Goddess?"

Gediyon peeks his head into view. "Er, Mayor, sir—"

"How do you even know that I'm this 'Goddess' of yours?" I ask.

"You look just like her!"

"Who, this angel chick of yours? I don't think so."

"She came from Tyme," Gediyon says. "I think she's here to help us."

The mayor looks at me sternly. "You shouldn't be here. We were born in a dormant Cycle."

"Whoa, whoa! Even if I am this *Goddess* of this game world of yours, you should probably be a bit more welcoming. I mean, three people so far tell me that I shouldn't be here. That's not much…*incentive* for me to be a good role model."

"We were supposed to live a peaceful Cycle," the mayor murmurs.

"Mayor, please. This must be a good omen. Michelle is Goddess, after all!"

When Gediyon says it like that, it makes me want to shut up and accept my video game rank. How bad can it be? The Goddess rank is probably higher than anything else.

The mayor sighs. "If only you understood, Gediyon." He looks at me, first shaking his head, then nodding with what I hope is some approval. "Then there's nothing we can do but welcome you back, Miss Goddess." With both of his hands, he reaches toward my arms and caresses them. I'm not sure if I would feel more awkward if he gave me a hug.

"Michelle. My name's Michelle."

"Goddess Michelle, then."

"Just Michelle." God, I hope I don't have to do this with everyone I meet.

He nods. "Well I'm afraid I'm not the most enlightened when it comes to the teachings of the Cycle. I presume you've mastered your abilities on Tyme?"

I see Gediyon smile and pull back into the kitchen.

"I have abilities? Are they cooler than Gediyon's?"

The mayor furrows his eyebrows, then smiles and shakes his head. He chuckles as he says, "Will I be the first to mentor Goddess in this lifetime? But I'm a disgrace!" He laughs.

I squint at him. "Can't Gediyon teach me?"

"I'd love to, Michelle, but—"

"He has a delicious meal to prepare, and he doesn't know the first thing about being Goddess."

And the mayor does? He pulls me away from the kitchen toward one of the mats.

"Hopes, dreams, imagination," the mayor says. "These lie in the heart of our Creator. Miss Goddess, you have the power of creation and destruction—the ability to manipulate Starrs at your own will. You would have so much more power, even over the Cycle itself, if Goddess Saei hadn't given up her immortality to become human."

"So, wait, *do* I have awesome magic powers like Gediyon? Can I even heal people?"

He looks toward the ceiling, and I think he's holding back another sigh. "She really is from Tyme, then? Why are we blessed with an incompetent Goddess in an awakened Cycle?"

Geez, I can hear you, old man. I guess this means I'm *not* as cool as Gediyon.

"In the past, when our Goddess was reborn, she was found and trained from a young age to help the people of Starrs. She could..." He takes what seems to be a painful moment, then splutters, "Fix things." Did he just dumb down his history lesson for me?

"And you want me to fix this dam of yours. All right. I've got it. Let me at it."

"Not so fast, Miss Goddess." It's *Michelle*! "You see, this dam is currently under tide. Only at midnight does the whirlpool open, granting you a safe path to the broken dam. But you are not prepared in your current condition. You see, this whirlpool lasts for only about twenty minutes, and if you do not have the proper skills to repair the dam in time, the water will rush in and not only destroy any attempted repairs, but also blast you full on with the Tainted Sea's toxin." He looks aside. "This single blast has even killed some of our best craftsmen in an instant."

I gulp.

"But we are running out of time. The rush fish stew will only help us for so long, and we can't depend on the Arriscyleans to provide us with fresh water forever. If we continue to let the toxin leak into our lagoon, the fish and coral will die. Not to mention, we may not survive very long, either."

"Then let me do this already!"

"I don't know if eleven hours is enough to teach you the necessary skills."

"I don't care, teach me! I'll learn."

He shrugs, nods, then reaches into his apron pockets. He pulls out two shells, made of similar material as the spatula. "Then use your imagination to repair this spoon as it was before." He hands the shells to me.

This was a *spoon*? I can see where it snapped in the middle of the handle, and it would probably be easy enough to glue back together—if I had any glue. Glue wouldn't make it flawless, though.

Oh yeah, sure, fixing this shell is gonna be a piece of cake—maybe if I actually paid attention in biology! How am I supposed to know how shells are made?

I look at the pieces from all angles and pretend I know what I'm doing. The mayor watches me with an amused, raised eyebrow. I'll teach you to be amused, old man.

I press the pieces together where they broke, and they align well, but they don't stick together. Actually, if I look closely, a tiny triangular fragment has broken off. If only I can find that tiny shard and smooth it over somehow.

Why can't this be easier like in normal video games? Why can't I have a tutorial that I can follow at a slow pace? Mr. Video Game Designer *badly* needs to rethink this part of the game.

How the heck are shells made?! I never thought they would annoy me so much.

I pull the two pieces apart again. Still not sticking.

Okay, tiny shard! Fly over to me right now, wherever you are, and stick into this freaking socket! Come on, fix already!

"Fix yerself, ya goddamn piece of crap!"

The mayor grumbles. I hope that my harsh words has granted me powers, but when I loosen my grip on the pieces, they fall apart again. Frustration beads as sweat on the tip of my nose. Losing my cool isn't doing me any good.

I take a deep breath and close my eyes. If I want to be a Goddess, I have to act like one—serene, poised, and wise.

Somewhere in this building has to be that tiny, triangular shard—the missing piece to this puzzle. Behind my closed eyelids, I imagine that the pieces in my hand glow and, like a powerful magnet, attract the missing piece from its hiding place. The key piece shines like a beacon in my mind—it's lodged between the floorboards in the kitchen. In an instant, I feel something whiz by.

With a clap of the mayor's hands, I open my eyes as if waking from a trance. "There you go."

The spoon! Just as I imagined, it's one piece again.

I gasp. "I did it!" I spring to my feet and skip to the kitchen, waving around the spoon. "Gediyon, I did it!"

Fire is coming out of the palm of his hand.

"Gediyon! You can firebend, too?!"

The mayor claps. "Well done, Miss Goddess!"

"Am I ready to fix the dam yet?"

"Not quite. The whirlpool opens at midnight, remember? I suggest you familiarize yourself with this ability, and tonight we can decide if you're ready."

"Fine, fine. Can I help Gediyon then?"

"Gediyon is a distraction."

Gediyon drops diced fish into a frying pan and laughs. "Am I, Mayor?"

"Why, if I was a young lady myself, I would let you distract me in a heartbeat."

Did the mayor just hit on Gediyon?

He chuckles, then puts a hand on my back. "Come, Miss Goddess, let's see to the villagers."

CHAPTER FOUR
A GAME OVER PLEA

I spend four hours with Mayor Rayel, stopping at every corner to fix something. I'm eager for as much practice as possible, until he asks me to grow a shell into the size of a car, then I know he's just amusing himself. He probably never knew that he'd live to see Goddess's return and wants to live his childhood fantasies. The walk pays off, though, because I learn to manipulate and fix objects a little faster.

A few times, we stop inside the huts, where he introduces me to the villagers. They're also shocked to see their Creator has returned, but they don't reprimand me like the others. They welcome me with hugs and even kisses on my cheek, which I think is sweet, until they smother me. Some of them are like sloths climbing down a tree when they release me from their hugs.

Well, I'm glad that not everyone thinks of my return as a bad omen or whatever.

I stop to chat with the other water mages, who give me the purest, most tasteless water I've ever dribbled down my chin. They tell me they're soldiers from the kingdom Arriscyal, where natives are born with mastery over a single element.

"Single?" I ask. "So how come Gediyon can control water and shoot fire out of his hands?"

One soldier responds, "We don't quite know ourselves, but Sir Gediyon has always been special."

Wow, Gediyon is even a "Sir"? Fancy. I want to personally ask him more about himself, but by the time Mayor Rayel finishes parading me around from hut to hut, Gediyon's done with the stew and has left to feed the villagers. Mayor Rayel won't let me go, saying, "You'll be a distraction to him, Miss Goddess."

He gives me a basket of food, and I exile myself to pig out at the top of Mayor Rayel's hut, high over sea level. I dig into the flat bread first. Still warm from the surrounding air, grainy and rough with flavorful seeds, and as soon as the first bite rubs against my tongue, I'm already drooling for more. Five circles of flat bread are in the basket, and they're all for me!

As I start on my third circle, I finally look at what else is in the basket. They're all the same fruit that Gediyon gave me on the boat, the pitrom. While I chew on a ball of grain, I take a bite of the fruit and let their flavors mingle in my mouth. I make disgusting, monstrous snorts as I chew.

Once I finish the whole basket, I wash my face and hands in a makeshift basin. These people are so cool, they can weave baskets like bowls; not a single drop seeps through the cracks.

I throw myself to the floor and rest my head against a cot. Overhead, in the center of the thatched ceiling, glowing insects circle one another. They flicker from teal to magenta.

Now what am I going to do? Gediyon still isn't back, and we have about five hours until the whirlpool opens. I would sleep, but I'm not tired at all.

Oh yeah. I'm in a video game.

Waiting in video games really blows. In one game, the password for an enemy hideout was three whole minutes of standing in place, perfectly still. I made myself a sandwich in that time.

But it's too bad this place doesn't have any ingredients for a sandwich.

How do I even save the game?

How do I…even turn it off?

"Aaron," I squeal. I jump to my feet and look around the hut. I don't even have any goddang buttons to press! No sack of BBs to pull off my eyes. I pat myself over, hoping to find an alien button somewhere, but it's just me and my skimpy summer clothes.

I've been playing for at least seven hours, and Aaron only played for twenty minutes? How the heck do I turn the game off?

"Aaron!" I scream overhead, hoping he can hear me. Maybe he's monitoring me from our garage. "Aaron! How do I turn this thing off?"

A young Arriscylean with ginger hair peeks his head over the hut ladder and asks, "Miss Goddess, could I help you with something?"

I flash him a smile. "No, I'm fine, really." Urg, no I'm not! "Just ignore me."

It's not like any of them can help me, anyway. They don't understand that they're characters in a video game.

I stretch out my arms and punch into the air. "All right, game! Are you listening to me? Power off! Now! Turn off now! Game over! Reset—oh, geez, no, I don't want to start all over."

The Arriscylean pops his head into the hut again. "Miss Goddess, are you certain everything—"

"Jesus, yes, everything's fine! I'm just trying to get out of the game. Leave me alone!"

Even if he is a video game character, I can't help but feel pretty stupid.

Maybe getting out isn't as simple as pressing a button or shouting commands. Maybe I have to fall asleep, or save my game, or complete my current mission.

But I still have five hours before I can fix the dam.

I plop onto the floor and sigh, then look at the basket. It still has three fruit pits, their skin, and the knife. Maybe I can actually use these next few hours to do something productive.

It's weapon making time!

I pick up the knife and examine it from all angles, just as I learned with everything else I fixed or altered. I never trusted myself with sharp things, so a sword is definitely out of the question, even though I could simply extend the blade. I need something blunt, something I can swing around carelessly and still not hurt myself.

As I picture my new weapon, the wooden handle of the knife extends and rounds until it reaches four feet in length. The blade broadens and multiplies, stacking onto itself several times until it's as thick as a football. I give the entire thing a shake and the sharp ends flatten, but the metal part also falls to the floor with its sudden weight. It leaves a dent in the boards—oops. I can fix that later.

In my hands is now an inverted, long-handled mallet. I smile and try to lift it up, but the metal is too heavy.

This isn't good! What use is a weapon if I can't even lift it?

I squeeze the handle tight and will the metal to be as light as a feather—or a football, at least. I can feel my warmth running through the wooden shaft, and gradually I can lift the weapon until it's the perfect weight. Now I can swing it as easily as a tennis racket, but it's probably ten times as destructive.

The mallet is still missing its finishing touches, so I temper the wood until it shines like a baseball bat. Now it shouldn't snap with my first swing. I create a leathery handle in the middle of the shaft for easy gripping, and for fun, I engrave both flat sides of the mallet with an angry emoticon. That way, when I smack someone, it'll leave an imprint like this: >:O

I can't help but dance around and laugh.

"This thing is so cool! I can't wait to use it!"

I twirl toward the window and look outside. Through the fog, I don't think I can see anything to fight out there. I could smash the fireflies or whatever they are, but they've been nice to me, so I don't want to attack them for nothing.

Below, I see someone in a flowing white cloak, and at first I think it's just another Arriscylean, when I notice his long dark braid.

"Gediyon!" I yell, but I don't think he can hear me. He's levitating a pot of stew behind him, and in his arms is something furry.

Jumping down to him from this height would be crazy fun, but I don't think I want to risk breaking my neck. I glance around the hut and pull a shell candle holder from a shelf, then, in my fastest manipulation yet, I fashion it into a grapple gun. For kicks, I make it blue and pixellated. With the mallet in one hand and the grapple gun in the other, I step through the window and aim for one of the raised walkways below me.

I squeeze the handle and the whole device rumbles in my hand as its cord releases. I feel the entire length of the sturdy cord wobble when the spike hits wood, and a second later, I fly through the window.

Half screaming and half laughing, I swing from the platform to the lower docks and kick Gediyon right in the chest.

He falls backwards and I land on top of him, but the pot remains in the air and the girl he was talking to kneels over both of us. Gediyon regains his composure at once. I try to apologize to him, but I laugh so hard, I don't think he understands a word I say.

"I see you've learned quite a bit while I was gone," he says, still mustering a smile.

I climb off of him and raise the mallet and grapple gun. The girl's mouth hangs open.

"Aren't they super cool? This will probably help out later with the first task."

"My, Miss Goddess," the girl says, "I never imagined you would be so bouncy." To Gediyon, she says, "Thank you again, Gediyon. It means so much to us." She starts down the dock, but a few steps later, she turns around and calls, "By the way, you're a wonderful cook!" Then she runs away.

I laugh and pat Gediyon on the back. "Looks like someone likes you."

He completely ignores that comment and raises the furry thing to me. "I regret that you can't eat the stew, so I found this for you. It's a cocoa nut, a delicacy, and it's the right season for ripening."

I look at the hairy thing. It looks like a deflated volley ball covered in coarse brown hair. Disgusting—but it smells like cake. My mouth waters.

"A coconut, you say?"

"Shall I prepare some for you?"

"Sure, why the heck not?"

He brings the pot and weird fruit to the side of the dock so we won't block anybody, then he pulls off a blue clay bowl hooked to the pot. He seems almost as excited to prepare it as I am to taste it. With cautious hands, he expertly slices open the fruit and scoops out a chunk into the bowl. It's a creamy brown color, like mocha, but it has the consistency of shortening.

"It's best to drink it hot," he says. "You would need a spoon to eat it cold."

With that, flames rise out of his fingers and surround the bowl. In a few seconds, the cream softens and melts into a thick drink. He pulls out a cloth from his vest, wraps it around the cup, then hands it to me.

"Careful, it's hot."

It smells divine. I let it steam my face and smile at Gediyon, who smiles at me as if offering me my first ice cream cone. Then I take a sip.

It's instantly sweet and warms me all the way down. It's like drinking the tropics. Chocolate, coffee, coconut, all blended in the perfect ratio into one creamy drink. I don't want to drink it all at once, though. I want to savor every sip, as if I'll never have another taste again, but I can just lift the bowl to my lips and drink more.

"This is amazing!"

Gediyon smiles wider. "My mother loved this for dessert. You mustn't drink too much, though, because the high sugar content can make you nauseated."

"Bah! This is the best thing ever!"

By the time I finish it, I feel like I never want another sweet thing near my mouth again, but at the same time I know I'll want another drink in a day or so.

We walk down the docks toward the mayor's hut again, when I see a group of people huddled in an area I hadn't seen before.

"What's that over there?"

"Lereli's Universal Mirror. Would you like to speak to it?"

"Speak to it? What, is it like the mirror in *Snow White*?"

"I'm sorry?"

"Is it magical?"

"You could say that."

As we walk closer, I see some of the villagers kneeling, some bowing in what looks like a shrine. The platform juts out into the water, but I don't see any mirror. Instead, three slabs of black stone are positioned like a three-way mirror. I guess the stone is pretty glassy, since I can see the torches flickering clearly on its surface, but otherwise it's not very reflective.

Gediyon and I stand on the dock, looking at it. Some of the glowing insects circle our feet.

"What does it do?"

"It connects directly to the cosmos of all six universes. We in Starrs are the only ones of the six universes aware of the Cycle, so we fabricated these mirrors. If we speak to them, we can lend our consciousness to connect the universes. We do this with the hope that in another life, we can recapture the memories we made on Starrs. It also helps ease our spirits. Goddess Saei's memories are in the cosmos, and when speaking to the Mirror, sometimes she appears in the reflection. Then we know everything will be all right." He looks at me. "That's also how we can tell that you're Goddess. You look like her."

I snort. "I wish. She's way too pretty." I cross my arms. "So basically, what you're saying is, this thing is a save point?"

"Come again?"

I groan. "If I talk to it, I can save my game. Maybe if I do this I'll actually get the option of stopping for now. Yunno, I want to try this."

I march onto the platform and dodge aside some, push others, making my way to the Mirror.

"Goddess coming through. Excuse me!"

The people kneeling in front scramble out of the way, and I set the mallet and grapple gun where they prayed. I rub my hands and clap them. My outline reflects in the glossy black stone.

"Okay, universe! Michelle here. Time to save my game. Want to know what happened so far? Well, let's see, I met this Goddess person, and then I fell from the sky, but Gediyon here helped me. Then we came here, yadda yadda ya, I figured out how to use my Goddess powers, blah blah blah. Don't want to do that again. And here I am! Game saved, right? Do I want to quit the game? Yes I do!" I hold my arms out, expecting to see a big flash, then

I'll be back in my garage, but nothing happens. I don't even see Goddess Saei.

"Game saved!" I shout. "Quit. Game. NOW!"

Still nothing.

I let out an ugly croak and turn around. "Gediyon, this thing is broken!"

I pick up my things and march back across the platform to the docks. The villagers look confused but smile apologetically as I pass.

Well, that totally failed. I guess I have two more options left: completing my first mission, and then sleep. If these don't work either, then I'm not sure what else I can do.

When another thought comes to mind, my stomach twists horribly. Maybe I actually have to complete the entire game.

Chapter Five
Damming Poison

Gediyon and I make it back to the mayor's hut and return the pot of stew. Some is still left, but everyone affected by the poison has already eaten some, and if they eat anymore, it could be dangerous for them.

Come to think of it, I didn't see any petrified people on our way back. I guess the fish really did help, after all.

For the next few minutes, I help Gediyon clean the cooking utensils and bowls. With Gediyon's water magic, we finish quickly, and by that time I'm ready to bounce off the walls.

The cocoa nut drink must've had caffeine in it. I love caffeine!

Gediyon says something about talking to the villagers for the next few hours, but I don't want to do that. I skip around outside from one rocky wooden walkway to the next, and when I find the right overhead platforms, I take out the grapple gun and swing my way around. The villagers must think I'm high, but I only had caffeine! They're the ones with the adrenaline rush, and they aren't even taking advantage of it. That's their loss.

I stop swinging around like Tarzan when I miss my footing and fall into the water. I don't know if I swallow any of it, but once an Arriscylean pulls me out, I'm calm again.

I guess I should spend the next few hours walking around the entire village and patching up all the damage I inflicted with the grapple gun. There sure were a lot of splinters flying around.

The villagers apologize to me that there's not much to do in Lereli now that the water is contaminated. They tell me at night, children usually capture lantern beetles in jars and they dive into the surrounding water looking for a coral that only glows at night. The adults, on the other hand, like to drink and toast in their huts while the sober recount their fishing accomplishments. Today, though, everyone is too fatigued to engage in normal activities, and they need to save the energy from the rush fish for tomorrow. One woman tells me that everyone must thank me and Gediyon, but I haven't even done anything yet. Still, hearing her say this makes me want to be a bit more respectful and stop grappling everything in sight. At least I repaired their wood.

Everyone starts disappearing from the docks, and the lights in their houses extinguish.

Now I realize that it's about half past eleven, and I only have half an hour before the whirlpool opens. I retrace my steps around the dock and look out to the sea where Mayor Rayel said the whirlpool would appear. The water is calm, not a ripple in sight, and I'm sure if it weren't for the fog, I would see the night sky reflected on the surface.

Hard to believe that somewhere under that flawless glass is a dam. How difficult can fixing it be, really? If it's anything like what I did with the small trinkets around town, it should be a snap.

I feel a hand on my shoulder and look up to see Gediyon.

"Are you ready?"

"I should be. I've been waiting around so long, this is all I want to do. I wanna get this out of the way."

"Michelle, would you like me to accompany you down there?"

"Really?"

He nods.

"Awesome! And all this time, I thought I was going to do this alone. Yeah, I'd love for you to come with me!"

I sit on the edge of the dock, rolling the shaft of my mallet back and forth over my lap. Gediyon stands beside me and asks me questions about Tyme, which I guess means my home. I don't think I'm breaking the fourth wall, since I've mentioned too many times that I know I'm in a game, so I tell him about Aaron and the virtual reality game. This time, though, he acknowledges the word "game"—did the laws of this game world just change?

Anyway, it relieves me that I actually know something that no one else here does. I explain to him what a video game is, but I don't think he really understands the concept.

"In some games, there are classes or ranks, and I'm pretty sure you'd be classified as a black mage. That means you have all kinds of offensive magic. Never came across a Goddess rank, though."

"Fascinating. I do hope I could someday experience this video game, myself."

I imagine Gediyon standing in front of a TV, flailing his arms while holding a Wii controller, and I laugh. It's like a marionette playing with his own strings.

I'm about to tell him about different consoles when I hear a funny sound like a giant slurp. I look to the water and, not too far away, I see a spiral forming. I rise to my feet and hold my mallet and grapple gun in each hand.

"It's about time," I say. "Should we tell someone?"

"Mayor Rayel comes now."

Around the corner of the dock, I see the little old man wobbling toward us. "Ah! I was worried you might have run off somewhere, but I'm glad to see that you're so punctual."

"Hey old man! Look! The whirlpool!"

"I may be old, but I can still see, Miss Goddess. I see you have made adequate preparations," he says, nodding toward my mallet and grapple gun. "With Gediyon at your side, you should have no problem with the Taesmal mutants."

"The Tay—*what*?"

"Taesmal mutants," Gediyon explains. "The variety here were once hatched as normal fish, but the toxins of the Tainted Sea have rearranged their genetic makeup and brain chemistry to become hostile creatures."

I snort. "Hostile *fish*? C'mon, they can't be as bad as angry birds!"

Gediyon and Mayor Rayel exchange uncomfortable smiles.

Gediyon tells him, "I will do my best to aid her."

"Then may both of you return safely. After all, we need at least one of the Cycle's players to reach the end."

Did the mayor make a video game reference, or was he being figurative?

Gediyon puts a hand on my shoulder. "Ready?"

"Now or never, right?"

To assure that it's safe, he takes the first step in water. I think he stands on coral. I hang the grapple gun from my wrist and take his hand as he leads me down to the sea floor.

We use the flat, circular coral as stepping stones. Someone must've arranged them this way since the path leads directly to the dam. As soon as we step below sea level, I feel the warm, tropical air suck away, replaced with the spray of the howling whirlpool.

Already, it's another world down here. I guess this is what it was like to walk with Moses when he opened the Red Sea.

Gediyon lights his entire right hand ablaze to guide our way. I'm afraid to let my mallet even brush against the whirlpool walls. I see the glowing eyes of fish on the other side, and they don't look friendly. I shudder.

I miss a step from one coral to the next, and my foot slides into the soft, sinking sand of the sea floor. Gediyon immediately helps me out, and as I bend down to shake the sandy mud from my leg, I hear the rush of water. Our twenty minutes can't be up already!

I spin around and see the fish leap from one wall of the whirlpool to the other. I hold the grapple gun and mallet ready, but before I can swing either of them, one of the fish rams into my side. It hurts as much as someone shooting a basketball at me, which will only annoy me if they keep this up.

The grapple gun dangles on my left wrist, and with both hands, I swing the mallet at the next fish that leaps out. It flops as it hits the wet sea floor. Ha! No more swimming for you, little fishy! My insides tickle when I see the angry face imprint on its scales. My eyes have to readjust to the darkness as Gediyon extinguishes his flaming hand to strike away his own assailants.

Another fish bounces off my head and I swing at it, but it leaps back into the water wall. I growl and reposition the grapple gun, following its glowing eyes before firing. Dark blood bursts into the water as I spear it, and when the cord retracts, fish guts cover the pointed tip. Ew. This game is more graphic than I thought.

Even though my hands shake, I take out about three more fish using this method, and then something strange happens. Through the walls, their glowing eyes follow each other. They're lining up.

"Get down!" Gediyon shouts.

I throw myself to the sea floor and scrape my arm against the coral. Ow, geez! Why does the pain feel so real?

Gediyon is still standing. If he doesn't duck soon, the fish are going to hit him all at once. I keep one eye open as I watch him.

A second later, the fish burst out of the water, but I can't see if they hit him or not. The spray of water, along with a flash of light, obscures my view. My hands fly in to cover my head. I hear a horrible crackling noise, the water stops splashing, and several things thump on the ground at once.

Slowly, I lift my head. Gediyon stands unharmed. All of the bulbous, glowing-eyed fish have fallen—some of them with black char marks. I see sparks of electricity at Gediyon's fingertips.

Water, fire, and electricity? He's definitely a black mage.

I push myself back to my feet, wobbling a little from the excitement, and look over the smoking pile of fish. I can't help but think that it smells yummy.

Gediyon bursts one of his hands into flame to light our surroundings. With the other, he reaches down for one of the fish. "Looks like I can make some fish stew for you to eat, after all."

"Are they edible?"

He laughs and drops the fish. "I'm not certain, but it's best not to risk it." He steps over the pile. "They haven't hurt you anywhere, have they?"

"Nah. I mean, I scraped my arm, but that's my own fault." I show him the cut on my forearm. It's bright red and stings, but it's not bleeding much. I've had worse.

Gediyon takes careful hold of my arm and looks at it. "I'm sorry that I have nothing on me to help you, but we can clean it up once we return to the mayor's."

"Yeah, that's fine. No biggie."

"Come now, we mustn't dawdle any longer."

Ugh. That's right. The dam. We wasted about five minutes here killing these stupid fish.

At least the dam isn't too far now, but it doesn't look how I expected. Gediyon lights both of his hands to help me see better. The dam isn't made of wood, but rather concrete and metal pipes. It looks so industrial that it's out of place on the coast of Lereli.

I can see through to the other side of what everyone calls the Tainted Sea, and the water really does look deadly. It's a murky, grayish purple, and seems to be consisted of half slime. Shadows swim through the muck.

I think I have about fifteen minutes left. Why can't I have a clock in the corner of my vision so I know how much time I have left? Why can't I have a diagram of the dam as it was before so I know what it's supposed to look like?

Standing close to the concrete wall, I examine the pipes: a large main one, five medium-sized pipes, about a dozen smaller ones, and countless others the width of my pinky finger. They intertwine like a plate of mixed pasta.

Suddenly, I don't think that thirteen minutes is enough to fix this damn dam! No wonder everyone else before me failed. It looks like someone threw a bomb into the largest pipe and blasted the rest of it.

Maybe that's it. Maybe I just have to reverse the damage of the bomb or whatever.

Part of me wants to create an actual undo button that I can press about a hundred times in the next ten minutes, but I don't know if that'll work, and I don't want to waste time on a dud button. But what's faster, figuring out how to undo damage, or examining each pipe and deciphering their connections?

Come on, Michelle! Stop thinking and do something!

Gediyon helps me climb onto the concrete, but my unsteady nerves nearly push me right back off. I put my shaking hands to the largest pipe. This and the medium-sized ones should be easy. Warmth extends from my finger tips as I smooth over the large broken pipe, curling the bent, blasted metal into one piece again. I reach all around the cylinder to make sure that it's sealed completely, then move onto the other pipes. Three of them are simple and straight like the largest one, while the other two snake around the rest. Fixing the tiny pipes is going to prove difficult.

Crap! Four minutes have already passed, and I haven't even gotten to fixing the concrete. My heart pounds faster and rattles my vision with every beat.

"I don't know if I can do this!"

"I know you can," Gediyon says.

Yeah, whatever. That sorta helps.

I don't think it's physically possible to fix the smaller pipes using the same method for the bigger ones. I jump off the concrete and put my hands to the smooth concrete wall and close my eyes, like I did when I first discovered my powers.

The concrete is rough, wet, and cold, like the sidewalk after a winter storm. I don't think I'll have a problem fixing the wall itself, but I still have to fix the pipes. I press my nails against the concrete and—sure, it sounds dumb, but I try to reach into its existence. Maybe if I try hard enough, it'll tell me how it functioned before.

You're a dam. A stupid dam, and I'm going to fix you, so help me out here.

In the darkness behind my closed eyelids, an orange flash outlined like an X-ray burns into my vision. It's a more vivid image than the soft glow I saw when I fixed the spoon. I open my eyes, and though the orange light disappears, I now know the placement of the pipes. I don't dare blink.

I raise my hands to the open area of intertwining pipes, and already I see the smaller pipes branching out to reconnect themselves. I'm not sure why—maybe I'm not breathing correctly, maybe my heart is beating too fast, or maybe I'm straining too hard to keep my eyes open, but doing this makes me lightheaded.

"Gediyon," I utter, trying hard to move as little facial muscles as possible, "how much time left?"

"Two minutes, I think."

"Okay, go. I'll meet you back on the dock."

"Michelle, are you—"

"Yeah. If I fail, I don't want you to get hurt too. Go."

"Michelle—"

"As Goddess, I order you to leave."

For a few more seconds, he stays behind me. Then I hear his boots squish in the wet sand, and he's off.

Several inches remain between the slowly connecting pipes. I'm sure I can make it. I have two minutes left before the poison of the Tainted Sea rushes in on me, but I can't start fixing the concrete yet, not until the pipes are fixed. I can't look away and lose concentration before they've fully connected.

Overhead, I hear water slosh around as the pipes connect. I think I have less than a minute now. I could just walk away for the time being—I mean, is the current so strong it'll blast away the pipes again? But I can't let this job go incomplete, not when so many people are counting on me. I have to stop this poison for them. This poison isn't going to kill me. I didn't wait twelve hours only to die here!

I finally blink and wave my hands over either side of the concrete wall. They multiply like crystal and the particles roll onto themselves to fill in the gap. Why can't this go faster? I only have about thirty seconds left!

With a growl, I put both hands to the repaired concrete and close my eyes. A large hole still gapes at me from overhead, but at this rate it won't fix in time.

An idea—maybe it's a single word or a memory—flies into me and I feel the wall pulse. I hear the rubbing sound of coarse stone against stone and look above. It's fixed!

But the water is ready to crash down on me.

My heart beats so fast that my hands shake, and I turn around and aim the grapple gun for the wooden dock. It's a messy shot, but at least it's sturdy. I feel myself flying over the cold sea floor as the whirlpool spills over to where I was standing.

Moments later, Gediyon catches me in his arms, and I feel the splash of the closing tide on my ankles. Just being on the dock, I regain the warmth that the water had leeched. Behind me, the water has filled in the pathway, not any more contaminated than it was before.

I rub sand onto Gediyon's clothes as I hug him and scream, "It's fixed! I did it!"

"You did very well, Michelle!"

"C'mon, let's go see everyone else!"

I pull on his arm and drag him over the rocky docks back to Mayor Rayel's hut. When I jump inside, I drop my mallet and grapple gun and scream, "I did it! I'm alive! I fixed your dam! Everyone is saved!"

It's too bad a cheering crowd doesn't rejoice, since everyone else is asleep, but Mayor Rayel thanks me with a hug, and I lift him and twirl him around.

"Miss Goddess Michelle, you truly are amazing! I apologize for underestimating you before."

"Whatever! It's cool." I let him down. "So I completely restored this village back to normal, right?"

"Well, you see, it should take a few days for the fog to dissipate, but now that the dam is fixed, the cleansing mechanisms can purify the water again." He walks to the opening of the hut and looks outside. "But the effects of this particular toxin are not reversible.

I mentioned before that the rush fish can help us only momentarily, as it simply alleviates the symptoms and doesn't cure it. The best of tonics won't even help us. For this, we need something more potent—more powerful."

"Mayor Rayel," Gediyon says, "may I suggest… a healer?"

The mayor turns around and smiles. "You follow my thoughts exactly, Gediyon."

"Then tomorrow, I shall return to Arriscyal."

I gasp. "Ooh! Can I come?"

The mayor and Gediyon exchange glances. Gediyon says, "If that is what you wish, Michelle…"

"Pft. Duh! What else am I gonna do?"

I'm not sure if they understand, but they don't deny me.

Gediyon nods to Mayor Rayel. "Michelle and I will return as soon as possible."

"Very well," Mayor Rayel says. "Then off to bed with you both. You have a long journey ahead."

The mayor leaves outside and Gediyon smiles at me before beckoning me up the ladder. I think I know what he's so excited about.

I might've completed my first mission, but of course there's more to this game. Another rank: the healer. I can see her already. She's without a doubt going to be prettier than me *and* she'll have bigger boobs. She'll probably be soft-spoken and so perfect and sweet that I'll want to barf every time she graces my presence. And Gediyon is probably in love with her.

Of course he is. He probably had to rescue her on many accounts and she won him over with her damsel-in-distress-like lifestyle. I don't know why this bothers me so much. I mean, I'm a little too young for Gediyon anyway, but I have a feeling I'll become the third wheel once she joins our party.

Maybe I'm so annoyed because I'm this so-called Creator and I can't even heal myself. I turn my forearm and look at the scrape. At least the blood isn't dripping. If the healer were already here, she would offer to heal me in a heartbeat, because she's oh-so-nice and doesn't like to see others hurt. Talk about sickening.

I wonder if I can refuse her.

As I climb the ladder, another thought bothers me. Mayor Rayel didn't give me the option to save or quit, even though I completed the first task. I guess I'll have to see what sleep brings.

Chapter Six
Trek to the Kingdom of Magic

Insomnia must run in my family—or weird sleep habits, anyway. My dad manages to fall asleep when he's doing the most mundane things, like watching TV or reading a book. He even fell asleep at a company dinner during the CEO's speech—I still cringe when I think about it. It doesn't matter what time of the day, he starts snoring somehow, yet he can stay awake until six in the morning, making one urgent phone call after another.

My mom hasn't displayed any strange behaviors, but Aaron and I always had trouble falling asleep and staying asleep. We never could doze off when our parents said it was time for bed, and I know that in his dark bedroom, he was building the Death Star out of LEGOs, and I was catching Pokémon.

My friends tell me I probably can't sleep since I have so much pent up energy, but I know that if I don't get enough sleep then I'm going to be sleep deprived and lethargic the next day.

It doesn't help that the lantern beetles keep flicking over my head. I would get rid of them, but Gediyon told me they keep away other bugs, and I don't want to wake up half-eaten by exotic mosquitoes.

It's also incredibly uncomfortable to sleep in denim shorts.

I roll onto my side and stare at the woven mat beside the cot I'm supposed to sleep on. I can see its geometric design in the beetles' light.

I don't know that if I do fall asleep, I'll wake up in our garage. How did Aaron do it? It's not that I miss home—I mean, I'm having a lot of fun here and it's basically a free vacation, but just having the option of leaving when I want to will make me feel better.

If I'm not home when I wake up—if I do fall asleep at all—then I'll have to follow Gediyon to this Arriscyal of his. I hope he can give me a piggyback ride the whole way.

I blow hair out of my face and sit up. The lantern beetles flicker brighter with my sudden movement. My scraped arm throbs for a second, but the pain goes away quickly. Gediyon gave me an ointment that healed my skin within minutes, but it's still numb.

The village has no clocks, but I think it's about three in the morning. In the next few minutes, I stand over the ladder into the hut below and debate whether or not I should go down. Eventually I do, surrounding myself with the deep breathing and light snores of the Arriscyleans.

Gediyon sleeps on the lower bunk beneath an older man, who mutters in his dreams. I feel a bit like a creep, standing over Gediyon and watching him sleep, but I can't help but notice how peaceful he looks, as if he hadn't had any trouble falling asleep.

I lower myself to my knees and put my hands on his arm, then shake him slightly. I whisper his name several times until he lifts his head and looks at me. In the dark, I can't tell that his eyes are red.

"Is something the matter?" he says in a sleepy voice.

"Sorry for waking you. I can't sleep. Do you have anything…?" I don't know what I'm asking for, but I don't want drugs.

He closes his eyes and smiles. "I know just the thing. One moment."

I stand back and wait for him to fully awaken. He sits up and tosses his loose braid over his shoulder, then reaches for a bag beside his bed. He pulls out a small tin and shows it to me.

"Claren tea, my own special blend. Let's go downstairs."

He leads me down the first ladder, and we cross a walkway along the tree trunk until we reach the ladder to the main hut. It's dark in here, but Gediyon lights a torch and brings me into the kitchen. From one of the shelves, he pulls down a shell teapot and two cups. Gosh, they're beautiful—they look as if they were imported from an undersea kingdom.

"My mother taught me how to make this tea," Gediyon says, still in a hushed voice. "We blend it from all parts of the plant—the leaves, roots, flowers and fruit, so it is especially potent. We consider it a cure-all for small ailments, like headaches, stomachaches, *insomnia*," he adds, smiling at me, "but moreover, I like how it tastes."

The water in the teapot is already boiling, and he sprinkles in some of the tea blend.

"I drink this twice a day, with breakfast and before bed. It helps me sleep too, and I haven't fallen ill once." He looks around the shelves and asks me, "Would you like some sweetener?"

"Yeah, I like sweet things."

He reaches for a jar and scoops out some thick red liquid into each cup. I guess it's some kind of honey. He hands me a cup and has that smile, like he knows I'm going to love this too.

I inhale the steam. It smells like a rose and apple bouquet. I put the cup to my lips and take a small sip. Delicately sweet, unlike the cocoa nut cream. Flowery, like chamomile, and a little spicy like ginger. At once, I feel like I can breathe deeper and my thoughts don't race.

Gediyon takes a few sips of his own.

"Wow. This is really good." Wow. I feel so calm.

He almost laughs. "Do you like it?"

"Yeah. I think I could drink this every night, too."

"Actually, not many people *do* like it. Others tend to drink it as a medicine because they find it too bitter or spicy, but my mother found the right blend of fruit to root." He takes another sip. "They admitted to liking it only when she prepared them a cup, herself."

"*You* made mine and it's awesome. But I like pretty much anything."

When I finish the cup, Gediyon leads me back through the huts. As relaxed as I am now, I don't want him to go away yet. I feel like a five-year-old when I ask him, "Can you tell me a bedtime story?"

"A…bedtime story?"

"Please?" I jump onto the cot and roll onto my side, watching him with wide eyes.

"Do I know any stories?" he asks himself, then asks me, "Do you know about the sea angel?"

"Nope. Tell me."

He kneels down beside my cot, looking overhead as if he's trying to figure out the story. I close my eyes once he starts talking.

"Long ago, a young woman was appointed to guard over a faraway sea. She guided sailors safely to their destinations and warned them if a storm was nigh. One day, like any other, a fisherman approached her, but instead of asking for her guidance, he asked her to tell him about her experiences."

Gediyon's voice sounds distant and I feel myself sinking into sleep. I'm not exactly sure what happens next, but I think the angel and fisherman fall in love. She creates a song for him that'll guide him across the sea, or something like that. I don't catch the ending, but I'm sure they live happily ever after.

The next thing I'm aware of is how warm I am. Even though nothing covers me, I feel sweat bead on the tip of my nose. Ugh, I feel disgusting. Aaron must've forgotten to turn on the AC before he locked himself in the garage.

I hear splashing and high-pitched laughter. Probably the next-door kids playing in their backyard pool. I wish we had a pool.

My lips feel wet. Guess I drooled through the night. It happens when I'm extra tired. I wipe it away and roll onto my back.

This isn't my bed.

My eyes shoot open, and instead of a shockingly white popcorn ceiling, I see a thatched roof. The lantern beetles no longer circle ahead, and are now latched to the wall beside me. Their lights are out—I guess it's their time to rest.

I sigh and cover my eyes with my hand. I'm still in the game. Three options have failed. How am I going to get home now? I guess I do have to finish the entire game, but what is this, a game of *life*? How will I know when the game is actually over?

I sit up on the cot and wipe the sweat from my nose. So far, the game isn't bad. It could be easier—then again, *life* isn't easy. I'm just glad I don't have to deal with someone I don't like.

I wrinkle my nose when I remember that today, Gediyon and I are going to meet our healer. Maybe I had a nightmare about her or something, but just thinking about her makes me want to throw her in a pit. If she proves to be as repulsively sweet as I think she is, then maybe I will.

I grumble to myself as I make my way to the window. Hey, the fog has cleared! It's still a bit hazy, but I can actually see the sunlight and even the farthest dock in the village. I guess it's about seven in the morning—ugh, I only got about four hours of sleep. I rub my eyes and yawn.

Already I see the Arriscyleans pacing around outside, but where's Gediyon?

I climb down the ladder and see that the hut is empty, save for a boy sitting on a lower bunk. Unlike the other Arriscyleans, he isn't wearing a white cloak, but I can tell he isn't from Lereli because of the gold and silver embroidery on his vest. He was the one asking me if I was sane when I was trying to stop the game, and I'm pretty sure I saw him the other night pouring water for the villagers. His large orange head stands out.

"Miss Goddess!" he exclaims, then sweeps down into a low bow. From this angle, his head looks like a pumpkin. He rises and says, "I have a message from the mayor, Your Divinity. He says these are for you." He lifts a bundle of cloth and hands them to me.

"I get cool Lereli clothes?" I squeal. I take the bundle into my arms; it's so lightweight. Something is neatly folded in a patterned bag. "Ah, this is awesome! I'm gonna change, 'kay? Don't watch me!"

He blushes and his eyes widen. "Of course not, Your Divinity!" He turns around and I climb back into my hut.

I can't help but feel distant to the other characters. Not all of them are part of the background. I guess I should get to know some of them. I say, "By the way, what's your name?"

"Mine, Your Divinity?" he calls from below. "It's Porter Golias, Your Divinity."

"Okay, cool. Now stop with that 'Your Divinity,' it's weird. Call me Michelle." I pull off my top and look into the bag. Awesome! My breakfast is the same thing I had for dinner. I can put my old clothes in here later.

"So Porter," I continue. "When are we leaving to this home of yours?"

"Oh, 'we,' Miss—M-Michelle? Actually, I think only you and Sir Gediyon are going back to Arriscyal. The rest of us need to stay here and help the villagers until the water is clear again." He sighs, then mumbles, "I'm not sure if my boss will be pleased."

I pull on a blue pleated skirt that falls past my knees. The hem is painted with a seashell design. "Your boss, huh? You got a job back home?"

"Yes, M-*Michelle*. I'm not cut out to be in the military, so I usually run the gondolas around the city. The king ordered water users to come here and help out, so here I am."

"Is it nice to be away from home?" I tie a red sash around my waist.

"It is exciting, yes, and I can't wait until the village is back to normal. Everyone says it's beautiful. I do miss my brothers, though."

"Aww. I don't really miss my brother yet, but I'm sure I will." Just saying this makes me miss him already. Then I think about how he dumps his dishes in the sink and leaves them for days without washing, and this annoying thought is enough to make me not miss him so much.

I'm finished dressing now. I wish I had a mirror so I could see exactly how I look, but just looking down at myself, I *feel* pretty darn awesome. The lightweight robe must be made of silk, and it has flared elbow-length sleeves. It should keep me cool and protect me from the sun at the same time. Since both my robe and sash are the colors of the sunset, I keep the red elastic headband in my hair.

I throw my old clothes and grapple gun into the bag beside the bread and fruit, then sling the bag over my mallet. I climb down the ladder more carefully than before since I'm wearing a skirt, and I twirl for Porter. "Well? Do I look travel-ready?"

"You…look…fantastic." He turns his head and is suddenly fascinated with an upper bunk. "Lereli has the finest dye around."

"Yeah, these colors are pretty snazzy. Anyway, do you know where Gediyon is?"

"I think he left for the northern docks—near the jungle. He didn't want to wake you, so he went ahead and passed around the rest of the stew."

"All right, cool. I'll find him." I lean my mallet against my shoulder and start for the exit. "Thanks Porter! Hope I'll see you soon."

"Y-Yes Michelle! It was a pleasure."

I make my way down to the bottommost docks. My clothes allow me to step lighter, even though I'm wearing more than I was before. It must be because they make me feel more graceful.

As I start on my second piece of flat bread, some of the villagers come up to me and give me a hug for fixing the dam. At least they're livelier today, but a few of them are still slow. Somehow, their delayed smiles make them even more charming. They give me more fruit and a bottle of nectar that I store away in my bag. Geez, if only I had magical hold-everything pants, I could store all this stuff without it weighing me down.

When they leave, I skip along to the jungle ahead. If I knew that helping people was so rewarding, I might've actually gotten off my butt to volunteer or something instead of playing video games.

Oh wait, I'm still playing a game, aren't I?

Not too far ahead, I see Gediyon walking down the dock toward me. He's smiling, as usual, and the loose strands of his hair fly behind him with his flowing cloak. It's hard not to stare.

"I was on my way to wake you right now," he says. "Did you sleep well?"

"Yeah, I think so. Are we ready to leave yet?"

"Nearly. Mr. Isel Mingon is preparing our Bubbles right now. Have you eaten breakfast?"

I show him the bag. "Got some more in here, too. Want some?"

"I've already eaten, but thank you." He looks toward the jungle. "Is there anything else you would like to do before we embark?"

"Nope. Let's do this."

I follow him down the dock toward the jungle. The trees tower over the village, and already I'm wondering what kinds of bugs are in there. I hope I don't cross any giant, mutated ones. I'm not prepared to protect myself from stingers and bites, and I think my mallet can only take so much before bug guts make it too slippery to swing. I hunch over and hold my mallet protectively in front.

Where the dock meets land stands a man, and floating beside him are large, iridescent bubbles about four feet wide. Even with his back to us, I can tell he isn't from around here. His clothes are almost modern. He wears striped pants, and on the back of his maroon vest is a large yellow circle with a happy face. He must hear our approaching footsteps because he turns around.

I wince at once. His squinty smile is obviously so forced, it's creepy, and he's greedily rubbing his hands like he wants more than our money.

"Ah! So this is our Miss Goddess! It's a pleasure! A pleasure, indeed." He sweeps into a bow and swings himself back up in an instant. He wobbles slightly on the ball of one foot and stretches from one side to another in the same awkward running position, but he's not running, just bouncing. He has a thin, up-turned creeper-stache. "Never thought I'd serve our Creator herself, not I!"

I guess he doesn't mind the weird look I give him because he goes on grinning like a maniac, bouncing from one foot to another and rubbing his hands as if we're going to make him a millionaire.

Gediyon says, "Michelle, this is Mr. Isel Mingon. He's a Bubble salesman."

"Huh. Are ya now? You gonna lead us through this jungle?"

He laughs—high-pitched and even crazier than his smile. "Not I, no! That's the job of these Bubbles here, you see!"

He snaps at the two giant bubbles floating beside him and they turn around. It's funny I can say that, because how can bubbles have sides? But they do—they have cartoonish faces that slide around the curves of their liquid bodies, and when one's eye falls too far out of place, it reappears where it should be.

"The heck? What is this, like Glinda's flying bubble?"

"It is also another Taesmal creation," Gediyon explains, "but unlike the mutants, Bubbles are docile. They may not look like much now, but we can ride within them, and they'll grant us a safe and swift journey."

"Awesome. Beats walking." I touch one and it pops, but it doesn't splatter me. It's solid now and it sits on the ground like a large ball of glass. Its eyes no longer fall all over its body and they stay in place. Inside, something gray fills out—a seat!

"Whoa! Cool!"

Gediyon touches the other and it does the same.

"The Bubble will carry that weapon of yours, Miss!" Isel Mingon says. "Hold it out like so..."

A transparent arm lashes out toward my mallet and grips it.

"Neato!"

"Fantasteriffic! Now you can smash things in your path! Bubbles are wonderful creatures, are they not? Hmm? Now once you step inside, just say, Miss, 'Destination: Arriscyal!' Routes are already programmed in the Bubbles, so you won't have to do a thing!"

"This is so cool!" I touch the surface of the Bubble like Gediyon, and the glass gives so I can reach inside. I jump onto the seat, and the glass closes over me like a shield. Isel Mingon says something—wearing that creepy grin—but he sounds like he's underwater. I throw my bag aside where it rests against the base of the Bubble.

"Destination: Arriscyal! Full speed ahead!"

The Bubble lurches forward, rising up, down, and around roots, vines, and tree trunks. Everything flashes by, and I'm sure that if I was on the highway back home, a CHP officer wouldn't hesitate to give me a ticket. It's a good thing *I'm* not driving, though. The Bubble knows what it's doing.

I look behind me, but see nothing but jungle. Aw, crap. Where's Gediyon?

I'm about to command the Bubble to slow down when I hear something crunch. The Bubble repositions the mallet, which is covered in pink slime and something that looks like a mangled insect wing. Ew. I guess there are giant bugs in this jungle after all.

"Yo Bubble, slow down and wait for Gediyon."

It gradually slows so it isn't jerking aside each second to dodge everything in sight. Now I can enjoy the beauty of the jungle. The sunlight cuts through the trees and casts white rays onto the large-leafed ferns on the ground. Vines hang down from every tree, and if the jungle weren't so infested with bugs, I'd like to try swinging around. Now I can actually see the bugs without smashing into them, and not all of them are terrifying. A golden one slithers through the air like a Chinese dragon, and another with glimmering rainbow wings changes colors in different angles of light. I even see a purple lizard with large eyes. It's kind of cute.

I guess the Bubble knows which ones to strike down because it smashes a blue-tinged bug with a stinger the length of a pencil.

"Good Bubble," I say. I look behind me again, but still no sign of Gediyon.

If only we had cell phones or something.

I slump in my chair and gaze ahead at the Bubble's eyes. I wonder if they can see inside its body and watch where it's going at the same time.

A plan pricks my insides, and I reach to the glass wall in front of me. The area I touch ripples for a moment and the Bubble makes a popping sound. I hope it isn't protesting. The glass pushes away my hand, and I see a control panel forming. Perfect! I keep my hands in place until it's complete, then I look over the control panel. It's pretty simple: a large red button reads "SPEAK!" with a pattern of tiny holes for the speakers. I push the button and say, "Contact Gediyon."

I imagine radio waves extending from my finger tips, through the button, and across the jungle. A moment later, the sound of rushing air fills my Bubble.

"Hello?" I say.

"Michelle? Is that you?"

"Cool, you can hear me?"

"How are you speaking to me?"

"I made a communicator thingy. Hey, sorry about rushing off like that."

"It's not a problem. I'm just glad that you're doing well. We should be following the same path, so I don't think we'll be separated."

"Good." I lean back. "So how long is it going to take to get there?"

"Twenty hours."

"Twenty hours?! Geez! I can't sit on my ass that long!" I groan. "I don't suppose there's anything fun we can do?"

"Most of us take a nap."

"Yeah, a twenty-hour nap. Sounds like a plan." I let out a hard sigh and straighten myself. "When you're playing a game, time passes *so* quickly. You can be a giant sprite on a mini world map. Walk a hundred steps or so, and bam! You're in the next town." I slump back again. "Well, this is a virtual *reality* game, so I guess I have to suffer through travels too."

"If you'd like, we can stop so I can brew you some more claren tea."

"Nah, that's fine. We'd have to step out with all these bugs around." I blow my bangs out of my eyes. "I think we just need some good traveling music. You want to listen to some music for the next twenty hours?"

He chuckles. "If you think it'll make an improvement, then I'd love to."

"Awesome!" I put my hand over the control panel. A few seconds later, another button pops up beneath my palm. It's yellow and reads "Music time!" I press it and command, "Play 'Voyage' from the Home World of *Chrono Cross*!"

Not a second later, the inside of my Bubble bursts into an electric guitar melody. I can get used to abusing my power like this. *Now* I feel like I'm on an adventure! I recline in my seat and gaze overhead at the jungle canopy.

For the next hour or so, I tell Gediyon about why I like playing video games so much. Real life is too boring. So I'm gonna go to school, someday find a job, and maybe even get married, but where's the excitement? I like escaping on adventures. It's more active if I can play through it, myself. I can fight battles, make tough decisions, and save the world. Then it feels like I've done something worthwhile when I reach the end.

After I finish talking, I close my eyes and Gediyon says something about defying the destiny that the Creator has set up. Whatever that means, I think he agrees with me that life shouldn't be passive. I know what he's saying is fascinating, but the Bubble is rocking me, the music relaxes me, and Gediyon's voice is so soothing that I fall asleep. I guess this is what it's like to be my dad.

I wake up a few hours later—probably noon—to Gediyon calling me and telling me we should stop for lunch. Outside, I see that his Bubble has finally caught up with mine and he signals me to stop ahead. We've finally passed the last stretch of jungle and the Bubble heads into a natural tunnel within the mountainside. On the floor of the tunnel, I see a narrow stream of shallow water. I guess over time, the water carved out this path.

The Bubble stops beneath a skylight in the cave. Now that it's safe, the glass is pliable and I can step out.

The tunnel smells rusty, but the wind that flows through is relieving. I take a swig of the nectar—sweet and tart like spikes on the tip of my tongue—and I split the flat bread and fruit with Gediyon, but he only takes a little. Then he points out golf-sized red spiders on the wall and tells me, "Here's our lunch!"

Eugh. Well, if Gediyon is going to cook them, then I'll try it. It seems like anything he gives me tastes good.

I spend the next half hour laughing like the Joker as I chase down the spiders. When I reach for them, I first scream when a swarm scuttles over my hand, but their sharp feet tickle, and I find them endearing, like shell-less hermit crabs. Maybe I just think everything is cute.

I feel a pang of guilt when I shake them off into a pan that Gediyon set up over a fire—but hey, it's lunch. Gediyon cooks and seasons them as if he eats them on a regular basis, then he scoops a handful onto a waxy leaf and hands it to me.

As I expected, Gediyon can make even spiders taste good. It's better than shrimp scampi.

When we finish eating, we restore the tunnel as it was before, and continue on to Arriscyal. It doesn't take as long to leave the tunnel as it took to travel through the jungle. Once we reach the other end, I can see that the green landscape spouts waterfalls from all heights. The tallest ones reach higher than skyscrapers, and the shorter ones fall serenely into lagoons.

We pass over rocky streams, dodge large majestic birds, and curve around a beach until we ascend cliffs that overlook an endless ocean. I press my nose against the inside glass and peer outside, admiring each wave that crashes below. I've seen the Californian coast countless times, but the water here *feels* cleaner, even from inside a Bubble.

Gediyon must notice my face smashed against the glass because he says, "This is the Chormetic Ocean, the largest body of water on Starrs."

"*Awe-some*," I say. "I guess this is like our Pacific."

Even after nightfall, the ocean remains clear. I don't see any boats, islands, or even whales. Once it's too dark to gaze at the falling waves, I turn my attention instead to the sky. It's not even completely black yet, but already I can see more stars than I could ever hope to see from my bedroom window. No wonder they call this place Starrs. It's as if someone took a bottle of glitter and scattered it across the midnight velvet above. It'll take an eternity to number them.

"Gediyon," I say softly, "the stars are amazing!"

He doesn't answer. I guess he's asleep.

I lean back, gazing overhead. As the sky grows darker, I think I can even see clusters of faraway galaxies. Through the trees on my right, every now and then I see two moons glowing through, one yellow and the other coral pink.

Two moons. This place is awesome.

After a while, I finally turn off the music and say, "Good night, Gediyon." Then I attempt to sleep.

I wake when I fall against concrete. My mallet and bag topple beside me.

I clench my teeth, fighting through the pain on the side of my body so I can figure what the heck is going on. I look overhead and see my Bubble floating, shrinking smaller and smaller until a giant bird pops it with its metal beak.

"Hey! What do you think you're doing?" I jump to my feet and immediately swing at the bird, but it blocks my attack with its massive wing, fortified with steel.

I hear an explosion as a fireball blasts into its back. Its flesh smokes and I smell a mixture of burnt feathers and hot metal. Gediyon stands on the other side of it—his Bubble has ran off, too. After his attack, the bird turns toward him, but I swing my mallet high and smash it into its head. I hear a crack, and just for good measure, I give it another swing, then it crumples to the ground.

I sigh and lower my mallet. It's an oversized seagull with steel-barbed feathers and a beak that looks like a knight helmet.

I groan and fall into a sitting position. Worst wakeup call ever.

"Another one of those mutants, huh?" I ask Gediyon.

"Unfortunately," he says, tossing some hair out of his face. He helps me to my feet.

I look around. We're standing in the middle of a long, concrete bridge, and I can't see either end. All around, water surrounds us, and below I hear clanking. I guess a train is passing by.

"What is this place?"

"The Intercontinental Highbridge," he says. He looks at the moons, still glowing in the sky but faded in the morning sun, and he points in the right direction. Good, 'cause I can't tell one end from another.

"We have to travel by foot, but Arriscyal is just at the end of this bridge."

I groan again, then follow him. This is going to be a long walk.

"Oh *no*!" someone moans from behind. "You! Why'd you do that? I can't bring this bird back in this condition!"

Whoever it is speaks with a slight accent—Russian? Swedish? Probably nothing from Earth. Whatever it is, at least I can understand him. I turn around and see short, somewhat pudgy man in a dripping wet, skin-tight brown and red diving suit with goggles. Did he jump out of the water?

When Gediyon and I turn around, the man stumbles back and gasps, "By…Lord Pesaeton, you two…" He looks to his left and right, then decides to dive over the left side of the bridge. Did he just commit suicide?!

"Huh?" I look over the side and see him kick into the water, then he's gone. "What was that all about? Do you know him?"

"I don't know," Gediyon says. "He appears to be a Taesmal scientist."

I look back at the dead bird. "You mean he made that thing attack us? What if he sends more monsters after us? Why didn't you kill him?"

This last question seems to break his heart. "You…would want me to kill him?" He looks aside. "Sorry Michelle, but I refuse to take another man's life."

"Oh. Sorry. Guess I got ahead of myself." Even if it is a video game, because it's virtual *reality*, I guess I would have a hard time killing someone too. I had enough difficulty throwing spiders in a pan. Now I feel guilty even suggestion that Gediyon should murder someone for me.

I keep my mouth shut as I follow him into Arriscyal.

CHAPTER SEVEN
ARRISCYAL

After telling him several times that my feet hurt, Gediyon starts giving me a history lesson on Arriscyal. That's a nice way to distract me from the pain.

"The kingdom used to be called the Coastal Lands of the Gifted."

"Is that what Arriscyal means?"

"Actually, Arriscyal is a compilation of the first two kings' names. They were brothers."

He goes on, reminding me that anyone native to these lands is born with the power over a single element.

"What, is there something in the water that makes everyone hokey pokey?"

"It's genetic, but abilities can vary greatly from father to son, or mother to daughter. At birth, an infant is bestowed with that single ability, but they must grasp it within the first minute of life, or the mother cannot pass on another ability until her next conception."

Now he sounds like a biology teacher. Well, I know that if Gediyon taught history at my school, none of the girls would fall asleep in class, and if he taught biology, girls would stay late for help with homework, whether they need it or not.

"So if they get a *single* element," I ask, "how come you have a bunch?"

"That, I do not know. My mother couldn't even explain it to me."

Ah, well, it doesn't make him any less cool if he doesn't know why he's cool.

When we reach the end of the bridge, I'm ready to dance and sing, and then I see the miles ahead of fields, farms, and spiking out of the ground every now and then, windmills. Farthest in the distance is a gleaming spire, and before that, a thin line of white running from as far as I can see from the left all the way to the right. I guess those are the city walls.

I sigh as we continue down a paved path that cuts between the farms, but I won't say any more. I've tortured Gediyon enough with all my complaining.

"Do you see that tower in the distance?" Gediyon asks. "It's the center of the Arriscylean Palace. It's also where our healer sleeps."

I spit hair out of my face. I almost forgot that we're here to recruit the healer, and it turns out that she's a *princess* too? I bet she also has a menagerie of beasts that she can summon in battle—probably in a closet along with ridiculously flashy gowns. Let's see you defend yourself in that hoopskirt, Princess!

I'm making faces to myself, gazing away over a farm with animals that look like walking mops, when I hear rattling in the distance. I look straight down the road and see something headed directly for us. Whatever it is, it's going to run us over!

I dash off the road onto some plush grass. I look back at Gediyon, but he's still standing in the middle of the road, watching me with a smile.

I wave my arms. "Gediyon, watch out!"

"It's the kingdom escort," he says.

In a flash, the silver carriage stops a yard in front of him without even a screech. Two large, muscular cats lower themselves into a sitting position, like lazy sphinxes. They're striped white and silver as shiny as the carriage.

The coachmen step off. They're dressed a lot like Gediyon, wearing the same emblazoned white cloak, and one of them also has long hair. Both of them are wearing an engraved, golden chest plate.

They salute us. "Good morning, Sir Gediyon Raidyne." They face me and bow. "Your Serene Divinity."

The one with longer hair says, "We have orders to escort you to the palace at once."

"You're certainly punctual," Gediyon says with a twang of amusement.

The other coachman says, "Madam Manasa informed Her Highness of Our Divine Creator's return."

I sigh and step back onto the road. "You mean I don't have to walk all the way to the castle? Thank God!"

They swing the carriage door open for me and help me step inside. Plush red velvet seats! Awesome! I squeal out of relief and fall back into them, but leave enough space for Gediyon. Ah, my throbbing feet! I rub my hands all over the seats and scratch happy faces into the pile.

The coachmen close the door again, and before I can call for Gediyon, the carriage is already speeding down the road.

"Hey!" I yell, pushing aside heavy red curtains and sticking my head out of the front window. "What about Gediyon?"

"Another carriage will come for him shortly."

"Why don't you let him ride with me? We're going to the same place, aren't we?"

"Sir Gediyon must report directly to Her Highness. On the other hand, Your Serene Divinity, we would like to treat you to some hospitality."

I gasp and pull back into the carriage. Oh God, how could I have been so stupid? My feet are tired, and a carriage conveniently appears out of nowhere? These guys aren't Arriscylean soldiers!

"You're kidnappers!"

Both of them are silent. Oh God! Why did I have to leave Gediyon's side?

I expect them to laugh or something, but they both gasp.

"Good Goddess, no!"

"That's preposterous!"

"We're such idiots!"

"We apologize for coming off as so hasty—"

"Miss Goddess, we would *never*—"

"One kidnapping is enough—"

"How could we present ourselves as such?"

I slide the curtains back. "So you guys *aren't* kidnappers?"

"No!" they say in unison.

They go on apologizing but I pull back and sigh. "Don't scare me like that! Still, you coulda let Gediyon come along. He did a lot of walking too, you know."

"We apologize, Your Divinity, but it isn't proper for our Creator to ride with a commoner."

"What's *common* about him?"

"In fact, we're hardly fit to escort you, ourselves."

I smack my forehead and groan. These people!

With the carriage speeding down the road, everything outside is a blur. A flash of feathery fields passes by, and then the carriage comes to a sudden halt. I nearly fly out of my seat.

The coachmen open the door for me, and as soon as I step out, they kiss the ground I walk on and spit out apologies.

"It's okay! Really!"

I pat them on the heads, then hear a flourishing fanfare to my right. We made it to the city gates, and closing in the space between the carriage and the other side of the wall is a lineup of heralds, blasting their lungs into their trumpets. Inside the city walls, the people that I do see are kneeling in a bow or flaring their skirts in curtsies.

A man dressed no different than the two men at my feet marches down the road and bows. "Your Serene Divinity, it is our greatest pleasure to welcome you back to the Kingdom of Arriscyal. If you will, we shall escort you to your chambers in the palace. Please follow me."

As I pass, the heralds bow one by one. The city is silent as I walk through the gates—the only thing I hear is running water. Straight ahead I see a carved silver gondola adorned with blue, green, and white gems. A young man stands in the boat, and though he wears a hat to protect him from the sun, his uniform doesn't look like a typical Venetian gondolier. He wears stunning coattails that glimmer with silver embroidery.

The channel of water in front of me stretches to the left and right, and I spot arching bridges cutting over them to the opposite street. Even on the bridges, people silently bow, and I look overhead into windows and see the tops of people's heads. Just looking at them sends a chill through my bones.

Before the guard can lead me all the way to the boat, I stop, take a deep breath, and make sure that everyone can hear me.

"Hey! Just 'cause I'm here doesn't mean that y'all have to act hella stiff, okay? Quit bowing and do what you normally do!"

The guard standing beside me looks like he wants to run away, but he stays in place, his eyes darting nervously from one person to another. It takes them a while, but a few people lift their heads and ask others if it's all right. They look at me—smirking with my hands on my hips like I'm Peter Pan—then decide that it's okay to move about.

I nod. "There ya go!" I start toward the gondola, then add, "Happy day to everyone!"

When I step onto the gondola, it doesn't wobble. I dump my things at the bottom of the boat and take a seat.

"This will take you directly to the palace," the guard tells me. "Good day to you, Your Divinity."

I wave after him. "Thanks man!"

The gondolier stands at the back of the boat, but he isn't holding a paddle. He angles his right arm toward the water and, like Gediyon, uses his water magic to propel the boat forward. It's an amazingly smooth ride.

I look over the side and peer into the water. It's clear, like the water at Lereli, but the water here is tinged green like it's supposed to be. Gray pebbles line the bottom of the bank and long, narrow fish swim in the current.

Even as I pass through the city, I don't think everyone is acting normal. Everyone bows or curtsies as I pass, and some of the women look stiff, but their tight corsets might be to blame. Girls and younger women, who are only wearing loose sashes around their waists, move a lot more gracefully. Their light, flowing skirts billow in the wind, exposing their strappy sandals that tie above the calves. I don't really know how the men manage in the heat, because most of them are wearing vests and boots. Their shirts seem to be made out of the same material as the women's skirts, though.

The gondola curves into a shopping area, and now I see the real magic. People exit shops, carrying glowing jars of some bright white jelly. Some rich-looking women, who have bought too much, lead their servants, who use their levitating powers to tow bags and parcels of merchandise. I stand up to catch a glimpse inside a restaurant and jewelry shop, where several people shoot fire out of their hands into ovens at the same time. In another shop I see two people simultaneously shaping enormous glass vases with fire and wind, and with a wave of her hand, a florist blooms flowers to the size of balloons on request.

"This is so cool!" I turn myself back and forth, facing one side of the street and then the other.

"Your Divinity, please have a seat. You may fall overboard."

Within five minutes of sitting in the boat, my stomach growls. All the oven-fresh bread, roasting meat, and tea shops we pass make me hungry, and I don't have any more flat bread, fruit, or nectar in my bag. I could really do with some more of those red spiders.

"I'm hungry," I mumble.

The gondolier tells me there will be plenty of food prepared for me when we arrive at the palace. It's nice having worshippers.

It takes about half an hour more to snake through the city, and we finally reach the base of the palace. From the channel, the palace seems to be in the sky. Water pours from underneath, so it looks like it's floating on top of a geyser. I think this is the source of water that cycles throughout the city channels. The gondola floats closer to the base of the waterfall, and I'm afraid we'll be pulled under, when the gondolier switches something on the boat. It seals us in a bubble of air before the waterfall even sprays us. The gondola slides into the waterfall and ascends.

The waterfall provides relief from the sun, but now I can't look around the city anymore. Watching the water spill over the sphere surrounding us is pretty mesmerizing, though.

When the gondola reaches the top, the last of the water spills over the side, and the gondola pops onto a calm stream. The gondolier pulls into a small cove at the base of the palace steps and he helps me step out.

As soon as I step foot on the pavement, I hear squealing and see three women running down the steps to greet me. One has graying hair, another is as old as my mom, and the third is a girl in her twenties. They're dressed more conservatively than the women in the city and wear blue pinafores over their dresses, but these are embroidered gold with what I guess is the royal family's crest. It's circular, with six crescents orbiting a single, six-pronged star set on a shimmering backdrop of a sea.

"Miss Goddess is here!" the women say, then curtsy in unison.

"This is wonderful!" the middle-aged one says. "Allow us to take you to your chambers at once!"

"Everything is prepared!"

"Whoa, I have a room here?"

"Of course! We always have a room prepared for when our Creator returns!"

"We've had to refashion it several times since Goddess Saei's time, but it's still as magnificent!"

They surround me and pull me up countless stairs. Wow, I can see the entire kingdom from up here—I can even see a forest and the Highbridge in the distance.

When we finally reach the top of the stairs, the first room that we enter looks like it can be part of any house. It's a spacious square room with a high ceiling, trimmed with more gold and silver, but there are no windows, paintings, or even tapestries. The most ornate decoration in the room is a chandelier that hangs over the center. The crystals themselves seem to be made of light and they float in a spherical formation.

I gape at it when the women lead me to the center of the room and touch another sphere. This one is blue and is about the size of a classroom globe. It floats above the center of an elaborate design etched into the white marble floor, and it glows when one of the women touches it. She prods it around in a few places, and then I see blinding light rise out of the floor design. I shield my eyes, and not a second later, the women lead me down an entirely different corridor. The sphere still sits behind us.

"Whoa! It's like *Star Trek*!"

The women just smile at me but continue down the corridor. More guards stand watch, standing on either side and bowing as we pass, but every other pair carries a halberd or saber.

As we continue down the hall, I notice that the walls aren't completely solid. They look like intricate, floral lacework and allow the sun to pass through, but I have a feeling that no ordinary sword can damage the carved stone, and the gaps are so small that I don't think a fly can squeeze in.

At the end of the corridor is a set of large glass double doors, with similar lace stonework. The last two men at the end bow to me and open the doors for me and my escorts.

The first thing I see is a fountain of food. I gasp and run toward it, but I don't know where to start. Fruit floats next to bonbons next to small pastries. Long tables on either side of the entrance hall support platters. The left has all kinds of meat dishes—breaded, stuffed, roasted, rare. On the right are vegetable and grain dishes, steaming and piled on top of each other with colorful garnishes. Some kind of broth calls to me. Standing around the room are young, stoic-looking boys holding pitchers of different drinks.

I hop from one side of the banquet to the next, but the first thing I bite into is a chocolate bonbon. The inside cream oozes into my mouth, and in the very center is something chewy.

I prance around the vanilla-scented fountain, pick up a flaky pastry, and make my way to the vegetable table. I scoop out something that looks like rice—reminds me of home—and I munch on tiny bread bowls full of what I think is broccoli cheddar soup.

The three women who come with me smile as I stuff my face, so I ask them, "You guys aren't going to eat any?"

"This was prepared only for you, Your Divinity."

"Well, you guys can have some. I don't mind!" I nudge the boy standing beside me, who carries a pitcher of what smells like root beer.

They don't move; I feel like a pig eating like this in front of them, and some sauce, cream and juice dribbles down my front. I have a feeling the only way they'll eat any food is if I feed them myself, so I take a white bonbon from the floating sweets fountain and hand it to the youngest woman.

"I saw you eyeing it," I say. "Eat it. It's delicious."

I stare at her until she puts it in her mouth, and then she smiles at me. "Thank you, Miss Goddess."

"Michelle, okay? My name is Michelle."

I break off the wing of a roasted bird, take a pitcher away from one of the boys, and hand him the meat. I do the same with another, but I hand him a long roll of bread. It takes them about ten minutes to loosen up, and by then they're enjoying the food as much as I am, and chat about the latest gossip.

"Then it's true that the prince has been kidnapped?" the youngest maid asks.

I almost choke on a fish tail. "The prince has been kidnapped? Is anyone doing anything about it?"

The middle-aged maid responds, "Why yes, Michelle, the troops are searching the Arakid Jungle as we speak, so you mustn't worry yourself about such matters!"

The oldest says, "Now let's clean you up before we show you around the kingdom!"

They shoo the boys away and then lead me into the rest of the Goddess suite. I take a few steps up into the bedroom: beautiful and mossy green. Curling, fragrant vines hang from baskets on the walls, and a carpet as soft as clouds cushions my feet as I walk toward the bed. It's the largest bed I've ever seen, practically the size of my whole room at home. It's green with specks of gold flowers. I brush my hands over the comforter. Cool and smooth silk. All of the cushions at the head of the bed look like a pillow fight's dream.

"Geez, and I can sleep in this?" I say under my breath.

"This room is only reserved for the Creator when she returns to our kingdom."

The women stand in front of a large mirrored door, with their hands folded in front of them.

"And how many times has she come back?" I ask. I guess it's more appropriate to ask, "How many times have *I* come back," but it sounds weird to me.

"Three times, since Goddess Saei. But *your* return is a mystery."

"How come?"

"Our Creator is reborn on Starrs every two hundred years or so, and her last incarnation left this world about only eighty years ago."

"Yeah, I guess that is pretty weird. Maybe my brother's invention messed up time on this world? Haha. *Tyme*."

I walk past the bed and push aside sheer cream-colored drapes that lead onto the balcony. These doors also have the same lace stonework, but they aren't as heavy as they look. With a single touch, they pull open, revealing a circular balcony as wide as my backyard. I run to the end and look over the railing.

I'm maybe fifteen stories high and I can see the palace gardens below. A pond cut into four parts lies directly below, and in the middle stands a statue. Smaller ponds are scattered here and there, but instead of a straight path from one to another, the paved walkways curl around each other. Some of the pathways look like fireworks, with bursts of colorful flowers and trees trimmed like stars. Another path is completely hidden beneath a vine archway that leads to a gazebo on top of a hill, where I see a couple walk hand-in-hand. Aw, that's sweet.

I bounce on the balls of my feet when I say, "I have to go down there later!"

"Yes, Michelle, but first let's clean you up."

They pull me back inside and lead me into the mirrored door. It's a bathroom! It smells like a florist's, and steam rolls around the top of a large, glowing pool. A small waterfall feeds it. Like the rest of the room, it looks like it belongs in a garden, but I think I'd prefer my bathroom to look like this than something super high tech or something that should belong in Versailles. The floor beneath me looks like pebbles, but it's as smooth as glass.

I feel awkward when the women undress me, but I melt in their hands when they lead me into the pool and give me a shoulder rub. Ah, being Goddess is amazing!

Their backs are turned to me as I wash off the travel of the past two days, wading around in the pool and sticking my head under the waterfall. After a moment of silence, the oldest one is daring enough to ask me why I've returned to Starrs. I don't know if it's a taboo subject, but her voice shakes. Without hesitation, I tell her about the virtual reality game. They probably don't understand, because they change the topic.

The women chat about taking me around the kingdom so I can help the farmers prepare for the impending famine, and then make speeches or something like that. The older women, whose names I learn are Simmy and Mirra, leave to pick me an outfit, but the youngest stays to keep me company. Her name is Canaria.

"Do you know where Gediyon is?" I ask her, swinging my leg back and forth underwater.

"Oh, have you met Gediyon?" She's smiling. Guess that's another one that has a crush on him. "I think I heard Mr. Baas say that he was sending him off to search for Prince Jaysonn as well."

"*What?*" I scream. I jump out of the pool at once, and my naked body spills water all over the floor. Ah, this is weird! But at least Canaria has her back to me. I wrap myself in a towel and say, "He's leaving without me?"

"Why yes, Michelle. It's best if you stay in the kingdom, where it's safe and you can help—"

"Screw side quests and mini games! *I* want to save the princess! I-I mean, *prince*!" I put on the same clothes that I came in. A costume change can wait!

I tie the sash around my waist as I ask Canaria, "Can you take me to Gediyon?"

"He may be in the throne room. Then you can speak with Her Highness!"

With wet feet, I march toward the door and Canaria follows. The other two women emerge from the opposite mirrored door, holding a pink gown between them, but I say, "I can get fancy later!"

Canaria excuses us. "I'm taking her to the throne room."

I pick up my mallet and bag off the floor in the entrance hall, which has already been cleared of the food, and we continue into the outside corridor. The men outside bow to us as we pass, and I don't care enough to tell them not to. I'm on a mission! I march to the floating sphere on the other side of the walkway, Canaria presses a few places on the orb, and we both appear in a bright room. It doesn't look like Gediyon is here, though.

Like everywhere else, the palace guards stand all around. The entire wall to the right is missing, and in flows a warm breeze from the gardens. At the opposite end of the room are two thrones; the taller one is empty and sits on the floor, while the other levitates high. I guess the person sitting in it is the queen.

Canaria and I step forth off the circular etching, and she curtsies. "Your Divine Highness Queen Trissa, may I present to you,

Her Serene Divinity, our Great Creator, Goddess Michelle." What a mouthful.

I can't help but curtsy as well. This is my first time in front of a queen! What else can I do? When I lift my head again, I see that the queen's throne has descended to the floor. As she walks across the silver carpet toward us, her heavy, dark metallic blue gown trails behind her like an ebbing tide.

"You bow to no one, Miss Goddess," she says. Her voice is strong enough to echo throughout the hall, but still warm and soft. As I rise, she leans herself into a lower curtsy, and everyone else in the room follows her lead.

I walk down the carpet and kneel in front of her. I take her hands, which have the smoothest skin I've ever touched, and she raises her head to look at me. Gosh, she's beautiful. Her almond-shaped eyes, which are the same color as her dress, are wide with surprise at my gesture. Pale blond curls frame her face, while the rest of it twists around her head in an elaborate updo. A crystal tiara sits on top of her head, but it looks like it could be made of water frozen in time.

"I may be Goddess," I tell her, "and I appreciate everyone's awesome hospitality, but this is too much. I was born a normal girl, and I never thought I'd ever meet royalty, so for someone as...*honorable* as you to bow to me, it's really weird. Can we all be a little more casual?"

The queen smiles. Wow, she's pretty! She has the kind of face I've only seen in movies.

"And before you start on that 'Miss Goddess' stuff, my name is Michelle, so call me that."

She nods. "I am Trissa. What brings you here?"

"I want to save the prince!"

"Oh, do you?"

"Yeah! I'm not gonna sit around and let everyone else do it! I want in on the action."

"Well, I'm not one to stop you." She looks at Canaria and says, "Canaria, dear, I don't want to burden you, but will you escort Michelle to the port?"

"Certainly, Your Highness!"

Wow, that was easy.

I stand up and the queen rises with me.

"By the way, you came here with Gediyon, correct?"

"Yup!"

"Interesting."

"He's saving the prince too, right? I can go with him, right?"

"Yes, yes you can."

I jump in place and punch my fist into the air. "Woo hoo!" I start toward the sphere when I remember something. "Oh, Your Highness? Gediyon and I came here looking for the healer to bring back to Lereli. Do you know where she is?"

Both Canaria and the queen laugh, but the queen says, "Michelle, my son *is* the healer."

"Oh," I say, then the meaning of her words sinks in. "Oh! I guess I don't have to deal with some perfect chick then!" I laugh and skip back to the sphere.

Yes! The healer is a boy! If he's not a pretty princess, then he must be a magical kindergartener and super adorable, considering how beautiful his mom is.

As Canaria punches away at the sphere, I can't help but think that something was a little off about the queen. She didn't seem too worried about her son, and there was something rather vacant about her eyes.

Chapter Eight
To Enemy Waters

The next place Canaria and I appear is the seaport. The wind blows back my hair at once, and I can smell the salt in the ocean. Docks made of stone and wood stretch out from the coast below the palace; cargo ships pull in and sailors pace. Men in white cloaks load a medium-sized vessel with barrels and crates. I guess that's where I'm going.

"This is as far as I go," Canaria says, stepping back to the sphere.

"Righty-o!" I wave to her. "Thanks for helping me out!"

She waits until I descend the steps before disappearing. Once she's gone, I gallop downward to the military vessel. Water sloshes beneath my footsteps.

"HALT! Where do you think you're going, missy?"

I turn around and see a tall, muscular, dark-skinned man running toward me with a megaphone at his mouth. A girl about my age, with long strawberry blond pigtails, runs to catch up with him, though she doesn't look away from some kind of clipboard. When the man sees my face, he trips and falls flat on his nose, and it's miraculous that the girl doesn't trip over him.

Actually, the man's bowing, but I guess he isn't very graceful. "Miss Goddess! I apologize!"

"Miss Goddess?" the girl gasps, looking up from her clipboard. She bows, hanging upside-down from the hip up, the tips of her pigtails brushing the docks.

I shrug. "It's cool, guys."

Both of them lift their heads and look at me. The man says, "Goddess, you're so young!"

"You don't look much older than me." The girl holds a hand over her mouth. Her nails are painted aqua.

The man rises to his feet and rubs his stubble, looking between me and the girl. "And I thought Jayse was young, but then—ah, maybe I'm just getting old."

"If I'm as old as Goddess, herself, then yes, you are old." The girl smirks, and the man grins sheepishly. Aww, he's just a big teddy bear!

He asks me, "How can I help you, Miss Goddess?"

The girl goes back to looking at the papers on her clipboard.

I say, "I'm looking for Gediyon. I'm gonna help him save the prince!"

"Y-*you*?" he chokes. "Did you speak to Trissa about this?"

"Yup, she sent me here."

He arches his back and yells at the sky, "*What* is everyone smoking?" I like this guy. He looks back at me and says, "Miss Goddess, that's dangerous! Everyone will be facing the Taesmals and their twisted pets! Maybe even the Taesmal King himself."

"Oh well! The more danger, the merrier!"

I think he wants to slap his forehead, but he ends up smashing the megaphone against his nose.

"Careful, Uncle," the girl sighs.

Uncle? There's no way she and Byran can be blood related because they look nothing alike. She has light skin with rosy undertones, and he's—well, he's a big black guy.

"Ah, Byran, Chili. I see you've met Michelle."

I look over my shoulder and see Gediyon, and I'm so excited that I hug him. Even the pigtails girl—I guess her name is Chili—says, "Hi Gediyon!"

Byran rubs his nose. "Well that's a sight!" Once I let go of Gediyon, who gives me a pat on the back, Byran says, "Gediyon, Miss Goddess wishes to accompany you!"

"You do?"

"Yes! And the queen let me come." So that makes *everything* okay!

Byran scratches the back of his head. "Can't really argue against either of them."

"It's going to be dangerous," Gediyon says.

"I've broken into Bowser's castle a bunch of times. I'm sure this is nothing." I look back and forth between Byran and Gediyon, then I shout, "As Goddess, I demand that I tag along!"

Someone on a cargo ship yells, "Baas! Get back to work!"

Byran points his megaphone at him and yells back, ten times as loud, "*You* get back to work!" He faces us, takes a deep breath, and remembers to lower his megaphone before deafening us. "Gediyon, her safety is on *your* conscience, got it? Don't say I didn't try to stop you! C'mon, Chili." He storms off and Chili prances after, sticking her nose back in her clipboard.

"Uncle, please be careful," she says when he nearly uppercuts a sailor with his wide-swinging arms.

"Who are they?" I ask Gediyon.

"Byran Baas, the head of the transportation in Arriscyal, and his niece Chili. They're in charge of the korelian coaches, the gondolas, the tele-spheres in the palace, and even this port. His family has been running it for over ten generations."

"He's…kind of funny."

Gediyon nods and laughs. "He and my mother were good friends. He was also close to the queen's brother, Prince Aloyin, who himself was in charge of the military."

"So he's kind of important then."

Gediyon nods again, then lowers himself on one knee before me, as if proposing. Warmth flushes my cheeks. "Michelle, are you certain you want to join our search for the prince?"

I shrug. "Beats making speeches."

"It's not that I don't enjoy your company, but the Taesmals are dangerous. If they're after Jayse's blood, there's no doubt they would want yours as well."

"Psh. I trust you guys to protect me. But here's a funny story about that carriage!"

I tell him about the kidnapping false alarm while we walk toward our ship and manage to make him laugh. I've never been on a military vessel before, but the boat isn't very big. It was probably built for a small crew of about forty or so, but I only see about ten people on board. You'd think that if we were on a rescue mission to save royalty, there would be a whole army; Gediyon tells me that many soldiers have already left.

It isn't long until the ship embarks, and I spend most of my time on deck since Gediyon tells me it's stifling downstairs.

"However, you would be safer below deck once we approach the Tainted Sea," he says.

I might as well get as much fresh air while I can. I've been to the beach before, but I've never been out to sea like this. It's even more breath-taking than I imagined, but I don't feel lost because we sail with land still in sight. It doesn't make me feel as insignificant as I do when I stare at the sky. The sea holds its own serene beauty.

I turn my grapple gun into a music player, and listen to a nostalgic world map theme. It adds to the ship's atmosphere, and I wonder what's beyond the horizon.

I stand at the bow of the ship, watching as it slices through the water ahead. If only I had a hot guy to keep me from falling overboard.

Screw that. I'm Goddess! I'll do what I want.

I clear my throat and clench my mallet tight. I reach my arms out to the side. The weight of the mallet tilts me to the right. I close my eyes, feeling the wind in my short hair, the warmth of the afternoon sun on my face. I start to whisper, "I'm flying!" but I end up snickering and lowering my mallet.

I hear laughing behind me and turn to see two boys, one who's laughing so hard that he falls over, and another lying on the deck, clutching his side. I think the one laughing is trying to say something, but he can't get a single word out. Both of them are wearing the white cloaks, but they don't look any older than I do.

"What's wrong with you two?" I ask.

The one rubbing his side says, "You hit me!"

I look at my mallet. "I did?"

The one laughing pulls himself to his knees and says, "You *idiot*! I told you not to sneak up on her!"

"I didn't know she'd attack me!"

The one who was laughing crawls to his friend and forces him into a bow.

"It's a pleasure, Miss Goddess!"

"We just wanted to say hello." They speak with an accent different than Gediyon's, Byran's, and the queen's. It sounds more common and casual, like a guitar to a lyre.

"Well, hi!" I wave frantically at both of them.

They rise to their feet. I don't think they're related, but they look a lot alike. Their hair is longer than mine and both of them wear it tied back, and the collars of their cloaks are popped similarly.

"Aren't you guys a little young to be in the military?"

"We'd only be too young if we couldn't swing a sword. This guy almost doesn't cut it." He nudges his friend in the side, who hits him back, and then he bows to me again, but this time from only the waist. "The name is Launce, by the way."

"I'm Nichols," says the other.

"Michelle."

Launce cracks his knuckles. "Anyway, we were wondering. What brings you here, Goddess Michelle?"

"Well, duh, I'm gonna save the prince."

They ask again, "How did you come to Starrs?" So I tell them about video games. This story is getting old, and each time I tell it, I think I go a little more monotonous. I let them know they should assume I know *nothing* about Starrs.

"So what kind of powers do you have?" I'd address them by name but I still have them confused. I think Launce is the one with brown eyes and Nichols has blue eyes.

They look at each other nervously, then Nichols says, "Actually, Miss Goddess, we aren't from Arriscyal. We grew up in Plaretta, but our families sent us here to join the military." So that's why their accents are different.

" 'Cause, you know, Arriscyal has the best training in the world."

"Not all soldiers have magic. That's why some of us still carry ye olde weapon."

I think back to the palace guards. "Yeah, I did see that."

They go on, talking about how they snuck on the ship to escape mundane palace-guarding duties. The way they talk about it, no wonder the prince was kidnapped.

"It's easier since the king isn't here," Launce says. "He's pretty strict about who goes where."

Oh yeah, I didn't see the king when I was in the palace. "Is he trying to save the prince too?"

They exchange looks.

"He left a while ago to his home in Yinidel to take care of some politics. I guess that's when they thought it would be perfect to kidnap the prince, 'cause that's when Prince Jaysonn went missing. But it takes at least three days to travel back, so he couldn't join the search himself."

Launce shrugs. "Sure he'd like to, though."

"So wait," I say, "the king wasn't born in Arriscyal?"

Launce shakes his head; he leaves the speaking to his friend.

"King Oresonn was born to the Duke of Yinidel," Nichols continues, "so he doesn't have any powers. Arriscyal thought it was blasphemous when they announced the engagement, but the Duchess of Yinidel and Queen Trissa's father convinced everyone that it would help unify the nations, magical or not."

"Guess it worked out, 'cause we only had one war in the past decade."

"But the last one was expected."

"A war, huh?" I say.

"Between the Arriscyleans and Taesmals. They're our sworn enemies—*they're* the ones who kidnapped Prince Jaysonn."

"What, are they trying to start another war or something?"

"Maybe. Or maybe the Taesmal King just wants to gain power."

"And he'll get stronger if he has his enemy's prince as a pet?"

They look at each other and smirk.

Nichols continues, "Gare told me that every few generations, someone in the royal family is born with extraordinary blood. It might be Prince Jaysonn this time—he can heal, after all. Anyone who has a taste of his blood can gain tremendous strength."

"Or they just want to kill him." Launce shrugs.

"*Sacrifice*, more like. I read that if someone sacrifices the special-blooded prince to Pesaeton himself, then that person will become the next Taesmal God."

"Who's Pesaeton?"

"The original Taesmal God, from Goddess Saei's time, eight hundred years ago," Launce says. He shrugs again. "Yeah, we've been enemies that long."

"Pesaeton isn't a physical being, but sometimes people say they can see his shadow in the Universal Mirror. We know his spirit is somewhere on Starrs, because once a year, maybe even twice, he initiates the Cycle with the first trial: the Dark Mist."

"And every two years, a month after the Dark Mist, we get the Famine."

The boys look at each other again, then look back at me.

"I heard the people in the palace say, because you've returned, Miss Goddess, you've triggered the full Cycle of the Six Moons, but I don't know how that's possible if the conditions aren't right."

"What conditions?"

"The players have to be present on Starrs at the same time."

"*Players*?"

"Three key people who awaken the Cycle with their presence. You and two others, but one already died eleven years ago, and we don't know if Jaysonn is the other for certain."

I sigh and take a deep breath. So much history! Even so, I'm glad to hear it.

I ask them to tell me about the Tainted Sea, since we're going there anyway, and they tell me it's contaminated because of the underwater Taesmal fortress called Sheirced. It was constructed generations ago. The Taesmals experimented so much that their byproducts seeped into the water, and over time it became toxic. It was abandoned for the past century, until the last Taesmal King renovated it for his new reign, and since then, the population of mutants has been on the rise.

"We know the Taesmals as the 'Masters of Toxins and Arms,' " Nichols explains, "but the etymology of 'Taesmal' doesn't break down into anything that means that, in any language."

"But that's what they call themselves." Launce shrugs.

Not long later, a man in a dirty apron marches on deck and smacks them with a spoon and a broomstick, and orders them to do chores below deck. Wow, that guy smelled like beer.

Now I'm lonely with nothing but the sea, but soon I grow bored of staring at it. I find Gediyon downstairs in a cramped kitchen—of course—and Launce is making a mess at the stove. Gediyon tells me the journey will take another eight hours, and I don't hesitate to ask him for some claren tea. After a few sips, I fall asleep by a shelf of packaged food.

I wake up a few hours later in another, dark room, lying on a cushioned bench. Somewhere, I hear the sound of a music box. It's so soothing, but sad.

I roll onto my side and scream when I see a horrible face. A munchkin witch is at my bedside! I fall off the other side of the bench.

"What the hell are you doing?" I yell at her, trying to steady myself on my feet.

The old woman clears her throat, but her voice is still croaky. "Since it doesn't look like you're going anywhere, I suppose it's best that I guide you through the Cycle."

I narrow my eyes. "How do you know so much, anyway?"

She digs into her clothes. "I've traveled the universes since before even our Creator herself became mortal."

Dang, then she must be *hella* old!

"I am."

Whoa, did she hear my thoughts?

"Yes, child."

A small yelp escapes my mouth. From her robe, she pulls out a glimmering blue stone hanging on a simple silver chain. "This belongs to the prince. Goddess Saei wore it long ago, but she left it here when she died. I gave it to Trissa when she was pregnant, and she gave it to Jaysonn."

She drops the stone in my hand. It's light blue, like the sky, but it sparkles as if it has millions of stars trapped inside. The brightest of stars twinkle in a perfect circle. There are twelve of them, and when I look closer, I see a thin arrow revolving from the center.

"It's a clock?" I say, but when I look up from the stone, the old woman is gone.

I look at the stone again. The time on the rounded side reads to be about a quarter past six. The flat side also has stars, and this one reads to be at exactly twelve. I guess the sides aren't mirrored, but why are they different?

I slip it around my head, and it falls around my neck, the stone hanging just below the front of my robe. I pick up my bag and mallet and start back to the top deck.

The music box I heard earlier is coming from here. I see Gediyon's silhouette against the orange sunset and start for him. In the palm of his hand is a small, round music box. On the inside, tiny ships circle around a sea as the song jingles away.

"It's so pretty," I say.

"It's the Song of the Sea Angel," he says. The song winds down and then he closes the top.

"The bedtime story?"

He nods.

I lean against the edge of the ship and stare out at sea. I wonder, if the sea angel were here, would she guide us to the Tainted Sea any faster?

"Madam Manasa gave it to me." The munchkin witch?

"She gave me something too," I say, and show him the stone around my neck.

"Goddess Saei's necklace?"

"I guess."

"When she appears in the Universal Mirror, we can see her wearing it."

"Guess it's special then. But the time is all weird." I twist it around to show Gediyon.

As he looks at it, I continue, "You know, all these people are saying that I might've 'awakened' the Cycle or whatever, and it doesn't sound like it's a good thing, but then everyone seems happy that I've 'returned' so I can 'set things right' and stuff. So what's the big deal? Is it a good thing that I'm here?"

He smiles. "You're the reincarnation of our Goddess. Of course it's a good thing that you're here." His words make me melt into a smile that reflects his. "Now, I wouldn't take your awakening the Cycle personally…"

Before he can finish his thought, several footsteps land on deck, and eight Arriscyleans stand ready for battle. Five of them hold weapons—one grabs my arm and pushes me toward the stairs. I remain in the stairwell, watching the scene.

Three gliders surface from below the sea, and instantly, seven others hop on board. They wear skin-tight suits like the man Gediyon and I met on the Highbridge, but I think two of them are female. It's hard to tell because they move so quickly.

The next thing I know, the soldiers shout commands at each other. One blocks an attack from a Taesmal, who retaliates and shoots what I think is a rocket, but another Arriscylean diverts the blast and sends the rocket into the sea. I see another explosion of water and the ship lurches to the left. I hope they didn't just blast a hole! Gediyon swings and dodges around one who throws knives at him, and just as they reach the edge of the ship, Gediyon blasts air at the man's feet and tosses him overboard.

Everything happens too fast, and I see one of them drop what must be a bomb. I jump off the stairs and ready my mallet to smack the bomb off deck, but I see a flash of steel, and then a smile from Launce. He just deflected a needle aimed at me. There's no time to thank him before he shields himself from another attack. I swing my mallet into the bomb and it flies off deck, but explodes before touching the water. I duck and cover myself from the blast.

At the sound of splashing, I turn around to see only two more Taesmals on deck. One is definitely a girl, and two soldiers are pointing a halberd and sword at her throat, and the other is collared in stocks of ice. Gediyon stands over him.

"Throw them overboard," the old man says.

The Taesmals actually appear to dive in themselves, but they're weaponless and admit defeat. Somehow, that seemed too easy. What else could they have wanted?

I guess this means that we're close to Sheirced now. Everyone asks each other if they're all right, and Launce and Nichols congratulate each other on their battle scars—two cuts each. Several men run back below deck to check if that earlier blast damaged anything. Gediyon continues to stare at the sunset, and I look at the water. Debris floats beneath the surface and an oily film slithers on top. Land isn't far, and I recognize the tall, tropical trees that were outside of Lereli.

I stand by Gediyon, watching the sea in case anyone else emerges, when I almost fall overboard. Gediyon takes hold of my arm and we look around to see what caused the sudden lurch. The ship has practically crashed on shore and the other soldiers immediately walk off the ramp for the jungle. I don't know why they're going there when Sheirced is in the middle of the ocean, and I look around the deck at Gediyon, Launce, and Nichols who are as perplexed as I am.

"Where are they going?" I ask them.

"Probably to find the other troops?" Launce says.

I look at the sea, then back to the jungle, where the last soldier disappears behind a trunk. Funny how they left like that, like they were in a trance. I point at the ocean and say, "But isn't Sheirced…?"

Gediyon steps forward and says, "Did you three have anything to eat on board?"

"Only the soup we were making," Launce says.

"Only the tea," I say.

"I'm starving," Nichols says.

"Perhaps there was something in the liquor," Gediyon says.

Something in the liquor that made them march into the jungle? What do we do now? None of us know how to steer the ship, and we don't know exactly where Sheirced is in the Tainted Sea, or if the prince is even alive. I don't want to go with them into the jungle because of the bugs, but we all leave the boat for the beach.

We stride into the sand, and I stare at the sea. The sun has already set and the horizon looks even more red with the pollution.

"I will go in and redirect everyone back here," Gediyon says.

As he starts off, I see something rise out of the water. It looks like a pin at first, but then the rest continues to surface with it. Domes, spires, and towers, of different kinds of architecture as if they were stolen from different countries, all melted onto one fortress. Its black silhouette in the red sky makes it look like something straight from hell.

CHAPTER NINE
SAVE THE PRINCE!

"Is that it?" I say under my breath.

Behind me, I hear a rustle and turn to see Gediyon drop his cloak. He starts for the water and Nichols shouts, "Are you going to swim all the way?"

"Gediyon, you aren't going in all by yourself, are you?" I add.

"I'll be fine. You three stay here and keep yourselves out of sight until I return."

Before he can step into the water, I jump at him and cling onto his back like a baby koala. "I'm not letting you go in alone!"

"Michelle, this is Taesmal territory. If I exposed you to such danger—"

"We're going, too!" Launce says, raising his fist with Nichols's limp wrist.

"Yeah!" I say. "We can't split up now! That's always when something bad happens. Who knows if something is waiting for us in the jungle, and will only attack when you're gone!"

"Strength in numbers!" Launce adds, still swinging Nichols's arm as an extension of his own—but Nichols looks like he'd rather run into the jungle. Launce continues, "Where are the rest of our troops? We are the troops! Now let's go. Time's a-wasting!"

Gediyon sighs and takes me by the hand, though much more gently than Launce clenches onto Nichols. "Then we must stay close. None of us can lose sight of each other."

We nod in agreement and Gediyon casts freezing air onto the water before us, creating about two yards of a jagged ice platform jutting off shore like a dock. Before any of us step onto it, I re-form our shoes with sturdy cleats. From here on, the poisonous water might as well be flowing lava.

Gediyon keeps a firm grasp on me as we trudge across the ice. He continues to build the bridge as we walk, and each time he raises it a little higher. It's a good thing that Gediyon is wearing gloves, otherwise I'd probably slip off because my hands are sweaty.

I keep my eyes on the ice, but I'm still clumsy from nerves and I trip over nothing. Gediyon immediately balances me, but my mallet topples into the water.

"No!" I gasp.

"Are you all right?" Nichols shouts from behind.

I sigh. "My mallet…"

"Stay close to us," Launce says, "and you won't even have to defend yourself!"

I'd still feel safer with something in my hands, though. At least I have Gediyon.

Now all four of us are extra careful. Luckily, no one loses anything else. About halfway between shore and the building, Nichols says, "That shell shaped structure? See the smoke and sparks?"

That's when I look up. Now the building could be the disguise of a volcano. In the rough center of the entire fortress is a conch-shaped building, spiraling toward the sky, but instead of a cone at the top, it's open and glowing smoke billows out. No streams of lava yet.

"The Taesmals supposedly hold sacrifices to an open sea and sky. Since Sheirced is normally underwater, and that appears to be the only open structure..."

Then that's our checkpoint. We can't drop in directly from above—who knows if we'll fall into a giant cauldron of soup?—so Gediyon decides that we'll break in from the side.

I don't know how much time has passed since we left shore, since I hadn't checked the time on the necklace when we left, but I hope it hasn't been long enough that they've already stabbed the poor prince in the heart, or whatever it is they're going to do.

We've made it across one obstacle, but many more will come. As soon as we step onto the conch, Gediyon melts the rest of the ice bridge. The surface of the conch is metal, but corroded and covered with something rough—barnacles? I return our shoes to the way they were before so our footsteps will be softer. The conch is several stories above the water, and if we slid off the edge, it's a likely spiky death from the spires atop the towers below. Luckily, if we stay close to the inner spiral of the building, we're somewhat safe from the fall.

I continue clinging onto Gediyon as he leads us forward, guiding himself with his free hand and feeling the curved wall for any weak spots. It takes no time at all before he finds a seam that slides open to a window. Of course glass covers it, and even if it weren't tempered, a metal grate protects it from harm.

That's nothing I can't handle, though! Gediyon steps aside and I put my hands to the metal grate, warming the cold bars with my too-sweaty hands, until the metal becomes floppy like clay. I break off the bars and roll them into a ball, then set it at my feet. It rolls off a moment later.

Next, the glass, and I try reminding the physics of the universe that we're fighting against the clock and that I can't make an art project out of this. Before my hands even steam the glass, it quietly shatters into a pound of sand that sprinkles over the floor on the other side.

Gediyon climbs through first, then catches me when Launce and Nichols boost me through. The two of them would have likely crushed each other falling through, but Gediyon cushions them with a pillow of air.

The hall is lit—with buzzing electrical light bulbs! I didn't think I'd see anything like these in Starrs. Launce and Nichols are taken aback by the scenery—I don't blame them. The walls are paneled with wood, not rusty metal coated in dried blood, and it's surprisingly well-lit.

Gediyon knows our priorities and seals the metal shutters over the nonexistent window, scatters the sand with a whirlwind so the grains aren't as obvious, then he continues downward. Launce and Nichols have to hold their equipment to keep them from rattling while we walk. Now I'm somewhat glad that I've lost my mallet; if anyone would fumble with a weapon and alert the entire fortress that we're here, it would be me.

We follow the spiral to perhaps one floor below, then come across a landing that leads into a hall, and a set of stairs that continues down the spiral. A man and woman emerge from the hall and head downward, and for a second I feel like screaming. Gediyon shoves me behind him, Nichols holds me securely, Launce is about to draw his sword, when Gediyon sweeps a gust of air at the Taesmals from the side and smashes them both into the wall. Like he did for Launce and Nichols, Gediyon softens their fall so others won't come running at the racket. They're both knocked out, so Gediyon lays them against the wall and sends sparks at the three closest lights to destroy the bulbs. Now if anyone passes through, they might not notice these two and keep walking, or so we hope.

"No need for casualties if they do not see us first," Gediyon whispers, eyeing Launce's hand on his sword, which he still hasn't drawn.

"There's no way we can't run into someone else," Nichols says. "We can't kill all the lights and hide in the shadows either—that's too suspicious."

"Say someone does see us," Launce says. "We have to get rid of them somehow, otherwise word will get out that we've broken in."

"We're here to rescue Jayse," Gediyon says, "not to annihilate the Taesmals. I would like for us to find him without alerting the others—let the Taesmals believe that everything is going according to *their* plan. We can't let them know we were ever here, or they'll come after us, if they don't stop us before we leave."

Right now the main issue is being caught. If only there were some cheat code I could use so enemies couldn't see us…

I look at the Taesmals at our feet. The woman is wearing a black cloak, and suddenly an idea strikes me. The others are still trying to figure out how to get by without killing anyone, while I work on the cloak. Now my childhood fantasies can come true and I can sneak around in my own invisibility cloak! For good measure, I make it extra long so it's sure to cover all four of us, especially since Gediyon is so tall.

I whip the material in front of me as if it's a bed sheet, and though it doesn't make my feet vanish, it blurs them into an indistinguishable shadow. Good enough, I guess. Maybe if we stop in the shadows between each light on the way down, we can avoid anyone seeing us at all.

We drape ourselves with the material, and with even a foot between each of us, the cloak still trails behind us like a wedding dress, extending the blurry shadow like a lurking grim reaper.

We descend about three more floors under the shadow cloak. Eight Taesmals pass us in that stretch, and none of them suspect anything. It's lucky for us, but I thought a lot more Taesmals would roam the halls for security's sake.

We hear a murmur of hundreds of voices echo hauntingly through the conch structure, then three more Taesmals emerge from one of the side halls. This time, they have a mutant with them. The four of us back against the wall, knowing that a fight is near. Though the mutant's eyelids are sealed shut, its nose makes up for its lack of sight, and it sniffs the air to find its next meal—mere yards before it.

In the shadows of the cloak, Launce and Nichols reach for their weapons. The Taesmals leading the dog mutant start for the ascent, but the creature won't budge. It's growling, tail twitching madly, saliva oozing through its lantern fish jaw…

Its tail fans out and whips at us, literally blowing our cover. It would have sliced Nichols's head clean off, but he ducks just in time, and I instead catch the cut in my left shoulder.

For a moment, I stand shocked, but Gediyon and Launce act immediately. My hand shakes as it hovers over my shoulder. It feels like it's on fire, but I don't want to look at it, especially since the monster is about to attack again.

Launce goes for the mutt, hacking while dodging its razor sharp fins that have extended in its fury. Gediyon blasts concentrated streams of water at the Taesmals' faces; one of them is unaffected by the attack and blows a whistle.

I hear Nichols mutter, "Damn it," before he leaves my side and takes care of the Taesmals who'll rise around the corner. Launce has already made a sloppy butchering of the mutant—looking at it makes me want to barf—so he runs down to help Nichols.

I decide not to touch or look at my cut until this is over. I run to help Gediyon, then stoop down to the fallen Taesmals. They're still breathing, of course. I shuffle through their belongings, then find a box of…eggs? They're cushioned, warm and speckled, about the size of baseballs. If they're the eggs of a monster like that dog fish, I won't feel so bad throwing them.

Inevitably, more Taesmals rush in from the side hall and from above. Gediyon takes care of those coming down the spiral, and I toss the eggs at those coming through the hall. It's a good thing I'm right-handed, since my left shoulder is injured. My first shot is lucky, and the egg splatters on the Taesmal's face. Two behind stumble into him while he tries to wipe it off. As for the rest of the eggs, I turn them as dense as lead and toss or roll them at their feet. I was always better at bowling than baseball.

I manage to sweep most of them off their feet, then Gediyon comes in and smashes the rest against the wall.

An army lies at my feet. Launce swings the blood off his blade; Nichols stands frozen, panting as if he'd just run a mile. The Taesmals surrounding them are dead—stabbed, dismembered, disemboweled. My head spins and I walk to the doorway of the side hall, hyperventilating and repeating, "Oh God! Oh God!"

"We need to get rid of them!" Launce shouts.

"There's no time!" Gediyon says.

They aren't even trying to whisper anymore.

"You don't want anyone following us, right? We have to get rid of them one way or another."

A rushing sound comes from this hall. I look up and see a few yards down a bridge above a pool of water. Aside from the blood, this smells like the sea.

"Guys," I squeak, "we can dump them here."

Gediyon takes a look in the hall, then goes back to round up the bodies in a wave of water, which helps wash away the blood. He rolls the wave toward the door, but Launce stops him.

"We'll take care of them," he says. "You go on ahead. We'll catch up." He nods at me. "You too. Can't let Miss Goddess dirty her hands. Go on."

Gediyon drops the wave; the water flows down the hall and seeps through the side railing, rinsing off red. "Thank you," Gediyon says.

He pulls me across the dripping bridge and I scream after the boys, "Be careful!" When we reach the other side, I knock out one side of the bridge's railing so it'll be easier for them to dispose of the bodies.

At the other end of the hall is another spiral walkway, only this one is narrower and since the descent is steeper, the path is made of steps. It's much darker on this side; only a few bulbs light the path—many of them have burnt out. These walls are bare stone.

I hear murmuring, so we must be close to the sacrificial chamber. Gediyon and I exchange no words; we only hear the sound of each other's breaths.

Eventually we catch a whiff of warm air and a burst of light. Gediyon pulls us through an alcove overlooking the center of the room. Even here, barnacles stick to the walls, so this entire area must be submerged when Sheirced is underwater.

The smoke rising is lighter from where we watch, and below is an area that might be the equivalent of maybe six Arriscylean throne rooms. No wonder we didn't encounter a lot of Taesmals on the way, because most of them were here!

Currently, everyone stands still. The Taesmals present are wearing black or royal purple robes. Some of them have white or silver faces—masks? If they aren't wearing masks, then they're wearing hoods.

A pool of water, maybe leading to the same one in the previous room, takes up about half of the room. Flaming torches line the half circle of floor and an aisle, which leads from the only doorway down to a black slab that hangs over the edge of the water. Lying on it is a boy, but I don't think it's Prince Jaysonn since he looks too old to be the healer. At least, he's maybe around my age, and the healer is much younger.

Are there multiple sacrifices happening tonight? Is that why everyone is standing around doing nothing, because they're waiting for the real sacrifice? So what's that guy doing down there, napping while everyone watches? Taesmals are weird.

Gediyon finally speaks. "We're just in time. It looks like they're still preparing."

Now I'm confused about how this is going to play out. I keep looking back and forth from the staircase behind us to the scene below, waiting for Launce and Nichols, waiting for the ritual to start.

Are Gediyon and I just going to watch while they kill him? Shouldn't we at least try to save him too?

Even though the crowd below is eerily quiet and still, I feel as if they're all madly chanting, and I hope no one is going to reach into that guy's chest and pull out his flaming heart. Thinking about it reminds me of the pain in my left shoulder. I reflexively reach for it; my palm feels like it's glued to it. Sticky blood. Gediyon hasn't noticed my injury yet, but I don't want to bring attention to it since there are more important things at hand. I still don't want to look at it, but now that I've felt it, I'm sure I won't die of blood loss anytime soon. Maybe an infection somewhere down the line.

I'm not sure how much time passes—maybe a few minutes—but then the massive doors crank open at the end of the flame-lit aisle, and in walks a procession of more silver-masked people, then one with the most ornate robe, wearing a purple and gold mask.

When he starts down the aisle, everyone except his procession bows, so he must be the Taesmal King.

Before he reaches the altar, we hear shuffling behind us, and even though I'm certain it's Launce and Nichols, I'm ready to run or jump or maybe fight if it's the Taesmals.

Gediyon and I are safe, though. They nearly pass us, but then Launce and Nichols scamper inside. Launce slides in on the other side of Gediyon, but Nichols falls to his knees behind me, shaking. Even though it's dark in the alcove, I see Nichols wipe away some tears. He tries to hide it, and I pat him on the back.

Gediyon reaches for Nichols and gives him a silent nod of thanks. This simple gesture makes me realize how much of a burden Launce and Nichols took for us. They dirtied their hands so we didn't have to.

I give Nichols a hug for thanks, but he awkwardly pulls away for a look at the scenery, because the king has started to speak.

It's hard to make out everything that he's saying since the reverb is so intense. He definitely mentions a sacrifice, then something about pure blood, the true king, and immortality.

Maybe making up for the hug he rejected me, Nichols leans close to me and whispers, very softly, "I think this is what he said. They're going to sacrifice his pure blood, which will deliver them the true king."

I whisper back, "What does that mean?"

"What I told you before. He thinks this sacrifice will make him a God."

"But I thought they had to sacrifice the *prince*?"

Nichols stares at me.

Wait a minute!

I look down at the boy on the stone slab. That *teenage* boy, not a toddler. But he has light hair, like Queen Trissa. I don't see a five-year-old prince anywhere in sight.

I gasp, then slap my hand over my mouth. That hot guy down there *is* the healer!

Now I'm blushing, my entire body is warming up, Nichols can probably feel more heat from me than the rising smoke… And the Taesmal King is bringing a knife to poor Prince Jaysonn's forearm. He slices it open, and I can't help but think what a muscular arm that is for a *healer*.

"Why aren't we stopping them already?" I hiss at the others.

"This isn't the sacrifice," Nichols whispers, much lower. "That's the king tasting his blood for his own benefit. They need His Highness to be alive when they send him to Pesaeton."

"Why?"

"What's a sacrifice if it's already dead?"

The Taesmal King bellows, "Accept this! My offering for you, Lord Pesaeton!"

On the other side of Nichols, I hear Gediyon, "We need to make them believe Pesaeton is watching."

"How?" I hiss back.

I see Gediyon shake his head and shrug. A moment later, the crowd gasps and pushes each other for a view of the forming whirlpool below Jaysonn. It glows aqua with streaks of gold and lavender swirling in like cake frosting.

"Are you doing that, Gediyon?" Launce asks.

Gediyon nods, keeping his eyes focused on the scenery.

The Taesmal King's laugh is perfect. Low, echoing, majestic and villainous. His servants roll Jaysonn into the whirlpool, and when he hits the water, Gediyon sends up a magnificent array of lightning bolts, which produces more gasps from the spectators. The Taesmal King steps atop the slab where the prince was, then raises his hands to the opening above.

Gediyon quickly tells us, "Meet me below only when you see me return. Cover your eyes, now!"

I guess he must blind them with some kind of flare, because I see the flash behind my closed eyelids. Then I hear him jump off from the alcove.

When I dare open my eyes again, Gediyon is nowhere in sight, so he must have jumped into the water when everyone was blinded. Into the poisonous sea?!

I bite on my folded fingers. To my left, Launce and Nichols peer over the edge of the alcove into the water, but it's too murky to see. Without Gediyon's full attention over the sight, the whirlpool has subsided. Many of the Taesmals are still recovering from the flash—some of them simply blindly feel their way out, or those who have regained sight lead them.

Though the rest leave, one remains: the Taesmal King. He stands on the stone slab, gazing upward through the opening in the ceiling. Now that he's facing our direction, I can see that his mask exposes his mouth but conceals everything else.

It seems like he's waiting for shooting stars to streak the sky to grant his wish, but no such thing happens. Does he feel any different at all? If what Nichols says about the prince's blood is true, then maybe he feels stronger, because several minutes after everyone else has left, he finally steps down the slab and exits, himself. When the door closes after him, it clanks as if it takes several mechanisms to seal it.

However long the king has been standing there was way too long for any normal person to hold his breath underwater. Maybe Gediyon has hidden gills—even if he did, wouldn't the toxin still affect him?

"He's taking too long," I squeal.

"He's probably using an air pocket," Nichols reassures me.

"Do you think he found the prince all right?" Launce asks.

Nichols says, "Just hope that there aren't any man-eating fish down there that also got a taste of his blood."

A deep clanking rumbles through the structure, and by the sound of the water rushing, it means Sheirced is sinking back beneath the surface. I shriek—which is sort of okay since the Taesmals are gone—Launce curses, and Nichols sputters nonsense. We frantically look into the water for any sign of Gediyon.

Nothing.

How fast can this building sink? If Gediyon doesn't return… If we can't find a way out, then the poisonous water is going to rush in and it'll be like Lereli all over again.

"They're gone!" Launce shouts over our panicked noises. "We can make our way down. Save time, if Gediyon…"

He doesn't finish his sentence. We follow him out of the alcove and hurry down the spiral staircase, which leads to one of the side halls in the sacrificial chamber.

Standing here where the other Taesmals were, even though the ritual is over, the entire situation seems much more grand. I feel so small down here. Overhead, we can see the night sky drifting farther away as we sink into the sea.

We rush to the stone slab, which is smeared with a small amount of the prince's blood, and we gaze into the water for air bubbles, light, anything.

Then, like a missile out of water, Gediyon lurches out of the water and lands quite dry several yards from us.

"Gediyon!" I scream.

"You did it!"

"You're all right!"

Gediyon is carrying the prince in his arms, who unlike Gediyon is soaked.

Launce starts, "The poison?"

"The water is purer here. It hasn't fermented with the rest of the sea yet." Gediyon lets out an exasperated sigh. "He's breathing well now. I had him cough up the water while we were submerged, but now it's probably best for him to sleep off the toxin and sedatives." He nods at us. "Hurry, we'll ride the current out. Stay close to me."

I cling onto Gediyon's arm, next to the prince's head. He's even cuter up close! Before I know it, Gediyon has surrounded us with a shield of shimmering air. In a steep arc, we lift off the ground and sink into the water. The world becomes dark, but I trust Gediyon in this different kind of transportation bubble to lead us to safety.

Since the air barrier is glowing softly, I can make out the prince sleeping next to me, safe in Gediyon's arms.

He's the Prince of Arriscyal—the healer we need to restore Lereli. He's nothing like the healers I've met in video games, but I think I prefer this turn of events.

Chapter Ten
The Healer

The underwater slope becomes shallower, and Gediyon warns us that he's going to catapult us out of the water. His warning is so abrupt I don't know what to expect. It feels like someone has dropped a ton anvil on the other end of a seesaw. I hear Launce and Nichols screaming, the ground is a sea of lights, and then I land on something lumpy but firm.

"Oof!"

It's Launce. My head is a bit sore from the impact, but it must be worse for Launce. As soon as I realize it's him, I try scrambling off, but my legs are entangled with his.

"Sorry!" I yell.

"No, no, no!" he groans. "Excuse *me*!"

Nichols scrambles up on his own and asks Gediyon, "Why couldn't we just *walk* out to shore?"

"I'm terribly sorry," Gediyon says. "If we had, the contaminated water would have flooded our shield and put us at risk of infection."

"So you *flung* us out instead? I mean, Michelle here—"

"Mehh, speak for yourself." I push myself to my feet and brush off sand. "We're dry and safe. Gediyon did the right thing." I look around the beach.

The five of us are the only ones on shore. There's no sign that the other soldiers had returned since we'd left.

Now beneath bright star and moonlight, we can clearly see Gediyon carrying the still-dripping prince in his arms.

"I apologize for not—" Gediyon starts.

"Don't," Launce says. "You're already doing more than enough."

I jump to Gediyon. As much as I want to look at the prince I feel like I'm not worthy enough to look at him directly.

I ask Gediyon, "Jason okay?"

"Jay*sonn*," Nichols corrects me in a quiet voice.

"He's with us now," Gediyon says. "I'm certain he'll be just fine."

Nichols is looking out to sea when he says, "Let's hide quickly in case anyone is keeping a lookout."

Gediyon starts for the jungle, but I gasp, "Not in there, please!" Who knows how long we'll have to stake out? I don't want to spend the night with bugs crawling through my hair!

"Where, then?" Launce asks.

I look at the ship. It's in plain sight, but it looks untouched since we'd left it. I think aloud, "If we can make it invisible…"

Gediyon doesn't doubt my abilities because he heads straight for it. Before I leave the beach, I grab Gediyon's cloak from the sand so it won't give away our position—that is, if I can even manage to make the whole ship vanish.

We use his cloak for the prince to lie on when we climb on deck. Maybe this is a little too out in the open, but we agree that it's much easier to breathe up here than it is below deck. Can't have our healer running any health complications before he even wakes up.

The prince is lying still, breathing steadily. He looks nothing like the little boy I imagined. He's probably about a year or two older than me, and since his shirt is so wet, I can see the definition of his muscles, so he must work out, or at least swing around a sword a lot. Ah, stop staring, Michelle!

Before my eyes, water droplets rise from his body like quickly evaporating steam. I look up to see Gediyon toss the mass overboard to sea. Launce quickly returns from below deck with a strong-smelling bottle of liquor.

"This was behind the others," Launce tells us. "I'm surprised they didn't touch it, since it has the highest proof, but that's better for us, right?"

We use the alcohol to clean our cuts. Gediyon rips part of the prince's sleeve and uses it to bandage his bleeding forearm. Nichols dabs the alcohol against my shoulder, which makes me hiss through my teeth in pain, then he also helps to dress my wound.

When we're done, Gediyon says, "Please come with me, Michelle. I'll help you turn the ship invisible."

We stand on the highest point on deck, and Gediyon sends a wind barrier around the ship. It shimmers, and I concentrate to make the inside invisible to outsiders. It takes longer than I'd like because I keep changing my mind about how I want it to work—whether it's a shadow, mirror, if it's impenetrable, if Gediyon needs to maintain it for the entire night… Once I'm satisfied, Gediyon and I walk through the wind barrier to the beach, and looking up, we can only see the sky. We did it!

"I'm going to search for the others," he tells me. "I shouldn't be long."

"What if someone *does* find us?" I ask. "Like if another mutant sniffs us out?"

"You, Launce, and Nichols will make a great team." He says it with such confidence, but I don't think the boys trust themselves that much. Then he adds, "Don't worry," and starts off for the trees.

"What about Jason—Jay*sonn*? Should we try to wake him up?"

"Let Jayse sleep it off, but keep an eye on him."

I sigh. "All right. Be careful, Gediyon!"

"Of course." He nods and then leaves. When I turn around, I have to crawl and feel for the ramp until I pass the barrier. On deck, Nichols holds a jar of some glowing jelly. He's reaching into it and throwing handfuls of it around the deck. In midair, they turn into brightly glowing balls of light.

Launce sits next to the prince, and I tell them what Gediyon is up to. Nichols repeats my concerns, but Launce tries to reassure us, "Did you see that smile on the Taesmal King's face when he walked out? He thought the sacrifice worked, so until someone else sees that the prince is alive, we should be safe."

It's a good thing that no one else can *see* us on deck here.

"We do make a good team," Nichols says.

The three of us look at each other in silent agreement.

I look at the prince—I mean, I can't help it. He seems to be sleeping fine. It doesn't look like he's having any trouble breathing…

Okay, I'm *staring* at him again, but can you blame me? I might be able to call Gediyon handsome, but I don't know if any words in the human language can describe Jaysonn's looks. I guess it's expected, considering his mom is so beautiful, but I don't expect her son would look so… so…

"Why didn't you tell me he wasn't five years old?" I blurt out.

Launce raises an eyebrow. "Who said he was five?"

"And all this time, I thought I was going to meet some annoying righteous perfect girl, or maybe an adorable little kid, but I get this guy as the healer? This is all wrong! He doesn't fit the role. I mean, look at him! He looks more like a hero than a support character."

Nichols smirks at me. "You like him, don't you?"

I turn my back to them. "This is wrong! This is *wrong*!"

The healer is freaking hot.

I scream and fall into a sitting position on deck before I realize it'll hurt my butt.

"This isn't right! Someone is screwing with me! Next thing you know, a meteor is gonna fall out of the sky and pop and shower everyone with candy and confetti!" I look over at Launce and Nichols. "And what are you guys, fairies? Oh and guess what! I'm your father!" I laugh hysterically.

Launce and Nichols exchange glances and keep quiet until I've calmed down. I keep my forehead on top of my bent knees and listen to them tell me how the prince and Gediyon were good friends when they were younger, before Gediyon joined the military and started helping everyone outside the kingdom.

"Gediyon is like an older brother to him," Nichols says.

"No wonder he was so quick to save him," I mutter back.

They go on, saying how it took a while to even realize that the prince was kidnapped since he's hardly ever home in the palace. He often leaves with his swords and slays Taesmal mutants in the Arriscylean forests and fields so they won't bother people in the city. After all, since the military deals with other people, and the farmers deal with their own livestock, who else is going to take care of the mutants? He's been out so long in the past that they stopped sending search parties to find him, because he'd return in the morning with several pelts to donate to shops.

"That's nice of him," I say.

"Gediyon's been gone for a while, hasn't he?"

I check the time on the stone. It looks like it's a little past eight, but it feels later. Maybe the time is set to another time zone?

"Do you think we should go look for him?"

I look back at them. "But what about the prince?"

Launce grins. "You're here, Miss Goddess. You can look after him."

"All by myself?"

"Ah, it's safe. We just have to make sure the others aren't giving Gediyon any trouble."

They stand up.

"You're leaving me?"

"I don't see a problem," Launce winks. "After all, you and His Highness here can become, uh, *better acquainted*."

"He's freakin' *asleep*!" I jump to my feet, but the boys run off deck and hop off the ramp for the beach. They race each other into the jungle, where I can hear their laughter drown out the insect chirping.

I growl and clench my fists. "You—you guys are mean!"

I stomp over to Jaysonn and sit in front of him. "Okay, so I'm alone with you, and I'm staring at you—I mean, I'm supposed to *watch* you, right? And YES! You're the best looking guy I've ever laid eyes on, and…"

And he can't hear a word I'm saying. Maybe I should save my breath for when he wakes up.

If he wakes up.

I poke him in the shoulder and then shove him. He rolls back, but shows no other response. Dang, he's really out, isn't he?

I kneel over him so my face hangs above his and I yell, "WAKE UP!" Nothing.

I groan and fall back onto deck, looking ahead at the stars.

"Ah, why did I have to get stuck with you?" I put my foot on his knee and give him a blind kick. Still nothing.

I crawl onto my front and face him again. "I'm just glad you aren't a pretty bimbo princess. I mean, sure you're kind of a pretty *prince*, but healers aren't supposed to look like you." I stand up and give him another tap with my foot. "Come on. Get up. You don't want me to smack you awake, do you?" I wouldn't dare.

I walk around.

"So, nice to meet you. My name is Michelle. Oh, your name is Jason? That's cool. Oh, you want to know my life story? Funny that, because I was about to ask you the same thing!" I scream and face him. "*Why* do you have to look like that?"

I only become crazier. I spew movie quotes and sing Disney songs, and after I've exhausted every one I know, the others still aren't back, and the prince still hasn't woken up. I hope I don't have to give him a kiss to wake him up.

Oh God! I gasp and my hand flies over my mouth. What if that *is* what I have to do?

I shake my head. That's stupid.

I keep pacing around the ship, wondering where the others are. I'm so bored that I use my powers to make a bed out of the deck, which has a bedspread the same pattern as the wood grain. If no one comes back soon, I'll probably have to sleep out here.

I sit on the deck mattress and to my surprise, it's springs back. I lie on it and stare at the prince, wondering if I should do the same for him.

Nah, he can sleep on the ground. That's what he gets for making me think he'd be a girl or little kid.

I yawn and reposition myself on top of the mattress. I wonder if my bed back in Arriscyal is more comfortable. I wonder how comfortable the prince's bed is.

Stupid prince.

The next time I open my eyes, the sky is bright. I'm surprised that I slept so well even though I'm outside.

What time is it?

I position the stone over my nose but don't bother looking at the time because I notice that beside me, the prince is gone.

I gasp and the stone smacks against my face when I drop it. With one eye open, I jump off the deck bed, which shrinks back to its normal state when I step away, and I look around the empty ship. Launce, Nichols, and Gediyon still haven't returned in the night, and now the prince has been kidnapped *again*?!

I scream and spin around to look for anyone on board. I'm the only one here. If the Taesmals bothered to take the prince again, why did they leave me here alone? Or maybe they actually killed me and this is the afterlife.

I look over the morning beach, vibrant in the early morning haze. It's absolutely breathtaking. Of course it is, if I'm dead! Keeping my eyes on it, I scream and turn on my heel—

"Easy there."

I scream again and fall to my butt, looking up at the prince standing over me like an angel, the rising sun glowing behind him.

He. Is. Beautiful.

His hair shines like antique gold and many strands hang over his eyes, which are a fresher green than anything I've seen in Starrs. Heck! Who dares call those perfect jewels "eyes?"

"Oh my God, you are so hot." Did I say that out loud?

He smiles, and I melt. "I wanted to take a look around, see if it's not just the two of us. I didn't want to disturb your sleep." His voice matches his angelic appearance. So clear, youthful, and mature at the same time. He reaches for me to help me to my feet, and I feel something like a pleasant spark. Is this what it's like to be touched by a healer?

Standing up, of course he's taller than me—I never had much going for me in the height department, but I can't help but think that he's a nice kissing height.

He then sees the bloody bandages on my shoulder and, without asking for permission, he hovers his hand over it. My skin tingles as he heals it, and I quickly unravel the bandages to see that my shoulder is flawless. He just used his magic on me! He's removed his own bandages, and like my shoulder, his own cut is gone. He really is a healer!

Then he talks again. Oh, speak more!

"You must be wonderfully skilled to have singlehandedly rescued me. Do I have the privilege of knowing my savior's name?"

I wonder if he even recognizes me as Goddess. Then again, I have a feeling that everyone in Arriscyal knew that I'm Goddess because Madam Manasa told them—same with Mayor Rayel and the villagers in Lereli. I mean, Gediyon didn't recognize me on first sight. I wonder if the prince can even see the pretty Saei in me, or was I born too average-looking for him to notice?

"I'm Michelle," I tell him, "but I'm not the one who saved you. Gediyon did the big stuff, but Launce and Nichols also helped, but they left with…everyone else and… I don't know where they are."

"Gediyon came?" He breathes out a laugh and looks overhead. "I thought that barrier looked like his magic. It'll be nice to see him again. Are you from Lereli, Michelle?"

I look at my clothes—that's how he can tell, but I shake my head. "Nah, I'm from California, from a small boring college town called Davis. Your name is Jason, right?"

"Jay*sonn*," he says, adding the emphasis on the second syllable that I keep forgetting. "But please, call me Jayse. Jaysonn is too formal, and I'm not worthy of the suffix."

"Suffix?"

" 'Onn.' In Arriscyal, it means I'm next in line for the throne. Oh, and please don't call me 'prince'—titles don't suit me either." Wow, he sounds like me.

He laughs a little and then smiles at me. Oh man, what a cute smile!

"So Michelle, think I can reward my savior with a kiss?"

I burst out into a horse laugh. "You can kiss Gediyon if you want, but I don't think you want to kiss me!" I laugh more. Good God, this guy is too much!

"Where can they be, anyway?" I wonder aloud. I reach down for the stone to check the time again, when I remember why I have it in the first place. I lift the chain from my neck and dangle the stone, reaching for Jayse's hand. "An old lady gave this to me to give back to you."

"Madam Manasa?"

When he reaches for it, I see the stone glow for a split second before he touches it. I feel the chain hit something, but something obscures my sight—

The old lady, Madam Manasa, in a cloak more ragged than she's worn before, hiding in the shadows beyond some bars.

As distinct as the image was, it disappears as quickly as it came. I stumble back when the sight of deck returns to me, and it must affect Jayse too because he falls to a knee.

I lower myself before him and ask, "Are you okay?"

He looks up and I see him smiling through his hair. Wow, that's sexy. "I'm fine." I want to ask him about the vision, but I've just met a really good-looking guy, and I shouldn't lead him on into thinking I'm crazy.

So I say, "Gediyon says there were all kinds of stuff wrong with you, like drugs"—I'm making him out to sound like a drug addict, so I quickly add—"and the Tainted Sea's toxin."

He huffs. "Really?"

I nod. "But anyway, you look really healthy now!"

He chuckles. "I *am* a healer."

This time, I help him to his feet. Now standing, the two of us can see some people emerging from the jungle—our soldiers! I run down the ramp and wave away at the invisibility barrier, hoping it'll disappear so they can see that the ship hasn't abandoned them, but Gediyon helps me to completely disperse it.

"We made it out alive!" Launce yells, bowing to the sea.

"What took you guys so long?" I ask, but my question is drowned out with exclamations of, "Your Highness!" when they see Jayse at the top of the ramp.

"The Taesmals must have set an illusory barrier around the jungle," Gediyon explains, "but it vanished with the sunlight. They must have laced the liquor with some kind of hallucinogenic so everyone would enter the jungle at landing, and couldn't leave to rescue the prince." He smiles at Jayse and asks, "How are you doing, Your Highness?"

Jayse sighs. "We might not have seen each other for a while, but you don't have to revert back to formalities."

"I apologize." Gediyon smiles, but it's not the usual polite one he puts on. I can tell he's truly happy when he says, "It's good to see you again, Jayse."

"Yeah. Thanks for saving my neck back there."

I look at the others, who are watching the three of us curiously.

"Weren't there a lot more of you?" I ask.

"Couldn't find 'em," one of the soldiers says. "We think whatever was in the liquor made them head back to Arriscyal."

"On foot," another snickers.

"So we're going back home?" Jayse asks. I can tell he's disappointed.

"Actually, Jayse," Gediyon says, "we are to take you back to Lereli to heal the villagers."

"So you fixed the dam?"

"Michelle here did."

I smile, but I probably look like a shark compared to him.

Jayse laughs. "Any detour is fine with me. Are we all heading to Lereli together?"

Nichols points back to the ship. "This is our only mode of transportation, so yes."

"To Lereli then." Jayse leads the men across the beach and thanks them for coming out to rescue him.

Launce circles around me like a scuttling crab. I think stalls heading for the ship because he wants to talk to me. When I start back, he runs up to me.

"So did you tell the prince that you're our Creator?"

"No," I say, wondering if I made a mistake.

Launce chuckles. "Just between you and me, he's scared of girls of a higher status."

I'm never going to get used to being a higher status than a *prince*.

I sigh. "I shouldn't tell him, huh?"

Launce shrugs. "Only if you want him to keep flirting with you!" His words smack me, and I blush. Jayse really was flirting with me, then?

Before I can ask Launce how much he saw, he runs ahead to the ship.

Ugh. Boys.

As I follow after, I notice a flash of red from the jungle, but when I turn to look, nothing's there. Maybe it's a bug. Funny how they don't emerge from the cover of the trees.

Chapter Eleven
Restoring Lereli

Once I step on board, the oldest soldier double-checks that all of us are accounted for, then he pulls up the ramp and we're off sailing.

Gediyon tells me that it'll only take an hour to sail to Lereli, which is a relief since all of the other traveling we've done so far turned out to be day trips. He tells me he'll start breakfast for everyone, but I stay on deck to watch the water.

Sailing through the Tainted Sea, ahead all the way to the horizon is sparkling clear water.

I contemplate whether I should go downstairs and help Gediyon with breakfast, when I turn around and Jayse approaches me. He makes eye contact with me—gosh, his eyes are so pretty—so I figure he actually wants to talk to me and not just steal my amazing viewing spot.

"Sorry to bother you, Michelle, but I was wondering… If you aren't from Lereli, does that mean you'll accompany us back to Arriscyal?"

"If that's where we happen to go next, then I guess so. You don't think there are any other princes in need of rescue, do you?"

He laughs. "I hope not. Say, where is it you're from again?"

"Uh…" I see Launce and Nichols peeking out from the stairwell. Launce smirks and nudges Nichols in the side, who punches him back. Why are they so weird?

It'll be easier for me to act like myself instead of a Goddess, anyway. I don't know Starrs enough to tell Jayse an outright lie, so I say, "Davis. Little farm town on the west coast."

"Oh." I can see him trying to find Davis on that mental map of his. "I don't think I've ever been there."

I shrug. "It's in the middle of nowhere." I lean back against the edge of the ship, but I forget that I already stepped away, so I stumble back against it. Yeah, real smooth, Michelle. I hide my dumb expression and face the sea, then ask him, "You been to Lereli before?"

"Once, but I was very young. I do remember a lot of seashells, though."

"Yeah, it was pretty cool. I hope all the fog has gone away. I bet it's really pretty now!"

"Oh, of course—you were the one who fixed the dam, right?" He pauses. "That's quite an accomplishment. How did you do it?"

I don't know how well I could explain it without mentioning my Goddess abilities, so I just say, "I have skills."

I make faces at the sea, hoping it'll make faces back and tell me what an idiot I'm being, when Jayse moves next to me to watch the same view. I immediately try to wipe my expression blank, but the smile that takes over isn't any more pleasant than my grimaces.

"Have you been to the Arriscylean palace yet?"

"Uh…" Well, yeah I have, but what kind of question is it? It isn't as if I had a formal tour of the entire structure, so I say, "Not really."

"Would you like me to show you around when we return? I know more secret passages than anyone else is willing to admit."

I smile. "Sure! Sounds fun."

Is he *actually* hitting on me? It might be because I'm the only girl on board, but if I were a guy, I'd leave myself alone. Still, I continue answering Jayse's questions as naturally as I can. So far, it doesn't seem like Jayse realizes that I *am* Goddess. I'm scared of how he might shun me if he did know.

I'm not the kind of girl who would keep talking to a guy if he approached me the way Jayse did. I'd ignore the guy and walk off. He was probably desperate anyway if he was hitting on *me*, because back home most people knew me as an awkward dork.

But here, nobody knows me enough to think that I'm acting weird, so I might as well get all of the flirting experience I can before applying it to the real world.

Heh. I wonder if I can accumulate flirting experience points?

We keep talking, and Jayse teases me about joining the Arriscylean army.

"I suppose we *could* use a bit more of this so-called 'female insight,' but you'll have to speak to the king before we can allow such changes."

"Fine, I will! In less than a month, our entire female army will be ten times as powerful as yours, and we won't even have to go to battle!"

"Yeah, it definitely sounds like you have a scary army there."

I laugh. "Aw, are you boys too afraid to draw your puny swords on a lady? Are your mommies going to spank you for not being gentlemen?"

Jayse sighs dramatically. "Mother will lock me in my bedroom and never let me out again. I won't know what to do until a brave female soldier comes to rescue me!"

I laugh and smack his arm. It's even funnier when I remember that Jayse's bedroom is at the top of the palace spire.

Launce and Nichols interrupt our conversation when they stumble on deck. Another soldier from downstairs is prodding them with the silverware in his hands, and Gediyon follows carrying a stack of small pots in his arms, and balancing plates on his other hand.

Gediyon suggests that breakfast will be more enjoyable on deck, since it's a lot more spacious and everyone can breathe. He sets up the pots and dishes for everyone to choose what they want for breakfast, and then he arranges a plate before going to serve the captain.

I fork at some kind of fruit dish. The fruit is firm and tastes like it's been pickled, but the tartness compliments the sweet breadcrumb crust. I would eat more, but I have a feeling the crew is hungrier than me, with their manly stomachs and all. I do pour myself a cup of claren tea, and I can't stop smiling when I notice that Jayse is the only one who also pours a cup. Then I notice Launce smirking and raising his eyebrows at me, and I fling some crust at him when he isn't looking.

It doesn't take long to arrive back in the Crystal Lagoon, and the clean Lereli is even prettier than I imagined. I thought that the water I landed in when I first met Gediyon was clear, but the water that flows beneath the docks is colorless. The only way I can tell it's water is the way it distorts the coral below, and their coral is even brighter than their dyed fabric. The water sparkles like diamonds in the sunlight, which is even hotter than it was the last time I was here.

I'm not the only one in awe at the sight. Even after the ship stops and the ramp reaches the docks, we stay on board admiring the sight until we realize we don't have to stay onboard. As I step off the rocky dock, I want to sit down and stare at my surroundings until I see it in all angles of sunlight, but I remember we're here for business.

I follow Gediyon and Jayse to the mayor's hut, but we lose some of our soldiers when they pass by the water users and chat. Launce and Nichols immediately run off, and I have a feeling they just placed a bet on a swimming competition.

As we walk down the docks, I don't notice any living statues, but some villagers move slower than before. Maybe they managed to move the statues inside before they solidified again.

When we walk into the mayor's hut, the old man runs at us with hugs, but he takes a longer time with Jayse, saying, "You've grown into such a handsome young man! I can't tell whether you look more like your mother or father." He continues patting Jayse on the back for about another minute before he stops himself and says, "Now then! Let's get you started on healing everyone!"

He leads Jayse out the doorway and I follow, but the mayor holds up a hand and tells me, "Now, now, Miss Goddess! It would be best if you stayed here. We can't have you being a distraction to Prince Jaysonn!"

Before the mayor pulls Jayse out of sight again, I see Jayse looking at me as if I ran over an entire box of his newborn kittens.

Well, I guess that game didn't last very long.

I look at Gediyon, hoping he has an idea of what we can do while Jayse expends his MP healing all the villagers. Gediyon is eyeing a basket of shellfish.

I put my hands on my hips and ask him, "You want to kill time and make everyone lunch?"

He doesn't hesitate before leading me into the kitchen. At once, he fires up the hearth and places a large pot over the flame, then fills it with hot, purified water. The kitchen is just big enough for the two of us to work comfortably, and I help him chop something that looks like green onion, only the outside leaves are fuzzy. I'm careful with the small knife he hands me, and I take pride in the small, perfectly even slices, but I'm still cutting one stalk when he already finishes a handful of vegetables that are like water chestnuts and bamboo shoots. Somehow, they look even better chopped than they did as whole plants. I look sullenly back at my own cutting board.

"You're doing a wonderful job, Michelle. Take your time." He takes his own cutting board to the pot.

"Hey Gediyon? Growing up, did you want to be a chef?"

He gives a small laugh. "I hadn't given it much thought as a professional career, but I do enjoy cooking. It relaxes me."

"So are you in the military 'cause of the money, or…?"

He lifts his shoulders in a slight shrug, then stirs the shellfish into the pot. Their shells rattle against each other.

"They've provided me with a room in the palace and allow me access to the kitchens, but I'm not doing it for the monetary reward. There are always others in need, and being in the military, I can travel farther and help more people."

I sigh. "Aw, geez, you're such a nice guy!"

"It's how my mother taught me to live. Besides," he chuckles, "I like being useful. Keeping myself busy keeps me from staring at the ocean all day."

I finally finish cutting one stalk. Now to move onto the other five! I pull another onto my chopping board and ask, "How long have you been in the military?"

"Six years. It was just before Jayse turned twelve, and…well… Byran, the man you met at the ports, talked me into enlisting. I still haven't fully thanked him for helping me make that decision." He comes back to the counter and helps me cut up the onions, and he chops one in less than thirty seconds. I don't want to give up just because he can do it better, and he doesn't take my half-chopped onion, so I guess I can keep cutting it at my snail pace.

"So have you known Jayse since he was born?" I ask.

"Only ten years. He was seven years old when we first met."

I squeal a little inside as I try to imagine what Jayse looked like as a little boy. Then I say, "And Gediyon, how old were you?"

"Fourteen," he answers slowly.

I nod. "So you're twenty-four now, right? And Jayse is seventeen, right?" I nod again. "All right. I think I can do with that."

"Sorry?"

I giggle. "Nothing!"

I wonder if guys get self-conscious about their age too, because Gediyon doesn't say much for a while. Then again, maybe he's too shy to continue talking about himself.

Once I finally finish cutting up the furry onions, I bring them to Gediyon and watch him stir the seafood soup. He does seem rather relaxed in the kitchen. He keeps that perpetual smile, but there's something trancelike in the way he moves. It's not like when I catch him staring at the sea, because that's the only time I notice his smile fade. When he is staring at the watery horizon, I see something nostalgic in his red eyes.

I'd ask him more about himself, but I have the feeling he'd change the topic.

After we put a lid on the pot, Gediyon asks me if I want another cocoa nut drink, and he asks me to keep an eye on the fire while he fetches the fruit. It's not as if the fire will burn out of control, but I would feel horrible if I walk away for a second and the entire hut turns into a smokestack.

While I'm watching the pot, some of the village children run inside to watch me. When I realize they're staring at me from around the corner, I spin around and make a hideous face at them, holding the spoon over my head as if it's a deadly weapon. They scream and run away laughing. At least they're lively. I wonder how many of them Jayse healed so far?

The next time the children run in, they give me a fruit to snack on, then run away again before I can thank them. It's a pitrom—

the first fruit I tasted on Starrs—but receiving it as a reward makes it taste extra special. I save half of it for Gediyon, and he comes back with the cocoa nut already sliced and a cup full of cream, but he suggests I should try it as a pudding.

As quick as he can chop onions, I lick the cup clean. I don't even give him the chance to hand me a spoon.

"These would make amazing cookies," I say, staring at the empty cup.

"That's a brilliant idea," Gediyon says matter-of-factly. "I never would have thought to do that with cocoa nut cream. It would be fun to try, but it's too bad we don't have any flour."

Hmm. I cross my arms and look at the sliced sack of cream in Gediyon's arms. "Can I see that?"

He hands it to me—wow, this thing feels weird. It's like touching the peeled scalp of a balding person. I try to shove that thought out of my head as I sit down with the cocoa nut and stare at it. The cream is thick—if only I could make it crunchy somehow, maybe even meltable like meringues, with the cute swirly pattern.

I stare at the cream with unblinking eyes, imagining the taste, texture, temperature and smell of these cocoa nut cookies. When the strain is too much for my eyes, I blink, but when I open them again, the cocoa nut skin is now full of about a hundred quarter-sized, drop-shaped cookies.

Gediyon laughs. "You're amazing!"

I pick up one of the cookies and pop it in my mouth. It melts once it touches my tongue. It's fluffy and would crunch if I bite into it, and it tastes like the pure cream of the fruit.

I drop the cocoa nut skin into a basket for stability and hold it up for Gediyon to try. We agree that it'll make a nice addition to the seafood soup when we bring it around to everyone.

Twenty minutes later, Gediyon and I make rounds through the village. He levitates the pot of soup behind us, and in his arms he carries the basket of cookies, while I hand servings to everyone.

The majority of villagers have gathered in the labyrinth of docks, and Jayse takes his time with every affected person. As we pass food through the crowd, I can see Jayse speak to the villagers as he heals them. With one hand on a cheek and the other over the sternum, Jayse smiles and passes his energy on to them. I can see the transformation. The villagers' faces brighten and I can tell that it's easier for them to breathe and move. I can't tell how Jayse does it, though, because it doesn't look like it drains him of any strength.

I smile as I watch them. At one point, he looks up and spots me right out of the crowd, but he quickly looks away.

Gosh, I hope he isn't upset about Launce's game.

At the rate he's going, it takes him all afternoon to heal the villagers. They appreciate the time he gives to each of them, and I see the young and old alike stare at him while he treats them. I guess they do have the right to fall in love with him; he is saving their lives, after all.

I suppose the villagers like me and Gediyon too, because they always hug us when we give them something delicious.

I spend the rest of the afternoon with the other Arriscyleans, talking about returning to the kingdom, Jayse's healing, and how beautiful Lereli is now that it's clean again. Once the sun sinks into the horizon, the other villagers gather inside the huts for celebratory drinks. They invite me too, but Michelle on caffeine is one thing, and I would probably embarrass myself if I drank alcohol. Besides, I always hated the taste of beer. I hope the adults don't drink themselves sick, because then Jayse would have even more work cut out for him.

I sit on the docks facing the sunset, watching Launce and Nichols splash in the water with some of the village children.

For a while, Gediyon sits with me, drinking a cup of claren tea. When I ask him why he isn't with the other adults, he tells me, "I don't drink liquor." Then he leaves to make sure everyone else is prepared for the journey back to Arriscyal in the morning. Luckily, this time we can take the ship instead of riding Bubbles for twenty hours.

Launce floats on his back like a dead man—looks like he lost the game with the village children—when Jayse starts around the corner dock to us. He doesn't look too exhausted, but now he looks as if *he* had ran over my box of kittens. I'm about to rise to my feet when Jayse falls to the ground. At first I think he passed out or something, but he's just bowing to me.

"I am so deeply, truly sorry for acting the way I did earlier, Miss Goddess. Please forgive me."

I have a feeling that Launce is smirking and raising his eyebrows again. I see him in the water, and he's only smiling as if he knows he did something wrong. I shoot him a sharp glare, and when Nichols sees me, he presses his hand on top of Launce's face and shoves him underwater.

To Jayse, I say, "You really didn't do anything wrong. You just didn't know I was Goddess, right? It's fine."

His forehead is still pressed against the wooden boards. "That's no excuse, Your Divinity! I should have known it was you, but I don't speak to the Universal Mirror often enough to see Goddess reach back to me. I should speak more often. I apologize."

I blow at my bangs and then step toward him. "It's fine, okay? You acted fine before. It's not like you were blaspheming my existence." I push him into a sitting position and pull him to his feet.

He won't even look me in the eyes. Gosh, poor guy, I guess he really is ashamed of his behavior. He looks so sad, I want to hug him, but instead I put my hand to his cheek and turn him to face me. I move my head into his line of sight, and when I see his pretty green eyes, I smile.

"As Goddess, I can assure you, you did nothing wrong."

"Still, I… I'll make it up to you. I'll do anything."

"Anything, huh?"

Now it's my turn to think like Launce. My smile turns into a wide grin. At first I think it's too daring of a request, but when else will I have the chance to make a gorgeous guy do what I tell him? I burst into a fit of giggles. If I don't get it out soon, then I'm never going to say it.

"How about…a kiss?"

His eyes widen and his cheeks glow pink. "A kiss?" he says. He barely breathes the words.

I nod, and I hear more splashing. It looks like Launce, out of both shock and payback to Nichols, tripped his friend into the water.

I cross my arms, smiling like an idiot, wondering if he'll do it or not. It seems that Jayse has already accepted his fate, and he steps toward me, then stops. I wonder if he plans to plant on one my lips or cheek. When it looks like he's decided, he takes another step toward me, but when his face comes too close, I cover my mouth with a hand and turn away, bursting into wild laughter.

Launce and Nichols must punch each other out of disappointment, because when I hear another splash, both of them are underwater. I keep laughing, but I stabilize myself and then slap Jayse on the shoulder.

"Sorry, sorry! I couldn't do that to you. Don't look so disappointed."

Jayse still looks like he doesn't understand my joke.

"But here's something you *can* do," I say. "Don't call me Goddess, Your Divinity, or any of that fancy crap, okay? Just Michelle is fine. You were fine the way you acted before, so let's forget these past few minutes happened and go on with our lives, hm?"

"If you say so, but it would be so disrespectful of me."

I shake my head. "It's not!"

"It's just…growing up, everyone spoke of our great Creator, and how we should treat her with respect, and this feels like it defies history. I always thought Goddess would—maybe, I don't know—throw us to the ends of the world if we disrespected her."

I snort. "I'm not gonna smite you just 'cause you hit on me!" I throw an arm around his shoulder and lead him down the dock. At least then, Launce and Nichols can stop punching each other with bets on what we'll do next.

"Look," I say. "I didn't grow up on Starrs. I came from a planet called Earth, but everyone here calls it Tyme."

"You came from Tyme?"

"Yeah, awesome isn't it." I hope he doesn't ask how. "Anyway, there, I was just a normal girl. As normal as any of these kids here," I say, gesturing as some of the kids run by with jars of lantern beetles. "Back home, I didn't have a big name to live up to. I mean, my parents were always comparing my grades to my brother's, but whatever. The thing is, I grew up as basically an invisible person, so it's weird when I come here and I have princes and queens bowing to me when I haven't even done anything astounding. I want to earn the respect."

"I see. Then I'll call you Michelle, but I'll treat you with no less respect than I treat any other lady."

Geez. So princely.

"So, do you want to talk to the Mirror?" I say, pointing my thumb toward the Universal Mirror. "Maybe if Saei does show up, you can tell me if I actually look like her or not."

I watch him walk across the platform to the Universal Mirror. No one is else is praying now, I guess because they're all celebrating. I sit on the dock across from the platform and dangle my feet over the water.

He probably has a lot to report back to the universe, because he talks to it for a while. I sit patiently and watch him, but I try not to listen to his words. He has a right to privacy, even if I do want to know what recently happened in his life.

The sunset is beautiful. It's probably the reddest sunset I've ever seen, since so much pollution hangs over the Tainted Sea, which deepens the red. Jayse's skin glows in the light and his hair looks even more like soft precious metal. The trees and huts around us become black silhouettes, and as the sun disappears over the horizon, the lantern beetles rise from underneath the docks. Streams of them swirl around the posts and torches, and when Jayse notices them, he turns around and looks at me.

"I didn't see Goddess Saei, but I don't need to."

I jump to my feet and hop to the mirror platform, then twirl in the light of the beetles.

"It's so pretty," I whisper, as if my voice will shut off their light, but they continue to fly and circle around the trees.

"Do you want to speak to the Mirror?" he asks.

I look at it. About twenty beetles are flying around it. Oh, why not? I could do with a game save. I walk toward it and smooth out my sleeves, as if wrinkled sleeves will offend the universe.

"Hello universe. Michelle again. Sorry I was so rude last time, but this is what happened since we last talked."

I tell it about leaving for Arriscyal, Gediyon's cooking, meeting Launce and Nichols, and then rescuing Jayse. When I start on about breaking into Sheirced and watching the sacrificial ritual, something odd happens. The Mirror shimmers as if from an internal light, and the opacity fades, exposing the water on the other side. I stop talking then, because I see another silhouette in the mirror, but it's impossible for anyone to stand on the water behind it, and I know it's not my reflection because of the stature and broad shoulders. I can't make out any distinct features, but it can't be Saei. I open my mouth to keep talking, but as soon as I take a breath, the Mirror turns black again.

"What was that?" I ask.

He keeps silent for a few moments, then says, "Do you really want to know?"

"Why not?"

He takes a deep breath. "We take it as a bad omen. It's Pesaeton's shadow."

"The Taesmal God?"

He nods. "But don't worry. Seeing his shadow doesn't mean he'll *smite* you. It probably only means the First Moon is close."

"The First Moon?"

"Of the Cycle. The first month of Pesaeton's trials, to punish those who cursed him. But the First Moon is harmless."

I look back at the Mirror, wondering if it'll change again. It stands there, black and glossy, but the only change I see in its surface is when a beetle flies in front of it.

Chapter Twelve
Long Live the Prince

We leave Lereli about an hour behind schedule because of the long good-byes with the villagers. Baskets full of fruit sit on deck, and spheres of water float beside them, swimming with fish. The rest of the water mages join us, and we all wave farewells as the ship pulls into deeper water. The villagers dress as colorful as a kindergarten's finger painting, but far beyond the docks and huts, I see a twinkle of red on the edge of the jungle. Must be the jungle insects again.

Gediyon tells me that the journey back will take about a whole day. I'm getting sick of these long journeys. While he takes some of the fish into the kitchen to prepare another seafood meal, I barge into the engine room with hopes that I can speed up the ship.

Instead of machinery, three soldiers sit around a tub of water, churning the waves in and out.

"This is your fantastic amazing engine room?" Sure, it's pretty cool that only three of them can power the entire ship, but it'll probably go faster if it were mechanized! Human beings can stand only so much labor, magical or not.

I sit among them, studying the tub. "Why don't you use actual machinery?"

"Machines belong to the Taesmals," one of them explains. "Why use enemy technology when we can use our abilities?"

I don't say anything until I pull away from the tub, finished with my alterations. Along with their magic, the tub churns water as well, and we can feel the ship pick up speed. They tell me it'll probably cut down our travel time to half a day. This still isn't fast enough for me, so I go back on deck and sit at the bow, facing the rest of the ship.

Behind my closed eyelids, the structure of the ship pulses in a cool blue light. If only I could take this structure and place it back at the ports in Arriscyal. That might be easier if I were a giant or something, but I'll probably crush continents if I do that.

The outline of the ship blurs and I think I've done something—the sound of the waves don't sound as harsh—but when I open my eyes, the ship splashes back into the ocean. I hear some gasps around deck, but I don't think I damaged anything.

I growl and pull my knees close, banging my forehead on top of them.

"Are you trying to manipulate the ship?" I hear Jayse's voice.

"It's too hard!" I whine. "I don't think I can teleport it." I roar out of anger. "I'm supposed to be Goddess! If I can make a ship disappear, why can't I teleport it?"

"I'm sure it takes practice, just like anything else." He sits next to me.

I look at him—sitting with his arms supporting him from behind, gazing at the drifting fluffy clouds. He has a really cute nose.

I look toward the same sky. Big tropical clouds look thunderous in the western horizon. Two moons that I've seen before are now both thin crescents. Another moon, smaller and white, is nearly full.

I sigh. "You were born with healing abilities, right? How long did it take for you to get used to them?"

He leans forward and rests an arm on top of a knee. Does he have to look like a model in every pose?

He says, "I didn't know I could heal until I was four. It was only small things then—cuts, scrapes, relieving pain before a bruise formed. I couldn't even do it for long. After healing a few cuts, I couldn't do it for a while, as if I forgot how. As I grew older, I learned how to channel it better, so I could heal deeper wounds, more soldiers—an entire village." He looks at me and shrugs. "Hey, it took me several years. You've only been here for about a week, right? And you fixed the Lereli dam on your first day!"

I sigh. "A week, huh? What day is it?"

"The twenty-sixth of Consier."

"Con-what-what?"

"Consier. The seventh month of the year. Do you call it something different on Tyme?"

"Yeah. July." I sigh again. "I left home July twentieth. I guess it has been almost a week already."

We discuss the names of the months, telling each other their respective names in our own worlds. He tells me my birthday is the twentieth of Hermise and his is the eighteenth of Jarnit, which is January. I keep a note to remember this date if I can't return home by then.

"So, I bet everyone asked you how you came back to Starrs from Tyme," Jayse says, smiling like he's prepared to ask the same question.

I have the virtual reality speech memorized now. "You too, huh?"

He shakes his head and laughs. What a cute laugh. "I want to know what it's like there. What you do for fun, what your towns are like, what kind of magic you do."

Even though I didn't want to at first, the first thing I talk about is video games. It's strange explaining Earth to him, because I never thought I'd have to tell anyone. I feel stupid telling him about everyday things, like a microwave, the supermarket, a car, school and vacations, but Jayse seems fascinated and asks me more about them. I didn't think anyone could find these things so interesting, but Jayse does. It's not that I'm complaining because I like the attention.

"Gare would love it if you could tell him some of this," Jayse tells me. "He's the librarian at Arriscyal and does a lot of research about the Cycle and Universal Mirrors."

"Gare is my buddy!" I hear Nichols from across the deck.

"What about me?" Launce says, and they start punching each other.

"In fact, I can take you to the library later!" Jayse says. "If that's all right with you, of course. My mother or the king might have different plans for you, though."

"Psh. I'll go with you. They probably want me to make speeches or something."

It turns out, being stuck on a ship for half a day isn't that bad, especially if I'm stuck with a hot prince and about twenty other attractive soldiers.

It actually feels like Arriscyal comes too soon, and the soldiers pull cheerfully into the port. The Arriscyleans at port don't look very welcoming, though. In fact, they look confused, and they gather staring at us like the ship is a car full of clowns. I even spot out the big man Byran in the crowd.

When they see Jayse step off the ramp, I hear gasps and squeals, and a swarm surrounds him and pulls him to the telesphere at the top of the walkway. As soon as they see me, they pull me into the crowd, and everyone shouts so much I can't tell what they're saying, except for Byran's, "You all came back alive!"

I see a flash and the next thing I know, I'm in the throne room, but this time both chairs are occupied. The king and queen are wearing dark colors, and the queen is as beautiful as the last time I saw her.

I try to remember their names so I won't have to sound stiff calling them "Your Highness" and stuff. His name is King Oresonn, and hers is Queen Trissa. Right.

Nobody knows what to say. Jayse steps toward his parents, and their thrones descend to ground level. The queen steps off first and rushes across the floor to embrace her son. She closes her eyes and smiles, but it looks sad, relieved, and happy all at the same time. The king stops a few steps behind her, and I get a good look at him.

Granted, he's old enough to be my dad, but I don't think it's much different than finding George Clooney, Johnny Depp, or Robert Downey, Jr. attractive. He is Jayse's father, after all, and I can see some of the resemblance, even though Jayse looks more like his mother. Behind the king's expertly groomed dark beard, I can see a similar jaw line, and they have the same cheekbones, but these features are softer in Jayse. He must know that I'm staring at him, because he looks at me. His eyebrows rise in intrigue as he recognizes me, and I see that his eyes are a darker green than Jayse's. It looks like he might say something, but Jayse speaks first.

"Why is everyone acting like they've seen a ghost?"

The queen pulls back and caresses Jayse's face. "We feared we would not see you alive again. The soldiers returned on foot, and when we found out about the toxin in the liquor, and that the Taesmals had already sacrificed you… How did you make it back?"

"Michelle helped me, but it was Gediyon…and all of the others we left at the port."

Queen Trissa gasps. "Then we must thank them!" She turns to the king and says, "Let us prepare for them a feast tonight."

Some servants already leave—I guess to inform the cooks. Queen Trissa hugs Jayse and says, "I couldn't bear it if I lost another son!" She looks up and smiles at me, finally leaves Jayse, and walks forward to take my hands. "Many, many thanks to you, Goddess Michelle. I knew we could rely on you."

Now King Oresonn steps forward. He nods at Jayse, who nods back, then says, "Indeed, our Creator has returned?" He has the voice of God. He lowers himself on one knee and bows, but I still feel like I should be the one bowing to him. "It is a pleasure to welcome you back to our kingdom. I regret that I was absent when you first arrived, but I hope our hospitality will make up for it. We are indebted to you for helping Prince Jaysonn."

"Thanks?" What the heck am I supposed to say?

The king rises and the queen says, "There is much you can do to help us with the kingdom!" And she starts listening what sounds like chores, each one more unappealing than the last. Do I really have to make speeches? What could I possibly say to make people feel better?

"Actually," I say, cutting her off mid-sentence, "can I just hang out with Jayse and Gediyon?"

Jayse clears his throat and starts for me, then says, "I'll show Michelle around, and you can tell everyone that I'm alive." He nods and pulls me toward the tele-sphere, and before anyone can stop us, we reappear in a rosy, wood-paneled corridor.

"Sorry about them," Jayse says. "They aren't much fun."

"Well, they're kinda cool. They're very…kingly and queenly."

"Like I said, they aren't much fun." He takes me across the hall and says, "Anyway, this is our library."

Our footsteps echo as we walk down the corridor. It opens into a wide lobby, with a wooden staircase ahead that branches twice to the three levels. I gape above at the pink and gold stained glass dome while Jayse leads me to the center of the lobby. I've never seen so many bookcases on display in my life. I don't even feel closed-in or trapped, because it's so well-lit.

"It's usually a lot busier," Jayse tells me, "but the library has been closed for a while because the king sent Gare away on a trip."

"To Mediscus Heights," says a man behind a counter. He's wearing strange, magnifying goggles and examines a sprig without looking up to acknowledge us. I guess he's Gare. "The herbalists there are a joke—not to mention, the large-chested women there are dangerous. How was your kidnapping escapade, Prince?"

"Can't say I really enjoyed it, but thanks for your concern." Jayse looks at me and shrugs, as if to say, "That's how he is."

"By the way," Jayse continues, "Michelle has joined us for the afternoon. She's our Creator, but skip the pleasantries and formalities."

Gare carefully places the sprig on top of a thin cloth, then lifts his head to look at me. I flinch at his goggles. He pulls them up to his forehead, revealing brown eyes with tremendously thick eyelashes.

"You look far too ridiculously happy to be Goddess." Who says something like that?

"Pft. Well, you look too young to be a librarian." He looks even younger than Gediyon.

He lowers the goggles back over his eyes and continues to sort through his briefcase of plants. "I have to start young, because it'll be my work that does me in. Gare Rotcod, pleased to make your acquaintance. How can I help you?"

Jayse leans against the counter. "See, I thought *she* could help *you*. She came from Tyme."

Gare looks up again. "Did you?"

I nod.

"Peculiar, but indeed fascinating. I do have a lot of questions, to tell the truth. Thank you for escorting her to me, Prince."

Gare raises his goggles and closes the briefcase, then beckons me to a round table. Jayse pulls out a chair for me and sits a few seats away so he has a good view of me and Gare. Gare eyes him strangely but sets down a large notebook with loose paper sticking out every few pages. When he realizes Jayse isn't going anywhere, he picks up one of his many pens and asks me all about my life on Tyme.

Even though Jayse already heard most of the conversation, he still sits there interested in our exchange. Gare madly scribbles in his notebook, and not once do I hear a pause in his pen scratching paper, except when he picks it up to move onto a new line. He even draws diagrams of the things I describe, which is amazing because I don't even describe them in much detail, but he seems to comprehend the concepts.

At one point, Nichols runs into the lobby and pats Gare on the back.

"Gare, buddy! I missed you! Listen, I'm going upstairs to read some."

"Must you? I believe the palace mischief is missing you."

Nichols laughs. "That's okay! I can put it on hold for a few hours, right?"

"Where's Launce?" I ask.

"Flirting with the new cook in the kitchens. If anyone comes in looking for me, tell them I'm with him stealing food." Then he sprints upstairs.

"I don't understand why he joined the military when he could have just come to Arriscyal to *study*," Gare mumbles. "He spends more time reading books than he does practicing with his sword." All the time he says this, his furious writing doesn't slow.

Gare reminds me a lot of Aaron, minus the Star Wars fanaticism. His brown eyes, the way he hunches over when he writes, and the way he concentrates when he's working. They're about the same age, too. Since I'm already talking about my home anyway, I tell Gare about my brother, but I don't tell him that he reminds me of him.

Actually, talking about Aaron makes me miss his nerdy ways, because Gare seems far too serious.

After telling him about the public school system, I ask Gare, "You know I wanna learn about? The Cycle. Tell me about it. I mean, if I'm going to help people, I need to know what it is, right?"

"Ah, yes." Gare slaps his notebook shut. "If Goddess Saei, King Cyal, and the true Taesmal King's reincarnations are born into Starrs within the same lifetime, Lord Pesaeton's residual spirit will set the full Cycle of the Six Moons into motion, leading to our universe's destruction. One moon leads to another, and on the sixth—*poof*." He says it quickly, as if he'd recited it, with as much certainty as saying the sky is blue, and I flinch.

"But that's not gonna happen, right?"

Gare shakes his head. "You needn't worry yourself. After all, the conditions *are not* met. Now." He rises from his seat and nods at me. "Thank you for your time, Miss Goddess, but now I must return to studying these plants."

"Wait, that's it? Can't you tell me more—why are you studying *plants*?"

"Because they are fascinating. Good day."

All right, then.

Jayse helps pull my chair out and leads me through the library. Several more people have come in while we talked, and they roam the shelves and read at similar tables. Somewhere upstairs, I hear laughter, and I think it's Nichols, but what could he be reading?

I'm about to ask Jayse where he's taking me, when I see that we're headed for a large stained-glass door. Through the glass, I think I see a courtyard, and I let him lead me outside before saying anything.

"I thought he could tell you more about the Cycle, but I guess he has his own agenda to follow."

The courtyard leads to a path through columns ahead, and long pink tendrils brush over the path. It looks like a pink willow tree, which has berries that twinkle in the sunlight. A smell similar to tangerines wafts down on us.

Jayse must see me staring at it because he says, "That's a muse tree. We plant it near scholarly buildings, like libraries. The scent is supposed to inspire us and give us the extra push to achieve what we want. I guess it works, because they use the extract to fight against the Third Moon."

"The Third Moon?"

"The Night Devourer. Pesaeton's third trial, from the World of Dremes. For a week, it sweeps over the entire planet. When we sleep, it robs us of all motivation—even motivation to live. Most people lose themselves to sloth, and some never wake up, but this tree here helps." He touches one of the draping leaves. "The Third Moon isn't as common as the first two. I've only experienced it once, when I was six."

"So can't you tell me about the Cycle?"

"I'm no expert. Your best bet is Gare, or even the priests in Dissett, or Madam Manasa, if you know where to find her. All I know is, if we get to the Sixth Moon, we're all dead. But we've only gotten that far once before."

"In Saei's time?"

He nods. "And she saved us."

He leads me down the path through the columns, which ends at a balcony overlooking the palace gardens.

"But I think the only thing you need to worry about as Goddess is helping others—fixing things like the dam in Lereli—because we were born in a dormant Cycle."

I lean against the balcony wall, looking below and remembering what others had said. "Actually, I heard other people say that I woke up the Cycle since I came here from Tyme."

"But how can that be?"

"Because 'all of the players' are present. But, it's only you and me in this lifetime, right? And the former Taesmal King… Didn't he die already?"

Jayse nods. "My uncle killed him in the last war."

I drop my head. "Launce said something like that." I bury my face in my hands and groan into my palms. "I don't get it. If I went back home, would it stop the Cycle? Would this world cease to exist? If I came back, could I start back up right here? Would it be like loading a saved game?" I sigh. "I don't even believe this is a game anymore." I lift my hands and look around, the world bright but bleary from the pressure against my eyelids. "Everything is so real."

Grinning, Jayse leans in closer and says, "I'm as real as they come."

I giggle and push him back playfully. He definitely feels like a real, living person, and the heat from my blushing is real too.

"To answer the rest of your questions, if you went back home, we would still be here. I don't know if that would stop the Cycle, though…and you would still be a whole world away."

He looks down into the garden, and I follow his gaze so I won't dwell on him wanting me to stay.

Through the garden, many people stroll by themselves, though there's also a mother and her son, a few couples, and—

"Aren't those…your parents?"

I see the king and queen, dressed in their dark clothes, walking close beside each other but not holding hands. A few attendants and guards follow several paces behind. They stop at the pond with the statue in the center and admire it silently. The statue is a man, dressed in armor and gallantly holding his sword high.

"Who's the statue?" I ask.

Jayse hesitates before answering, "My uncle."

By the tone of his voice, it sounds like his uncle had died. Why else would they have a statue of him? Jayse said that he had killed the previous Taesmal King, but maybe he had never returned from the war.

Jayse looks more interested in a bird than watching his parents. The king leads the queen away from the pond, picks up a flower from a shrub, and hands it to her. She thanks him with a kiss on the cheek and I can't help but sigh, "Aw, they're so cute."

Jayse grunts.

"I wish my parents were like that. The most romantic thing they do anymore is argue who's going to do the dishes."

Jayse grumbles.

"Ah, there you are, Goddess Michelle!"

I turn around and see my maids walking toward us from the library path.

"Good afternoon, ladies," Jayse says.

They bow to both of us, and Simmy, the oldest, says to Jayse, "Excuse us, Your Highness, but we have orders to prepare Miss Goddess for the banquet tonight. You should also ready yourself."

"I get to be all fancy just for dinner?" I say. I can't help but squeal out of delight when they nod.

Jayse leans into me and quickly whispers, "Meet me behind the Universal Mirror afterward."

"We'll steal her away from you now, Your Highness." Canaria takes my arm and the other two giggle. "Good day."

Jayse sighs, flips the hair out of his eyes, and crosses his arms. "Well, Michelle, just between you and me, let's see who'll show up to the banquet more beautiful."

Of course he'll win, but I say, "Ha! You're on!" I put my arms around my maids and drag them back to the library. "Come on, we have a lot of work to do!"

Once we walk back inside, Simmy says, "Well, Prince Jaysonn is certainly friendly with you, Goddess Michelle!"

"You mean he isn't this friendly with everyone?"

Canaria laughs. "He is, but he seems to quickly lose interest in one girl and speaks to another the very same minute."

So Jayse is a player, huh? At least he likes girls, I guess. I imagine him prancing across town, hitting on a flower girl then a seamstress and a milkmaid, but he turns into a shy puppy at the first sight of an empress.

"Well of course he's going to pay more attention to you, Michelle!"

" 'Cause I'm Goddess?"

"Why, because he's destined to fall in love with you!"

Chapter Thirteen
Royal Strife

I burst out laughing, and I can tell that Gare is glaring at me behind his goggles.

"Didn't you know, Mirra?" Simmy asks.

"You don't mean that—"

"Prince Jaysonn is the reincarnation of King Cyal." She prods the tele-sphere and we reappear in the corridor leading to my room. "Could you not tell? The tell-tale signs of his healing abilities."

I still can't believe that Jayse is *destined* to fall in love with me—like we're supposed to have the greatest love story of all time. That's the stuff of Shakespeare.

I'm still snickering when I say, "Wait, wait a minute. Who is King Cyal?"

"Our very first king, the one after whom Arriscyal is named. He and Goddess Saei were lovers."

I laugh again at the word she uses—like the tarot cards or something.

They lead me into my room, sighing over fated romance, but I don't buy into any of it, especially since it's concerning *me.* I don't want to fall in love because of some old legend. I'm barely old enough to even have kids. Plus I don't want anyone forcing Jayse to fall in love with *me*, of all people, just because his past incarnation fell in love with mine.

Sure, he is *really* hot—and I like the attention he gives me, and he's nice to me, and he actually seems genuinely interested in me, but… But I can say the same about Gediyon, so there.

I'm still smirking about it when they lead me to the bath, when they must understand that I think it's a joke, because they stop talking about it.

Well, with their change of topic, maybe I prefer the forced romance, because they give me a list of requests for Goddess's help: a broken windmill, barren farmland, inefficient furnaces… I groan as I keep listening to the mundane list. Why don't they involve killing zombies—or more relevantly—fending off Taesmal mutants? At least then, Jayse can show me how he swings a sword, or Gediyon could roast the mutants for a feast.

After my bath, my maids spray me with all kinds of pretty-smelling liquids. Before they start on my makeup, I take out my music player and simply ask for something upbeat. It starts playing a song I've never heard before, but hey, it works.

They seem far too excited to do my makeup, but I'm sure whatever they do to me, it'll be better than what I can do to myself, as long as they don't make me look like a clown.

I sit with my eyes closed and hands clutching the arms of a plush chair. Canaria prods at my face with pointy and fluffy brushes. The powders she uses smell like candy. Mirra tugs on my hair as she tries to figure out what to do with it, but there isn't much length to do anything. Simmy prepares my dress, shoes, and accessories.

And to think I'm only dressing for dinner.

Once they finish with my hair and face, they keep me away from the mirror and force me into a pink dress. It's the same dress

Simmy took out the last time I was here, and I guess it's fitting for a royal banquet, even though it's too pretty, and all I want to do is stuff my face.

It's a flashy princess dress. The fabric feels wonderfully smooth—and expensive—and in different angles of light, the pink turns to peach and then gold. The hem is embroidered with fine gold lace and pearly beads. It feels far too heavy when they lace it up in the back, and I'm afraid I'll trip over it walking to the dinner table, but Mirra whips some air in her hands and blasts it underneath my skirt. The hem floats outward, and I feel cool wind around my ankles.

A petticoat made out of air! This is awesome. Not only does it cool me down, but also spreads out the skirt enough so I can walk without tripping.

The women bring me in front of one of the mirrored doors. At first I feel like I'm looking through a window, but the girl in front of me does everything I do.

My eyes look bigger than ever and my cheeks glow, not only with a light dusting of blush, but also with sparkling highlights on top of my cheekbones. My lips look full, young, and glossy. Mirra did something to my hair so it looks wavy, and Simmy sits a glittering headband on top.

The dress is a warm rosy color—not too pale or bright—so it complements my tan skin and dark hair. It's hard to look at myself at first, but once I see how perfectly the dress fits, I can't look away. I hop and dance in place at my reflection.

"I'm so cute!"

"Prince Jaysonn has some difficult competition this time," Simmy says.

I wouldn't call myself beautiful. I still don't think I look like Saei, but I can't deny that I look adorable. "I look like a fairy princess!"

They laugh with me as they escort me down to the banquet hall. It's a good thing I have them with me, because I still don't think I can use the tele-sphere without ending up somewhere I shouldn't be.

As soon as they've escorted me, they curtsy and leave again.

This new hall is bright white, and a melody dances along the walls from the room at the end. It sounds like others have arrived before me.

My two-inch heels click as I walk down the hall. Halfway through, Gediyon walks toward the other end. He's changed into a dark suit and his hair isn't braided, but tied back loosely with silver twine. I run after him and yell, "Gediyon!"

He turns around and smiles. I can't help but think that he looks even more attractive in his suit, like a magician ready for the stage. With his hair pulled back like this, I can see piercings on each ear. A bead as red as his eyes dangles from his left ear.

"Why, good evening, Michelle! You look very pretty."

"And you look super hot! Who knew a sweetie like you could have a bad boy side? Where did you get all those piercings?"

He touches the bead on his left ear but still doesn't know how to reply to me.

I change the topic. "Jayse and I are competing to see who can come to dinner prettiest."

He nods. "Then you've won."

"Did you even see him yet?"

He laughs and shakes his head. In his right hand, he holds a small, brown leather book and I ask him what it is.

"Gare found it for me," he says. "It's my mother's recipe book."

Why would he bring a recipe book to dinner? Maybe he just didn't have time to go back to his room and put it away. But what was Gare doing with it?

As we walk down the hall, I tell him about my afternoon, and he tells me that he's to leave in the morning for Mediscus Heights. I'm about to ask him if I can go with him, but someone waits for us at the end of the hall.

A girl holds a silver tray of frosty glasses. She curtsies, keeping all of the glasses upright, and greets us, "Right this way, Miss Goddess and Sir Gediyon."

As soon as Gediyon takes a glass, I take one as well. The water is flavored with some kind of herb that makes it even more refreshing, like cucumber mint water.

"Thank you," Gediyon says. "I don't believe we've had the pleasure of meeting before."

She curtsies again. "My name is Kalei, at your service, sir. I began work here in the kitchens just the other day."

She's in her late teens or early twenties, with olive skin and big, deep blue eyes and long lashes. She has the prim demeanor of most Arriscyleans, but her many, intricate braids makes her look exotic, and she actually looks a little too athletic to be a cook. Then again, Gediyon cooks a lot, too, and look at him.

"You're the new girl that Launce was hitting on?" I ask, remembering what Nichols said in the library.

She blushes. "Um… if you come this way, I'll lead you to your seats."

Once we enter the banquet hall, everyone goes silent and rises to their feet, even Queen Trissa, who's the only other female at the table. Even the orchestra stops playing to honor my arrival.

King Oresonn opens his arms welcomingly. "Ah, now let us welcome Her Serene Divinity, our Great Creator!"

Everyone breaks into polite applause, and Kalei leads me to the opposite end of a long table. The tablecloth is so clean, white, and expensive-looking that I wonder how anyone would dare eat on top of it. Throughout the room, orbs of light float around and sparkle occasionally. Baskets of bread rolls are placed every few feet, and some of the soldiers are already smothering them with whipped butter and munching away.

I wave at Gediyon to sit next to me. Once I take a seat, everyone else does as well. King Oresonn sits at the head with Queen Trissa; Jayse is nowhere in sight. Gediyon sits to my left, and I'm happy since I can ask him about proper etiquette if I need to.

Once we're seated, the band resumes playing. The music makes me feel like I'm in a dream. I lean on the table with both forearms and stare at the glass ceiling while everyone else continues their conversations. Is the dining room in the middle of the garden? Trees with glowing flowers tower outside.

Gediyon hands me a basket of rolls, and I grab one, immediately covering the entire flat top with sweet, fluffy butter. The crust has the perfect amount of crunch, and the inside is fluffy and moist. I try to keep my crumbs to a minimum so I won't soil the tablecloth, but after a few bites I give up.

It seems that I came a little early, or maybe everyone else comes late. The oldest soldier scolds Launce and Nichols, who shove each other into their seats. They've also changed into nicer clothing, and I catch Launce winking at poor, bashful Kalei in the doorway. A few other soldiers run in late, bowing and spewing apologies, but the oldest soldier isn't as harsh on them, and the king simply ignores them.

The only person we're missing now is Jayse. I spread the bread crumbs on the table, telling Gediyon how hungry I am, and he tells me not to worry, that plenty of food will come, but it seems like we won't start until Jayse comes.

I think everyone else must be getting hungry too because the head chef walks in and announces, "Many apologies for the hold-up! We'll soon begin with a salad course."

Just as the servants walk down the long table, Jayse walks in. Like they did for me, the orchestra stops playing at his entrance. He's wearing princely clothes—a fine, white-collared shirt with a fitted, embroidered dark blue vest. Though I prefer the more disheveled look, like when we first met, the way he combed his hair makes him look more like a prince and less of a swordsman.

He also looks like he'd rather be anywhere else in the world.

"Jaysonn!" King Oresonn laughs as he takes a sip of red wine. "You took so long, your mother and I were afraid you had been kidnapped again!"

Some of the soldiers chuckle.

"Ha, ha," I hear Jayse grumble. He takes the chair that is meant to be placed across from his mother and walks with it halfway down the table. He shoves it between two soldiers, forcing one side of the table to scoot down and make space for him. The hall fills with clatter until everyone settles down with their chairs and respective plates again.

Queen Trissa clears her throat politely, then raises her crystal goblet of red wine and says, "You are all invited here on account of two occasions. First, I would like to thank all of you for helping Prince Jaysonn return to Arriscyal. A toast to you."

Everyone picks up their goblets and clinks them with their neighbors. Gediyon and I are the only ones who pick up our glasses of water. Even Jayse, Launce, and Nichols toast with wine, but Jayse doesn't sip any, and the other two unflinchingly gulp down half the glass. Jayse looks like he'd rather still be kidnapped than sitting down.

I know this next toast is coming, but I can't help but feel bashful when Queen Trissa announces it.

"Now let us toast to honor the return of our Creator. To Her Serene Divinity, Goddess Michelle. May we have a peaceful Cycle."

I stare down at the napkin on my lap as I raise my glass with the others. The clinking of glass is so loud, I'm afraid that someone will break something.

King Oresonn has already finished his first cup of wine and he says, "Then let the feast begin!"

The orchestra blossoms into a cheerier song and everyone talks louder. It isn't long before we're served salad, wrapped in thin slices of some kind of melon, sitting on tiny plates.

"It's so small," I mutter, poking at the melon slice with my fork.

"The entire banquet consists of small plates," Gediyon tells me.

All right, that's cool. I guess there is no main course, but at least we get a small taste of everything.

It turns out, everything is delicious. I never thought I could experience so many tastes, textures, and different temperatures all in one night. After the salad comes a soup, then some sorbet to cleanse our palate, meats prepared in all kinds of ways, seafood—I think they even used some of the fish we got from Lereli—all varieties of pasta, more sorbet, exotic plants… I'm filling up quick, but I hope I won't pop a seam in my dress.

I can't help but think that Gediyon's cooking is made with more love. I tell him this, and he smiles and thanks me, but I think I just embarrassed him because he lowers his face parallel with his plate. Aw, he's so adorable.

Every time Kalei refills our drinks, Launce and Nichols toss her compliments and grow more lewd with more wine. "Your fingers are beautiful on that bottle," Nichols says, while Launce reassures her, "I'll sleep *so good* tonight." She keeps escaping to our corner, and Gediyon and I try to make her feel more comfortable with small talk. I catch her staring at Gediyon, either because he's so handsome or because he's the only man who treats her with respect—maybe both.

When dessert comes along, Launce and Nichols display that they can't hold much liquor at all, and half their bodies slump over the table while they slap each other and laugh stupidly.

The king is a lot more composed, but he drank twice what they did, and his face is red. Gediyon has politely tasted everything on his dessert platter, but he only melts candied flowers in his mouth. Jayse, on the other hand, is scraping the sides of a bowl that once held a salty and sweet custard. I noticed, in the entire dinner, it was the only thing he finished eating.

He looks so devastatingly bored, I want to do something to cheer him up. He's been ignoring the soldiers who have been shouting at and over him, and he's too far down the table that I don't think I can speak to him without yelling and getting squeaky.

I look at my plate. I still have a lot of candied flowers left, so I piece them together in the shape of a small person. After staring at it for about a minute, it lifts itself off the plate and clumsily walks across the table.

I laugh as I watch it slip by arms, goblets, and forks. Only Gediyon and Kalei notice it and watch curiously. When it finally reaches Jayse, he notices it right away. The flower person waves at him, and he looks across the table at me. I smile and wave too, then the flower person climbs into his bowl and spins around. As it does, the bowl refills with another serving of the same salty custard, but it dances on the surface and scrapes a happy face. Then the person falls apart, scattering petals over the top of the bowl.

Jayse looks at me again but this time smiles. He also mouths, "Thank you."

I mouth back, "You're welcome!" and he starts to eat the custard.

He barely swallows a few spoonfuls before King Oresonn roars over the table, "Jaysonn! Why so quiet? One would suppose you'd have a lot more to say after an adventure like yours. Surely everyone here tonight would like to know what happened!"

Jayse takes his time with another spoonful before he says, "If everyone wants to know what it was like, they can get themselves kidnapped."

"Jayse, darling," Queen Trissa says, "your father has had a bit much to drink, but he's only concerned about you."

"Yeah? If he's so concerned, why was he back in Yinidel instead of looking for me? All the troops went astray, and if it weren't for Gediyon, Michelle, and these two idiots, I *would* be dead!"

The other soldiers sip their wine as if they aren't listening. Gediyon and I sit silently at the mentioning of our names.

"Jayse, dear, you know that the time it takes to travel—"

"Travel time—whatever! I appreciate *everyone*," Jayse says, addressing the table aside from his parents, "for helping me out, but I'm really not that useful or great of a crown prince."

"The future of Arriscyal needs you, Jaysonn—"

"Don't call me that!" he snaps. "No one needs me. They're fine with you! Why don't you just send Gare out somewhere else so you can finally find that plant that'll grant you eternal life? Then *you* can be king forever, and I won't have to worry about anything."

"Jaysonn—"

Jayse slams his palms into the table and stands up. The king rises as well, but in a split second, I hear a *shing* and see a flash, and both of them have drawn swords on each other.

Queen Trissa sighs and stands up as well, then says, "What is this? These knives are far too big for the dinner table."

"If you strike me," Jayse enunciates, "I *will* fight back."

"Then we can finally test whether your uncle's training was enough," King Oresonn replies. "But seeing as a child killed *him*, no wonder you couldn't defend yourselves against the Taesmals."

Queen Trissa's mouth drops—albeit beautifully.

Jayse says, "You would insult your brother-in-law in front of your own wife?"

King Oresonn narrows his eyes and Jayse winces, as if that look sent daggers through his chest. Jayse sends back another glare, then sheaths his sword and bows to the rest of the table. "I apologize for the spectacle, everybody. Good evening." He turns and leaves.

The king and queen lower themselves to their seats, but nobody else moves. Even one soldier, who's in the middle of chewing a cookie, is as still as a statue.

I clear my throat, stand up, and everyone else rises with me. "Well this is incredibly awkward! I'm gonna leave now. Thanks for the food, everybody!"

I run down the hall, prodding in random places on the tele-sphere. I don't care where it takes me, as long as it takes me someplace else.

A moment later, I reappear in a dark brown corridor. No idea what this place is, but at least I can look through the tele-sphere without anyone watching me.

In its resting state, the tele-sphere is actually an overhead view of the palace. When I press one area, it zooms in and shows another cross-section, but in the default view I can see the different levels. When I select one, it zooms in again but shows another floor plan. Whatever this floor is, I don't think it leads to the Universal Mirror.

I stand in front of the tele-sphere for about ten minutes, zooming in and out, trying to find the most logical way to the Mirror. I learn that the library is in the first quarter of the north wing on the third floor, and the kitchens are in the central quad on the first floor. My room is in the west wing on the sixteenth floor leading from the second tower.

At last, I find the large label, "The Temple of the Universal Mirror," and I press it. Lights flash around me and I reappear in a dim, wide room.

Several people pray quietly. The Universal Mirror here is about five times as big as the one in Lereli, but it also faces the ocean. The sound of the waves is such a contrast to the dinner orchestra. The temple isn't an enclosed space; only large columns support the roof overhead, no walls. There aren't any seats, like I'd expect to find in a church, but the floor is carpeted. It smells like orange blossoms—the muse tree?

Jayse is nowhere in sight, but he did say to meet him behind the Mirror.

I step off the carpeted floor and walk down some stairs. The temple is to the right of the palace entrance, where the gondola stops. From where I stand, I can only see the kingdom from the northern coast to about a quarter of the city. The streets glow with soft light, but they aren't strong enough to cast a halo overhead and block the view of the stars.

I walk along the side of the temple until I reach the back. The grass is softer than the temple carpet, and the bright moons lead the way so I don't trip over anything. From here, I can see the other side of the Mirror, as black and smooth as from inside the temple. I look around—maybe Jayse is sitting on the ledge over the cliff—but then I see a path sloping, hidden behind the ledge.

I follow the path, which hugs the cliff and curves with it. I hold onto the rocky wall as I descend the slope. It isn't steep at all, but I've never been good in heels, no matter what height.

From the bottom of the path, I hear something whooshing through the air, and when the path curves in the right direction, I see Jayse slicing through invisible enemies. He stops when he hears me coming and lowers the sword.

"I didn't think you would still come," he says, averting his eyes as if he's ashamed of what happened at dinner.

I shrug. "I tried to leave as soon as you did. It was really awkward."

He sighs. "Sorry, that was my fault. Never liked palace affairs much."

"Why not?"

It sounds like he says the first thing that comes to mind, which is, "It's boring," but I don't think that's the truth. Not the whole truth, anyway.

He looks around the cliff landing, sits on a rock, and then says, "I think you beat me in that competition."

I look down at myself and snort. "Yeah, after a lot of work."

I stand in place, quiet. Now *I* feel awkward. Maybe he changed his mind about asking me to come here.

In the silence, I can hear a voice: "Please protect my farm from the Famine."

I look up. "Is that…?"

"From the temple," he says. "They can't hear you from down here. You hear all kinds of things. Who needs help, who hates this, who hates that, who wants to succeed and who's failing…" He looks at me. "People ask a lot of you, you know. It's a lot of responsibility being Goddess."

I sit on another rock and the wind petticoat whips against the grass. "That's what I'm supposed to do, right? Help everybody?" I pause. "Can I even help *everybody*?"

"Your predecessors tried."

I laugh. "My predecessors?" I want to ask him if this means we're all the same person, if we're reborn, or if it's something else entirely, but I lose myself in my thoughts, I forget to ask him.

He then says, "Do you think I can leave? To your world, or any other? Just be reborn there without having to fulfill the responsibility of this life."

"There's probably a way." I look toward the sea. "I don't know why you would want to, though. This place is a lot cooler. But…" I look back at him. "I guess you're right. About the responsibility thing. I've never been this responsible before."

When he doesn't say anything, I stand up and look at the sea. The two earlier moons have disappeared, but the small third one is full. The water shimmers beneath it. For some reason, it doesn't look as bright as it should.

"I wonder, out there, if there's still that sea angel?"

"Did Gediyon tell you the story?"

"Yeah."

"It's sad."

I turn around. "It is? Why?"

"They both die."

"Oh geez, really? I guess I fell asleep before I heard the end."

"He told me that story a long time ago. I didn't pay attention much then, but it makes sense, why he watches the sea."

"Why?"

"It's the last thing he remembers."

"What do you mean, the last thing he remembers?"

"He…" Jayse looks at me, as if he isn't the one who should be telling me this, but he goes on. "He doesn't remember his childhood."

I stare at him. "*What?*"

"He doesn't remember anything from his childhood," he repeats, "except the sea angel and her song. It's not that big of a deal anymore, since everyone knows him as the person he is now, but I know he still wonders about his past." He sighs and gazes at the moon. "Because he still stares at the ocean."

"Oh geez! That's so sad! He doesn't remember *anything*?"

He shakes his head.

"God. Well, I hope he can remember someday. At least you guys took care of him."

I stare at the ground, thinking ahead and planning what to say to Gediyon the next day. Oh wait, he's going off on another mission. Maybe I can tag along.

The ground darkens. I look up, and Jayse notices it too. We both look at the moon, which is fading into the sky, and Jayse starts for me.

"It's the Dark Mist," he says. "It won't hurt us, and it can't get inside the palace."

He takes my arm because he knows we won't be able to see soon. Within a minute, the surrounding light goes from dim to pitch black. I know my eyes are open because I can still blink, but I can't see anything in front of me. I feel Jayse's hand in mine as we cautiously feel our way up the slope. I'm thankful the Mist doesn't sting my eyes.

I'm not usually afraid of the dark, but for some reason, my heart is pounding. Jayse can probably feel my pulse through my hand.

Somewhere from the sea, I hear something that makes me think of a large whale grumbling.

"Does that usually happen too?" I ask him. I hope my voice doesn't squeak too much out of fear.

Ha! Who's afraid?

Yeah, okay, I am, because his silence tells me no.

Thunderous wind rushes into our ears and I feel Jayse's arm around my waist. He shouts, "Stay close—we'll be okay."

Just as he says this, the wind becomes harsh and rips us apart. I leap forward and reach for him again, but I can't grab onto anything.

I fly off the ground. I scream and thrash in midair, and my mind races too fast for me to use my powers.

"Jayse!" I yell.

Somewhere far away, I can hear him calling me back. The wind pushes me in all directions, and I feel myself ascending higher and higher until it's hard to breathe.

No matter where I look, even in my thoughts, all I see is black.

Part Two
The Creator's Role

Chapter Fourteen
Deserted

I feel like I've been forced through a tiny pipe.

I am in pain. I try not to wonder how many bones are still intact.

I smell something burning. My entire existence is on fire.

"Eat this, child."

Ugh, what a horrible voice. Listening to it worsens my pain.

Something presses against my lips. Maybe it's food, but I don't have enough energy to chew—much less open my mouth.

Just let me die here.

"Child, I will not let you die," the voice croaks.

Something else presses against my lips. This time it slithers into my throat. It warms me on the way down, stinging the back of my throat, and after a few seconds, it turns icy cold.

I bolt upright and cough, trying not to choke on the liquid. Whatever it is, it's given me enough energy to move, but as soon as I realize I can sit, my head spins with pain, and I feel myself sinking.

Someone catches me before I fall and shoves something into my mouth.

"Quick, swallow."

It feels like a grape that I'm bound to choke on, but I do as I'm told. It's stuck in my esophagus. More liquid pours down my throat, and the lump goes down. I can finally lie back and I feel and hear bones snapping back in place.

The next five minutes make me want to die, and when all the snapping is done, I just want to sleep.

"You can sleep later, once you're safe."

I open my eyes. I don't ever remember my eyes taking this long to focus before. I see a small figure curled over a fire.

"Mm… Mmm…" I know what I want to say, but it's not coming out.

"Madam Manasa, yes, it's me," she says.

Oh God, I've never felt so crappy in my life.

"You'll feel better soon." She hands me a teapot. "Drink more."

From where I lie on my side, I try to pour more of the hot-icy liquid into my mouth, but a lot of it spills onto the ground. I'm lying in dirt.

After a few more sips, I have the energy to sit up. Besides the small fire, I only see a dark, leafless tree nearby. The rest is barren. In the horizon are the shapes of black mountains against the bright, starry sky.

"Where are we?" I manage to choke out. I drink more of the liquid to moisten my throat.

"The Bandits' Desert, outside the Tufos Canyon." She looks away from a stick she's carving, and I see the outline of her large nose in the firelight. "We're on the Riesen Continent now. Far, far away from precious Arriscyal."

My eyes widen. "How did I get here? I was just with—"

"Prince Jaysonn, yes. That was three nights ago."

"Three nights?!" I gasp. "How did this happen?"

"The First Moon," Madam Manasa says. "On your sixth day here, Pesaeton decided to strike. His shadow possessed the Dark Mist and stripped you and the prince from the safety of Arriscyal. It's a phenomenon rare even for the First Moon; however, Pesaeton's hatred toward you is strong." She chips off another piece of wood into the fire. "Don't worry about your prince; he can take care of himself. As for you…" She hands me the carved wooden stick. Her tone becomes harsh and threatening. "You can keep thinking that this is a game, and put yourself in danger, or accept that this is your new reality, because if you don't start taking the Cycle seriously, you'll never return home."

I swallow hard. "What do I have to do?"

"First, find yourself shelter for the night, because there are more vicious Taesmal mutants here in the desert than back in sweet Arriscyal. Plus, if you don't get any rest, you won't make it to tomorrow's sunset." She eyes me up and down. "You may want to do something about those clothes, too. A princess isn't suited for this terrain."

I look at myself. I'm still wearing the pink dress, but I no longer have the air petticoat, and much of the skirt is ripped, tattered, and stained with my blood. It's a shame.

"At daybreak," Madam Manasa continues, "follow these mountains south until you reach the canyon. Follow the river downstream to the West Wind. You can take a boat there back to Arriscyal."

I keep staring at the wooden stick.

"That is for your protection. It shoots fire at your grip and will."

I point it into the distance and give it a squeeze. Sure enough, fire blasts out of the top like a flamethrower, but I'm not in the right mood to laugh about it.

"Besides the mutants, thieves and vagabonds roam the mines and caverns of the canyon. Be careful about who you trust."

"Can't I just teleport myself back to Arriscyal?"

She narrows her eyes at me. "Try it." With that, her image twists itself into a small thread and she vanishes.

"Wait!" I yell, pushing myself to my feet. "Please don't leave me."

But the old lady isn't coming back.

I sigh and fall back to the ground. Now what?

I pick up a nearby rock and stare at it for a few seconds. Maybe because I'm so weak and exhausted, but it remains a rock. I want it to be a transporter or a communicator, but even after deep, calming breaths and trying to forget my frustration, I can't transform it. I can't even smooth its jagged edges. I hurl it back into the dirt.

Damn. I'm really alone, aren't I?

Now isn't the time to cry. I look around me and take a deep breath. If not for the fire, I would be shivering. As Madam Manasa said, I need to find shelter, though it doesn't look like there are nearby caves, or enough wood on the lone tree.

I lower myself to all fours and scoop dirt around me in a wide circle, creating the base of a dirt wall. I try several times to use my powers and raise it into a building, and each time I fail to make anything happen, I feel myself sink closer to tears.

Finally, once I close the circle of dirt, I manage to raise and harden it into a clay dome, with the fire sitting in the center. A hole at the top allows the smoke to escape.

If I were in a better state, I would be able to create a comfortable bed and a proper cottage, but this is all I can manage for now. I gather the skirts of my tattered princess dress and try to curl up for sleep, but the dirt floor is hard and the fabric is too lightweight. My stomach grumbles with the little food Madam Manasa gave me to eat, though I'm too tired and disheartened to try to make food from the rock.

I can't help but think that this is how Goddess dies, this is where the game ends—but Madam Manasa is right. I have to accept that this is my new reality now.

No more games now. I'm out in the wilderness, with no one to guide me. I have to survive.

I tell myself not to cry, but I can't help but get teary-eyed as I fall asleep.

CHAPTER FIFTEEN
A CYBORG AND HER WOLF

Sleep rejuvenates me, and I find that I can turn a rock into the blandest oatmeal I've ever tasted. I wish it had raisins or cinnamon—even a little bit of sugar—but in my weakened state, I can't even manage that. At least it's warm and doesn't make me throw up. It fills my stomach with enough energy to start my day.

I kick a hole through the clay walls of my dome and crawl out into the bright, open desert. Madam Manasa said that I should follow the mountains south. Since I slept in until about midday, it's hard to tell where the sun had risen, so I mark the edge of the tree trunk's shadow in the dirt while I alter my clothes.

I stay in the little shade of the barren tree while ripping the skirt of my dress to my knees. I still can't use my powers to change them with a simple snap, but I can finish the edges so the material doesn't unravel. I wrap the excess fabric over my shoulders, smoothing out the wrinkles until it becomes a capelet with a hood. I tug on my shoes until the material stretches into knee-high boots that are suitable for the desert.

By the time I'm done, the mark of the tree's shadow has moved slightly, so I calculate my bearings and decide which direction is south. I pull the hood over my head to protect me from the sun, hold Madam Manasa's fire stick in front of me, and cross the desert for the mountains.

After walking across flat land for what seems like forever, I finally climb upward. The sun has drifted further westward, and it beats through my lightweight capelet and hood. I should've stayed asleep for another twelve hours, and travel at night when it's cool, but I'll see how far I can travel before the heat becomes unbearable. I can't even count how many times I've had to wipe the sweat from the tip of my nose since waking up.

About five minutes later, I see some coyote-like creatures descend the slope. Whether they're Taesmal mutants or not, they sure aren't friendly. I squeeze the fire stick and blast fire in their direction. They keep far enough, but I don't want to know what they'll do if I let the fire die. The stream seems pretty constant, though, so I don't think I'm in danger of running out of fire fuel.

What if I do, though?

That thought makes my stomach tighten, even more so since I'm trying to climb uphill. As I pass them to higher ground, I keep blasting the fire in their direction. They follow me with their eyes and inch closer, maintaining the same distance between us. Once I climb to the top of the slope, I slowly reach down for a rock. Adrenaline boosts my abilities and I transform it into a large, raw T-bone steak. Quickly, I toss it in their direction, and they bound on it. I keep an eye on them as I back up onto the mountain. Not too quickly, otherwise I'll slip on loose rock.

I make it to the top of the slope and slide out of their line of sight. They wandered off since finishing the steak, so I think I should be safe.

I look around the top of the mountain, trying to catch my breath. I groan when I see that I have to cross many more mountains, and no canyon in sight. The view is dizzying. It's like I'm in a completely different world of dirt and rock, compared to the watery and lush land that I thought covered Starrs. The mountains are dry and red like terracotta, and they could be pretty if they might not be the death of me. I continue southward, stepping loudly and lazily until I realize, snakes might be out here.

So far, I've only encountered coyotes, I'm not that hungry, I *am* a little thirsty…

I pluck out the thinnest blade of grass and turn it into a green, leathery canteen of water. It tastes like the smell of freshly cut grass, but I still I guzzle it empty, then refill it. I spread dirt over it to change the bright green into the color of desert soil. The color sticks like paint. As much as I'd like some company, I don't want to attract the wrong sort.

I continue walking for about three hours, stopping every now and then for a water break, turning more rocks into bland, boring oatmeal because I still don't have the mindset to turn them into delicious sandwiches. Still, all around me, I see nothing but mountains and desert.

Hours later of traversing the mountain range, I notice ahead something that looks like tracks. I look down the mountain and see—there are people! I gasp out of excitement, thinking that maybe I'm finally close to civilization, and then I see a few take out guns and shoot the others dead.

Okay, so they're people, but they aren't civilized. I stop jumping and pull back so they can't see me. If they already did, I hope they thought I was a wild animal.

I continue down the tracks. It's a good thing the tracks also lead southward, so maybe if I can make a cart and speed downhill, I'll arrive at the canyon faster.

To my luck, I find a mining cart. It's a big metal one that I imagine would be used to transport giant gems, or act as a vehicle in a mine-crumbling rollercoaster chase.

I look inside. It's empty. It must've come from the tunnel in the mountain, but I don't see any lights inside, so there probably isn't anyone around.

With some difficulty, I climb inside. I reach over the side to release its brakes, then I hear some shouting and see two people running for the cart. I immediately duck, though it might be a better idea to jump out, because the other two also jump in and the cart starts to roll down the tracks.

I hide myself under my cape hood, hoping they won't notice me, but how could they miss someone dressed in this shade of pink?

One of them—a girl with a strange voice—is shouting, "Do you set it? *Did you set it?*"

"Yes!" replies a man.

"If you didn't—"

"I'm still sober! I didn't forget!"

A few seconds later, I hear an explosion and I yelp out of surprise. The girl whoops with laughter, but the man puts his hand on my shoulder.

"Hey there," he says. "You one of the girls they were gonna sell off? Musta been pretty smart to escape them!"

I look at him, but try not to reveal too much of my face. He smells like liquor and has large biceps and even a black tattoo that covers most of his left arm. It looks like some kind of animal.

"It's okay!" he says. "You're in good hands now!"

"Damn it!" the girl says. "There are more coming after us!" The cart picks up speed on its downhill roll. I hear a whir, several clicks, and she starts shooting.

"What's your name?" he asks.

When I don't answer, the girl says, "She's prolly mute."

The man continues, "You can call me Wolf. This here is Dre."

"That's Lady Dreana het Codget Ivy Bescur, Champion of Tyrique to you, little girl," she scoffs.

Who does she think she is? I look up at her, blasting behind us with not a gun, but her entire right arm. She glances back for a second and I see her face. Her eyes are icy blue, with pupils like a cat, and beneath her left eye are four round red gems of graduating sizes. This girl is a cyborg!

"Whoa," Wolf gasps. "Aren't you…?"

I cover my face again, but he says to Lady Dreana hit—oh, whatever her name is, "Dre, I think it's Goddess!"

She grunts as she dodges another attack and shoots back. "Isn't she kind of little?"

Little?

"Weren't you supposed to be in Arriscyal?" Wolf asks.

"Well, yeah, but—"

"Oh! She speaks!" Dreana laughs condescendingly.

"Hey," Wolf says, brushing my hood off. "We're experts 'round here. We'll take care of you."

He has enormous blue eyes and blond hair tipped with black, as if he had dyed it some time ago. Now I notice that his tattoo is a stylized wolf, and he has a large sword strapped to his back. He's about ten years older than me.

"You trying to get back to Arriscyal? Then we'll help you!" Wolf fist pumps.

Dreana shoots one more person and then we slide into a tunnel. It's dark and the wind blows all around; it's a relief from the sun. We pass some vents in the rock, which allow us light for a second, and then Dreana reaches for something in the track. Maybe she's changing our course.

Whatever she does, it leads us to the end of a tunnel, where I see a set of humongous, round black doors lit by torch. The door is cracked and wind whistles through. Has someone already been here not too long ago?

Dreana and Wolf hop out, and Wolf tells me, "Stay here!"

I peek over the top of the cart and watch them approach the vault. Dreana holds her robotic arm close. When she whips it out again, a bright silver blade extends from her hand. It's not thin like a katana, but broad like a giant chef's knife.

Before they can even touch the door, others burst out with curved blades of their own, and they strike at Dreana and Wolf, but they're no match. Dreana and Wolf dispatch them as easily as slicing down foliage. Wolf fights like an animal, using his brute strength against the others—I guess that's how he got his name. Dreana, on the other hand, is extremely graceful. She fights as if it's a dance, and her deep red hair spins around her as she twirls.

Watching her, I feel really—well—*naughty*, and I can't get over how sexy she is. She's so incredibly badass, fighting in form-fitting clothes, and…okay, she has the most extreme hourglass-shaped figure I've ever seen. Her waist is tiny and her boobs jiggle when she moves, but at least she has the decency to try to cover her cleavage.

She and Wolf are dressed so much differently than the people in Arriscyal. I haven't seen anyone with a tattoo like his or embedded skin jewels like hers, but it is another continent.

Once they leave their enemies bleeding and groaning on the ground, Wolf beckons me over and I hop out of the cart after them. I'm careful to avoid the bodies. I don't even look at them.

"Does she have to follow us?" Dreana asks.

"She's Goddess! We can't just leave her behind!"

"So, what are we gonna do? Take a giant detour and bring her back to her fancy royal people?"

"It's Arriscyal, Dre! *Arriscyal!*" He says it as if it's Disneyland.

They start whispering to each other so I can't hear what they say. I follow them deeper into the vault.

It doesn't look like a lot of obvious treasure hides in here. No glittering stacks of coins or heaps of golden goblets. Many portraits lean against the walls, though, framed in beautifully carved wood. I look around and see a lot of woodwork—some jewelry boxes, some framed mirrors, even wardrobes. Many of them are encrusted with gems. Draped here and there over furniture are long fur coats. One of them catches Dreana's eyes, and she hesitates as if contemplating picking it up, but it's far too hot to wear a fur coat. They continue looking around, whispering to each other, pushing over everything to see what lies beneath.

At one point, a hidden man jumps out with a large axe, but Dreana slices his neck as if it's second nature. I hold my own neck protectively as I watch him go down, blood spurting from behind his fingers as he tries to keep it in.

She tosses mirrors and headboards over her head as if they weigh no more than a shoe box. Wolf has to dodge some of them, and I stay behind at a safe distance.

"So little girl," Dreana says. "I take it you *have* met the Arriscylean royal family."

"Yeah."

"What are they like?"

"Well, they're all very good-looking"—they laugh at this—"and they're pretty polite, I guess, but the king drank a lot at dinner—"

Dreana laughs. "The Arriscylean king getting drunk in front of Her Serene Divinity!"

"Anyone else?" Wolf asks, and Dreana elbows him. That alone makes him double over.

Anyone else? "Well, there's Jayse?"

"The crown prince? Is that what they're calling him now?" Dreana spits. "I hear he's quite a dish. Is that true?"

"Well, yeah—"

They laugh again and I feel blood rise to my face. What's so funny?

"How about—" Wolf starts, but Dreana elbows him again. She rises from a pile and holds a baseball-sized dark metal orb. She places it inside of a jewelry box, then drops it inside a black cloth bag.

"Now we just need the stone."

"What is that?" I ask.

They pass me for the exit. "None of your business," Dreana says.

Wolf and I climb back into the cart while Dreana switches a lever on the tracks, then runs and jumps into the cart. She holds onto the edge, her legs in the air like a gymnast, then she flips inside. I watch her wide-eyed, then realize I'm staring, and I look away. Her cat eyes are cold.

"So," I say. "You guys treasure hunters or something?"

"Treasure hunters get themselves killed," Dreana says.

Wolf sighs dramatically. "May their souls find peace in another life."

Dreana rolls her eyes and slaps Wolf in the forehead with the back of her robotic hand. Now he looks like he's going to have a migraine.

Maybe they're thieves, but at least they aren't trying to kill me. I should probably keep my mouth shut and not annoy them, in case Dreana wants to use her knife on me. While huddled in the cart, I look at her robotic arm. Despite all the blood and use it must've seen, it gleans as if new.

"Impressed?" Dreana says in that strange, slightly robotic and seductive voice of hers. She raises her arm and twists it to show me the buttons and switches on its surface. "This is what helps me win the championship of the Tyrique Tournament every year."

"It's very cool," I say.

"Cool?"

"Uh—it means neat—yeah, impressive. Whatever."

" 'Cool.' Is that what you kids say in Arriscyal these days?"

It's what we say in California, but I don't tell her this.

Wolf almost leaps at me with excitement. "You should come to the Tyrique Tournament! It starts the last week of Hermise."

Hermise is September, I remember from what Jayse told me.

"Uh, okay?" I say, not sure whether I can smile or if it's okay to make a promise. "Where is it?"

"In Tyrique," Dreana scoffs, as if it couldn't be more obvious.

I don't want to ask them what kind of tournament it is, but the way Dreana admires her arm, I have a feeling it involves lopping off heads.

"What, have you been living under a rock?" Dreana says.

"I…wasn't born on Starrs."

Wolf looks at Dreana, as if he's waiting for her permission to gasp, but she just curses.

"No wonder," I hear her mutter. She turns on me with her cold, scary eyes and shouts, "Then what are you even doing here? Do you want us all to die?"

I curl away from her. "I—I don't even know!"

She groans out of frustration. "What, so you came here like now, right? And you're just a kid! The Cycle has already started, and do you even know what you're doing?"

"No, I don't!" I snap back. "But if somebody actually told me, maybe I would!"

Dreana smothers her face with her robotic hand and shakes her head. "Oh Lord, and we have to babysit you?"

I stand up, then realize it's dangerous with the cart moving, but I'd rather not be below her. Even when both of us stand, she's still a lot taller than me.

"You don't have to," I say. "I can find my own way back to Arriscyal. I'll leave you alone, once you stop this cart."

"Dre," Wolf says, widening his eyes like a puppy. "Stop being so mean."

She tosses her hair and crosses her arms. "Fine." She looks at me and snarls, "*Sorry*. Let us at least find you a ride back to your frilly kingdom. We can't just leave you to die out here—everyone'll hate us." She eyes me up and down. "Now sit. I'm the only one allowed to stand."

I glare at her but do as I'm told. It's probably for my own good.

Sometime later, the cart stops at the end of the tracks. Wolf and I stand up to find ourselves in a valley with a dried up riverbed. Downstream is the start of a canyon. I pull out my compass, and south points straight in that direction.

Wolf helps me climb out and Dreana walks ahead, using her fingers to whistle loudly. I raise my hood.

"Gum!" Dreana shouts, her voice echoing. "Mr. Gum! Get your ass over here!"

As if he has been hiding in a nearby tunnel, the man that I know as Isel Mingon approaches us, smiling and rubbing his hands.

"Ah, if it isn't Lady Dreana and her Wolf!" Isel Mingon says.

"Gum Gum, give us some Bubbles now."

He rubs his hands again, continuing to smile, but one of his eyebrows twitches. "Well, I just sold my last to a few men back that way."

Dreana grabs him by his shirt collar and spits in his face, "You sold them to *thieves*?"

He shrugs. "They had money?"

She growls. "Then how do you expect us to get out of this desert?" She said that kind of funny—does she have an accent?

Isel Mingon keeps shrugging. "Wait until the Bubbles come back to me?"

"That can take days, Gum! We might as well walk." She lets go of his collar and shoves him to the ground, then heads back to me and Wolf.

"Please don't call me that out here, Lady Dre," Isel Mingon says, dusting himself off.

"Oh sorry, *Isel Mingon*," she says. She waves to us and points toward the canyon. "This way, then."

Isel Mingon stays in place, waving after us. "I'll make it up to you later, Lolli! I'll buy you more clothes!"

"Thanks Gummy!" Dreana waves without turning around.

"Have a fantasterrific day!"

What is he, her sugar daddy? And why does she keep calling him Gum?

We continue walking down the valley, and the sun is so hot I wish I hadn't left my canopy behind. Dreana doesn't seem to like the sun very much either, and I don't blame her. Her clothes are really tight, after all, and her light skin looks like it can be burnt easily.

We take a break in the shade. Dreana turns her arm into a fan, waving it at herself and complaining to Wolf about how it takes so long to walk everywhere. Whatever accent I heard earlier, it's not so apparent now that she's talking slower.

Come to think of it, some of the Arriscyleans also extend their vowels, but maybe that's a result of living near the palace and trying to sound regal. I notice Gediyon sometimes does something strange with his R's, and the people in Lereli don't speak their S's and T's as sharp as they could. If they were from my world, they could probably tell I'm Californian right off the bat, but I can't place a regional equivalent to their accents.

I don't think we're going to move much farther unless Dreana has shade for the entire way, so I pick up a dried leaf and expand it until it's the size of a beach umbrella. Dreana and Wolf watch in awe as I transform it, then I take hold of the end to shield us from the sun.

Wolf gasps like a little boy seeing Santa Claus. "You really are Goddess!"

I smile but say, "Let's keep going."

I think Dreana appreciates what I've done, because she stops complaining. We continue walking downstream, until the dry riverbed leads over a cliff. This might've once been a waterfall.

We look to the left, right, and below, but it looks too dangerous to climb down.

I bend the leaf umbrella into a glider shape, and a long, wooden handlebar spouts from its center. I fasten my fire stick to the belt around my waist, grab onto the handlebars and tell the other two, "Come on, let's glide!"

I feel them grab on, and I run toward the edge of the cliff, certain that it'll carry us to safety, but just as I lose footing, Dreana and Wolf let go.

"Wait!" she screams. "There are Taesmals down there!"

"Aw, crap!"

Sure enough, atop a plateau, I see a band of people dressed in skin-tight suits with their mutants waiting close by. I try to twist the glider back around, but the wind is already carrying me into the canyon.

"Be careful of the Mysiochs!" Wolf yells.

"What's a Miss Eye Hawk?" I yell back, but whatever he says, I can't hear it.

I grunt, trying to turn the glider around, but the wind is merciless. I'm about to fly right into the Taesmal's line of vision, so I guess right about now would be a good time to turn invisible.

I still don't have enough strength to do that, and I groan in frustration while flying across their sight, which ensures that they notice me. I'm sure the sight is hilarious to them, and I would be laughing too if they weren't dangerous. As I glide past their plateau, I can't tell if they're amused or not, because metal masks cover their faces. None of them move, though. I guess they didn't think anyone could be so stupid.

As soon as I fall out of their sight, I hear them move, but I try to redirect my glider far from their plateau. It takes about two more minutes until it's safe to land, and then I hop off and leave the leaf glider behind. I won't need it; it'll slow me down.

I pull my fire stick out of my belt and jump into a sprint. I hope the Taesmals aren't fast runners.

I'm alone again.

CHAPTER SIXTEEN
THE PRINCE IMPOSTER

If I stop now, I know I won't be safe. As I run, I see the shadows of the Taesmals jumping overhead. I don't know what else to do, so I hold my fire stick over my head and squeeze fire relentlessly, hoping it'll scare them away.

I know it's only a matter of time before they find their way around it. At once, two Taesmals drop in front of me and land expertly. I almost fall, stopping myself from crashing into them. Dust curls between us. They rise unscathed and aim some kind of gun at me. The tips of their needle ammunition twinkle in the sun-light.

Before they fire, I kick a cloud of dust in front of me, which solidifies into a wall that blocks their attack. I guess in dire circum-stances, adrenaline boosts my powers.

I immediately turn around and sprint for another plateau, pray-ing—to myself, of course—that my next plan will work. I can hear snarling and a bark—mutant pets are after me too, but I have no time to look around and see how close they are. I keep my eyes on the sedimentary wall ahead, and I gasp in a breath of relief when I see a hole opening. I don't even wait until it's as big as a door—I leap into it and hear a large body thud against it. I look behind and see the large, drooling mouth of a mutated coyote before the sedimentary wall seals me in darkness.

I exhale a sigh of relief and throw myself against a wall. It feels as if someone has stacked rocks on my chest. Trying to catch my breath, I take the fire stick and start a little flame so I can see where I trapped myself. I'm completely closed in, but at least I'm safe.

I drop the stick and choke. The fire extinguishes, but if I keep burning it, I won't have any more oxygen to breathe. I close my eyes—not that it makes much of a difference—and I put my hands to the stone cold walls. Somewhere overhead, I hear crackling and some rocks fall inside. I look above and see some sunlight where a vent has formed.

I sigh and slide to the ground. The Taesmals are probably surrounding me outside. They know I'm trapped inside; I can't stay in here forever. What if there's an earthquake, and the walls crush in on me?

I don't know if they expect it or not, but I can probably make a tunnel and find another way out on the other end. If they're smart, though, they'll surround the entire plateau, waiting for me to come out.

I look toward the ceiling and the small ray of sunlight coming in from the tiny vent. They probably won't expect me to go upward, though.

I fasten the fire stick to my belt and feel the stone walls. I push aside a few feet of crawl space at a time, careful to stay close to the outside wall so I have access to air. The empty space behind me seals in once I've made more space. I feel like a mole in the Chuck E. Cheese sky tubes.

I don't know how long it takes me to do this, pushing rock and crawling, but when I reach the top, all I want to do is sleep. I seal the tunnel to protect myself while I catch up on rest.

I must fall asleep for a few hours, because the next time I open my eyes, my burrow is completely dark. I reach for the ceiling and press against the rock, and it falls to the sides. I peek out to the top of the plateau, like a prairie vole, and it's silent and seems safe. Stars twinkle overhead.

As quietly as I can, I climb out of my burrow and crawl to the edge of the plateau. Below, as I expected, the Taesmals are camping out, waiting for me. I sigh and look around. I'm safe here for the time being, but I need to keep moving.

I check the compass and follow the plateau to the southernmost edge. Across the gorge, another plateau is lower than the one I'm standing on. I pick up a thin blade of grass from the ground and pull on it until it stretches out into a full-sized glider, as green as the grass it once was. There's nothing blue I can use to change it into the color of the sky, so I'll have to be quick. I shake it by the handlebars, making sure that it's steady, and then I walk back to the north end.

I start into a run, holding the glider over my head, hoping that it'll work, and then I kick off the edge of the plateau. I gasp from the sight and try not to scream—I can't bring attention to myself like last time. The glider holds steady, but I don't know if I can reach the other side. Just when I think I'm going to smash into the rock wall, I kick my feet out and run up the wall, hoping the glider has enough wind to keep me airborne.

I run to the top of the plateau, then stumble to the ground. I look over the rocky ledge at the Taesmals, who haven't seemed to notice. Their mutated coyotes are howling, though.

I take the glider to the next southern edge, hoping to travel as far as I can at this height. While in midair, all I can see ahead are more rocky plateaus against starlight. Is this as big as the Grand Canyon?

It doesn't take long before my muscles and foot soles fall victim to use. Resting takes too long, and I try to make painkillers out of rocks so I can keep walking. I transform them into similar-looking tablets that are probably only sugar pills, until I take a few minutes to meditate with them in my hands. They'll have the same properties as Tylenol, I tell myself. They'll numb my pain and I can keep walking.

After swallowing a couple, it takes a long time for them to kick in, and the relief is only slight, but it makes walking bearable. I wonder if it's a good thing that I don't know how stronger painkillers would affect my body.

I lose track of how many days pass, and I still can't see the end of the canyon. I like to think that I cover about twenty miles a day. If it weren't so hot, I could probably walk ten more, but I don't want to push it, especially because I haven't seen the Taesmals since I left their camp. Every now and then, I come across some mutated giant birds and snarling coyotes, and I chase them off with my fire. At one point, I hold the fire stick a little too enthusiastically and end up roasting a coyote. I haven't had any protein for days, and I pick apart its flesh to eat. The taste makes me gag, but I manage to swallow. I don't linger too long next to its corpse, because the scent of fresh barbecue attracts other animals. I rip off a piece of its leg for food on the go.

The protein gives me more strength, and that night, I find that I can now turn rocks into plain chicken breast, which is just as bland as my rocks-turned-oatmeal.

Every night, I sleep inside rock walls, and each new bed is more comfortable than the last. I guess I'm getting used to this solo-adventurer thing.

On about the fifth day on my own, I wake up and manage to make oatmeal with cinnamon. I sit inside my cool burrow, scooping the spicy, sweet mush into my mouth, when the wall explodes.

I choke on the mouthful and everything happen too fast. I can't breathe, several arms pull me out, some prick me with long needles that dig down to my bone, and I try to scream, but a bird screeches louder. Rock scrapes against my bare arms as someone drags me, and I realize I can't move at all, much less breathe.

I can still hear, though, and barely see through the hair over my eyes. People are screaming, making guttural noises, and a dog yaps out of pain. They fall silent. I hear several thumps in the rocky ground, then footsteps. They're light, but not cautious at all, as if the walker is fearless.

Whoever it is jabs several spots on my back and neck, and I can move again. With the first gasp of air, I choke on the oatmeal and end up spitting it out. When I look up, I feel like throwing up again, because lying all around are headless, dismembered and stabbed Taesmals, bleeding into the rocky soil.

The person who releases the pressure points helps me to my feet and I look at him. He turns away as I lift my head. His clothes are a dusty brown, good camouflage for our surroundings. They're loose and airy in the hot weather, and he wears a scarf wrapped around his head, hiding his face. As he walks away, he sheaths his bloody sword into the scabbard strapped to his back.

"Thank you," I cough out, but he doesn't reply and keeps walking.

My arms and legs are scratched and red, but it's nothing compared to what I went through the first night. I'll live. I look at the corpses—flesh cut to bone, ribs ripped out at sickening angles—and I decide to follow him. He's my only ally now.

He doesn't say a thing, though. I wonder if he's some kind of assassin, if he's even here to help me, or if he was just passing through. I can tell from his height and build that he's still young.

"Sorry if I'm bothering you," I say, more politely than ever. "But I'm trying to get to Arriscyal. Someone told me that if I keep heading south, I can catch a boat or something. Could you…help me?"

He stops and turns to me, but I still can't see his face, not even his eyes. He nods and waves his hand for me to follow, then continues walking.

I gasp and run to his side. "Thank you so much!"

Even though he doesn't say anything, I'm relieved to have him at my side. It's still nice to have someone to walk with, but I find myself missing Gediyon. At least he had the patience to explain things to me.

When I need to take a break, I tell him and he follows without a word, leaning in the shade as I sit down. I finally catch a glimpse of his eyes when he's surveying the landscape, and they're strikingly beautiful, an intense blue-green. He must realize that I can see them, because he turns away from my view.

Several breaks later, and I offer to make him a pastrami sandwich, but to eat he would have to unwrap his scarf, and I guess hiding his face is more important than nutrition. But why would he be hiding it? He couldn't be completely disfigured, could he?

"I'm Michelle, by the way," I tell him after a few bites. "Goddess, your Creator, if you haven't figured it out."

He just nods.

We continue walking, and after some time, we turn a corner and spot a stream. Other animals have already made it—mutants. The largest bird sips water from the stream, while the groveling coyotes tear away the insides of their docile counterparts. I hold my fire stick ready, and the scarfed man draws his sword. When the coyote bounds for us, I blast and he slashes, but the bird swoops in overhead. Its talons catch him in the head. I burn the feathers and the bird flaps away, feeding the flame.

At least we got rid of them quick. I look back at the masked man, but—

"Jayse?" I say.

He turns away. His body language tells me he's about to run away, but he stands still. After all, I've already seen his face. Then, slowly, he faces me and smirks.

"Hey babe."

He looks a lot like Jayse—they even have the same voice—but then I get a better look at him. His hair is shorter and more brown than a faded gold, and his skin is lighter. He even has a scar running from below his left eye to his jaw—Jayse would've healed himself before a scar could form.

I guess he realizes that it's useless to cover his face again. He walks toward me with open arms as if he wants a hug, but I step away.

"Why do you look so much like him?"

He shrugs. "Does my beauty bother you?"

"Are you like his brother or something?"

He turns his face to the side to show off his scar. "I don't have any Arriscylean powers. Could I be his brother?" He starts back for the stream.

"It's crazy how much you look alike!" I follow him. "Why were you hiding your face, though?"

Suddenly, I find myself against the wall. He isn't touching me—one hand rests on the wall above my shoulder, and his face is an inch away from mine. My eyes grow big as I stare back at him.

"See my beautiful face, Miss Goddess?" he asks. "I can't share it with just anybody. But you…" He swipes a finger down my cheek and stops at my lips, which makes me gasp and wonder how stupid I look. "You're special." He leans as if he's going to kiss me, and I'm ready to push him off, but he winks and pulls away, then laughs.

My heart is pounding like crazy. I raise my fire stick at him and shout, "Don't ever do that to me!"

"Oh, is little Miss Goddess a little bashful? Don't want dear princey boy making any moves on her, does she?" He cackles again.

I growl. "Shut up!"

"I love having this face!"

"What, did you steal it from him?"

"Maybe," he says, then starts away from the stream.

I march behind him and whack him in the shoulder. "What did you do to him?"

"I didn't do anything. I just happen to have the same beautiful face as him."

I blow steam through my nostrils, but it wouldn't be a good idea to piss him off now. I walk behind him in silence for a few paces, then ask, "What's your name?"

"You don't need to know."

"It would be nice," I say. "You're the first person I've encountered out here, besides the Taesmals. I was with someone a few days ago, but I lost them."

"They must've wanted to get rid of you. It's dangerous escorting Goddess around these parts."

I think about it. "Yeah, I guess those guys probably wanted to get rid of me. I don't think Dreana liked me very much."

He stops walking and I bump into him. "Wait, Dreana?" he says. "As in, Lady Dreana het Codget Ivy Bescur, Champion of Tyrique?"

"Wow. You know her whole name?"

"She's the Champion of Tyrique! Of course I know her. And you met her out here?"

"All the way back there," I say, waving my arms all behind me.

"Of course I would miss her," he sighs, then continues walking.

I let a few seconds of silence pass before I say, "So are you gonna tell me your name?"

"No."

"Fine, then I'll just call you the Prince Imposter!"

He turns this to his advantage and acts like a caricaturized version of his idea of Jayse. I'll admit, it's funny, but I feel bad for laughing, because he presents Jayse as narcissistic, obsessive about his looks, and overconfident with his lady skills. Every now and then, he whines like a spoiled brat about hating palace life.

"Stop being such a jerk!" I say, whacking him with my stick.

Then he turns on me and tries to seduce me with a deep voice and gaze, but I punch him in the stomach and push him away. I'm sure it doesn't actually hurt him, but he pretends to cry like it's the end of the world.

And he reminds me that since I'm here, it soon will be.

This thought depresses me and I don't say anything for a while, but he feeds off my silence.

"Don't you know, the Second Moon has already started? What is Goddess doing, taking a stroll in the desert, when people out there are starving because of the Famine?"

"The Second Moon already started?"

"It is Ellio." It's already August, is what I understand.

"Cities out there are probably falling to starvation," he goes on. "Where oh where could our Creator be? Oh, what was that? You say she's in the desert on a picnic with her darling prince? What a responsible Goddess she is! Now let's hack up what's left of Grandma so we won't starve tonight!"

I slap him. Hard. "I would help them if I weren't stuck out here. It's not my fault I'm out here, and it's not yours either, so shut up!"

"You shouldn't have come to Starrs in the first place," he says, his voice serious.

"I don't need you to tell me that, too."

We continue walking, and I'm thankful he doesn't say anything, but just hearing his footsteps in the gravel behind me makes my pulse throb. I reach to the ground for a handful of rocks, turn them into packaged chicken sandwiches, and shove them in his arms.

"A thank-you for walking me," I say. "Now good bye, Prince Imposter."

I march forth, determined to be alone this time. Maybe three more days, and I'll finally be out of the canyon, and I don't need a guide.

Not long later, I hear quick footsteps, then turn to see him, the scarf wrapped around his head again, running ahead as if it's a race to the finish line.

He waves at me and says, "See ya!" and I notice that he's dumped the sandwiches behind.

What a bastard.

Chapter Seventeen
On Canyon's Edge

I'm glad I'm alone now. Honest. It's better to be alone than to hang around someone who pisses you off.

I can probably sing and dance and otherwise act like a complete idiot, because I'm alone—but I don't because it'll attract mutants.

I march forward, only looking back to check if any animals are stalking me. Nobody in sight, especially not that scarfed jerk.

I hike uphill and finally I see more vegetation. I pass spindly trees and even hear some birds chirping—the cute, small kind, not the large vultures soaring overhead. The edge of the canyon mustn't be too far now. I even see some clouds! Never thought I'd be so happy to see clouds. They're peachy pink like my clothes, since the sun is about to set soon.

Unfortunately, the scene that greets me at the top of the hill isn't a lush forest—of course not—but in the distance I finally see ocean! It's still quite a way, but I'm closer now than ever.

I hop a little downhill as I survey my surroundings. The small stream I passed earlier has curved around a long way and it flows into a wider river that heads southwest. This is a good time to make a boat.

I snap a leaf off a tree and, like I did with the gliders, pull on its blade until it broadens. I mold it into the shape of a simple boat—green, translucent, and lightweight. When it grows too big to hold in my hands, I fling it toward the river and run after it. It lands by the bank, where I continue stretching it out until it can fit my whole height. I flatten the bottom and push it into the water, hopping inside as the current pulls it along.

It's a slow river, but it beats walking. I lie back, using my capelet to shield me from the sun while I sip on water from my canteen.

Then I realize that I'm extremely vulnerable, so I sit up and hold the fire stick, looking all around in case any mutated coyotes want to bite my boat like a chew toy. So far, nothing hurdles down the slopes after me, but I do see a shadow circling on the ground. I hope it's a normal falcon or something.

The boat is doing its job well, and I refill my canteen with river water, which I then purify in my hands. The water sizzles within my canteen, though it isn't hot. Specks of dirt and microbes fly through the opening and fall back into the river.

Sometime later, the sun sets over the mountains. I've been too lazy to check my surroundings, so now's a good time. Ahead, I see coyotes and birds near the river. They haven't noticed me yet, but I hold the fire stick, ready to blast. That's when I notice something strange.

As the boat drifts closer, the water turns red and I realize that all of these mutants are dead. It looks like they were killed with a sword, too, so the Prince Imposter must've been this way. There are so many of them, though, I wonder if it was an ambush.

I push some of the floating bodies aside to let the boat pass through. The water continues down the gorge, and I hope that it continues straight to the ocean, but I don't think my boat can handle sea waves.

Thinking it's safe, I lie back in my boat, waiting for the stars to appear in the sky. I hum myself a song and, by luck, the next time I look up, I see the Prince Imposter walking down the riverbank. Funny, I thought he would be a lot farther by now. The scarf has unraveled from his head.

"Hey, jerkface!" I yell across the water. "Looks like I'm going to beat you to the ocean!"

He doesn't say anything and keeps walking, ever so slowly, but I know he heard me.

I throw myself back into the boat. Yeah, I'm comfortable here, and yes he's a jerk, but I can't help but feel pretty mean about not offering him a ride.

I sit up and look back upstream, but he isn't walking anymore. I see his clothes against the rocky gray ground, and I spot a red stain in his side.

Oh God, what happened?

I look down the river, then back at him. I'll never forgive myself if I leave him, so I use my fire stick as an oar and paddle for shore. It takes a little while fighting against the current, especially since I've never done this before, but once I'm close enough, I jump into shallow water, pull the boat onto the rocks, and run back to the Prince Imposter.

He's lying on his front and when I turn him over, I see that his face is ashen. I roll up his shirt and see three deep, bloody gashes. It looks like one of the birds attacked him. His clothes have soaked up a lot of his blood, so I don't exactly know how much he's lost, but at least he's breathing. His pulse doesn't feel very strong, though.

I start hyperventilating. What am I supposed to do?! I'm Goddess, not a doctor! If only I had Jayse with me. He might freak out over how much they look alike, though.

I should probably start by cleaning his wounds. I run to the river and pick up a rock. Maybe because adrenaline is pumping through my body, I find it doesn't take as long to turn it into a crude teapot. I dunk it into the river to fill it, then bring it back to the Prince Imposter and gather scarce twigs along the shore. I set them ablaze with the fire stick and place the pot on top.

While it heats to a boil, I crawl back to the Prince Imposter and look at his wound. I hope it didn't reach any major organs. I feel weak just looking at it.

I rip a strip from his scarf and wind it over my fingers until it turns into a roll of bandages. He's unlucky to have me—of all people—looking after him, but at least I'm trying. I zig-zag them over his wound and tightly wrap them around with the rest. I hope it's enough to help the bleeding.

I check his pulse again and listen for his breathing. Still steady, I think. He lets out a groan and I gasp when he opens his eyes. They're more of a turquoise compared to Jayse's bright green.

He must recognize that it's me because he says, "What are you doing?" Is it wrong that I'm a little pleased his voice is so weak? At least now he can't be so mean.

"I'm trying to help you, dumbass!" I pick up a small rock and say, "Do you think you can swallow anything?"

He flinches and reaches for his side. I'll take that as a yes. I'll force it down his throat if I have to.

I close my eyes and hold the small rock in both hands, praying so hard for the medicine that Madam Manasa gave me that I'm starting to chant. I feel the rock smoothen in my hand, but I won't let go of it just yet. I put my deepest wishes in this pill, hoping it'll do the same thing for the Prince Imposter that it did for me.

I give it a kiss for good luck before handing it to him, then realize maybe he doesn't even have the strength to reach for his own mouth, so I put the pill to his lips. Well, that's an indirect kiss. I tell him, "Take this," then I scramble back for the teapot.

I don't know if the water is hot enough now, but does it even matter? I take it off the fire and stick a pinky inside. Warm enough for a bath, but probably not sanitary. My fingertips shake with my quick pulse as I concentrate on transforming it into the same liquid Madam Manasa made me, and the steam stings my eyes.

The Prince Imposter chokes, "You trying to kill me?"

"I might as well, with the little I know." I bring the teapot over and put the spout to his lips. "Drink this, it'll help it go down."

He does so, but I don't think he likes the taste. I give him a few more sips, and I think it helps the pain go away.

I tell him, "I'm going to clean your wounds," then I unwrap the bandages around his waist. They've already soaked up even more blood. I hope the medicine is doing its job.

I completely remove the bandages and then pour some of the liquid over his wounds. He cries out and his face turns white, then he falls completely still. I shake his shoulder lightly. Oops—I think I just made him pass out. I might as well pour the rest of the liquid over his wound, though.

Before wrapping the bandages back, I wonder, how much blood has he lost? I look at the blood on the bandages and sigh. The thought makes me feel sick, but it's better to suck it up than be too squeamish and let him die.

I take deep breaths before I can manage my next move. I still feel shaky with adrenaline, but as soon as I feel calmer, I pull the blood out of the bandages into a floating jelly sphere. It's probably full of fluff and bacteria from the bandages, so I cleanse it of impurities between my hands. Like the river water, the foreign matter flies out of the sphere.

My hands are still shaking, but over the next few minutes, I make the blood multiply so it's probably enough to fill a carton of milk, then I surround it with a giant, sterile syringe. I make sure to remind myself "sterile" so he doesn't contract some kind of infection. The syringe rests on my lap while I take his arm and try to look for a good vein—maybe the one inside his elbow, but I have no idea what I'm doing and I'm pretty sure I'm going to be sick soon.

My hands shake as I bring the needle to his vein. I have to do this right. I want to look away as the needle pierces his skin, and I feel the blood drain out of my own face when I see a drop of blood. Geez, only a little drop of blood! I press down the plunger slightly, then angle the syringe into his arm so gravity can take care of the rest. I leave it floating in the air.

I look back to his wounds, which have stopped bleeding, but are still wide open. I don't know if it's a better idea to air it out or cover it, but I don't want anything crawling inside, so I thin out the bandages and rewrap him.

When I'm done, I check his pulse again. I think he's doing fine.

I look down the riverbank. The sky has grown darker, and I think we'll have to stay here for the night.

Like I did on the first night of being alone, I build a circular dirt wall, only this one's much larger than the first one I made. It isn't a perfect circle, but it'll do. Soon, the walls rise and close into a dome. I have the energy to raise a bed beneath the Prince Imposter, but I'm still not in the right state of mind to make it any fancier than a dirt platform. I kneel beside him and rest my head against the platform, making sure that he's still breathing. In time, I fall asleep as well.

Chapter Eighteen
The West Wind

"What in the world is this thing?"

I jump back into my senses and sit up. I guess I had rolled to the floor in the night.

The Prince Imposter is still lying on the dirt bed I made for him. His face is pale, but he's smiling and pointing at the giant floating syringe. Only a little blood is left at the bottom. I think he's trying to hold back a laugh—it's probably too painful for him.

I sit up and carefully pull the needle out of his arm. "This thing saved your life," I tell him. I turn the syringe into a happy face Band-Aid and stick it over his open vein. I cover it with his sleeve. "How are you feeling?"

"I've had worse," he says, winking then immediately flinching.

I shake my head then lift the thin bandages over his wound. It's still wide open, but he isn't bleeding as badly, and he's not dead.

"Maybe the pill Madam Manasa gave me was just for healing bones," I mutter.

He groans. "That old hag?"

"Yeah. She saved my life when I first landed in the desert." I rise and cross my arms. "Well, good morning! You hungry or anything?"

He takes a deep breath and stares at the rounded ceiling. Nothing's up there but stone, so what's he looking at?

Then he says, "Why did you help me?"

"Well, I'm not gonna leave you to die. You helped me, too. Life for a life?"

He sighs. "I guess you're not that incompetent of a Goddess after all."

I blow at my bangs. "So, you hungry or what? 'Cause I am! I'm gonna have some cinnamon oatmeal. What do you want?"

"Whatever you think I should eat. I haven't eaten in days."

"You—" I start, then moan out of annoyance. "You need to take better care of yourself! If you keep trying to be a badass, you'll get yourself killed."

"Thanks for the advice," he says, and I walk outside.

The morning is cool and the air is refreshing by the river. The gorge looks a lot different in the morning sunlight than it does after sunset. The light feels ordinary, rather than fiery. I pick up two rocks and turn them into identical bowls of oatmeal, then a thought hits me before I go back inside. I'm well-rested and in a better mood than I was last night, so I manage to transform one of the bowls into the salty custard I had at the banquet. It's even in the same gold-rimmed palace dish.

I bring it back inside and hand it to the Prince Imposter, who's still lying on his back.

"What is this?" he asks.

"Some kind of pudding," I say, then take a seat. I take a big slurp of oatmeal and once I've swallowed, I say, "What, do I have to spoon feed you?"

He narrows his eyes at me, then pushes himself up. I guess the pain is too much for him because he falls back with heavy breaths. I offer to feed him, but he grudgingly places the bowl on his chest and feeds himself.

"Why would you feed an injured man dessert?"

I laugh. "Thought you'd like it. I mean, Jayse likes it."

As soon as I say that, he throws the spoon back in the bowl and doesn't touch it again, even though I'm sure he enjoys it. I know he needs to eat, and I probably should feed him something healthier, so I take the bowl and turn it into a chicken sandwich. He eats it without a word.

I make him some more of the medicine I gave him the night before. This time, I let him only drink it and don't pour it over his wound again. When we decide to leave, I drag the boat closer to the dome shelter, then spend a long time helping him to it. I think the medicine helps his pain, at least, because some color returns to his cheeks.

After a while, I settle him in the boat and then push it back into the water.

"You take it easy," I say, then jump into the boat. The stream is still slow, but I don't want to attach a motor to the boat, because I'm afraid it'll spin out of control.

I hold my knees close to my chest, enjoying the view ahead. The Prince Imposter is quiet, and I turn around every now and then, only to see him gazing at the water. I stare at the sky and make note of the sun's position, making sure that we're still headed south. The river doesn't branch, so I should trust it to carry us to the end.

"Do you want to know something?" he asks.

I turn around and face him. "Sure."

He keeps gazing at the water. "When we separated, and I ran ahead, I knew the mutants would be there. It's downhill, so of course the river would widen, and wild animals and mutants alike would want a drink."

I stare at him. "So you ran ahead 'cause you knew they would be there."

"I had to save you the trouble. I didn't realize how much trouble it would be for myself."

I look away. "Thank you."

We continue drifting down the stream in silence.

"So are you gonna tell me your name?"

He shakes his head but smiles. "Not today. Someday, but not today, Michelle."

"Fine!" I turn back around.

A minute later, he says, "I apologize for underestimating you. I think you can actually do it—learn how to be Goddess before the Cycle kills us all. You can probably even save a lot of cities from the Famine."

"What *is* the Famine?"

"The trial of the Second Moon, from the World of Florrish. It's not any normal famine, since it's Pesaeton's punishment. We have to prepare for it after the First Moon every two years, and that usually means storing food. It's harder to come by food that isn't preserved, because crops become fragile and wither with the smallest temperature changes, fish refuse to be caught, and many livestock fall to an epidemic. Taesmal mutants are fine, though, as I'm sure you've seen."

"Does the Famine last forever?"

"No, thank Go—thank *you*, I guess. It only lasts for about three weeks before the crops grow back, and the fish come out of hiding, and the animals get better. It can be devastating, though, especially where food is so scarce to begin with, people can't afford to preserve anything."

"So that's where I come in, right? I can give people all the food they need."

"Yep. And we're headed to the West Wind. Let's hope they mind their manners."

He tells me that the West Wind is a rogue port town. It used to be a peaceful place, but since the Bandits' Desert to the north got its name, the same thieves moved south to travel. Some of the ships that dock there also trade with Arriscyal, so there's a good chance that I can hitch a ride.

As we ride farther down the river, we pass more trees and even some small, run-down buildings. I spot some crooked fences, which must close in pasture for grazing animals, but no animals are in sight. Probably sick, like the Prince Imposter said.

When we pass beneath a crumbling bridge, he tells me to put my hood on, and he wraps his head with the scarf. Taesmals might be roaming the West Wind, and we don't want them hampering my journey back. So I won't stand out as much, I turn my clothes a grayish blue and lengthen my skirt. I also remove the blood from his clothes.

Before approaching the actual town, I pull the boat aside to shore. This way, people won't spot us in the boat and know that we came from the canyon, because then they can assume two things: that we're thieves and we have treasure on us, neither of which are true.

I help the Prince Imposter out. He's still slow and cautious with his movement, but he tells me that it's nothing. Yeah, and period cramps feel like a foot massage.

I help support him while we walk toward the noise of town. I can tell by the way he gasps every now and then that he's still in pain, so I take a moment to make him a bottle of the medicine I gave him earlier. He drinks some before we enter the town, and then we make sure that our faces are covered before we walk any farther.

Apparently, disguising ourselves like this, we actually fit in. Many of the people we pass also obscure their faces, either with hoods, veils, or scarves like the Prince Imposter. Some do expose their faces, like burly sailors carrying cargo from their ships, or a few peddlers who only wear head wraps. The funny thing is, I don't see children anywhere. The Prince Imposter and I are probably the youngest people here, and that doesn't exactly make me feel safe, especially since he's still hurt.

"Keep your eyes ahead," he whispers to me. "If you keep looking around, they'll know you're not from around here and try to take advantage of you."

I keep my nose pointed straight ahead, but I can't stop my eyes from wandering. I imagine that this place is worse at night. In broad daylight, some drunken men are already stumbling into brawls because one of them looked at another in a funny way. A lot of bodies lie around, some definitely sleeping, but others I'm not so sure. Many of them look unhealthily thin, too. Could the Famine have already killed them?

The Prince Imposter leads me down one of the docks and says, "This looks like an Arriscylean ship. You stay here and I'll see if they'll let you ride."

I stand stiff at the side of the walkway, letting sailors pass onto ramps. While the Prince Imposter is away, I hear some of the sailors talking about the Famine, how the Taesmal mutants are getting out of hand, and of course the weather. Some of them try to strike up a conversation or wolf-whistle at me; I stay completely still as if I'm deaf.

After a few minutes, the Prince Imposter comes back.

"They refuse to let anyone on board," he says. "No matter how much I offer them."

"Did you tell them I'm Goddess?"

"It's too risky. It might be an Arriscylean ship, but someone in the crew may be working for the Taesmals." He crosses his arms. "They can't guarantee you a safe passage, either. Some of the waters they travel are dangerous."

"If only there were a sea angel…"

"Can't you make your own ship?"

"Uh." I look at him. "I'm not sure if I can do something that sophisticated. I can do simple things easy, but I don't know how to engineer a ship. And I haven't really been in the best state of mind, so it's even harder for me. Plus, if Taesmals are around, wouldn't it be kind of dangerous to do something out in the open like that?"

"I guess you're right. We'll have to keep looking then."

Farther in town, I catch the scent of something delicious. It smells like barbecue, and I can taste the spices as the smell wafts into my nostrils. I'm tempted to find it and eat whatever it is—I can do with some organic meat, after all, instead of stuff formed from a rock—but the Prince Imposter pulls me along, saying that it's a trap. During the Famine, the smell of good food only draws people in to get their throats slit and wallets nabbed.

As we walk down the street, some people try to peddle things our way, but the Prince Imposter ignores them and keeps walking. I do whatever he does.

When we pass by a large house, someone flings a box out of a window and it lands by our feet with shards of glass. The Prince Imposter bends down to pick it up, but then a heavily rouged woman with a chest that's about to fall out of her top stomps down the front stairs, yelling at someone behind her.

"It's the forsaken Famine!" she shrieks. "What makes you think we're going to get any business if no amount of money can buy us food?"

"Then why don't you just call our Creator?" an older woman shouts back. "She's sure to do something about it. Oh wait, she's in Arriscyal like she always is when she's reborn, enjoying her magical lifestyle while the rest of us suffer. Do you really think she's going to help us?"

"Hey!" the Prince Imposter shouts. He hands me the fallen jewelry box and marches up to the woman. "How dare you speak ill of our Creator! She's only a young girl, but she is trying her best."

"Oh-ho! Look at this boy, trying to be all gallant and faithful! Why don't you shove your faith up your ass and see if your precious Goddess helps you then?"

I really want to throw the box at the old lady and break her nose. Then maybe she can die from her own hideous face and blood loss before starvation overtakes her, but I really ought to do something good. I place the jewelry box on the ground and transform it into an insulated cooler that looks like a treasure chest. Inside, I place loaves of bread and cold slices of meat.

The Prince Imposter and the old woman are still arguing. He walks toward the busty younger woman and holds the handle of his sword toward her.

"Here, Miss," he says. "Why don't you do yourself a favor and cut up Grandma here for your dinner?"

She laughs but says, "How dare you!"

"Hey, Imposter," I say, rising from the ground and holding my hand out to him. "Let's go."

He turns around and points his sword threateningly at the old woman, then sheaths it and comes to my side. I tap the younger woman on the shoulder and say, "You dropped this," then take the Prince Imposter's arm and run away.

I hear the woman say, "This isn't…" Then she screams upon seeing what's inside.

I pull the Prince Imposter into a small space between a house and shed. He's gasping out of pain and holding his side, then throws himself against the wall for support. At least his wound isn't bleeding. I hold my breath until he breathes normally again. Then he looks at me.

"Did you do what I think you did?"

I smile. "I filled it with bread and meat."

He chuckles and pats me on the shoulder. "Word will spread quick. We should keep moving." He pushes himself away from the wall and beckons me to follow.

"Are you okay, though?"

"I want my mummy, it hurts so much!" Then he pretends to cry and I smack his back. "No really," he says, "I'm fine."

We start back for the coast in the hopes of finding a fisherman, but on the way, something grabs my attention. On the outskirts of town, I find a barren field and a young animal lying in dried grass. It looks odd—the snout and tail of a pig on the body of a cow, with black spots on a pinkish brown body.

"It's a moink," the Prince Imposter tells me. What an adorable name! Without hesitation, I climb over the fence and drop to the calf's side.

"Oh, you poor thing!" I say, brushing the calf's head.

"Michelle," he says, but when he sees that I won't move, he climbs over the fence too.

"I wish I had actual healing abilities," I say, putting my ear to the calf's body and trying to listen to its breathing. "Instead of guessing, I can actually do something worthwhile."

"You worked a miracle on me," he says.

"But you're still not fully healed." I sit up and brush the calf's head. "Poor thing. I know if I help it now, they'll still slaughter it later."

He looks around the field. "They already took his family."

Worthless or not, I still want to save the thing's life. I break off a dried piece of straw and turn it into a large baby bottle full of warm cow's milk. I have to offer more, though, and I cradle the bottle as if it were a baby, praying into it as many vitamins, minerals, and herbs that I can think of, praying that the formula will give the calf the strength to fend for itself and grow up, even if they end up killing it. Once I'm done, I make sure that it tastes sweet so the calf will want to drink it all, then I hand it to the Prince Imposter.

"Feed it," I tell him.

"Why me?" Before he can give it back, I jump to my feet and run across the field.

"What are you doing?" he yells at me, holding the bottle in the calf's mouth.

From where I stand, I don't think many people in town can see me easily. I hold the fire stick tightly in both hands.

"Thank you, fire stick," I say to it. "You've been extremely helpful to me these past few days, but now it's time for you to ascend to a higher purpose."

Holes break into the top of the knob on the end and it feels heavier. I hold it like the fire stick, but when I squeeze it, water sprays out. I jump and laugh when I see that it works, and I spread the water all around the field, soaking the ground. In a few moments, the shriveled straw grows green, and stalks rise out of the ground.

"It's working!"

I prance around the field and spray everything in sight. The stalk turns into blue corn, and the grass near the calf grows lusciously. I hop over the fence and water other crops, which turn out to be leafy greens, melons, and beans. By the time I'm done watering every crop in sight, I have to push the plants aside to make my way back to the Prince Imposter.

The calf is now standing, rubbing its head against the Prince Imposter affectionately. Even though his face is covered, I think he smiles at me.

"Let's go before anyone notices the mess you've made."

We decide to escape through the fields to shore, because we spot some townspeople running in our direction. When we reach the end of the fields, we climb over the fence and walk down sandy ground toward more docks, but these are smaller and quieter than the ones with cargo ships.

He eyes each boat as we pass. Even though I see a comfortable ship and its married owners, or a robust one and its brother captains, the Prince Imposter stops at the smallest boat whose captain is drinking himself red on deck.

"This one should do," the Prince Imposter says.

He hops on deck and helps me aboard, approaches the captain and unwraps his scarf.

"Good day to you, sir. I am His Divine Highness Prince Jaysonn Cordin Abelus Traetels, heir to the throne of Arriscyal." That's Jayse's full title? Sheesh. "See my lovely face? Yes, it's true. Now see here, this is my dear friend"—he brings me forth—"Her Serene Divinity Goddess Michelle, our Great Creator. Got it?"

The captain points his bottle at the Prince Imposter and babbles, "You're the prince!"

"Indeed. Now see, I need you to give Miss Goddess here a ride to Arriscyal."

"Wait, aren't you coming with me?"

"My friend and *I* need a ride to Arriscyal. Think this is the job for you? All right then, chump! Let's get going!" He slaps the captain on his shoulders and forces him into the cabin. I hear the Prince Imposter say, "Miss Goddess can repay you with all the sip you can drink later. Just get us there safely."

"Buh wait! There's sea—big serpent in sea—"

"Yes, and the weather is lovely too. We'll take care of it later."

I hope sailing drunk isn't the same as driving drunk. I think the Prince Imposter actually walks the captain through his maneuvering, because we pull out of the docks smoothly. Once we're in the open sea, the Prince Imposter comes on deck.

"It should take us five days to get back to Arriscyal," he tells me. "It can take us as little as three, but two days buffer time in case the seas are bad."

I smile at him. "You know, Madam Manasa told me that Jayse can take care of himself, so maybe he's already back in Arriscyal. You want to meet him?"

"Pft, yeah, and tell him how much he's ruined my life." He sighs. "Everywhere I go, 'Prince Jaysonn? Is that you?' Gets too annoying, I have to resort to covering up my beautiful face."

I laugh. "It's a shame!"

"Isn't it? Maybe if I meet him, I can talk him into switching lives for a while. He'd like that, wouldn't he? I always hear rumors that he isn't in the palace much anymore." He looks me in the eyes. "You know him, right? What's he like?"

"I haven't known him for very long, actually. But he's nice." I shrug. "You remind me a lot of him…but he's a lot nicer than you!"

He leans against the edge of the ship and gives me that look like he's trying to seduce me. "Who do you think is better looking?"

I slap him on the arm.

"Seriously. Me or him?"

I start into the cabin and say, "You look the same!"

"Miss Goddess sure knows how to pick her men!"

"You're not a man!"

"Ouch. Excuse me while I go cry."

A hidden hatch in the captain's cabin leads below deck. Down there are more discarded bottles of liquor, and a large table as if someone once held conferences. A map hangs on the farthest wall, defaced with tacks and rips. Several cabinet doors hang open, and I see long coats in one of them.

It's not ideal for spending the next five days, but it beats the desert.

At night, I sleep on top of the conference table. It's huge and can fit six more people. The Prince Imposter says he'll help out the captain while I sleep.

It seems like I only close my eyes for a second when I hear loud rummaging and the Prince Imposter shakes me awake.

"Michelle, wake up!"

"What time is it?"

"The captain is dead."

"What?" I jump off the table, but the Prince Imposter keeps me from going to the ladder.

"They're Mysiochs," he whispers. "Taesmals. I don't know if it's me or you they're after, but you have to stay down here, okay?" He pushes me toward the coat closet and shoves me inside. "Trust me, I'll take care of them, but you must not leave this closet—no matter what, do you understand?"

"But you're still hurt!"

"I can take care of them. Trust me."

"But they're Taesmals!"

"And I'm the Prince Imposter." He winks. "I'll give them what they want."

He pushes the door in. Before he closes it completely, he holds it ajar for a moment, then opens it again. He looks at me in the dim candle light, and I'm scared and wide-eyed and uncertain of what's going to happen. Then he steps closer, leans in to me, and gives me a light, gentle kiss on my cheek. He looks at me one last time before shutting the door.

Now in complete darkness, I gasp and hold my cheek. That's the first time a guy has ever kissed me, even if it wasn't on my lips. My heart beats even faster, and I'm scared, too. I want to help him, but I trust that he can take care of the Taesmals on his own. But with his wound?

I lean against the back wall of the closet, trying to breathe steadily, but my heart feels like it's going to ram into my ribs.

Then I hear voices. I can't tell what they're saying, but I hear shouts and swords drawing. Something heavy thumps into the deck above, and I hear more voices and footsteps.

Whatever it is they're talking about, it's keeping them from fighting. I press my ear against the closet door and try to make out something in their conversation. I think I catch the word "king" several times, and I hear the Prince Imposter shout, and more hard footsteps and swords clanging.

More bodies fall and the Prince Imposter yells in protest, then it's silent. I stop breathing, wondering what's happening. Even though I can't see anything, my eyes are wide.

Then I hear footsteps—soft, calm footsteps, and another voice murmurs. A second later, I don't hear anything.

I hope again that I'll hear some more footsteps and the Prince Imposter shouting that he's gotten rid of the Taesmals, but I don't hear anything. I don't think they're even waiting for *me*.

I don't care what happens. I burst out of the closet and stumble across the room, tripping over liquor bottles as I make my way for the ladder into the cabin.

The captain is sitting in his chair with a large silver stake protruding from his chest. I have to cover my mouth to prevent myself from screaming, then I push the door to the deck.

No one is here. I run onto deck, looking out at the ocean and hoping to find another boat somewhere, but all I see are waves.

I stop breathing when I spot something fluttering on the deck. The Prince Imposter's scarf. I fall to my knees and take it into my hands. It has his blood on it.

Taesmal King. That's what they were saying. Did they actually mistake the Prince Imposter for Jayse? Are they taking him back to Sheirced to spill his blood, in hopes that it'll strengthen their king?

I believed that he could take care of himself. But he couldn't even fight them, because he was still hurt, because I'm not smart enough to help him heal completely. And what the hell did I do while he fought? I stayed in the closet like a coward when I knew I could've helped him!

I can't stop the sob that comes forth. I curl forward, clenching and twisting the bloody scarf in my hands as tears stream from my face. Crying like this hurts my head, and I scream and pound on the deck.

I'm *Goddess* and I still couldn't even save him! He never even told me his name.

I don't know how long I stay curled up, sobbing every last tear in my body, shivering from the cold of the night. I finally move when the ship crashes into something.

Eventually I push myself up and see that the boat has crashed on shore. The plants glow here.

Dragging the scarf behind me, I stop crying and walk off the boat. I don't know where I am, but maybe if I keep walking, someone will find me.

I climb up shore and start onto a grassy path. Some of the grass is flattened, so maybe I'm close to a town. People must come down here to see the water.

I walk for a few minutes, then when I see a glowing tree, a crying fit takes over my body again. I sit on a log and cover my face with my hands, my tears falling into the scarf.

I don't know if I can ever move from this spot. How can I ever face the world again? I'm a failed Goddess. I'll probably die of dehydration before I stop crying.

"Michelle?"

Chapter Nineteen
Runaway

I look up and see the person I just sent to his death.

"What happened?"

His voice sounds the same, but it's gentler. Through my blurry, teary eyes, in the soft glowing light of the tree, I can make out longer and lighter hair, different clothes, and no scar running down his left cheek.

I don't know what I could possibly say to him, so I bury my face in my arms and—if it's even possible—I cry harder. Sobs wrack my body in trembles, and I don't care how loud I bawl.

Eventually Jayse sits beside me and rubs my back. With his touch, I can feel warm energy spreading from my back through my limbs and down to my toes, tingling as it heals everything in its path. This makes me wail, because it reminds me of my failure and how the Prince Imposter couldn't heal himself.

Jayse must see the bloody scarf in my hands because he puts both arms around me and holds me close while I continue to cry. Maybe he understands that I just lost someone and I couldn't do anything to help him. What would he think if I told him about the Prince Imposter?

I keep crying until I'm too tired, and Jayse holds me gently the entire time, letting me rest my head on his shoulder. When the worst has left me, all that remains are shuddering gasps with every breath. Warm tears still fall down my cheeks.

When I've calmed down enough, Jayse helps me to my feet and brushes something from the top of my head. Glowing fluff from the tree has fallen on us. I don't say anything while I watch them fall to the ground.

He leads me up the path and down a small road, and I see a house. It's bigger than the shelter domes I've made, though not by much. I see lights flickering inside. I could tell Jayse that I can make our own cottage so we don't have to break in, but I can't find the words, and I don't think I can concentrate enough to make the cottage.

It turns out, the front door is unlocked. Maybe Jayse had already been resting here when the boat crashed.

He leads me to a too-soft sofa and I lie down. He blows out the candles, covers me with a knit blanket, then takes his place on the floor, supporting his head with his arms and staring at the ceiling.

I can't sleep. Every time I look at him, I see his eyes sparkling in the moonlight, and I know he isn't close to sleep either.

I think two hours pass, and in that entire time, I had been calm, but suddenly my lip trembles and I have to cover my face to hide the incoming tears. I hear Jayse sit up and he puts his hand on my shoulder.

"I can't do it anymore!" I scream. "I can't be Goddess anymore. I'm no good at it. I want to go back home!" I sob, but choke out, "I didn't think it would be like this. It's too much to handle. I'm Goddess, and I can't even save someone's life?"

"I'm sure you did everything you could."

"It wasn't enough! How can I face anyone if I keep failing? How can anyone bow down to me and call me Goddess when I don't deserve it?" Jayse sits next to me and puts his arm around my shoulders. "I'm just a girl! I can't handle this kind of responsibility!" I throw my arms around him. "I want to go home! I miss my friends." I hold him tight and tremble, then scream, "I miss my brother!"

Jayse is far too sweet, letting me squeeze onto him as if I'm clinging onto life itself, letting me drip my tears all over him.

He runs his hand over my head. "Michelle, I can learn a lot from you. There are problems to face, and you deal with them. Me, I just run away." He sighs. "Still, I can see that this is a lot for you. I know that you can show everyone that you're capable as our Creator, even if you weren't born in Starrs—especially because you weren't born here. But if it's what you really want, I can help you find a way back home."

"Really?"

"Just for you. It's the least I can do as the Prince of Arriscyal. I mean, what other use am I?" He lets out a dry laugh. "As soon as we return, I'll talk to everyone. There must be a way. After all, you came here from Tyme." He releases me and brushes tears off my cheeks. "Don't worry, okay? And just so you know, I think you're a great Goddess." He smiles then scoots back to the floor. "Try to get some sleep. We have a long way back home."

I lie back and pull the blankets over me. I keep thinking about the Prince Imposter, how I can prove to others that I'm not a failure, and Jayse's words. Then I realize, I'm exhausted.

"What are you doing here?"

A man is pointing a shotgun at us. Jayse jumps to his feet and blocks me from the man, but when he sees our faces, the man lowers the gun and curses.

He looks outside the door and shuts it, then says, "The Taesmals will hit jackpot if they find this house." He hurries to a shelf and pulls a book off—only it isn't a book. Inside is a number pad and he dials some buttons, then the entire bookcase sinks into the ground.

Jayse reaches for his two swords. I hold the blanket close, and the man faces us. He's sweaty, looks and smells as if he hasn't bathed in weeks, and a bushy sandy gray beard hides most of his face.

His voice is kinder this time. "Your Greatnesses, what are you doing here?"

I look at Jayse, who draws a sword.

The man clicks his tongue. "There's no use for that, really. If you want to keep your necks, follow me." He starts down the secret passage.

He has an accent—a noticeable one, too, one that lingers with every syllable. Jayse must notice something off about him, because he hasn't lowered his blades.

"Why should we trust you?" he asks.

"They already want my head for treachery, so I might as well help ya out." He takes a few more steps into the passage. "Besides, I don't want the Cycle to kill us, either. Hurry before they take you back to their king."

"Who?" I ask.

Jayse starts to say, "The Taesmals," but the man cuts him off with, "Mysiochs."

Before I can remember where I've heard that word, Jayse pulls me to my feet and drags me into the secret passageway. I take one step down, then decide to run back and grab the bloody scarf, and a window shatters. The man grabs onto my capelet and throws me downstairs, where Jayse catches me, then the passageway slides shut. We hear an explosion not a moment later, and I can't see anything, but I feel rough hands grab me and drag me down a dirt tunnel.

I stumble over what I think are roots and rocks, and then I see a bright flash. The man has ignited a flare. Once it's lit, he pulls me after him.

"Not so rough!"

I hear metal scraping and turn to see Jayse drawing one of his swords. He points it at the man and demands, "Let her go!" but the man keeps dragging me along.

"Don't jump the gun, Your Highness, I'm here to help you. We can talk later, but they're after us."

"Do you know him, Jayse?"

"He's a Taesmal!"

I gasp and the man grunts, like he realizes we want an explanation now.

"I swear on my life I won't turn you to the Taesmals. You have permission to kill me if I hurt either of you."

"You're hurting her right now!"

The man lets go of my arm and says, "Apologies. Strike one for me."

He continues leading us through the passage, and I see bright light at the end, but the man takes a sudden turn into another hidden hall. We step a few feet, then he reaches for the ground and digs his hand into a crevice. I hear a click and then a rumble as a dirt wall rises and reveals a room. The man pushes both of us in and shuts the door behind.

It smells like cedar in here. Wooden panels cover the circular walls and a metal grate hangs over us. Far beyond it, I see the bright blue sky.

The man presses more buttons and the ground beneath us shakes. I hear gears grinding, and then the entire room shifts.

Above, the skylight stretches farther above, then disappears as the room moves to the right.

Jayse stands in front of me and draws both his swords, heaving as if he'd run uphill. In the light of the flare, his large shadow flickers on the wall behind us. When the man faces us, Jayse is at his throat in an instant, and the man laughs. It's an almost despicable laugh—low and worn, joyless.

"Jayse, what are you doing?" I shout.

"This man is a Taesmal!"

The man stops laughing and watches Jayse. The look in his eyes—what is it? Pride?

"Taesmals are made, Your Highness, not born like you Arriscyleans. Allegiance doesn't run in my blood. It's best you remember that."

"What are you saying?"

"I left. I'm a traitor. They want my head as much as yours."

"Why did you leave?" I ask, taking a cautious step forward and wondering if it's okay to interject. Jayse doesn't lift his blades from the man's neck, and I'm afraid he'll scissor his head off.

"My allegiance died with our last king," he said.

I put my hands on Jayse's shoulder and he backs off the man, but doesn't lower his swords.

"Can't stand the new leader," the man continues. "He's a tyrant."

"So just like that, you left?" Jayse asks.

The man takes a seat on the ground, maybe to show his humility. "I ran away ten years ago. Faked my own death. A few months ago, someone found out I'm still alive, and I've been running since. They must really want me dead, because they sent Mysiochs after me."

"Mysiochs," I repeat. "What are they?"

"Genetically modified human beings. Dangerously strong, but mindless. They are only capable of one thought, and that is their designated mission. Usually it's to assassinate someone."

Suddenly I find it hard to swallow. The Prince Imposter said the Mysiochs were after him.

Jayse still doesn't lower his guard. "So why are they after you? You can't just be any normal runaway if they sent the Mysiochs after you."

The man looks down and I hear his low, grumbling laugh. The next time he looks up, I think he smiles.

"My name is Brunan Cholans. I used to be on the council for our former, true king, but when our current leader took over, he decided he didn't need a council. He ordered our executions—all but one of us. Didn't want us revolting against him. I escaped, though. I've been trying to live neutrally, not taking any side in this incessant strife, but I still can't let go of Taesmal technology." He gestures at the room.

"Where is this taking us?" I ask.

"Far enough," Brunan answers. "Once we stop, the Cross-Sorantic Highbridge won't be far. You can take it back to the Irenn Continent. Mediscus Heights."

I look at Jayse. "Gediyon went there. Maybe we'll run into him!"

The man does his closed-mouth laugh. When we look at him, he shakes his head. "I hope you find your friends soon. It's a long way back to Arriscyal. You'll need all the guidance you can get."

Jayse doesn't lower his swords. I offer to make them breakfast, since the adrenaline has stopped pumping and I'm hungry, but when I turn strands of my own hair into oatmeal, I think back to the canyon. The other two take the bowls ravenously—Jayse manages to eat it while still holding one sword out—but I sit with the bowl in my lap. I'm not hungry anymore. I feel for the scarf hanging around my waist.

After about ten minutes of darkness, we see sunlight overhead again, and the room slows down. The room ascends, and Brunan and I rise to our feet. Jayse is already standing. As soon as Brunan opens the door, Jayse walks out.

Brunan looks at me. "Up the slope, you'll see the Highbridge not too far away."

I nod, fiddling with the scarf. Before I step out, I stop and say, "A friend of mine… The Mysiochs got to him. Do you think—"

"If it was the Mysiochs, then he's good as dead. I'm sorry, Your Divinity."

I nod. "It's just… He looked a lot like Jayse. So maybe…" I start out the door. The room has stopped in a seaside cave.

"Your Divinity," Brunan calls, his voice bouncing off the rock walls. "Ignorance is bliss, but the Cycle requires you to suffer for the sake of all the universes."

I look back at him, unsure of what to say. My voice is monotonous when I say, "Thank you, Brunan."

"Thank you, Your Divinity. The entire world takes you for granted." He bows. "Safe journey." He presses a button on the inside and the door shuts.

I hear the room continue to rumble wherever it goes, and then the sound fades away.

Outside the cave, Jayse stands in sunlit sand, looking out at protruding rocks in the ocean. His tattered clothes whip in the wind.

"You ready?"

"He was a Taesmal," he says, so quietly the ocean waves nearly drown him out.

"Ex-Taesmal."

His hands start to shake, and then his shoulders. He reaches for one his swords and slashes it out, slicing the air in front of him.

"I could kill them all!"

I jump back. "Jayse!"

"The world would be such a better place without them! Why don't they all just die?" He impales the wet sand and falls to his knees, holding his hands tight on the hilt. "I want to take away everything from them that they took from me!" He throws himself into the sand, pounding it with heavy fists. His entire body trembles.

"Jayse."

He keeps his head on the ground. "They killed my little brother." His voice cracks and I can tell that he's crying. "He was only six! And my uncle…" He gasps several times and throws another, weaker fist into the sand. "Why couldn't I do anything?"

Seeing him like this makes me cry, and I feel hypocritical when I kneel beside him and say, "Please don't cry!" I lift him from the sand and hold him like he held me, only this time we're both crying.

While kneeling on the beach, I can hear some faraway voices. Maybe somewhere farther down, people are playing in the sand, but I realize it's not a normal day for building sandcastles when I hear fast rushing water.

Jayse and I pull apart and look up to see a sea serpent rising onto shore.

Jayse wipes his tears away and spits, "Damn it." He pushes himself to his feet, pulls one sword out of the sand, and draws the other. "Another reason the Taesmals should die. These bastards won't go away until they stop experimenting!"

I wonder how he's going to fight that thing with only his swords. I wonder how I'm going to help him when I'm still unarmed. We both jump back when the serpent claws into the beach with its front arms. I guess it's more lizard-like than serpentine. It twists its head into the air and screeches.

I think Jayse is ready to jump at it with full-blown slicing, and I'm trying to think of a suitable weapon. A crossbow, maybe? Not that I've ever shot one.

Jayse runs at it, and someone shouts, "Bombs away!" Something falls and explodes in the water. The serpent writhes and screeches, but I think it's more furious than hurt. Before it can attack us, Jayse grabs my arm and runs with me away from the rock wall.

At once, we see the big man Byran with about three round, black bombs in his arms—something out of a cartoon.

"Baas!" Jayse exclaims.

He only goes, "Hee hee," then lights one of the bombs with a flame at the tip of his fingers and hurls it at the serpent. It dodges, and Byran curses.

"How did you find us?" I ask while he lights another.

"A bit of searching, a lot of luck. We have almost all the troops out again." He throws another, which explodes midair near the serpent's head. It screams and sharp scales fly toward us. Byran shoves both of us behind him, prepared to block the attack, but suddenly a large wave of water splashes down on the scales, but leaves us dry.

Jayse and I look up. Standing at the top of the cliff is—

"Gediyon!" we say together.

"Yeah, look who I ran into!" Byran says.

Gediyon flashes us a smile but doesn't divert his attention from the serpent, because it still isn't dead. Though half its head is bloody, spikes have formed on its back. It lurches forward, spitting something at Gediyon. He jumps down the cliff next to us to avoid the attack. Byran puts his arms around me and Jayse and pushes us down the beach to safety.

We leave Gediyon, who must be concentrating on another attack, because he's standing completely still.

Then something scary happens. The sky, which was clear only a moment ago, turns black and cloudy. I hold tight onto Jayse's arm when I see electricity flickering in the clouds. Then booming, cracking lightning shoots down from the sky and electrocutes the serpent. It only takes a few seconds for the sky to clear again, and the serpent screeches almost as loud as the lightning that hit it. It reels around and then releases the spikes on its back, which shoot out in all directions. This time, Byran is determined to protect us, and I only look up when I don't hear them flying anymore.

One of them has shot into Gediyon.

He stumbles back into the rock wall, gripping around the spike, but I don't think it'll be easy for him to take out. Before anyone can stop me, I dash forward, screaming his name. I immediately curl my fingers around the spike. First of all, it pains me because this is the same place where the Prince Imposter was wounded—on the left side of his midsection—but the spike is also sharp all around and cuts into my palm. I wince, but I won't let go—I can't let someone else I care about die!

Byran pushes my hands aside, and since he's wearing gloves, he clasps onto the spike. Gediyon doesn't even flinch when Byran yanks it out, and Jayse immediately heals the wound. I stare at my palms, red and sticky with both mine and Gediyon's blood. When Jayse is done with Gediyon, he takes my hands and heals them. The cut closes, sealing in all the blood, and my palms tingle with warmth.

"Gediyon, are you okay?" I ask.

He looks as if nothing had happened, but his clothes say otherwise. "Are you hurt?"

"Gediyon, you were stabbed!" I almost feel like crying again, but to stop myself, I leap at him with a hug.

"Does it really not hurt," Jayse asks, "or are you just good at hiding it?"

Gediyon laughs. It's probably the latter because he says, "It's good to see that you're both safe." Just like him to change the subject instead of saying "ow."

Byran whoops. "What a great day! Time to go back hooome!"

He marches down the beach, swinging his arms wide. I look at Jayse and Gediyon, try to smile, and then follow Byran. I skip after him to lighten my spirits. When I catch up to him, he joins me, and we both skip up the slope. It's tiring and strains my legs, but still fun.

Below, I hear another rush of water, and I think maybe the sea serpent has come back to life, but it's just Gediyon stepping through shallow water. He stops when the water reaches his knees, then looks around—at the ocean, up the cliff, in the cave.

"What are you doing?" Jayse asks.

Gediyon looks back at one of the rocks protruding from the ocean. He points at it and says, "Did you not see that girl?"

Jayse looks up the cliff at me, then back at the rock, but I don't see anyone. No one was ever there—no one else has been on the beach but us.

"What girl?"

Part Three
The Quest for Tyme

Chapter Twenty
Pit Stop at Mediscus Heights

Byran and I wait for Gediyon and Jayse at the top of the cliff. Jayse tries to heal him again, reaches for his forehead to see if he has a fever, asks if he's been drinking too much claren tea…

"Sorry for startling you, but I really am fine!" Gediyon dodges Jayse's healing hand and I laugh. "It was probably only a trick of my eyes."

"And eye tricks can fabricate whole girls," Jayse says. "I don't think you're *just fine*."

But he looks fine.

"*Hellooo*!" someone sings, and I jump. Behind us, Isel Mingon stands, surrounded with about a dozen floating Bubbles. "It's my favorite entourage!"

"Mingon!" Byran wobbles over and slaps the man on his back. "Lucky, lucky day! Listen, we need four Bubbles!"

Isel Mingon wiggles his fingers, palm-up, at Byran. "Hand over the money!"

Byran reaches into his pockets for change, and I walk up to the Bubble salesman. He bows, and I ask him, "Do you know what happened to Wolf and Dreana?"

He stuffs coins into his vest pockets and says, "Why yes! Yes I do!" He rubs his hands and does a strange jig. "I saw them again not too long after you left, and I was worried when I didn't see you with them! It was lucky for them, only two hours later, and two Bubbles come floating back to me!" He pushes four of them in our direction and Byran hugs one as if it's a stuffed toy.

"I am certainly very relieved to see that you're doing swell, Miss Goddess…with my favorite entourage!" He shoots his arms out in excitement, but pops one of the Bubbles. It springs back a moment later. "But fret not about Lady Dre and her Wolf! I am certain they're on their way back to Tyrique." He lunges at me with his hand at the side of his mouth and loudly whispers, "You *should* come to the tournament, by the way!"

I look at the others and say, "Uh…"

"I've always wanted to go," Byran says. "But city duties and all." He rubs his stubbly chin. "Maybe I can get my niece to cover for me."

The three other Bubbles float toward me, Jayse, and Gediyon, but since Byran already made contact with his, it's almost fully formed. Byran is the first to point out that something is different about them.

"Ah, you noticed!" Isel Mingon says. "I thought I would send them all in for an upgrade when one popped back to me with this thing attached!"

My own Bubble has formed its seat, and I can see what the other two are talking about. "My communicator!"

"Indeed! I knew it had to be our great Creator's ingenuity! I can connect these four Bubbles so you can communicate among yourselves during your journey. Others have reported back to me with much praise!"

Awesome! Something *I* did is catching on.

We thank Isel Mingon and then enter our Bubbles, ordering it to the long journey to Arriscyal.

I have a feeling that Byran badly wants to tell me what kind of work needs to be done in Arriscyal, but Jayse knows better than to let him bombard me with requests. Byran finally shuts up when Jayse hushes him about the Famine. Gediyon, on the other hand, has only announced that it would take about two days to reach Arriscyal. I ride behind him on the Highbridge, watching him looking over the horizon.

Was there actually a girl there, or was he hallucinating? Is he even thinking about her, or is he just staring out at sea like usual? I want to ask him about it, but our communicators aren't exactly private, and Jayse is worried enough, even if he does cover it with levity.

For the next several hours, we ride across the Highbridge, and every new song that plays over our communicators doesn't make our crossing any more novel. All we see is water, concrete, and sky. Three times, our Bubbles pass other packs traveling in the opposite direction, but we speed by too quick to really acknowledge them.

By the time we reach the end of the bridge, the sun has already reached the other side of the sky. Not too far ahead, I see mountains, and I find myself feeling the material of the Prince Imposter's scarf, which is still tied around my waist. I look away from the mountains and realize, I'm just glad to be on land again.

I didn't want to say anything to the others while we were still crossing the bridge, but I desperately need a stretch break. I'm sure the others will appreciate it too, but I don't know when would be a good time to stop.

The Bubbles enter a linear valley with mountains that cut the sun from view. It isn't densely populated with houses, but I can tell by the terraced fields on either side of us that it isn't a neglected valley either. The steps in the mountainside are beautiful in themselves, like they were made for giants to climb the sky, but the plants that grow in the fields look pitiful. As we keep riding through, I see a young girl carrying bushels of wilted plants, balancing them on rods over her shoulders.

For the first time in hours, I press the plain red communicator button—these models aren't printed with "SPEAK!" but I can still talk to the others.

"Guys, what is this place?"

"Mediscus Heights," Gediyon answers immediately. "Usually, the view is more stunning, but the Famine…"

"Let's stop," I say. "We could use a stretch break, right? And…we can help these people."

"Stop right here?" Byran asks.

"No, no, let's pull off to the side, somewhere nobody will see us."

I hope they don't give much thought as to why I don't want to bring much attention to us. The four of us tell our Bubbles to slow down and we curl into the curve of the mountain, where the Bubbles let us step out. I'm the first to push myself through its flexible membrane, and I immediately hide my face with my hood, then yawn and stretch away the past hours I spent sitting.

Luckily, nobody else is out here, but I still keep my hood on as I look around at the landscape. All of the steps are dry and golden brown, but here and there I see a splash of color: something lucky green in heartier plants, the dull red of dried flowers… It would be easier bringing them back to life if I had the water stick I used in the West Wind, but I left that on the boat…

Where I left the Prince Imposter.

I take a deep, sharp breath and try to push him out of my thoughts, even for a minute. I kneel down and examine one of the nearby crops.

It's dry, as if it simply didn't have enough water and baked in the sun, but the soil beneath it is perfectly moist. If it weren't for the Famine, these crops would be thriving. It would be inefficient to go through the fields and stop on each terrace to restore its crops. There must be a well somewhere with water I can change to restore any plant it touches.

Jayse, Gediyon, and Byran are still watching me, standing ready as if they're prepared to follow orders. I ask, "Can you make sure nobody is watching?"

They keep a look out as if I'm stealing from a bank vault.

I look back at the crops. The fields can't be supplying their own water, so there must be some kind of irrigation.

The water slowly trickles downhill, from one step to the next below. I look to the top of the mountain and start climbing, my boots squishing one step after another.

When I reach the top, Jayse calls, "Should we follow?"

"Yeah, maybe!"

Up here is a slow, steady canal. The water looks like it flows down on an incline. On the highest hilltop for at least a mile in each direction is a rough cone-shaped rock. Similar rocks poke out from other hilltops all around the mountain pass.

The others catch up to me and I continue up the canal for the big rock. Maybe it's the source of water.

With the angle of sunlight, it isn't until I'm only a few yards away from the rock that I notice a small body at the base. I run ahead as quick as I can and call, "Jayse!"

It's an unconscious boy of about six or seven. His breaths are shallow and raspy, and his lips are dry. It looks like he had climbed up the steps to fetch some water, because two fallen buckets lie at his side.

Jayse dashes to my side and takes the boy into his arms, while I take one of the buckets to the rock. Water spouts from the top and cascades down the sides, filling the canals. I hold the bucket beneath the flow of water and while it fills, I look at Jayse on his knees, holding the boy's body. Gediyon kneels beside them and Byran stoops over.

"Aren't you going to heal him?" I yell, trying not to sound panicked.

They look at me like I just said something preposterous, but I don't know how it's a stupid suggestion. Jayse is a healer, after all.

Then Jayse says, "When I heal someone, they have to be aware of the healing process. It's the pain they feel that draws my power to alleviate them. I have to make a kind of connection with them, so I know what I'm doing." He repositions the boy in his arms, then says, "I can't use my power to revive him, but…"

The bucket is overflowing. I look at it, then back at the boy, and I realize it's a bit cruel, but I've seen people do it in movies all the time.

I dump the cool water on him and he wakes up with a start. Before they tell me how mean or dangerous it is, I completely turn my back to them, then fill up the bucket halfway. I hand it back for the boy to drink.

"You all right now, big guy?" I hear Jayse.

"Who are you?" the boy asks.

I put my hands to the rock and close my eyes. Cool, refreshing water flows atop my fingers and gently massages my wrists on the way down. I know this water is pure, but I need to fortify it so it'll help all the crops—no matter how withered—flourish back to life. No, I want this water to make them grow larger and more nutritious.

"Where's your home?" Gediyon asks the boy.

"Down there," he says. "What's she doing?"

"This is Goddess!" Byran says. "She's going to—"

"Don't tell him!" I snap. Now I've lost concentration!

Right, big crops. Tomatoes as big as melons, melons as big as beach balls, but I can't have them growing to the size of cities. Behind closed eyelids, I can see the water reaching into the soil, blessing roots with new life, and nutrients glowing through stalks, vines, and leaves as it reaches the fruit.

I open my eyes and look at the water flowing down the canal. At its slow trickle, I doubt I'll see any results for maybe an hour. I look across the valley, counting the other rocks on the hilltop. At least eight. It's going to take me a while to climb all of them, though.

I look back at the others. Gediyon smiles like he's confident I've done it, Byran watches me wide-eyed like a kid at a circus, and Jayse is still kneeling down with the boy, who's no longer dripping wet. Gediyon must've dried him.

Then I remember what Jayse said to me at the beach, and with the boy so close to him, I can't help but see Jayse as a big brother.

"You all right?" I ask the boy.

He looks away from my eyes and nods. "Are you really Goddess?"

I shrug. "Let's see if I can fix—"

A deep horn sounds. The boy immediately jumps to his feet and looks around.

I look at Gediyon, hoping he'll have an answer, but the horn continues. The sound rumbles in my chest.

The boy says, "Come on! You haveta get inside!" He hops down the steps so quickly that he trips and rolls down a few, then jumps back to his feet and hops the rest.

"The brush bugs!" Gediyon says.

"*What*?" the rest of us say.

"They're panicking over little bugs?" Byran shouts.

"*Bugs*?" I repeat. I run down after the little boy.

"They mentioned it to me earlier," I hear Gediyon. I hope they're following me! "They said they never had this mutation before—"

As I step down, something breaks through the next step. At first it looks like a sickle, then whatever it is shakes the dirt off. For a second, I see what it is—it has a gray-brown, flat oval body and a sharp tail like a scorpion, but beneath its body are countless, spindly legs. It's the size of a boar. It snaps its front pincers at me. I scream and jump back to the others.

"What the hell is that?!"

Byran is the closest, and somehow I've managed to climb to his shoulders like a monkey. I squeeze around his neck and clench my eyes shut, hearing more of them emerging from the ground.

No way am I gonna fight them! I can't even open my eyes. Byran complains that I'm choking him, so I release my arm around his neck, but I dig into his collarbone with my nails. I hear metal clanging, so I guess Jayse is fighting them off—hacking them apart, I hope, but by the sounds of things, their armor is thick. I still haven't heard anything from Gediyon or Byran. Maybe they're hesitating to use their magic because fire or lightning will send the dry crops into an inferno.

"They're everywhere!" Jayse yells, and I shriek even more.

Finally, I hear a terrible screech, and then a crumpling thump.

"There ya go!" Byran says. He shifts triumphantly, but I clamp onto him tight. "We have to stab them from below! Good job, Gediyon!"

I shudder, realizing how many are closing in. I hear their snipping pincers, their sickle-like tails slicing through air and crops, their many legs squishing in the damp soil. Why don't they go away?! Stab them from below? Okay, but how are we going to expose their stomachs?

Suddenly, I see the irrigation rock in my head—tall and pointed, sticking out of the ground, and then it's quiet. I hear Jayse swinging his sword some more, but then he stops.

"Michelle," Gediyon says, "was that your doing?"

"What happened?" I squeal, too afraid to open my eyes.

"Well, they're dead," Jayse says.

Still holding tight onto Byran, I slowly open my eyes. I lift my head and look at the fields, where *hundreds* of brush bugs are impaled on sharp rocks. Some of them are stuck on spears of ice. Their bodies curl in death, but some of them still twitch.

"Can I have my back back?" Byran asks.

I slide off, but as soon as I touch the ground, I hop about, brushing myself off even though nothing touched me.

"Ew! Ew! Ew! *Disgusting*! Did the Taesmals do this too?"

"Brush bugs have mutated in Taesmal labs," Gediyon explains, "but usually, they grow no larger than the palm of your hand. The townspeople here told me that giants come out at night to terrorize them."

"Must be the Famine's doing that grew them so big," Byran says.

"But they're all dead now," Jayse says.

He kneels over one of the dead bugs, examining the water coming out of the rock that killed it. It trickles like the larger ones, but since it's closer to the crops, it already changes them. The stems of the plants perk up and fill with water, actually glowing for a moment with the same bright green of Jayse's eyes. Then they curl up toward the sky, and their large fruits and vegetables swell, but they stop growing before they burst.

I spin around, looking at the fields. The plants are only restored in this stretch, where I've fortified the rock, but they've grown so lusciously, I don't think I can walk without being in danger of stepping on a fruit.

"Now let's fix all the others!" I tell them.

We have to walk down a lot slower now, avoiding the bug corpses and trying to protect each plant as we pass, but I end up squishing a few on my way down, and I notice Byran's boots are covered with pulp and seed.

An entire town greets us at the bottom.

I hear them say things like, "Our Creator has saved us!" and "She hasn't abandoned us after all!" So much for my disguise, but at least I've actually done something to merit their respect.

I lower my hood since they already know it's me. The others stand behind me, proud, and I wonder if they expect me to make an elaborate speech. All I say is, "I guess I should start on the rest of your fields!"

"Miss Goddess, but this is far more than enough!" someone says. I look through the crowd and see an old lady. "This alone should help us through the Famine, and then the rest of the fields will restore themselves."

A murmur of agreement spreads through the crowd.

"You sure? 'Cause I can stay a bit longer to do the rest of your fields, or else we're gonna head back to Arriscyal."

The crowd murmurs again, and the woman says, "Arriscyal is still a day's and a half journey, even on the fastest Bubble. Please! Rest here for the night. It's the least we can do to thank you."

I look at the others, who are looking at me for an answer, and I say, "All right."

As soon as I give them the go-ahead, a flock of younger women hurry back to their houses, and the children scatter. There aren't many men here.

Gediyon talks to the woman who spoke—maybe she's in charge here. Whatever he tells her, it makes her gasp and cover her mouth with both hands. Gediyon nods, then she kisses him on both cheeks and hurries back to town with the others.

"What did you say?" I ask.

"I'm going to prepare a feast for them," Gediyon says. "Would you like to help me?"

Chapter Twenty-One
Bonfire Feast

I have a feeling that even if we told him no, Gediyon would let us off the hook, but how can we make him do all of the work? Byran tells us he'll help the townspeople fire up their ovens, Jayse says he'll see what kind of game he can catch, and I follow Gediyon back to the fields to help him pick some crops.

All of the fruit and vegetables look equally as big to me, but Gediyon is more selective when it comes to color and firmness. I let him pick them while I pull around a basket that I made, which floats around after us like a small hot air balloon.

It's just the two of us now, and I ask Gediyon, "What's up with the girl? The one you saw at the beach?"

"There was no girl. You saw, yourself."

"But *you* saw her. I don't think it was just your eyes tricking you."

I see his smile has faded a bit. He continues to look over each vegetable with gentle hands, careful not to pick immature vegetables from their stalks. He doesn't say anything, and I don't want to ask if he's okay, because that would imply that something is wrong with him.

Instead, I ask, "What was she doing?"

He pulls up what looks like a veiny yellow bell pepper. He smiles slightly, but it's not his usual friendly smile. It looks nostalgic.

"She was singing," he says, then picks off the pepper and places it in the basket. "It was the Song of the Sea Angel."

"*Really*?"

He nods.

I remember what Jayse told me before the Dark Mist separated us, that the sea angel is the last thing he remembers. As much as I want to know, I would feel uncomfortable asking him to talk about it.

Gediyon should challenge someone on *Iron Chef*. I don't know if he knows what he's going to make beforehand or if he improvises with what he finds, because the meal he describes to me seems to utilize everything we've picked so far, from salad to dessert, and he even allows alternatives based on what kind of game Jayse can catch.

After picking a fruit the size of a beach ball, Gediyon leans closer to me and says in a hushed voice, "I have a secret."

My eyes widen and I whisper back, "What's that?"

He keeps a straight face, and I'm afraid he's going to tell me that he has some kind of brain tumor and that's why he's hallucinating. He goes on, "You know how I carry a tin of claren tea wherever I go?"

I nod.

"Well"—his straight face turns into a sheepish grin—"I can't go anywhere without my box of spices, either."

This makes me laugh so hard that my voice echoes in the valley. Maybe it was the way he told me, like it's his dirty little secret, or maybe it's his proud but embarrassed smile. Maybe it's so funny because wherever he goes, he wants to make sure that food tastes good.

Whatever it is, I'm glad I didn't bother him more about the sea angel.

By the time we finish, the basket is three times its original size, and we've still managed to fill it. The sky is dark now, and Gediyon holds out a palm of fire to light our way back into town. He tells me about his first trip as an Arriscylean soldier, and how his captain found his secret stash of spices and mistook them for drugs. Gediyon prepared him lunch, which dubbed him as the troops' traveling cook.

Where most of the people have gathered, I don't see any buildings, but children run in and out of doors set into the mountainside. Cool, do they live in hollowed out tunnels? I want to check out their homes, but it looks like we're going to eat outside.

Byran has set up a bonfire in the middle of the valley, and little girls dance around it in a circle, holding hands and singing a song about a fire that people walked in to feed each other. Ah, morbid children's tales. Gotta love 'em.

Byran is laughing with one of the few men I see, but when three little boys scare him, he chases them like a bear, on all fours with a convincing roar. Jayse is already back with his hunt. Long-tailed bunnies are skewered on his sword.

My jaw drops but Gediyon says, "I hoped that he would find hopieti. Now we will certainly have an excellent dinner!"

One of the village girls helps Jayse unskewer the bunnies. She's about his age, and she's laughing with him. I turn away and stay on the other side of the fire, where they're out of my view. I sit down in the dirt.

I'm not jealous. If I am, it'd mean he belongs to me or something. I don't even really like him. I mean, of course I like him—he is a nice guy, after all, and he's pretty cool with his swords, and he has a sensitive side, and he's drop-dead gorgeous... But do I *like* him, like him? Probably not. Liking someone is chasing a boy at recess, or passing notes to him in class, or completely making out with him in the back of his pickup truck during lunch while all your friends talk about homecoming or term papers.

Jayse is cool, but I don't like him like that. But the Prince Imposter...

I pull my knees close to my chest and stare at the base of the fire, where the light flickers against the ground. I raise my hand and brush it against my cheek, where he gave me that good-bye kiss.

Jayse is definitely sweeter than he is, and I only knew the Prince Imposter for, what? Two days, was it? But maybe I did like him a little.

Did? *Do*? Maybe because his...his...his separation had such an impact on me that I...

We were companions in dire circumstances. Maybe that's it.

If that *was* all, how come I can't let go of his scarf?

"You're Goddess," I hear a high voice. I look to my left and see a girl, about five, standing next to me. Her friends are standing behind her.

I smirk at her. "Yeah." I pat her on the head. "Are you hungry?"

She swings her arms around. "Little, but my tummy's more happier. Auntie gived me fut." I think she means *fruit.*

"Well, my friend is going to make everyone really yummy food." I point Gediyon out to her; he's at an outdoor table cutting vegetables, and some teenagers—smiling bashfully—have joined him with their own knives and bowls. I resist the urge to roll my eyes. "He's the pretty man there with long hair."

The girl giggles. "Man can't be pretty!"

I shrug. "Some guys are." I pick up a clump of dirt. "You wanna see a magic trick?"

She gasps and her friends move in closer. I hold up the clump for them.

"You see this?" I say. "I want everyone to give it a little blow—just a little! We don't want all the dirt to blow away."

I hold my hand out to them again, and they each get their turn, some blowing too soft, others nearly emptying my hand of dust. When they're done, I blow it myself and say, "Now tell me what it is!"

They babble all at once, but collectively I hear, "Dirt!"

"Yup!" I squint at the tiny mound. "Now, on the count of three, you're to turn into something delicious. One, two, three… Presto change-o!" Nothing happens. "Aww. Looks like my magic trick failed!" I hold out my hand to them and with a pop, it turns into a warm loaf of honey oat bread. "Just kidding!"

The girls exclaim and gasp in amazement. I hand the loaf to the front-most girl and tell her, "Now you all be good girls and share it, okay?"

They stare at it, maybe wondering if it tastes like dirt. I take the loaf back, tug on it a little, and it slips into several slices. I take one, carefully hand the loaf back to the girl, and then put the bread in my mouth to demonstrate.

"Mm, yummy!" I say with a full mouth. Actually, I want some more!

They gasp more and each take a slice, devouring it like it's the best thing in the world. Some of them jump up and down with joy, others run off to tell their mothers or older sisters, and the rest thank me before joining them.

"That was really cute," I hear a voice from behind.

I jump and see Jayse standing near the fire. "You were *watching* me?" I squeal.

He nods and shrugs at the same time.

"So," I say. "I saw your, uh, your *kill*."

"It's not easy knowing that most girls want to hug them," he says with a hint of a laugh.

"Listen." He steps toward me and lowers his voice. Nobody else can probably hear us, especially with the fire roaring. "You're doing a good job. I know I said it before, it's a lot of responsibility, but you shouldn't be *afraid* of being Goddess." He puts his hands on my shoulders and my heart jumps. "Show a little more pride. Don't hide your pretty face."

His words take my breath away, but I still croak out, "O…kay." I have to sit down. I turn away from him and stare at the fire, holding my knees close. He sits next to me.

My face burns, and it's not because I stuck my head in the fire.

I almost completely hide my face behind my knees when I ask him, "Do you really think I'm pretty?"

He laughs like it's the stupidest thing he's ever heard, and I expect him to say, "*Your* face? What a joke!"

But he says, "Am I not allowed to?"

I don't answer him. Is there anything I can say without being awkward?

Hey Jayse, I think you're super hot. Wanna…hang out sometime?

Yeah, this isn't California.

I still haven't said anything. Jayse laughs again, probably realizing that he's embarrassed me. Neither of us say anything to each other for a while, but Gediyon and Byran cook over the fire. At one point, Byran comes around to our side and makes a noise as if he's going to tell us something hilarious, but he turns right back.

Now I smell the bunnies cooking.

"Jayse," I say at last. "Are you… Are *you* afraid? Of being the crown prince?"

He smirks. "No one is supposed to know that." He looks back at the fire, and slowly, he nods.

I stare at him, wondering if he'll tell me more, but I don't want to push him. Finally, he sighs, and in a voice so low it would be impossible for anyone else to hear him, he says, "It's the king." He looks around as if that was horribly insulting, then he scoots closer to me so he can speak even quieter.

"I don't know if I can live up to everyone's expectations when I finally take the throne. I don't know enough about politics or governing the most powerful country in the world. I'm afraid that it'll fall." He sighs. "Maybe I'm just afraid of being like him. All I want to do is fight for what's right—fight, and get rid of the Taesmals. My uncle was like that, too. *He* was in charge of the military when he was still alive, and it was fine for him because he was second born. My mother was always interested in governmental affairs, maybe because she knew she was going to be queen. But I'm not interested. I don't even have any siblings to pass it on to." He rests his elbows on top of his knees and supports his chin on top of folded fingers. The reflection of the fire dances in his joyless eyes.

"My brother was always the brains in the family," I tell him. "He knew he wanted to work for NASA when he was seven. Crazy. But he knew what he wanted and he knew how to get there. He's still not there yet, but he's working hard. My parents were *so* proud of him, always bragging about his first-place science fair projects to our relatives at holidays. And then there's me." I have to take a deep breath.

"I'm not as smart as him," I continue. "I don't even know what I want to do with my life. I like to draw and write and make things and play video games, but I'm not *especially* good at anything. I've never said it to anyone—not to my brother or even my friends—especially not my parents—but I feel like…" My throat tightens, and I choke out on a sob, "A waste of space."

"You're not," Jayse says, patting my back. "I'm sure if they could see you now, they would be proud of what you're doing."

I shake my head. "They wouldn't know who I am! They don't know me. They just see me as a girl who likes to play video games. I don't tell them about the other things I do, because they stopped caring. If they saw me here, all they'd say is, 'Why does this girl look like our daughter?' " I hide my ugly, crying face behind my arms now. "I really miss my brother! He'd say, 'It's okay! You can live with me once I get a job, but you have to cook for yourself!' Why wasn't I nicer to him?"

Jayse has stopped patting my back and he's hugging my weird, balled-up body. Once my crying subsides, he says, "Do you want to know something I never told anyone?"

"What?" My voice is hideous.

"The king blames me for my brother's death," he says. "He never said it directly, but I know that's how he feels. It's why he's so cold to me. I grew up thinking that it was *my* fault—him *and* my uncle. When I realized I couldn't have done anything to help them, that it *wouldn't* be my fault… That's when I started to hate the king."

Biting my lower lip, I lift my head and look at him. There's a shining, flickering streak on his cheek where a tear has rolled. I raise my hand and brush it off, then force a laugh. He looks at me, his eyes still rimmed with tears.

"We're despicable," I say. Then I actually laugh.

He wipes his tears away and laughs with me.

I say, "I don't usually cry this much. I swear!"

"Me neither!"

We laugh until our sides hurt.

When Gediyon tells us that the food is ready, we're both a pathetic, laughing mess.

We join the others on the other side of the fire, where different dishes sit in bowls and on large platters. As nice as the palace banquet was, this is a lot cozier and even smells better. Byran is telling a loud story about what he sees at the Arriscylean seaport on a daily basis, while Gediyon and the younger locals serve everyone dinner. Jayse and I sit on cushions, and one of the nearby women tells us about Mediscus Heights.

Soon, everyone quiets down while they eat, but the woman talking to us eats slowly so she can keep up the geography lesson. According to her, Mediscus Heights got its name because it's abundant in medicinal plants. Even the claren plant is native, but travelers took the seeds to plant elsewhere.

"Why, just a week ago, Sir Gediyon was showing us how Mrs. Raidyne prepared her cup of claren tea!"

"Mrs. Raidyne?"

"His mother," Jayse tells me.

The woman tells us more about plants, then says, "The Taesmals come by as well to use the plants in their tonics."

"You mean 'toxins'?" Jayse grumbles.

"You just let them take it?" I ask her.

She shrugs, defeated. "We have a truce. We give them what they ask for, and they keep the mutants away."

"So what about the giant bugs?"

"We don't know for certain if they were the ones who mutated them further," she says. "They came by recently looking for placido, oboedre, and forget-my-will, but they'd withered to the Famine. The women say the Taesmals sent us the giant brush bugs as a token of their disappointment, but we can't prove it was them."

"Who else could've done it?" Jayse says, but I know he's already pointing fingers.

"They may have mutated on their own," the woman says. She smiles at me. "Thank you again for exterminating them."

I nod, but I don't smile. I'm still thinking about the name of that plant. Forget-my-will? Like a sick parody of forget-me-not.

CHAPTER TWENTY-TWO
COUNTER-FAMINE

I open my eyes before sunrise. I know I have a long journey ahead and I need more rest, but since my brain isn't cooperating I might as well get up.

The straw-filled mattress rustles softly when I move. My bare feet brush the top of a rough, woven grass mat. Both Gediyon and Jayse are on the floor, lightly snoring and snuggled in fluffy blankets. I step over them and pick up my boots by the door, then fasten them before heading out of the tunnel house.

I only want to take a stroll in the twilight, but I end up walking to another water rock far from the one I already fixed. By the time I finish climbing to and repairing this one, everyone rises out of bed.

After breakfast, the townspeople pack us with some crops for the journey. Gediyon receives a fresh bundle of claren plants. We wish them luck and remount our Bubbles for Arriscyal.

Our Bubbles pass through the valley and cross over some rivers, then we're back in what seems like endless fields. Out here, we can't see the ocean anymore, but at least the view changes, unlike the Highbridge. The Bubbles scare away a herd of what they tell me are moink—the same cow-pig hybrid that the Prince Imposter and I took care of at the West Wind.

I hope they haven't slaughtered the calf yet. It would be nice if they kept it as a holy cow since it survived the Famine, but that might be wishing for too much.

Since I'm in better spirits today, I tell the others that I'm going to try to be a *good* Goddess and help the Arriscyleans with their fields like I did in Mediscus Heights. Of course, they think this is a great idea, and Byran names off other things I can do—like making speeches—but Gediyon politely cuts him off, reminds him that I can only do one thing at a time, and then offers to help me.

The next town we pass is called Plaretta, which—as Gediyon reminds me—is Launce and Nichols's home. This place is a lot bigger than Mediscus Heights, though, so I don't think I can easily find their families.

It turns out, the townspeople here are well prepared for the Famine, and they have stocks of preserved produce and dried meat. For lunch, Gediyon offers to cook for the entire town. I wonder if he ever gets tired, because trying to fix plants and animals for a whole town is tiring enough for me. At least he's enjoying himself.

I multiply their stock, so Gediyon won't have to deplete their rations, and then I multiply the fresh produce from Mediscus Heights so they don't have to eat only preserved food. Since it's midday, we don't linger too long and let them celebrate the feast on their own. They thank us with dried pasta and jars of jams and sauces.

Before we leave on the Bubbles, I pluck a small fruit from one of Gediyon's claren plants and eat it. I wince as if I'm swallowing a golf ball. The plant is already bitter, and the immature fruit tastes something like a dried lemon pickled in beer. Note to self: only consume anything claren when it's a tea that Gediyon prepared.

Still, it helps me fall asleep for the next few hours. I need to stop depending on this plant before I get addicted.

We arrive in Arriscyal in the afternoon of the next day, which is the ninth of Ellio, according to Byran. When we reach the city walls, an escort team is already waiting for us.

Among them is Nichols and Launce, who's so close to a pretty girl, he's practically holding her hand. The girl has dark hair in a large braid that swings from the back of her head. The braid consists of even smaller braids, and one segment weaves around like a tiara, with specially placed pin curls looking like flowers. I know I've seen her somewhere before. As soon as we emerge from our Bubbles, Nichols and Launce step closer and I notice the girl inch farther from Launce.

Byran hops out of his Bubble and sobs, "Chili!"

His teenage niece, still wearing her strawberry blond hair in loose pigtails, drags her feet forth and allows him to hug her.

"What's going on?" I ask Nichols and Launce, who's inched back to the dark-haired, pretty girl.

She answers for them. "We've succumbed to the Famine, as well, Miss Goddess. Our food stock is inedible."

I suddenly recognize her. "Oh I remember where I've seen you before! You were that girl these bozos kept hitting on that one night at the banquet."

Her smile softens. "You remember me?"

"Her name is Kalei," Launce says, his voice stupid and lovesick.

Jayse steps forward and asks, "How did this happen?"

Byran's niece, Chili, tenses her shoulders and her cheeks turn red.

Nichols says, "It must've been the Taesmals."

I scream, "*What*?" but Jayse says, "Show us what they've done."

The guards lead us forward, but Byran stays behind for a moment. He pokes each of the Bubbles and says, "Dismissed!" At once, they pop out of view.

We all pile onto a gondola, and the gondolier says, "It's such a relief that you've returned!"

It's Porter, the young water mage I met back in Lereli. I say, "Oh hey! What's up? I mean, how are you doing?"

"Still healthy. Now that you're back, we can hope that everyone else returns to health."

My shoulders sink. "It's the Taesmals' fault again, huh? Like Lereli all over again."

"Actually," Kalei says, "it isn't poison. They released some kind of bacteria. Many of us ate the food before it showed signs of rot, but now it's inedible. Those who ate it are now sick…"

"Dang, that sucks. If only you guys had perfect immune systems, then maybe you could eat all kinds of garbage."

I feel like it's my duty as Goddess to come up with some kind of solution, but right now all I can think of is a medicine to help people recover, and I'm not a pharmacist.

We don't even ride the gondola all the way to the palace. The soldiers lead us into a bakery, where the baker looks like he's going to throw up. He leads us to the back of the building and shows a pile of foul-smelling mush that I guess must have once been bread. I can't tell if the bacteria has reduced the bread to such a mess, or if several people threw up in the same spot.

The others talk about how the bacteria has affected the kingdom, while I get to work. I hold my breath and kneel in front of the pile, hovering my hands over it because I don't think I want to sink my fingers into this stuff. I close my eyes.

I know how to transform this stuff into fresh bread. I know the texture, scent, and taste of Arriscylean bread, and turning this rot into something palatable is going to be a piece of cake.

When I open my eyes, I see pretty loaves of bread stacked like logs, but floating above them is a slimy, swarming mass of bacteria. I jump to my feet and say, "Eugh! Gediyon, can you burn this?"

For a few seconds, the mass ignites before all the bacteria disintegrates. Everyone else watches from inside the bakery. Once the mass is gone, the baker wobbles forward to take one of the loaves, tears it down the middle, then laughs.

I smile at everyone. "If I keep doing this, everyone will be fine, right?"

Both Byran and Chili yell something about restoring the kingdom by nightfall. I don't have a problem with it, but Gediyon says, "Perhaps it would best to see the king and queen first."

Jayse sighs. "It's more important to make sure everyone has something to eat than to listen to whatever the king has to say."

"Maybe he'll have a better solution?" I say.

Jayse grumbles.

The others tell us that while we report to the throne room, they'll hand out rations of bread until the king gives further orders. Launce sings that he can help Kalei in the kitchens, and Nichols begrudgingly follows.

Porter waits for us at the gondola and gives me, Jayse, and Gediyon a ride back to the palace. On the way there, he tells us how many people have contracted infections. Not many of the ill can keep down any food, if there were even any fresh food left to eat.

My stomach sinks—not only because I'm a little hungry, but the Taesmals are so cruel to do something like this. If they hadn't attacked, Arriscyal probably would have been the most fortunate city during the Famine. I wring my fingers through the Prince Imposter's scarf.

"Hey Gediyon," I say. "You think you can use some claren tea to help everyone get better?"

He chuckles. "It would be a good idea, but claren tea is best as a preventative tonic for illness. However, we can use it to keep everyone's strength up."

"My healing won't help much either," Jayse says. "I can make them feel better, but I can't kill microorganisms."

"I could cook everyone some dird blood soup," Gediyon says, "if the dirds have not also fallen to the Famine."

All this responsibility is making my head hurt. I could really do with a bath, but this is more important than how nice I smell.

Once we reach the palace, Jayse reluctantly climbs the steps. I see him staring off at the Temple of the Universal Mirror, but he decides to come with us after all.

Only the king is in the throne room, though. As soon as we see this, Jayse looks like he's going to escape through the telesphere, but he makes eye contact with me and stays put.

Gediyon nods to King Oresonn, and whether anyone wants me to or not, I curtsy. Then we walk toward the thrones; the king has already descended his to the ground.

"I knew I could count on you, Gediyon, to bring them back safely," King Oresonn says. "A job well done."

"Thank you, sir, but I couldn't have done it without Byran. He was with us our entire journey back, and he regrets that he can't report to you as well, because he's helping the others with rations."

"I see. Then I must commend him personally when his schedule allows." King Oresonn looks at me and I can't help but jump at his gaze. "No doubt, Miss Goddess, you were behind these rations? You must be weary after such a long journey."

I shrug. "No biggie," but I know he saw me fumbling with the bloody scarf.

"Please trouble yourself no more. It must be unpleasant for you to return to even more hard work. As for you, Jaysonn, your mother would like to have a word with you. You may find her in the garden."

Without making eye contact, Jayse nods and starts out of the hall into the garden.

I shuffle my feet and wait until Jayse is gone. "Your Majesty, you're right that I'm tired and all, but I don't want to sit around while everyone is sick and starving. I have to do something."

"My men will take care of it, Miss Goddess."

I sigh. "Aren't you hungry, too? You don't even have healthy livestock or crops, and now all your food is rotten. I've eaten enough. If I rest and wait until tomorrow, it might be too late for some people."

I take the furrow in the king's brow as a sign that he's touched. He nods and says, "Very well." He looks at Gediyon and says, "I have already instructed the soldiers to deliver claren tea to everyone in the kingdom, but no one can brew it quite like you."

Gediyon smiles. "I have a fresh bundle from Mediscus Heights. It'll be my pleasure to brew it for the kingdom!"

King Oresonn nods. "I could do with a cup, myself."

"Certainly, sir!"

King Oresonn looks at me. "Now, Miss Goddess. I'll leave it up to you to determine how best to restore our food stock, but I advise you to look to the fields first. After all, only the Famine touched our crops."

I blow at my bangs. "Okay." I turn to Gediyon. "So you'll make everyone happy drinks, right? I'll see if Jayse wants to come with me."

The king laughs. "Good luck."

I don't really know if the king means good luck with trying to restore the food supply, or good luck to dragging Jayse along with me. I won't ask.

I say good bye to Gediyon, who returns to the tele-sphere, and I hurry into the garden.

As soon as I step out of the throne room, the heat overcomes me and I move sluggishly. I realize how nice it would be to sit down. As I step over soft, thin grass, small insects flutter into my path. My footsteps must activate the fragrance of a nearby plant, because the perfume grows stronger as I keep walking.

"What's wrong with the way I've done things before?" I hear Jayse's voice.

Through some plants, I see him and his mother standing by flowery shrubs shaped like starbursts. Her voice is too soft to make out what she's saying. She isn't even looking at him, instead concentrating on the flowers, turning the wilted ones brighter and larger than they were before drying up.

So the queen can manipulate plants? Could she stop the Famine herself?

Jayse speaks again. "What if that plant does exist, though? Then I won't have to worry about it."

Queen Trissa pulls away from her flowers and takes her son's shoulders. Whatever she tells him, it must be shocking, because his eyes widen. She kisses him on the cheek and starts deeper into the garden, looking as serene as ever.

Jayse stands in the same place, shaking his head. I jump out of my hiding spot and start for him.

"Did you hear that?" he asks.

"Not really," I admit.

He shakes his head again. "She told me to find the plant that'll give the king eternal life. She's been acting strange lately, but *this*… She said it as if such a plant actually exists."

I see the splash of her blond hair among plants; she's out of earshot, at least. I say, "So she doesn't always act this weird?"

"She didn't when I was younger. Perhaps she's grown too tired… I hope she isn't losing her mind." He suddenly straightens his back. "I need to talk to Gare. Do you want to come with me?"

"Well, I need to help feed everyone."

"Right. Of course."

I look at one of the flowers she enhanced. "So your mom can restore plants, right?"

He nods. "She used to visit and help more unfortunate towns, but I don't think she has the strength to travel anymore."

I pluck off one of the flowers. "It does take a lot out of you. I don't even think I can do it, but people shouldn't just die of hunger. If only I can be in more than one place at a time…"

The flower in my hand is cool and moist. I close my eyes and imagine the flower as it was before, and try to feel how the queen had enhanced it. The end result isn't far off from what I did to the crops in Mediscus Heights. If I could somehow use this flower as a prototype…

The lush flower dries and cracks into a fine powder. Jayse raises an eyebrow. I smile at him and say, "I did it. Don't worry."

I look around the garden for the most withered plant and find a dried-up crawling vine. I sprinkle a pinch of dust near the roots, and Jayse carries a handful of water from the pond. The powder dissolves as soon as water touches it, and within seconds, the vine grows plump and green. I bounce on the balls of my feet, still holding some dust in my left hand.

"Do you know what this means?" Jayse asks.

"We can ship this dust all around the world?" I cover the dust with my other hand and grin at him. "I'll talk to the king! He'll know what to do, right?"

I can tell that he's holding back a sigh, but he nods instead. "Do you want me to come with you?"

"It'd be nice, but you don't have to. I can go by myself. I'm a big girl," I say with a wink.

He smiles and takes a step back. "Sorry, but a prince is entitled to his own fears. I'll be in the library. Tell me how it goes."

He disappears somewhere into the garden and I carefully hold the pile of dust in both hands, walking back through the garden to the throne room. I barely make it through the columns when I say, "Your Highness! I made this dust, and it can restore any plant. Do you think we can ship it all around the world?"

His low laugh echoes through the hall from his high throne. As his throne descends, he says, "Did you just now find a way to counter the Famine?"

"Yup! At least this is one thing out of the way, right? We can all have fresh food and not have to worry about the rotten stuff."

He laughs, steps off his throne, walks toward me, and I show him the pile of dust. He nods and says, "You needn't demonstrate. I trust your abilities." He gestures with his entire right arm toward the tele-sphere and politely nods. "Let's discuss the transportation matters with Baas."

With his gesture, I don't know if he means for me to go ahead, so I feel awkward running toward the tele-sphere. Both of my hands are full, and King Oresonn expertly presses several points on the sphere.

We reappear in a rowdy workhouse that smells like a barn. Mostly men run around, checking files in their arms, and some of them are too busy to notice that the king and I are here. The few women I do see are carrying baskets of what must be food, and they nod toward us as they cross the workhouse. Now I see why it smells like a barn—to the right are stables for the large korelian cats. Chili is on her knees hand-feeding some cubs milk. At least they look healthy.

King Oresonn leads me forward and nods "good evening" to several people we pass. I keep turning my head to catch a glimpse of different coaches and magic technicians doing repairs or upgrades on tele-spheres.

Upstairs on a catwalk, Byran shouts orders on his megaphone. Some poor guy is already hunched over, carrying a stack of papers, and Byran marches after him, threatening to stamp him over.

"Baas!" King Oresonn calls, and everyone falls still and silent. "Miss Goddess here has a wonderful breakthrough." He hands me a small metal pail—I guess to hold the dust—and I clap it off my hands inside.

Byran makes his way downstairs, and King Oresonn asks him about how many fleets he can send out tonight. The king must be thinking ahead of me, because how can this small pile of dust restore all the barren fields of the world? I put the pail on the ground and kneel over it, holding it on both sides and concentrating on changing its properties.

This simple pail is going to be special—forever. Even after I'm gone, the pail will refill itself when empty, with the same dust that can restore all dead plants that have fallen to the Famine.

The pail is now the size of a barrel and the rim is engraved with the words "Counter-Famine Fertilizer." Funny—the words look a little strange to me.

The dust fills it to an inch to the top. This much dust is probably enough to restore the plants of a single farm, but if it works properly, then the dust should refill itself when only an inch layer remains at the bottom.

I look up and see the workers watching me. Some whisper to each other, and a woman holds her hands to her mouth in delight. King Oresonn and Byran talk to each other with their eyes on me.

I rise to my feet and say, "It'll refill itself forever."

"Everyone is to take a barrel and fill it with this dust," King Oresonn tells us. "You are to load every last vessel with as many barrels as you can. Fleets will be assigned later."

I run over to Byran, take his megaphone, and tell everyone, "When you bring it to people, tell them all they have to do is sprinkle it over the roots and give it some water. It should be pretty self-explanatory, but does anyone have any questions?"

Some of them shrug, others shake their heads, but everyone murmurs. Then a man asks, "How much do we charge them for it?"

I spin in the direction of the voice and yell, "What do you mean *charge*? I'm making this stuff for free! It's the freakin' Famine! It's life or death—you don't expect people to actually *pay* do you?"

Someone else says, "There are still labor costs. Our fleet can't sail for cheap."

I groan. "This is like the richest kingdom in the world! You are *not* going to charge anyone for this stuff, okay? This bucket is going to sit here for the rest of eternity, and if anyone wants some, they can just take it. *Okay*?" I look at the king, lower the megaphone and say, "Can you make sure nobody charges anyone for it?"

King Oresonn clears his throat. "Everyone will be compensated later, but by our Creator's will, no one is to charge anyone for this product, or they will be sentenced to…" He looks at Byran. "To three days in solitary confinement."

"Well, geez, that's kinda harsh," I say. I raise the megaphone again and shout, "You got that? Now this is what we're going to do. Take the barrels and follow me!"

The workhouse bursts into clatter as everyone drops their current tasks. The barrels are in another long, stony hall that smells a bit like wine. Instead of carrying a barrel back to the fertilizer, I bring it down the breezy hall to the shipyard. It sounds strange when I order the others, because I don't have the same commanding voice as King Oresonn or Byran, but they do as I tell them.

Once we've loaded enough barrels on a ship, I return to the fertilizer and tell the others to continue what they're doing. King Oresonn is gone—he probably left to the throne room. I take a small bucket of the fertilizer and run it back to the ships, where I sprinkle a bit into each barrel until I run out. Then I return to the barrels and multiply the dust inside until they're full, and I repeat the process for all of the other barrels.

The others catch on, and they help sprinkle the barrels with fertilizer while I spend time multiplying the rest. They actually finish loading the ships before I finish filling the barrels, so while I'm still working on the fifteenth or so ship, they bring the bottomless container from the workhouse and carry it around, filling barrels.

We finish loading the sixty military vessels around midnight. Even though I'm exhausted, I have a feeling that I won't be able to sleep, and I doubt Jayse is still in the library. I have no idea if Gediyon is still giving everyone claren tea at this time of night. They're probably both sleeping, and now isn't the time to be a creeper and watch them while they dream.

Instead of going back to my room, I say good night to the workers and head to the Universal Mirror instead. No one is here since it's so late, which is a good thing since I can talk to the Mirror in peace. I step across the carpeted temple. Even though I was shivering at the port, the air is warm here, even in the middle of the night.

I wring my fingers through the Prince Imposter's scarf. His blood is now a dark reddish brown, and some of the fertilizer has gathered in the threads. I dust some of it off, then look above at the Universal Mirror towering over me.

"Has anyone ever captured their memories from speaking to this Mirror?" The open space swallows my words, which aren't strong enough to echo. If someone were down the ledge, though, maybe my words will be answered.

"Prince Imposter," I say. "If you are... If you really are...dead... Then maybe somewhere in the Universe, you can catch my words again. I just want to thank you—for everything, and I'm so sorry that I couldn't help you. I hope, in another life, maybe we can meet again." I pause. "But we won't know each other, will we?"

I drop the scarf from my hands, letting it hang around my waist. I gaze deep into the black stone and see the outline of my reflection.

"Saei. If you're there... I want to know... Are we the same person? In a past life, did you do the same things I did? If you really are the Creator, and I'm you, why was I reborn human? Would it even be okay if I went back home? The Cycle will cease without me, right?"

I gasp when I see the Mirror glimmer white. I think it's Saei coming to greet me, but the light bounces away from the Mirror and shoots through me.

Roots. Snow. A red sea. A man with dark hair.

A city at a warm coast. A dungeon. A man with fair hair and a blue pendant.

When the light leaves me, I find myself on my knees, supporting my upper body with hands clawing into the carpet. I look back at the Mirror, black and glossy like it usually is.

"What was that?" I say. I jump to my feet, running at the Mirror and pounding on it. "Saei! What was that? Talk to me!" No light reappears, so I pound on it again and shout, "If you want me to stop the Cycle, then you have to tell me what's going on!"

Saei doesn't appear. Nobody does. I slide to the ground and rest my head against the Mirror, trying to make sense of the vision.

The man with the dark hair, standing over the snowy cliff above the ocean… He looked a lot like Gediyon, but his eyes—they weren't red. They were blue. Besides that and his paler skin, he looked just like him. Long dark hair, the same smile…

The man with the blue pendant… That necklace was the same that Madam Manasa gave me to give back to Jayse, and the man looked like Jayse, though older. His hair, on the other hand, was pale blond like Queen Trissa's. He also had a mischievous smile, like the Prince Imposter, but I haven't seen Jayse smile like that.

I reach back to the Mirror. My warm hands leave steamy prints where I feel the Mirror.

I whisper, "Saei, what was that?" When no one answers me, I pound again and shout, "If anyone wants me to do anything, I'm going to need some answers!"

I probably have to figure it out for myself, but I still have no idea what it could mean. I stand up and drag my feet across to the tele-sphere, then reappear in my room.

The soldiers still stand guard, but inside, no Simmy, Mirra, or Canaria greet me. I'll take a nice long bath in the morning, but for now, I want to sleep. My dusty traveling clothes will definitely soil the bed sheets. I untie the scarf from my waist and fold it. I stare at an empty spot atop some drawers. On one end of the surface lie my clothes that I wore when I came to Starrs. On the other end is a large vase of flowers.

Before setting down the scarf, I give it a kiss good night.

Chapter Twenty-Three
A Gourmet Duty

Around ten in the morning, my maids, Kalei, and a few other female cooks deliver breakfast to my room. I gasp at the delightfully decorated pastries and cups of carved fruit that look like gems.

"We wanted to thank you with an extravagant breakfast for your work last night," Canaria tells me.

"So everything's getting back to normal?" I ask.

Simmy nods. "It's getting there." She and the others set the trays down on the tables in the entranceway, just like when I had come to Arriscyal for the first time.

"Kalei's too shy to say it herself, but she wanted to show off her artistic plating," Mirra said.

"You did all this?" I say, gaping at the trays set before me.

"Oh, no, no, no." She shakes her head. "I only helped."

"The girl's got a special eye," another cook says. "We provide the food, she makes them works of art."

There's way too much food for just myself, so I invite them to stay and eat breakfast with me, and even pull the guards outside to snack on some treats. I notice Kalei shooting nervous glances at me as I nibble into a pastry decorated with a floral, puree swirl.

"It's really good," I assure her with a smile.

She smiles back and takes a breath as if she's about to rave on about how she made it, but she looks away shyly before she can start.

"So are you and Launce, like, dating?" I ask her.

The other women keep their forks in their mouths and stop chewing while waiting to hear the answer. The guards scarf down their breakfasts, snorting like pigs.

"We're just friends," Kalei answers.

"Ahh." I eat more of the pastry. "He seems to really like you, but I get the whole—yunno—'just friends' thing. He's probably too immature for you, anyway."

Kalei giggles. "I do enjoy spending time with him. I've learned much more about Arriscyal than just your culinary arts because of Launce."

Once Simmy has had her fill, she shoos the guards out of my room, and the cooks soon follow. I eat the rest of breakfast in the bath. I wade back and forth in my giant bathtub, grabbing some teacakes and swimming back to wash my hair under the waterfall. Canaria keeps me company, talking about what it was like when she got sick from eating the infected food. Just as Porter had told me, Canaria couldn't keep anything in her stomach, but she recovered after a few days of rest.

Simmy and Mirra, meanwhile, find me a dress for the day.

While I munch on the last teacake, Simmy and Mirra come into the bathroom, not holding any new clothes. Simmy is giggling, which is funny in itself since she's so old, and Mirra shakes her head.

"What's up?" I ask, globs of cake still stuck to my teeth.

Simmy takes a breath to speak, but she ends up giggling some more, so Mirra has to say, "Sir Gediyon is waiting outside your chambers."

I jump out of the bath and splash water over the floor. I still feel weird being naked around them, but they don't take it as a big deal. They dry me and hand me a flowy babydoll dress, which is enough to cover me but I wouldn't dare go in public wearing only this. My hair is still dripping when I head out of the bathroom door.

"Michelle, don't you want to get dressed before speaking to him?" Mirra asks.

"This is enough," I tell her, then march down the entrance hall to the double doors.

Gediyon is outside, talking to the guards. When he turns around, his brilliance shocks me and my legs forget what it's like to stand, so I slip to the ground in glee.

"Michelle!" he gasps. "Are you all right?"

He's no longer wearing his military cloak or even a long-sleeved shirt. Instead, he's only wearing a navy and gold vest, which is tight enough to show his defined muscles, and sleeveless to expose his biceps. He's carrying something green in his arms, which nearly makes me squeal because it looks like a bouquet, but it's actually a stalk of green onions. A brown leather bag is slung over his shoulder and his hair is tied back loosely, like messy chic.

My maids try to help me back to my feet. I giggle like Simmy, covering my face with my hands and peeking through my fingers at Gediyon. He still looks worried.

It's hard trying to stop myself from hyperventilating. I can't stop smiling and laughing and my heart is pounding so hard, I almost feel like jumping for joy.

"Is everything all right?" he asks.

I snort out my words. "Gediyon! You're…you're so hot!"

He looks around him, then feels his forehead and says, "I suppose it is rather warm this morning, but is it so hot that you find it difficult to breathe?"

I laugh. "No! No, Gediyon! 'You're hot' means—like, you're super good looking! Like totally gorgeous!"

Behind me, my maids laugh, even Mirra, but Simmy is the most high-pitched. Gediyon chuckles too, but I can tell that he's embarrassed, and he even blushes.

"Oh," he says. "Is that what 'hot' means? Well, um… Thank you."

I laugh again and jump at him for a hug. "Aw, you're so cute! What are you doing here, anyway?"

"I was wondering if you would be interested in helping me make dird blood soup for everyone. I'll be heading to Mrs. Featheroak's farm. She takes care of the majority of the livestock in Arriscyal, and because of the Famine, they aren't doing well."

"Of course I'll help you!"

"Once we bring the dirds back to health, we'll bring them back to the palace kitchens to cook soup for everybody." He shows me the green onion.

"Okay, cool! I like cooking with you."

"I'll wait for you here until you're ready."

"Righty-o! I'll be right out." I close the doors and look back at my maids, who burst into laughter again. I giggle with them as we make our way to my department-store-sized closet.

"He should dress like that more often," Canaria says.

"Does everyone have a crush on—I mean, does everyone like him a little?"

"It's hard not to fancy him," Simmy says. "It's just a shame that none of us can have him!"

"We think he promised himself to someone long ago," Canaria says. "And until he finds out who she is, none of us stand a chance."

The sea angel? The girl who sang the song? Does anyone else even know who she is?

Since I'm going to a farm today, they don't dress me in anything too elaborate. They give me a blue gingham dress and a pinafore similar to theirs, then hand me a white sunhat embellished with similar blue checked ribbon. I can't help but jump around at my adorable reflection.

When I'm ready, I meet Gediyon in the outside corridor, and by the sounds of things, the soldiers were teasing him about us, but Gediyon is a good sport. He guides me through the tele-sphere to the stables, where Chili lends us a small korelian coach. We ride it down the slope on the perimeter of the city, where it leads us back to the farmlands.

I ask Gediyon about his last night, and he tells me how relieved and grateful everyone was for his claren tea. I can't help but think they were actually excited to see *him.*

In only five minutes, we arrive at Mrs. Featheroak's farm. At least the old woman can walk, but considering her pallor, I wonder if she had eaten contaminated food too.

She leads us to a pond next to a coop, where several long-necked brown birds rest on wet soil. They breathe quick and shallow, and some of them have ruffled, unhealthy-looking feathers and bald spots.

I bend over them and say, "I forgot to send medicine for all the animals."

Gediyon puts his hand on my shoulder. "It'll be fine. You've done more than enough for the crops."

"Don't fret, Miss Goddess," Mrs. Featheroak says. "Every year, I raise these animals, even though I know that the Famine might do them in every two years or so."

I reach down and pet one of the birds. It coos at my touch, and then I walk to a coop to see what kind of food they have. Yellow and brown seed sit in a long tray and I put my hands inside, combing through it and turning it into a super food. The outside coat takes on a golden sheen and I bring a handful to the bird that Gediyon is holding. I have to lift its limp neck and place its head into my palm so it can eat. It pecks slowly at the seed first, but after eating a few, it flaps its wings and sits upright in Gediyon's arms, devouring the rest in my hand.

Once it's strong enough, Gediyon lets down the bird. He and Mrs. Featheroak help me feed the rest. We reach inside the coop, grab a few, and then move on to the other twenty coops. After recovering, they squawk at each other and feed themselves.

Their feathers still look unhealthy, but at least they move like normal birds now. Gediyon smiles at me, and I can't stop a sigh from escaping.

"We'll come back later to take the dirds to the palace," he tells me. "For now, let's attend to the others."

Mrs. Featheroak leads us to the barn, where we find moink and what Gediyon calls gozi—horned animals with a shaggy mane, like a walking mop. He tells me that the gozi produce a tart milk that we can use for the soup, and we can milk them when they're feeling better.

I'm pretty sure one moink is dead, and Gediyon carries it outside while I fill their mangers with fortified food. I laugh when I see Gediyon carry the moink overhead, since it's more than twice as big as him, but he must gain his muscles from somewhere. Besides, his powers must make it easier for him.

It looks like the main thing these animals eat is hay, and after I'm done sifting through the entire barn with a pitchfork, the hay also turns gold. Like with the dirds, Mrs. Featheroak and I have to force-feed some of them before they happily eat on their own. After some time, Gediyon returns and helps me.

When we finish in the barn, the animals are loud—still smelly—and we pet them. After all this work, my stomach rumbles, but I don't know if I want to eat any animals after working with them.

I take a deep breath of fresh air when we walk out to the fields. Mrs. Featheroak helps us carry ten dirds to the korelian coach, and I worry when one of the cats stands up. I hope they don't decide to snap at the carriage behind them to eat the birds.

Gediyon looks a bit too happy as we carry the dirds. I can see him mentally preparing the soup.

The dirds squawk and flap around inside the coach, which I think is funny until they peck at my legs. I kick my legs around to stop them from pecking and shield my face with my arms. I'm not sure what it is that he does, but Gediyon manages to calm them down. They coo and sit in the carriage like feathery footballs with long necks.

When we reach the palace, I remain curled in a ball until Gediyon leaves with the dirds. I follow him out, watching the dirds file after him as if he's a drill sergeant.

"How do you do that, Gediyon?" I ask.

He smiles at me and pulls out a sachet from his vest pocket. It contains dried, crushed blue flowers.

"Oboedre," he tells me. "When I started to help out on the farms a few years back, my mother told me I could use this plant to tame the livestock."

I raise my eyebrows. "Snazzy."

On the way to the tele-sphere, we pass palace servants, who lean against the walls to make way for us. They snicker at the obedient birds, but I'm still cautious in case the flowers wear off and they decide to attack me again.

The tele-sphere brings us to a catwalk overlooking a kitchen as big as a factory. I imagine that this place would be a lot busier if they had food in storage, because all I see them working with is fresh produce. Even so, all around, I see cooks young and old, male and female, thin and chubby, all wearing perfectly white clothes. Everyone moves with grace and dexterity, but some are more cautious, and others even appear to dance as they carry chopping boards from the counters to stoves.

The room glows with the afternoon sunlight of the dome ceiling, and lanterns float over the marble counters, where the cooks need light the most. Everything is clean like the kitchen of a five-star restaurant should be, but the kitchen still manages to look regal. As I make my way down a metal spiral staircase, I catch decorative motifs in the railing and even the trim of tables and counters. Nothing about this kitchen is plain—not even the pots or the furnaces.

As soon as we descend a metal, spiral staircase, many heads turn toward us. I see faces of relief and amusement, but I'm leaning more toward amusement myself. It's funny watching the dirds hop down one step to the next.

The other cooks don't even need instruction. They're already chopping vegetables or heating pots. Some of them even take the dirds to prepare them.

Gediyon fetches me a clean apron to wear over my clothes, then both of us thoroughly wash our hands. Even though I'm sure Gediyon is going to do most of the cooking, it would suck if I still contaminated the food after all our hard work.

Gediyon pulls over a large pot that someone else had placed for him. Everyone else is already contributing their share to this community soup, and I don't know what I can do that they can do better, so I just stand aside and watch Gediyon.

From his leather bag, he pulls out a box of spices and gives me that funny, innocently guilty smile of his, and I laugh. He sprinkles a combination into a spice bag and throws it into the pot of boiling water. Three other cooks walk over for the same combination of spices and he hands them off without hesitation.

I sit on a high barstool, watching the other cooks slice even pieces of vegetables. They're experts with their knives, but they seem like cooking is more of a chore, while Gediyon looks like he's really enjoying himself.

He strokes the bird in his arms to calm it down, then lays it over a chopping board. He smoothes out its long neck, then with a quick, hard stroke, he chops the head off.

My jaw drops. I watch him lift the body of the bird over a ceramic bowl to catch its blood. It splashes inside with some vinegar, and not a single drop falls outside the bowl. When the blood is drained, Gediyon waves a misty hand over the bowl to cool it down and places the body back on the chopping board.

"I'm sorry you had to see that," he says.

I can't help but gasp, "Poor birdie!"

He lifts the disembodied head by its beak. "Would you like me to fry this for you?" he says, like it's a deep-fried Twinkie.

My mouth still hangs wide open. "No thanks." I don't know if I ever want to eat meat again. I look aside and watch another cook chop happy vegetables. At least they can't feel anything—or scream.

He starts plucking and gutting the bird, then tells me, "This is likely our equivalent of what you did for the livestock. The blood helps us regain our strength, especially during a bout of flu or other infectious illness. Many people are appalled with the idea of dird blood soup, but it really is delicious!"

"Of course it is, Gediyon, you're making it." I wonder if everyone else's batch will taste as good as his?

He has slimy insides all over his hands and he places different parts into the spiced, boiling water. While that cooks, I tell him about going to the Universal Mirror and what I saw.

"Perhaps they were Saei's memories," he tells me.

"Yeah, but I saw you too. At least, it looked like you, but your eyes were blue."

"Oh, that's interesting. Though I believe my eyes have always been red."

I'm about to ask him if he *believes* or *knows* this, but we're happy here cooking and I don't want to upset him about the past that he can't even remember.

He doesn't seem to know anything about what I saw in the Mirror though, and by the sounds of it, he hasn't known anyone to receive a flash from a past life. Is it even possible to retrieve memories from a current life?

Gediyon skims scum off the surface of the soup. Some other cooks even stop and look over his shoulder to see if they're correctly preparing the soup.

While that simmers for the next hour or so, I walk around the kitchen and see what everyone else is up to. Two aisles are dedicated to the dird blood soup. The soup varies in each pot I pass, either in color, scent, or the sizes of the diced meat and vegetables. On the other side of the kitchens, cooks plate small arrangements of fresh and candied fruit.

Launce and Nichols are even here, bothering Kalei, who I can now see in action. She's artistically piping magenta puree on a plate of near-frozen fruit, even though Launce is chatting her ears off.

"It's our Goddess friend!" Launce says, and Kalei looks relieved to see me.

"A little too busy to steal food, are ya?" I say.

Launce laughs. "What are you talking about? I never steal food!"

"Enjoying the sights, then?"

Launce laughs more. Nichols slaps Launce so hard in the back that he almost stumbles onto Kalei's plates.

She curtsies behind the counter. "A pleasure to see you again, Miss Goddess."

"Not too long ago, Kalei moved here from Lade to study culinary arts," Launce explains, as if it's the most fascinating thing in the universe.

Kalei smiles and even blushes. She continues swirling floral patterns on the rim of the plate. Launce watches her as if she's performing magic.

I ask her, "Do you want these two bozos to stop bugging you?"

"It's him she should worry about," Nichols says.

Launce grins like an idiot, then tells me about how Kalei decided to come to Arriscyal instead of Yinidel, which is a lot closer to Lade. She could've learned traditional culinary techniques in Yinidel, but they can't prepare food like Arriscyleans.

"Of course," Launce says to Kalei, "it's our pleasure to welcome you to the Arriscylean kitchens! Them folks in Yinidel probably wouldn't have appreciated you as much as we do."

I'm not sure if his hovering is more cute or creepy, and I feel weird for suggesting that Kalei and Launce were dating. Nichols looks annoyed that Launce is still bothering Kalei. Too bad I missed out on Launce's initial stalking because I haven't been in Arriscyal since the Dark Mist.

Launce's hovering must be contagious, because now I'm doing the same. Even if she doesn't have magic of her own, she pipes puree like an artist, and I'm in awe at how easy she makes it look. It's as if the vines and flowers were blossoming out of the plate.

While finishing the fourth plate, she looks over her shoulders in both directions. She smiles at me and slides the plate toward me.

"I hope you like it," she says.

"Just for me?" I ask.

She nods.

Launce gasps when I prod a berry with a fork. All three watch me expectantly, but there's no way I won't like it. When the sugared berry touches my tongue, I taste a burst of sweet followed by fruity tartness. I then pick up a small, partly-frozen cake and dab it into the fruity puree, which has the same tastes in reverse but different textures.

I smile at Kalei. "This is awesome! Ngh, you should team up with Gediyon in a cook-off!"

Launce nearly throws himself onto the counter. "Can I try too?"

I slide the plate toward him. After the first bite, he looks like he's going to cry, and a waterfall of endless praise flows from his mouth.

Seeing him so smitten makes me want to see Gediyon or Jayse again. I walk across the kitchens back to where everyone finishes the dird blood soup.

Even though I was adamant about not eating it, when they pour some, I try some to be polite. Gediyon helps the others carry the pots to the tele-spheres so they can serve the kingdom, and I cautiously bring the spoon to my mouth, as if I'll detonate a bomb if I eat it too fast.

It doesn't taste much like metal. Instead, it's a bit tart with the vinegar and gozi milk, and a tad sweet with some fruit juice. The meat is tender and juicy, and the vegetables melt in my mouth. The spices make my mouth water for more. As soon as I swallow the first spoonful, I know I'm going to eat seconds. It warms me and washes away the fatigue from working in the barn.

"Do you think Jayse will want some?" I ask Gediyon when he comes back. Then I pause. "Do you even know where he is?"

Gediyon looks away from me and gazes above at one of the hanging lights.

"Hm?"

He smiles and says, "Sorry, I'm a poor liar. He told me not to tell you where is, but I—I can't…"

"Why doesn't he want me to know where he is? Is he mad at me?"

"No, of course not! He's…uh…"

"Is he still in the library?"

He holds back a laugh. "I'll tell him you figured it out on your own."

"What's he doing?"

"It's a surprise."

I snicker. What could it be?

I want to skip to the tele-sphere, but I don't want to bump into anybody and make them spill the dird blood soup. I wait until all the cooks have left, then take the tele-sphere to the library.

A lot of people whisper. It's probably busier than it was when Jayse brought me here last. The rosy light is the same.

Gare isn't at the lobby desk, but I ask someone if she's seen Jayse, and she escorts me upstairs, then points to a wall. Small offices are lined up, some of which are empty, others with frantic soldiers or small study groups. Jayse and Gare sit in one at the very end. Books are piled on top of the center table, but they aren't reading any. Jayse is talking and Gare scribbles notes.

The door is ajar and before I reach for the handle, I realize I can eavesdrop. I quickly grab a large book from a nearby shelf and hold it open, covering my face.

As soon as I open it, I glimpse at the written words, then do a double take. This is probably my first time reading anything from Starrs, and the script looks different. It doesn't look anything like English or the alphabet I know, but somehow I can still comprehend the words. This book is about textiles.

Gare continues writing and asks, "Might he be one of our own?"

"It's not an Arriscylean power though," Jayse says. "It didn't have an elemental heart. It was like a pull on the body."

For a few seconds, they're silent, then Jayse says, "Can the Taesmals fabricate potions to give them powers like ours?"

"They say that's what Pesaeton did, but he used the Universal Mirror. The very first one." Gare pauses. "We don't have any documented powers like that, so it must be something they've concocted on their own. But what kind of twisted person would create a specific power just to torture someone?"

"The Taesmal King."

So the Taesmal King has his own ability to torture people? Without even touching them? I wonder if that's what he did to Jayse when he was kidnapped?

"I'll see if I can search for anything else," Gare says.

At once, he's at the door, and I don't get the chance to run away. I'm so shocked that I drop the book. The next thing I know, he's eyeing me stoically and says, "How do you do, Goddess Michelle?"

Jayse runs out the door, his cheeks pink, looking horrified. He shouts, "How did you get here?"

"Please keep your voice down in my library, Prince." Gare bends down to pick up the book I dropped.

I grin. "It wasn't Gediyon, I swear! He tried to keep it a secret, but I figured you would be here, so… What are you up to?"

"You didn't hear our whole conversation, did you?"

"Just that the Taesmal King has his own special power."

He sighs. "That's all?"

I cross my arms. "You hiding something?"

The two of them look at each other.

Jayse sounds guilty when he says, "I'm making something for you."

"I hear the Counter-Famine is going quite well, Miss Goddess," Gare says.

"Gare! You can't drop hints like that!"

"A smooth transition, Prince. She'll never guess the two topics are related."

I laugh. "Yunno, I can hear everything you say."

Gare nods at Jayse and says, "Your Highness, why don't you lead Miss Goddess on a walk through the garden? I'll continue my work here." He shuts the door to the office.

I lean close to Jayse and nudge him with my elbow. "You're making something, huh? What is it?"

"I can't tell you. You might change your mind."

Before he pulls me away, I look back into the small office and see Gare climbing through the pile of books. On our way to the tele-sphere, I keep trying to bug Jayse about what it is he's making me, but he only says, "I'll show you when we're done."

The tele-sphere brings me to the garden, right in front of the statue of Jayse's uncle.

"Have you had a tour of the garden yet?" he asks.

And so my tour starts here. He leads me closer to the statue and points out the pond. Four sectors represent the seasons. Right now, most of summer is closest to us; water lilies float on the surface, and blue and green fish swim in the clear water. Autumn is coming around clockwise, with red, orange, and yellow fish. The surface shimmers with an illusion of fallen leaves. Winter is on the farthest side, with slow white and silver fish and a frosty surface. Spring is to the left, with pink and yellow fish, frogs, and colorful underwater plants.

"When one takes the tele-sphere directly to the gardens," Jayse tells me, "my uncle greets them here." He takes a deep breath and sighs, admiring the bronze statue.

The man depicted in metal looks a lot like his sister, though much more masculine, of course. He was pretty young—around Gediyon's age—and though he had some delicate features in his face, he had a strong, well-built body—perfect for a swordsman.

"His Divine Highness Prince Aloyin Soat Abelus of Arriscyal," Jayse says. "General of the Arriscylean military at only age twenty-five. Power of wind. The man who taught me how to fight. He greets garden visitors as the hero of Arriscyal, the one who put an end to the last war and killed the Taesmal King, himself. It was a suicidal mission."

In the corner of my eye, I see that Jayse is looking at me, and I drop my gaze from Aloyin. I start to say, "How," but I can't take back that word.

"Stabbed in the back. They said he was killed after finishing off the Taesmal King."

"But now there's a new king."

"With powers of his own." Jayse nods. "He's probably trying to start a new war. Probably thinks it's his right, as the representative of Pesaeton, to purify the world of Arriscyleans."

"What does that mean?"

"He wants to annihilate the 'Gifted' people—the ones who Saei blessed with these magical abilities—leaving only those who are…*normal*."

"Isn't that kind of hypocritical if he has powers too?"

Jayse shrugs, shakes his head, then says, "He's not going to get what he wants. I'll kill him with my own swords. I hope it's as prince, so I won't have to inherit this war as king."

I watch him as he gazes at the pond, probably thinking about his future; he doesn't look very happy about it. I tug on his arm, give him a big cheesy grin and say, "Come on! Show me the rest of the garden."

CHAPTER TWENTY-FOUR
THE FIFTEENTH OF ELLIO

No more breached dams. No more kidnapped princes. No more falling out of the sky and landing on another continent.

Adventure is winding down, and now I have time to appreciate Arriscylean culture, as well as dwell about my role in this world. I ask Jayse about bringing me back home, and he says he and Gare are still figuring it out. He says it so openly, so I don't think that this is his gift to me after all, but at least he's thinking about it.

I spend a few days with Gediyon making sure that everyone is eating all right and recovering from the contaminated food. Compared to the villagers in Lereli, everyone has recovered tremendously fast. It must be the magical blood. While we're at it, I help shops repair broken furnaces or strengthen their roofs, and Gediyon helps them unload merchandise, or delivers it across the city.

One day, Jayse meets me outside my room. He tells me that since the king has given Gediyon too much work, the day is his and mine.

Under the watch of chaperones, Jayse takes me out to the coast where tall grass hides fox-like animals, others that burrow, and sharp-beaked birds. Jayse points out which are mutants—not all of which are vicious. Some of them are downright pitiful, so we put them out of their misery and dump them in a pile near the chaperoning soldiers. They turn their noses up at the bodies, but the city shops will appreciate them. At one point, Jayse decides to play a joke on them, and we run away to a hidden cove by the shore. They aren't too pleased when they find us—not as if they have the right to reprimand us.

The next day, neither Gediyon or Jayse greet me in the morning. I guess maybe Jayse's parents grounded him for potentially putting me in danger, but I still want to know how Gediyon is doing. My maids don't know anything, so I march to the corridor outside and demand, "Take me to Gediyon!"

Four of them give up their posts and take me to the palace steps. I run to the bottom, waiting for a gondola to come, then ask them, "Where is he?"

"It's the fifteenth of Ellio," one of them says. "He'll be at Mrs. Raidyne's house."

When the gondola comes, it's Porter who steers it, and he's cheerful and friendly, asking us where we need to go, and when one of the soldiers says, "Mrs. Raidyne's house," Porter goes sullen.

I don't know what the big deal is. What's so special about the fifteenth of Ellio, and why are they so quiet about Gediyon being at his mom's house? They don't tell me anything except, "It's too disrespectful."

The gondola flows through the city into a quiet residential area. The canal narrows as it reaches the northern coast, and the voices from the marketplace fade away as the sound of the sea takes its place. The drop in temperature is noticeable. The ocean breeze is a relief from the warm city streets, though it also washes away the scent of fresh vendor food.

Plenty of space stretches out between the small houses. It looks like many of them belong to fishermen, too, because I can see small docks and boats behind their houses. Trees tower overhead and shade the rows of houses.

The soldiers stop in front of a house and one of them says, "This is as far as we go."

"Sir Gediyon may be in the garden if he's not inside."

I look at the house. It's two stories, but small and quaint—a summery blue with white trim. Some of the old paint is chipping away, but that only adds to its rustic charm. Flowers overgrow their pots in the front, and birds have made a nest on top of the front doorway. I walk forward past a short white picket fence. The gate is open and rattles against an old, broken rowboat.

To the left of the house is the garden. Unlike the palace, this garden grows untamed shrubs; that's not to say it looks wild, just more natural. I have to push flowery tendrils out of my way as I make my way through. A small channel runs water over the ground from one planter to the next, and I have to be careful not to step in them.

The plants here look innocent, pure and unspoiled by man. I won't be surprised if I run into fairies. The atmosphere calms into serene bliss.

The sound of running water grows stronger, and after I pass a dead tree, I see Gediyon. He kneels in front of a formation of rocks, over which water cascades and fills a pond. In the middle of the pond is a smaller rock, about the height of Gediyon's torso. Some yellow flowers float near the base of the rock. Is it a headstone?

I step forward and Gediyon hears my footsteps. He looks at me, but he isn't smiling.

"I would give her bliden blossoms, but they aren't in season." He looks at the dead tree behind me.

When I reach his side, I kneel with him and read the headstone.

Alina Fae Raidyne
12 Dofility 781 – 7 Erodise 856
To the Harmony that Brings Unity

"Your mother?" I say.

He nods. "Not by blood, but I owe my life to her." He rises to his feet and helps me stand.

"Everyone's making a big deal about you being here."

"Is that so? I tried to be discreet."

"Why?"

He sighs. "Come with me. I'll tell you."

He leads me through the garden, and I can't help but be startled at how sad he looks. He opens the back door of the house and I walk right into the kitchen. Small but homey, organized and clean except for some dust. Dustiest of all is a liquor cabinet hanging between the kitchen and the next room.

Gediyon pulls a chair for me at a small round table and I sit. His mother's small recipe book sits on top, and he takes it when he sits down. He doesn't say anything for a while, and I feel heartbroken because there's no trace of joy in the way he holds himself.

"I don't really know who I am," he finally says. My insides twist.

"I don't remember anything from more than ten years ago," he continues. "It was the fifteenth of Ellio when I awoke upstairs, and I didn't know anything about myself except my name and the girl who sang that song."

"The Song of the Sea Angel?"

He nods. "She was young. I remember her screaming my name and running to my side. It was snowing. Then I saw her, standing by a bliden tree in full bloom, telling me about the sea angel and singing her song."

"That girl," I say. "Was she the one you saw at the beach?"

He nods again. "I don't know anything about her. Not her name, where I can find her, or if she's even alive today. All I know is, she was important to me." He sighs. "I don't understand why I would see her there, though. I only had a lingering memory, and all of a sudden, she reappears."

He turns his head and looks at the kitchen. "My mother—Mrs. Alina Raidyne—was baking muffins here when I awoke that day. She told me that she had found me washed ashore, but no one would claim me, so she took me as her own. She always wanted children, but her husband died young.

"I wouldn't wake for two weeks, and word spread through the kingdom that there was a boy with red eyes. They wanted to banish me for it."

"Because your eyes are *red*?" I scoff. "But Gediyon, Saei's eyes are, like, *gold*! And that Dreana chick has *cat eyes*!"

"It scared them. My mother believed in me, though, and everyone loved her. They thought she was going insane. But she persisted, even after I was ready to accept that I didn't belong here. She taught me how to cook, I learned her values and helped anyone I could, just to prove myself and form an identity that didn't include my forgotten past. They wouldn't let go of their prejudices until after she had passed away. Even then, they blamed me for her death.

"I'm fortunate that Jayse is my friend, because he believed in me. He, Queen Trissa, and Byran helped me recover…"

I stand up and cross the table to hug him. "And you've done a great job, because everyone accepts you now." I pull back and put both of my hands on his shoulders. "I think I understand why you smile all the time. You don't like upsetting anyone."

"It's a habit of mine."

"Well, you don't have to hide everything behind a smile."

He puts a hand to mine and—of course—smiles. "Thank you, Michelle."

I take my hands off him. "Still, you wonder about your past, right? Maybe I can help you. I mean, I am Goddess. Maybe if I talk to the Mirror, it can spit out something for you, too."

"I'm trying what I can, too. Others are helping me as well." He hands me Mrs. Raidyne's recipe book and says, "She also used it as a diary. She said some things about me, but… See for yourself."

I open it, careful with the loose pages. I flip through recipes—all kinds of baked goods like cookies and muffins, more intricate things like candied flowers and latticed sugar bowls, and scribbled notes about how many spices to add to pasta dishes. Some "diary" entries are simple reminders about what to do in the morning, but the first page I stop at mentions Aloyin.

18 Turccise 851

Don't forget to bake nilegin muffins for Nicenne!

21 Turccise 851

Everyone is celebrating that the war is over, and that the Taesmal King is dead. I know I should be rejoicing like everyone else, but Prince Aloyin sacrificed himself to kill the king. I find it hard to believe that he would lower his guard and let a child stab him in the back. Everyone does.

Queen Trissa and Baas are devastated, but I'll do what I can to lift their spirits. My muffins should do the trick!

I snicker a little, because I have a feeling that Gediyon would do the same thing.

I keep flipping through the book, carefully replacing loose pages and skipping over more recipes. More one-line reminders, and then at the end of Consier, she wrote more.

27 Consier 852

There are times when I wish that I had asked Willem to teach me how to catch fish. The fish in the market are great, but I miss the quality of the fish that he used to bring home. This casserole requires that I have the highest quality ingredients, so tomorrow morning, I may take Will's equipment and attempt to catch some of my own. I'll just have to wake up early so I won't make a fool of myself!

28 Consier 852

I found a boy washed ashore. I feared the sea had taken his life, but he's alive, though comatose. It was early morning—couldn't bother waking anyone—so I surprised myself when I mustered the strength of my youth and levitated him down the beach. As I write this, he's lying in the room down the hall.

No one knows who he is, but I will take responsibility for him. Perhaps he can even be a son to me.

I look up from the book at Gediyon. He's watching me read, not smiling or frowning. I flip the page, but something is wrong here.

30 Consier 852

Jeroff examined the boy today

Jeroff is certain that Madam Manasa will lend us one.

3 Ellio 852

No matter what happens, I've sworn to Jeroff that I will do everything I can

Jeroff will inform the king and queen,

The boy is safe, at least.

one day, when everyone lives in harmony, he'll remember who he is.

I hope he will

15 Ellio 852

The boy awoke this morning. He told me his name is Gediyon, and indeed, that is one of the few things he remembers, besides the singing girl.

I must admit, I feel a little guilty asking him to call me mother,

What happened to the rest of these entries? She wrote in pen, so it's not like someone simply erased it. The blank spaces are perfectly smooth, not scratched and not even showing the imprint of where a pen might've written. It's like someone stole the words from existence.

After the last entry on the fifteenth of Ellio, a few more pages are blank, and then it returns to short but full entries that only mention mundane things, like her and Gediyon baking things for everyone.

"What happened to it?" I ask.

Gediyon shakes his head. "Madam Manasa gave it to Gare, but words were already missing when he looked at it. He couldn't figure anything out, so he gave it to me."

"So, wait a minute, is Madam Manasa *trying* to hide things from you? 'Cause I would've liked to ask her to help you out, but…"

"A cryptic one, she is."

I close the book and hand it back to him. "Well, I can't figure out what this means, but I'm not gonna give up! I'll ask the Mirror for you and see what I can get."

"Thank you, Michelle. I really appreciate this."

I shrug and pull him out of the chair. "Now, you wanna get something yummy to eat?"

Since no one has lived here for a while, there's no food except for the liquor cabinet, but I don't think Gediyon wants to touch it either, so we head back into the city. I mention the restaurants I saw on my way to his mother's house. Of course Gediyon knows which ones I'm talking about, and he say that we can go to all three: one for tea, another for the main course, and the last for dessert.

We walk along the gondola channel back to the city. I skip forward, thinking about delicious food and knowing that reality will far exceed my expectations. Gediyon is smiling, probably because I'm so happy, but I know he must still be hiding pain behind the smile.

While walking up the slope of the tea shop, I see white cloaks fluttering behind three men. Arriscylean soldiers dash to us, alarm painted all over their faces, and terror sinks into my stomach. The one who reaches us first says, "Mysiochs have infiltrated the palace!"

Chapter Twenty-Five
Palace Schemes

My first thought is to keep my feet planted right where they are. After all, if the Mysiochs are *in* the palace, then I'm safer out here, right?

I look at Gediyon and the other soldiers, who look back at me. Gediyon says, "You'll be safer—"

"Let me come with you!" I blurt. To the other soldiers, I say, "Are they killing people, or…"

One of shakes his head with uncertainty, but another says, "It seems like a mere attack of terror."

I don't waste any more time standing around and contemplating what I'm going to do. I follow the guards alongside the channel until we catch up with a gondola. We don't wait for it to slow down for us and we hop in the back, ordering the gondolier to work his fastest.

I hold on to the edge of the gondola. Everything around me is a blur. My nerves leave me shaky, anticipating my reaction to whatever's going to happen next. The soldiers don't have that stoic, confident look in their eyes, either. Do they even know how they're going to stop the Mysiochs?

Then something occurs to me.

"Did the Mysiochs attack just now?" I ask.

"We watched them vanish in the training grounds," a soldier says.

"Or have they been in the city since they poisoned the food stock?" I continue.

They exchange glances in silence.

Gediyon says, "They're usually quite stealthy. They tend not to linger after their work is complete, and to send the Mysiochs for such a simple mission like poisoning our food stock…"

I sigh. "Maybe they were waiting for something else. Like trying to assassinate the king and queen."

I don't like this thought any more than they do. I feel a little guilty, though, when I realize that I'm relieved they're not after me. Their plans might still change, so I can't drop my guard yet.

Someone must have cast a barrier around the palace because a golden light shimmers above the waterfall. It allows us through and sucks away most of the sunlight's warm beneath the barrier's protection. When we reach the tele-sphere room, the soldiers decide where to take us.

We reappear in the throne room, which I thought would be the most obvious and dangerous place to go when the enemy is trying to kill the king and queen, but the room has changed. The entire right wall, which used to lead straight to the open gardens, is now completely sealed. The walls and ceiling flash with the same golden barrier as outside, and the hall echoes more than before.

I'm surprised to see that Jayse and King Oresonn actually take refuge here. Both scabbards are strapped over Jayse's shoulders, and the king relaxes his hands atop the hilt of his single broadsword.

I rush toward Jayse. "Are you okay?" he says, while I start, "Where's the queen?"

"Safe," King Oresonn replies. "Goddess Michelle, it would be wise to join her."

I shake my head. "I'm not the best fighter, but I can't stand back and let you guys protect me all the time!"

Jayse sighs. Maybe he'll be more comfortable if I went with his mom, too. I mean, it's not like I'm going to jump out and put myself in danger. I'll only fight if I have to.

"Do you guys know where the Mysiochs are? What if they teleported in here, or got to the queen?"

"Trissa is safe," King Oresonn says so firmly that I want to shrink in a ball and scuttle away.

"What if they try to poison the palace food?" I say in a small voice. "But not just super bacteria, but like actual deadly poison? Have you checked the food stocks yet?"

A soldier confirms, "Your Majesty, the kitchens are a primary target."

I clench my fists. "Then let's go there and protect the food!"

The king narrows his eyes with disapproval, but it is his kingdom that I'm trying to protect. He can stay in the throne room and formulate battle plans all he wants.

I'm relieved when I see that Jayse and Gediyon follow me to the tele-sphere, and they guide us to the kitchens. Our accompanying guards are the first to step down the catwalk. I nearly step down the spiral staircase after them without thinking, but I take a look at the kitchens. It seems that my intuition is correct.

Order and discipline has now declined to chaos. Anything goes in battle, and I watch Arriscylean soldiers advance on the tight-suited Taesmals—on countertops and even crossing stoves. The Taesmals retaliate with quick bursts from guns, and I even see one shoot jelly at an Arriscylean, who makes a mistake when he uses his fire magic. The jelly ignites, setting his own clothes ablaze.

I hurry down the stairs, but Jayse pulls me back by the shoulders and I nearly fall. He says, "Michelle, you aren't armed!"

"Whatever—you have to heal that guy!" I jump the last few steps to the floor and let Jayse pass me.

Since everyone else is too preoccupied fighting each other, I run down the meat-preparing aisle and pick up a meat tenderizer. I swing it once through the air, and the shaft lengthens with the momentum. With another shake, the spiky head grows five times its size, but still weighs as much as it did before.

I turn around, and a Taesmal heads after Gediyon with a tubular weapon. I swing the meat tenderizer onto the man's forearm, disarming him immediately. His weapon clangs against the ground, but he doesn't bother picking it up because he's staring at Gediyon. And for whatever reason, Gediyon stares back. I take the opportunity to kick the Taesmal's chest and whack his face with the rows of small pyramids, then I pull Gediyon along with me.

I'm not sure what was up with their staring contest, but the next time we come across the Taesmals, Gediyon knocks the Taesmals off their feet with a blast of air, and we continue forward.

If we can't kill the Taesmals, we have to round them all up somehow. Maybe if Gediyon's oboedre worked on humans, we could calm them down and walk them outside, but I have a feeling that won't be so easy—especially when I see a Mysioch.

As soon as I spot one, two more appear. The three of them float above, wearing vacant silver masks. In an instant, they shoot to the floor. I hear some screams, battle cries, then gradually the other Taesmals disappear. I spot some of them pressing a device—must be a teleporter.

Once they're gone, falling pots and pans clatter as they fall, but the battle cries have stopped. The cooks and soldiers mutter in confusion, no longer fighting.

Jayse marches forward and says, "Nobody touch the food, not even the water—not until we know that it's safe."

"Where did they go?" I say under my breath.

Someone shouts, "They've taken some of us with them."

A low voice replies, "No, they didn't take us. They were taking their own people back!"

"What?" I say.

The deep-voiced man walks forth and grabs the long braids of a cook—Kalei! "She's one of them!"

"What are you talking about?" she shouts back, shoving him off her hair.

"Don't feign innocence! I saw you talking to them. And what's this?" He rips off her choker and throws it on the ground. I hear a small shatter, then a sizzle and a quick stream of red smoke. "Poison for His Majesty?"

Kalei gapes at the poison vial in disbelief, but I'm not buying this story. It looks like he had planted it on her.

No one else seems to grasp what's going on either, but the man takes Kalei by her hair and drags her across the kitchens toward the tele-sphere.

"What are you doing?" I scream.

"Throwing her before His Majesty!"

"You have no proof!" Kalei shouts back.

"The poison vial is more than enough. They were right to leave you behind!"

Gediyon stands before the soldier, which is enough to stop him. "You're not thinking rationally. Whether she is a Taesmal or not, your behavior is inhumane."

With a handful of her hair, the man shoves Kalei aside. Gediyon helps her stand, and she seems bashful at his touch.

"We will leave it for King Oresonn to decide what to make of your accusation."

I see Kalei swallow a big lump, but she looks much more relieved with Gediyon leading her instead. They start up the stairs for the tele-sphere. Before following them, I look at Jayse. He doesn't seem to know what's going on, either.

I have a feeling that King Oresonn will cut her some slack, so I take my time walking back to the tele-sphere. Jayse doesn't look so confident, though.

When we arrive at the throne room, I'm not sure what to think, because no one is even discussing the matter. No one speaks, but in the silence, every other sound has an intense echo—our footsteps, and even the inhalation of breath.

King Oresonn, flanked by his soldiers, stands at the base of the throne platform. Kalei stands directly across from him, stiff with tight fists, shoulders trembling.

Their staring goes on for so long, I wonder if they have mind-reading powers. I can't see Kalei's face, but King Oresonn is scrutinizing her, as if sifting through her thoughts to see where her loyalty lies.

Then he says, "Lock her in a cell for questioning. I will help with the interrogation tonight."

Kalei shrieks. "No! You don't understand! This is *his* plan—*he's*—"

I understand where the first scream came from, but this next one is so frightening, unexpected, and full of agony that I nearly fall to the floor in surprise. I hold onto Jayse's arm for support, then I see Kalei crumpled on the ground between two Arriscylean soldiers. I didn't see either of them strike her, though. They also look confused, but they pull her to her knees and then drag her to the tele-sphere.

Before they even leave, I step forward and say, "Your Majesty! This is ridiculous! This looks like a setup. Kalei even said it herself, it was somebody else's plan." I want to point at the guard who had accused her first, but they're already gone.

"Goddess Michelle, we will check on the girl's background—"

"Yeah, but do you have to lock her up? Like she's an *animal*?"

"Your Divinity, you have nothing to worry about, because when we no doubt find her innocent, we will let her go."

I scoff. "Without an apology, I bet! She won't even be able to show herself anywhere in the city without people spitting at her."

"Michelle—" Jayse tries to cut me off, but I take another step forward.

"She'll have to go back home! Do you know she came all the way from"—I try to find the name, then shake my head. "Whatever, but it sounds far!"

"That is enough, Goddess Michelle," King Oresonn commands.

I suddenly feel his overpowering gaze, and for a moment I fight to maintain eye contact. His piercing, dark green eyes make me shrink inside, and my nerves make me want to look to the ground, but I'm not going to back down just yet.

"She's been here for about a month," I say firmly, controlling the volume of my voice. "If she wanted to kill you or the queen, she would have done it already. She could've killed *me*. She made me breakfast. Me and my maids and guards—we all ate it. If she was really a Tasemal, she could've poisoned all of us, but she *didn't*."

King Oresonn nods, and I finally wimp out and break eye contact when she speaks. "Thank you for that information, Your Divinity. I'll consider it when we question her. Understand that this is part of our procedure of maintaining the security of my kingdom."

"Of course." I nod and turn around.

The tele-sphere is the only way I can leave now since the garden is blocked off.

The entire way, I keep my eyes aimed at the floor, and when I see the etched design surrounding the tele-sphere, I also see another pair of black boots.

It's Launce.

"They already took her away," I whisper to him.

Anger replaces the worry in his eyes. "This has to be a joke."

"I hope so."

"I need to stop them." Then his voice explodes, "Where is Kalei?"

"She is in good hands, Launce," the king answers.

I whisper to him, "They're keeping her in a cell for questioning."

Launce wastes no time. He doesn't even ask me to step off the tele-sphere circle before he redirects us to another bright hall.

Unlike the throne room, this place is narrow. It looks nothing like how I imagined the entrance to a dungeon: dark, wet, and cold with dim, flickering torches and rats chewing on their dead relatives. Actually, the walls are made of marble and it's lit with the same bright spheres found elsewhere in the palace. It looks like the only way inside is through the tele-sphere. At the end of the hall are two guards posted at a gate that must lead farther into the dungeon. They wear the same uniform as Launce, without the white cloak.

"You're making a mistake!" Launce yells, marching toward them. He's at least a foot shorter and ten years younger, but there's nothing laughable in the way he holds himself.

One of the guards says, "No one is to enter the dungeons without permission from His Majesty."

"What if your Creator tells you to step aside?" I say.

The men exchange glances, then the other says, "It's for your safety as well, Your Divinity."

"This is a *mistake*!" Launce yells. "There's no way Kalei can be a Taesmal!"

"That is for His Majesty to determine."

Launce growls and draws his sword. I barely even hear the *shing* before I see that the other two guards have blocked him with their swords. Nearly as quick as he drew, Launce resheaths his sword, and turns back to the opposite end of the hall.

"Launce!" I call.

"Please leave me alone until this is over."

Chapter Twenty-Six
Immoral Justice

I'm uneasy for the rest of the night. Gediyon helps the soldiers search the palace and city for any traces of poison or other evidence that can lead to the real culprit, while Jayse lets himself off his princely duties to help put my mind at ease.

Launce needs more help than me, though, but more than anyone, Kalei needs justice.

Jayse and I lean against the railing of my balcony. He looks at the starry sky and the almost prismatic clouds while I overlook the garden.

"Baas told me about this happening before," Jayse says. "They were innocent, of course. It can't be any different this time."

I sigh. "I hope so. And I hope Launce isn't beating himself up over this, either."

"He'll bounce back to his usual self when this is all over in a day."

"Your Highness," I hear Mirra. We turn around and see her in the balcony doors, the drapes flowing behind her like fairy wings. "I apologize for intruding, but perhaps it would be best for you and Michelle to go to bed now."

"What time is it?"

"Eleven."

I look at Jayse, then say to Mirra, "If you're tired, you can go ahead and sleep. Jayse and I are going to say good night. You don't have to wait for us."

Mirra nods with a curtsy, then disappears into my dark room.

We don't speak until she's completely out of earshot. I mean, it's not like Jayse and I are going to pounce on each other and make out, but still.

Jayse stands in front of me, both hands on my shoulders, and he says, "Don't worry. Everything is going to be okay."

"If you say so."

"Look, I'll be here first thing in the morning. Don't lose any sleep over this, okay?"

I shrug.

"All right. Well, I'll be heading out. Good night."

When he leaves the balcony, I feel weird not hugging him or even walking him to my door, but I'll feel even weirder if I chase after him.

I decide it's a better idea to go straight to bed and take a bath in the morning. I change into my silky pajamas and slide in bed, hoping that I'll feel better when I wake up.

Five minutes pass, and I'm even more awake than I was before. Maybe a bath would be a good idea. The warmth will relax me, and since my maids are in bed, I won't have to worry about anyone else seeing me naked.

I step into the warm, fragrant bath. It tingles and I feel more relaxed, but also rejuvenated. If everything I do makes me more awake, then I'll never get enough sleep.

I'd like to ask Gediyon for some claren tea, but he's probably sleeping too. I could try making my own from memory, but it won't be the same.

It's a long night.

The first thing I'm aware of is sitting on the throne room steps, gazing out at the garden. Did I sleep walk my way here? At least I managed to change my clothes before embarrassing myself.

The guards look at me funny, then they tell me that the palace is safe again, so the throne room is open to the public. All the food has been checked for poison, and it's safe to eat.

When I ask them about Kalei, they tell me to wait until King Oresonn announces her verdict.

I run at him when he enters from the garden. "Kalei is innocent, right?"

He looks somber. I guess this means she confessed, or they found evidence that painted her hands red—but I refuse to believe that.

"Kalei is no longer with us."

I speak in monotone. "You sent her back home."

"Goddess Michelle, she is dead."

My tongue is frozen. I choke out, "H-how? What happened?"

"She was a Taesmal after all. She killed herself. She must have kept a vial of poison in the event we found her out."

"No way."

"Believe what you will, but we are now safer without her." He starts for his throne.

I shake my head. "But she... This isn't..." The next swallow is like taking a pill. "Where's Launce?"

"He has already been informed."

"Where is he?"

King Oresonn sits on his throne and it rises toward the ceiling. A soldier answers me.

"The library, Your Divinity."

I nod and make my way to the tele-sphere. As slowly as I navigate through the holographic palace, I have to backtrack a lot because I keep pressing the wrong areas.

Eventually, I make it. I stagger down the hall to the lobby. A pit is in my stomach.

I'm not even sure what I mean to do, but I have to see if Launce is okay.

Gare is at his desk over a pile of notebooks. The question I ask is probably hard for him to understand, because he takes a while to answer.

"He's with Nichols in the back. At the end of this aisle."

He doesn't even add a snarky remark. This can't be good. I continue down the aisle for the glass wall facing the garden courtyard.

Sure enough, Launce is at a table with Nichols. Nichols has a small pile of thin books, one of which is open-faced; he's too busy watching his friend to enjoy it. Launce leans back in a chair with his feet on the tabletop. He's scraping the tips of his nails with his sword; he doesn't even look up when I approach them.

"Hi Michelle," Nichols says. His tone is joyless.

"Hey." I take a deep breath. "How are you guys?"

"I'm sick of people asking that," Launce says. He kicks back and sits with feet planted on the floor. " 'How are you doing? Is everything all right?' Of course! You don't see blood dripping from my ears or nose or any other orifice, do you?"

"Don't be such a jackass," Nichols says.

"Everyone expects me to be distraught and mopey like it's the end of the world! Just because Kalei is dead? She was a Taesmal. The bitch got what she deserved!" He shoves the table away—producing a horrible screech—and rises to his feet, then storms out of the doors into the courtyard.

Nichols and I watch him march off. The door closes on its own.

I take a seat.

"It's not your fault, Michelle."

"But didn't he like her?" My lip trembles, then tears pour down my cheeks. I wipe them away as they come.

"Don't…cry…"

"But it's not fair! What did Kalei do? She made plates look pretty! Sure she might've been a Taesmal, but did she hurt anybody? Was it really her who contaminated the food stock? And Launce just throws her away like this!"

"It does hurt him," Nichols says. "A lot. He really liked her a lot, even if it was puppy love." He sighs. "But we joined the military to grow strong so we can fight the Taesmals. Whether she did any of that or not, Kalei…was our enemy."

When I stop crying, I change the topic and ask Nichols to tell me about the books he's reading. I'm sure my crying made him feel uncomfortable, but he perks up when he shows me the open book.

They're actually plays. He tells me that in Plaretta, they had only heard of the famous playwrights and their stories, but nobody there has the actual texts. Studying literature was the main reason Nichols came to Arriscyal, even though his best friend talked him into enlisting with the military.

Nichols is reluctant when he tells me that he wanted to be an actor, but I think it's cool. In a world where military seems to be more dominant than anything else, it's refreshing to see someone interested in the arts.

When we start to talk about culinary arts, both of us grow quiet.

Launce still hasn't come back.

CHAPTER TWENTY-SEVEN
GODDESS GIFTS

I nearly break down again when they tell me that they burned Kalei's body. I suppose it's no different than cremation or a ceremonial burning, but I can't help but feel that it was done out of animosity, like they burned her for her sins.

It would've been nice if they had given her a painless burial or cast her out to sea, but since she's the enemy, I guess I can understand.

Still, the entire situation leaves me restless.

When Launce decides to be sociable again, I hang out with him and Nichols more than I do with Jayse or Gediyon. Jayse is still working on his special gift for me, and King Oresonn keeps Gediyon too busy for me to even say hi. Besides, Launce really needs the support.

None of us speak of Kalei, and Launce puts on a façade that everything is all right. He doesn't snap at anyone anymore. Even though he and Launce continue with their palace pranks—and even include me in their escapades—Nichols and I agree that he isn't quite himself.

We're all much happier, but I feel stifled because I can't talk about Kalei around them. It's been about ten days since I last had a decent conversation with Gediyon, and now I think would be a good time to see him.

The other soldiers tell me he went to his room, and I can't help but smile stupidly and bite my lower lip when they tell me they'll escort me to him.

They guide me through the tele-sphere to a corridor in a courtyard, and like the entrance to my room, only one door is at the end. I walk down the path, looking at the water lilies floating on the ponds in the courtyard. Long-legged birds perch eagerly on wooden plants, watching the fish swim below. Some of them glow in the dimming, sunless courtyard. Palace guards also line this corridor, though not as many as outside my own room. They nod to me as I pass.

The door at the end stands on its own with a polished brass handle. A stained glass design of the same water lilies and birds behind me decorate the middle panels, and two lamps of pure white light hang overhead. I knock a few times on the wooden frame.

On the other side, I hear something crash, and then footsteps. I look back at the guards down the corridor, but they're blank-faced as if nothing is out of the ordinary. I hear some clicks on the other side of the door, and Gediyon opens it.

Some loose black hair hangs over his face and his braid is messy, unraveling toward the bottom. He hasn't bothered to button up much of his shirt, and he looks like he just woke up.

"Oh, good morning, Michelle."

I snicker. "Actually, it's still night." I hold up the basket. "The others told me they didn't see you at dinner, so I brought you some!"

"Oh, goodness, thank you. Would you like to come inside?"

I nod and he steps out of the doorway for me.

"I apologize. It's rather messy—excuse me while I tidy up."

Actually, except for the few things that fell, it looks neat—a lot cleaner than either Aaron's or my room. He marches upstairs and pulls his curtains aside, flooding the room with orange light. He stares out the windows for a moment, as if he's still confused about the time. I walk upstairs and watch him pull white light from a jar—moonglow jelly, I learned it's called—and he tosses a few spheres around the room.

His bed sits in the center of this circular, upstairs area, right beneath a stained glass dome of red, blue, and purple, depicting a cloudy, twilight sky over an ocean. Three large windows sit behind his bed, overlooking a pond somewhere in the palace. Out on the bank of the opposite end, I see some girls lying in the grass, reading books.

His room smells like sweet spices. Most of his furniture is dark wood—masculine and sophisticated. On top of his desk, I see the open, unwound music box that Madam Manasa gave him, next to a stack of books and the bag he carries his spices in. When I see this, I feel for the pin at the collar of my shirt, which I'll give to Gediyon later.

His bed is unmade, and on the floor beside draped blankets is his mother's diary. It's fallen open-faced and some pages have scattered nearby. Near the top of the stairs is a hexagonal table with four chairs, one of which has fallen over. I put the basket of food on top, next to a pot of what's probably claren tea, and I bend down to lift the chair. A broken teacup lies next to it, and I fix it immediately.

Gediyon emerges from another room, rebraiding his hair. To my dismay, he's put on a vest over his now-buttoned shirt.

He has a slight laugh as he says, "I'm sorry you had to see this," then he bends down to pick up the diary and scattered papers.

"It's kinda early to be sleeping, doncha think?"

"I suppose," he says, placing the diary on his desk. He hurries back to make his bed. "How have you been these past few days?"

I take a seat at the table and take things out of the basket. I say, "Well… Jayse has been busy, and Gare won't tell me anything about it. I hung out with my maids for a bit. Canaria and I went shopping the other day, and she kept saying something about the Ceremony of…something."

"The Ceremony of Crescent Starrs?"

"Something like that."

"It's a festival we have every Hermise, to honor Goddess Saei. Usually, it takes place in Dissett."

"Sounds cool," I say, but I'm not too enthusiastic because I doubt I'll even make it. "Anyway, last night I was with Byran at the docks, and we watched the last few ships come in from sending the fertilizer all around. So like, the Famine is officially over, right?"

"Three weeks have passed since it started, so yes."

"Yeah. I've been hanging out with Launce and Nichols a lot, too. All they want to do is cause trouble. Today, they brought me to the gondola storage room, and we played a mean trick on Porter. Hid in a boat and scared him when he started his shift, but"—I laugh—"it was fun. And then we stole some stuff from the kitchens. They got in trouble, but they gave me a whole basket of dinner."

Gediyon sits at the table and I hand him a napkin of still-warm bread. I pick apart pieces from a roll while he sets up a plate, watching him take delicate bites from everything. Maybe he isn't hungry.

"How is Launce doing?" he asks.

"He was…pretty bad for a while. He's better now." I lean back in the chair. "Actually, I still feel bad about Kalei. I can't talk to them about it, and even though it's all over and done with, I feel like there was something missing." I shrug. "It's so unfair. I never thought she could've been a Taesmal. It was like somebody framed her."

Gediyon nods. "Many Arriscyleans will treat Taesmals that way. Taesmals treat us the same. The way I see it, a life is a life. No one has the right to steal it from someone else. It would've been immoral to keep her captive—even more so if we converted her to our lifestyle. To kill Kalei is to stoop to the level of our enemies."

"King Oresonn said she killed herself," I say.

"Is that what happened?"

"That's what he said."

"That alters our perspective, then."

"No matter how she died, I'm still kind of scarred. I mean, back home, I hear people die all the time, but I don't really *know* them. But with the Prince Imposter and Kalei—it didn't even phase me that I might not see them again, and then...they're gone."

"It is difficult to accept at first, but even if it seems like it's the end of the world, you will move on." He pauses. "Acceptance is important. With everything you accept, you understand more and grow more mature."

"Maybe," I sigh.

"I know it's hard at first, and it's easier said than done. Think about it as a learning experience rather than a setback." He pours himself a cup of tea. It must be cold, since he warms it up with his flaming hands. He takes a sip, then sets it on the table.

I ask, "How did you get over your mom's death?" Regret immediately sinks my stomach and I feel like banging my head against the table. "Sorry," I groan.

He shakes his head, smiling. "It's okay." He pushes his teacup farther from the table edge and chuckles. "I didn't take it well at all.

I tried to distract myself with work to block my grief, but it still caught up with me." He sighs. "I believe it was thanks to joining the military. I traveled elsewhere to help others, towns that grieved the losses of family due to disasters like the Famine, children who became orphans. I saw them at their lowest and watched them spring back up. I needed to be resilient like them. On the outside, I smiled to help them cheer up. At times, I even believed myself, but the grief still broke me down on the inside. I told myself, I can't let this define me. I wanted to forget my mother's death so I wouldn't know how deeply it could hurt me, but if I ever lost someone dear to me again, I wouldn't know how to cope. I needed to accept it and learn from it. Life goes on. You grow older. Those you care about pass on into the next life. They won't remember you, but they live on in the memories of those who loved them."

I nod. "Yeah. Thanks." I giggle. "I love talking to you. You give such awesome answers."

He blushes. "Thank *you* for hearing me out."

He's so cute. "Anyway, I've been talking to the Mirror. I said a prayer for Kalei, and that put me at ease—just a little. It never talks back, but you're right about it being like therapy. I talk to it without expecting an answer, and it still hasn't given me anything, but I'm not like disappointed. I asked it about your past, but I still haven't figured it out."

"Even so, thank you very much for all your efforts. I really appreciate it."

I shrug and smile, then say, "Still, I feel hella bad about not getting any results, so I made something for you!" I unclasp the pin from my collar and hand it to him. It looks like a red and gold envelope, rectangular and no larger than a postage stamp. He takes it and I say, "It's a spice pin! Look, lift the flap."

He has to open it with a finger nail, and as soon as the triangular flap lifts, the pin enlarges and takes on a new form—a lightweight metal box of the same red and gold, with twelve compartments. In each of them is a small glass bottle.

"This way," I tell him, "you can store all your spices without having to carry around that big box! You can just pin it to your clothes, and when you need it, take it off and open it. When you're done, just close it"—I flip the lid over and shut the box—"and it shrinks again!"

Gediyon smiles as he opens and enlarges it again. "Thank you so much, Michelle. This really means a lot to me."

I shrug. "I thought you'd like it!"

"Really, I'm honored to call you my friend. Even if you weren't Goddess, you would still be a wonderful person."

I giggle. "Aw, Gediyon! I can say the same thing about you, and you *aren't* Goddess!"

He laughs.

He never finishes his dinner, but he explains his spices to me as he transfers it from his old box to the spice pin Three of them are strictly for dessert, another six he can use for any dish, and the last are for savory dishes. All of them fit perfectly, and when he's done organizing them, he closes it and pins it to the breast pocket on his vest.

When it's time for me to leave, I give him a hug and say, "No matter how people treated you in the past, just keep in mind that people appreciate you so much now. You help so many people, and you don't ask for much in return. I promise, one day, you'll remember your past."

"I don't know how many times I can thank you before it wears out."

"It won't." As soon as I let go of him, I jump up, kiss him on the cheek, and then run down the stairs for the door. "Good night!" I hurry out.

I walk down the corridor to the tele-sphere and giggle like a creep. It wasn't a romantic kiss, just a friendly one. Not like kissing a brother—not at all. But not much different than the kiss the Prince Imposter gave me.

By the time I reach the tele-sphere, my smile has turned into a frown. I sigh when I touch the tele-sphere.

The next morning before breakfast, my maids tell me that Jayse is at my bedroom door.

I groan when I see him. "Why do you always look perfect when I see you?"

He smiles and takes a breath to say something, then stops and raises an eyebrow. "Hold on. Was that supposed to be an insult?"

I snort. "You can take it that way if you want. What's up?"

"As soon as you're ready, I'll take you for breakfast in the garden. I have a *very* special day planned for you!"

I put my hands on my hips. "Ooh! Do ya?"

He crosses his arms. "Let's see, in terms of splendor, if you can plan me an even better day."

"Ha! It should be easier for me if I'm going second!" I slam the doors in his face and tell my maids, "Hurry and get me dressed!"

They must think that Jayse and I are going on a date, because they take special care in choosing a dress and preparing my hair and face. They put me in a sage green chiffon dress, curl my hair, and clip on a flowery headdress. My face shimmers with sweet-smelling dust. Again, I look like a fairy princess, but I waste no time in front of the mirror and nearly trip on my way out of the entrance hall.

When I step outside, Jayse stares at me for a moment, then shrugs and says, "I suppose the wait was worth it."

I slap him on the shoulder and say, "You hungry? 'Cause I am!"

He takes me to the garden, where we trip over each other trying to hurry to the other side. When I nearly fall into the pond, I jump on his back and he gives me a piggy-back ride, running through the garden to a gazebo on a hill, overlooking another pond. Some palace servants stand here, carrying trays.

"Your Highness!" a stern old woman says. "Mind your manners!"

Jayse clears his throat and lets me stand. "My apologies," he says. When we look at each other, we snicker.

Sitting in the middle of the gazebo is a round glass table and two cushioned wicker chairs. The servants seat me and pour us a drink of something that smells familiar—a cocoa nut drink! They serve us tiny pastries for breakfast and I devour anything chocolate.

When we grow full and our eating slows, Jayse and I talk more. I try asking about what he's been up to, then he changes the topic back to me. I tell him about seeing Gediyon last night, and he sighs and shakes his head.

He looks around the gazebo at the servants, then leans in to me and whispers, "Do you want to know something?"

"What?"

"Sometimes," he whispers, "Gediyon makes me…*really* angry."

I hold back a gasp. "Why?"

He looks as if Gediyon has been pissing him off for years, and I'm afraid about what he's going to say. Then the corners of his frowning lips tighten and twitch, and he bursts into laughter.

"What?" I say.

He snickers, "It's 'cause he's so much better than me!"

I scoff and throw my fork at him. "You dork! Don't be mean to Gediyon!"

"*Honestly*, though! It's like he should be prince instead of me. More people are familiar with him, and all I am is the lazy prince who likes to hunt Taesmal mutants."

"You're more than that."

He leans back in his chair and sighs. "No, he doesn't make me mad. He never does. I'm just jealous."

"Like a big brother you look up to and everyone expects you to be like him?"

"Yeah. Exactly like that."

"I know the feeling."

After we're done eating, Jayse takes me to a courtyard where the Arriscylean soldiers train. It's outside underneath some kind of barrier that distorts the sun, so it won't blind them with its direct light. Jayse and I watch them from a balcony above, and it startles me to watch them fence with such little armor. The fencers are elegant but a bit stiff, and I find the halberd users much more fascinating. They swing and twirl their weapons with grace, jumping and kicking to parry their imaginary opponents' attacks.

Jayse tells me when Aloyin was young, he used to skip his school lessons to join the practice, and it was inevitable that he would become the next leader of the military. After his death, King Oresonn took over, and though the military is still strong, the king can't give it the personal attention that Aloyin did.

He next takes me to the royal menagerie, and I wonder how large the palace actually is. This place looks like a giant greenhouse, encased in glass with plants and birds that look like they might be from Lereli. I catch some short-tailed cats running around and a fair amount of lizards. Some small bears climb trees.

Byran's niece Chili must take some responsibility over these animals, as well as the ones for transportation, since she gives us a small tour of the habitat.

I ask Jayse and Chili if people can summon these animals, and they say that the birds can be trained to follow a certain whistle tone, which I guess is cool, but I doubt they can unleash a full-blown attack in battle. Chili gives us food for the animals, and we pet them, then come across something that looks like a giant armadillo with a saddle-like shell. I climb on top and yell, "Go, mousy, go!" But it's as slow as a tortoise.

Jayse finds another and we race each other, shouting at our rides and scaring away other animals. Chili watches and laughs, then the keeper tells us that we're being disrespectful and asks us to leave.

Until lunch, we stroll down the northern beach near Mrs. Raidyne's house. Every few steps, we pick up shells and try skipping them over the waves. Jayse tells me that when he was younger, he used to escape the palace to this beach. It was where he first met Gediyon, where Gediyon first told him about the sea angel, and where they spent most of their early friendship.

We eat lunch at a restaurant in the city, and the people here are a lot friendlier than the servants in the palace. We gather a lot of stares and I hear people whispering about "how darling" we look together.

When we start back to the palace, I'm already planning Jayse's amazing day, but he tells me there's more to do. We take the telesphere to a mysterious hall that echoes with every step. Chandeliers hang above, but only a couple are lit. Darker rectangles are spaced evenly along the wall, where portraits might've hung in the past.

"Our ancestors used this more than we have," Jayse says.

"What is it?" I ask, but Jayse wants me to find out on my own.

The room at the end is dark, but Jayse takes out a small jar of moonglow and lights our way. The room is spacious and staircases curve in wide spirals. Jayse leads me to a door, and on the way, we pass a ticket office. Is this place a theater?

The door leads into a narrower hall, probably backstage. As we pass by smaller rooms, I see the reflection of the jar light stretch along the walls and mirrors. These must be the dressing rooms.

Then a thought hits me, and I have to bite on my lip to stop myself from laughing.

"Did you see that?" I squeal, trying not to sound too happy.

"What?"

"I think it was a demon!"

"A *what*?" He swings around and shoves me behind him, lighting the hall with the jar, but nothing is there.

I laugh, slap him on the back, and say, "Just kidding! Ah, you people are funny to play with."

He glares at me.

"What are we doing here, anyway?"

"It's an extra special surprise," he says in a high voice, continuing down the hall.

"Are you making fun of me?"

He only laughs.

One more door is at the end of the hall. I can tell that the room on the other side is humongous because of the echo when he opens it. I follow him closely on stage. He puts down the moonglow jar behind one of the wing curtains and pulls me center stage.

"Don't worry," he says. "No one is watching."

I look out to the audience, where I see nothing but black. Besides the dim glow from the jar behind the curtain, it's hard to see anything else. My heart beats faster, and despite what Jayse just told me, I'm afraid the lights will turn on and expose the entire kingdom watching us on stage.

But what are we doing here?

Jayse walks downstage and picks something up. As soon as he touches it, it radiates a pale peach light. It looks like a crystal box the size of a grapefruit.

"This was one of the things I was working on," he says. "You saw the rest of the ships return yesterday, right?"

"Uh-huh."

He hands me the box. "This came with the last of them. Open it."

The box is multi-faceted and the light casts prisms on the wooden stage floor. I release the box latch and lift it open.

I nearly drop it when I see what streams out. Warm light streaks out into the theater, dancing around me in a circle, and as it's exposed to the air, it takes on a new form—bodies, smiling faces. It speaks to me.

The first woman recorded in light says, "Your Serene Divinity, you've truly blessed us with this gift. We have barely survive the Famine in the past, but this gives us hope."

A man says, "I've lost many sons in past years, but this is the first time I have faith that I may live to see grandchildren."

A young girl simply says, "Thank you, Miss Goddess!"

As soon as they're done speaking, the figures swirl away and someone else replaces them. Some of them overlap each other, all thanking me and telling me that I've restored their hopes. I recognize some of their clothes from Lereli, the West Wind, and Mediscus Heights, but I see many more in exotic fashion with piercings, tattoos, and outrageous hairdos. They have different accents, some are dead serious, and others scream in joy. A few even apologize for thinking that I was an incompetent Goddess, because my Counter-Famine proved them wrong.

"Thank you, Goddess."

"Thank you."

"You have blessed us."

When they're done speaking, their faces vanish into swirling light, which hangs in the air like smoke.

"This is something people will never forget," Jayse says. "It's a selfish thing to ask, but if you can eliminate the Famine, then we would love it if you'd… Did I do something wrong?"

I was hoping he wouldn't notice, but it's probably hard to miss my screwed-up face. I sniff and smile, but I can't hide my falling tears. I wipe them away and say, "No, it's fine! It's awesome. It's just… It's stupid, but I am happy! I'm not sad at all."

I let the box slip out of my hands and it clinks against the stage. I let out a sob and Jayse hugs me.

"It's stupid! I don't know why I'm crying."

"As long as you're not upset, it's okay."

"I didn't think I'd have this big of an impact on so many people." I rest my cheek on his shoulder. Unless my makeup is magically waterproof, it's probably smearing all over his expensive clothes. "Thanks Jayse. I'm fine now."

He steps back and picks up the box. Some of the residual light is still swirling around us, dimming. He waits for me to dry the rest of my tears and then he leads me back to the lobby.

"Are you sure you're all right? If I knew it was going to make you cry—"

I shake my head. "Really. That's one of the sweetest things anyone has ever done for me."

We don't say anything until we reach the tele-sphere. By then, my tears are gone, and I force myself to smile. I wait for Jayse to take me back, but he still looks upset.

"There's something else I need to say. Though everyone would love it if you'd stay here, it's your choice." He looks me in the eyes. "Do you still want to go back home?"

I have to look away from him. This might be one of the most difficult questions anyone has ever asked me. I already know the answer, and I've been thinking about it for so long, but I don't know how to say it now.

He says, "You can think about it, if you need to. You don't have to answer—"

"No. I *need* to go back." I almost choke when I say, "I can't die here. Maybe…maybe the Cycle will stop, too."

He takes a deep breath, then slowly nods. "Everyone back home probably misses you."

I laugh and shake my head. "Not everyone. Just a few people."

He sighs. "Well, everyone here will miss you." He touches the tele-sphere. "Now there's something else I need to show you. The second part of my gift."

The light surrounds us, and we reappear in the Temple of the Universal Mirror, but now equipment lines the perimeter of the building, leading up to the Mirror. It vaguely resembles what Aaron did to our garage.

"Gare finished it today," Jayse tells me. "It will reverse your trip to Starrs, and take you back to Tyme." He looks at me. "You can go as early as tomorrow."

"But Jayse! I haven't given you *your* super awesome day!"

He shrugs and grins. "That's okay! Because, uh…" He looks around in case anyone is eavesdropping, then says, "After I take care of a few things, I plan to go to your world as well."

"*Really*?"

"Then we can have a…*super* day there. But don't get your hopes up yet. It might take a while to convince my parents. And if they say no, I'll just run away."

I laugh. "You're really gonna do this?"

He shrugs. "Are you?"

I lower my gaze. "I have to go home."

He sighs and pats me on the shoulder. "Well, if it's your last day in Starrs, then we need to make sure you say good bye to everyone who'll miss you!"

Chapter Twenty-Eight
The Tyme Portal

I suggested to my maids that I could simply wear the clothes I wore when I came to Tyme, but they jabbered away about dishonoring themselves and me, so I followed through with their exuberant plan. I'm dressed more like I'm going to a cotillion than returning to Earth.

The gown reaches the floor. Yards of fluffy, almost weightless tulle drapes from my hips, and like last time, Mirra has whipped an air petticoat for me. It's so airy, I'm almost afraid that I'll take off flying.

The bodice is form-fitting and makes my waist look tinier than ever; it's beaded and embroidered with the finest lace I could ever imagine, like a genius spider spun the threads. It's more revealing than the other dresses I've worn, but my maids cover my bare shoulders with an elaborate and heavy diamond necklace that accentuates my collarbones. I know I could gain a fortune if I auction off the necklace, but I wouldn't dare myself to let go of it once I'm back home.

The dress is white and silver, beautiful by itself, but in the slightest glow of sunlight, the dress casts an aura around me, like I'm an angel. Like a Goddess.

"You're such a doll!" Simmy squeals. "I'll miss dressing you, and fetching you food and clothes…"

Mirra and Canaria nod, murmur, and sigh in agreement. I look away from my reflection and turn to face them.

"You guys are awesome—I'm gonna miss you guys, too." I spread out my arms. "C'mon! Group hug!"

They surround me, but they're careful about what they touch, because they don't want to disturb my hair, jewels, or clothes. It's an awkward hug, but I can tell how much I mean to them.

"Now let us move you along! The entire kingdom is waiting!"

Hold on, the entire kingdom? No one told me the entire kingdom was going to see me off. I guess that's why they dressed me so fancy. Now I jitter with nerves. My hands sweat through my delicate lace gloves, but at least my feet stick to the insides of my heels; they won't slip off while I walk. I follow my maids to the tele-sphere.

Instead of the Temple of the Universal Mirror, they lead me to the palace entrance. The king and queen wait there for me, also wearing white, gold, and silver.

"All of Arriscyal is present to bid you farewell, Goddess Michelle," King Oresonn tells me.

"Byran has connected auditory spheres to the one at the end of this platform," Queen Trissa says. "Everyone in Arriscyal can hear your good-bye."

"So I'm making a speech?" I say.

They nod.

Funny, I don't feel as dreadful as I thought I would have, maybe because I actually know what I'm going to say. I hope I don't mess up in front of the entire kingdom.

They lead me through the room, but instead of stepping down stairs, we continue onto an almost transparent walkway that floats above and stretches beyond the palace waterfalls. The floor of the platform has a white design engraved into it, like what surrounds the tele-sphere.

Byran and Jayse stand at the end of the walkway. Jayse is dressed like his parents, smiling at me in anticipation, and my brain thinks it's appropriate to make every footstep, bird chirp, and crowd murmur sound like the wedding march. At least I don't have a veil.

I try hard not to look like a gracious bride, so consequently I look even more clumsy. I swing my arms, bounce on the balls of my feet, grin like I don't know what a smile is, and I say, "Hey guys."

A split second later, I hear my voice echo throughout the kingdom. I guess the clear sphere that floats between Byran and Jayse is a microphone.

"Are you ready?" Byran asks, grinning like me.

I shrug, saying nothing because I'm afraid I'll sound stupid.

Jayse steps close to me and whispers, "The king and queen already announced your arrival, so they're ready for your speech when you are."

He steps back, allowing me to reach the auditory sphere, but he underestimates its sensitivity when he says in a normal voice, "By the way, you look magnificent," because his voices echoes and the kingdom murmurs with laughter.

Byran guffaws and I try not to laugh as I watch Jayse escape the platform. His cheeks have turned a very cute shade of pink.

With someone else's embarrassment at my disposal, I feel more comfortable walking to the bubble. I look at the kingdom surrounding me and try to brush away the vertigo when I look straight down.

"Good morning, everyone," I say, but my voice sounds different—like it ought to belong to a goddess. At least my appearance matches.

"I've heard many thanks for helping everyone in the past few days," I say. "But really, I should be thanking *you*, for making me feel like I'm actually worth something. Back home, I'm nobody, but you've helped me see my potential. If there were an easier way, I would love to stay here and continue helping you, but… I don't belong in Starrs.

"I need to go back home to my friends and family. You've helped me grow up here, but I need to live a normal life again.

"I know someday I'll return, and that's when I'm actually meant to live in Starrs—when I'm reborn here. I wish I could save all the memories that I made here. I wish I could remember them when I come back. But if I can't, then I promise you, when I do come back, I'll be a better Goddess for everyone. I'll learn the ways of the Creator and do what Goddess is supposed to. I won't be incompetent anymore."

I lower my head. "I'm sorry this speech wasn't any longer, but I'll keep it short and sweet. Thanks again, and I don't ever want to forget any of you. Good bye."

As soon as I step away from the sphere, the kingdom bursts into a deafening roar of applause and cheers. I purse my lips and try to stop myself from crying. I meet King Oresonn and Queen Trissa halfway down the platform, and they say something to me, but I can't hear it.

We have to take the palace entrance tele-sphere to the Universal Mirror. Taking it this time feels different—maybe because I'm in the presence of not just any couple, but the king and queen. They stand behind me when we enter the tele-sphere. Maybe it's so weird taking it because this is the last time I'll use it.

Now I think about all the "lasts." The last time I rode the gondola, the last time I saw Gediyon use his magic, the last time Jayse healed me… I wonder, if he does make it to Tyme with me, will he still be able to use his powers? I know I won't.

Gediyon waits by the entrance of the Universal Mirror, and as soon as I see that he's here, I run toward him and give him a hug. We already saw each other the night before when I said good bye to everyone, but I feel special knowing that he's seeing me off here. I feel a stronger flush of warmth when I see that he's wearing the spice pin on the lapel of his vest.

"Your speech was wonderful," he tells me.

I squeeze him harder. I'm short enough and he's tall enough that I can hear his heartbeat in this position. His simple warmth reminds me of a kitchen, tea, and cookies.

"I'm going to miss you," I say, even though I already told him last night.

I feel his hand on my head and he says, "We're all going to miss you, and everyone wishes you the best of luck on your normal life back in Tyme."

Yeah, I might need it. The first week of the new school year has already passed, and who knows if I have a missing person's report? Returning to a normal life isn't going to be as easy as I had hoped. I know people are going to ask me questions, like did someone kidnap me? But I'll say no, I'm perfectly fine, I just needed some me-time.

But what about Aaron? What if the cops had arrested him for manslaughter or something? I wrap my arms tighter around Gediyon when I think about this. I'll have to explain everything to the authorities, then.

What about Jayse if he makes it through?

I pull away from Gediyon and look back at Jayse. He stands next to the mirror with Gare, and Queen Trissa stands on the other side. King Oresonn is talking to my maids.

I lower my voice and say, "Jayse said that he's going to try to visit me. Do you think, maybe, you can come too?"

"I would love to see your world, but with my power, I don't know if that's the wisest decision."

"That's the thing, though! Back home, no one has any kind of power, so maybe yours will disappear too."

"Perhaps…" Gediyon sighs and places his hands on my shoulders. "Even so, it'll be difficult for me to leave this world behind."

I sigh too. "That's okay. I want you to stay here and figure out about your past. I just don't want this to be the last time we see each other."

"It won't be." He smiles. "In another life, we'll meet again."

I smirk. "Okay then." I hug him and pull away, holding his hands. "I'll never forget you."

"Good bye, Michelle."

"Bye, Gediyon."

I turn away and have to stiffen my lips to prevent myself from tearing up. I step across the carpet to the Universal Mirror. Gare sets a heavy metal block on the floor in front of the Mirror, and Jayse walks toward me.

"Are you ready?"

I shrug. "Let's assume that no matter what I say, I don't really want to leave, but this is something I have to do."

He smiles.

Gare says, "Mind your eyes," and bright lights flare up around the perimeter of the temple. I have to shut my eyes for a while. When I reopen them, Jayse is glowing.

I guess I am too, because Jayse says, "You truly are Goddess."

"I'm nobody back home."

He hugs me and whispers, "I'll see you there. I'll search for you."

"Tyme isn't like Starrs. People will think you're crazy."

"Well, I'm not. I'll find you."

I really want to kiss him, but I feel like that will seal something, like this will be the last time I see him…like the Prince Imposter's good-bye.

So no. I vow that this won't be the last time I see him. I can kiss him later.

"You'd better find me," I say. "If not, I'll find you."

"How about between you and me, whoever can find the other first…"

"That's not really fair if we're both looking for each other!"

Gare clears his throat. "I can't leave this open forever."

Jayse and I back away from each other. I whisper, "I'll see you again," and he mouths, "I know."

The light that surrounds us is like a dream. I can't see beyond the temple pillars, and Gediyon and the others at the back are mere silhouettes. Gare nods to me and he instructs me to kneel before the metal block, which is directly in front of the Mirror's central panel.

This is much more grand and beautiful, but the set up of the light and mirrors is a lot like what Aaron did in our garage back home.

"Miss Goddess, if you will," Gare says, "bow forward and place your forehead on the block."

I do so, and I feel like I'm pressing against a cloud when I lean into my dress. In the bowing position, I can't see anything but darkness. I feel my lashes press against the cold metal.

"Thank you, Gare."

I don't know if he knows how to say "You're welcome," because he just clears his throat. I hear him press some things, then he says, "Farewell, Goddess Michelle."

My senses accelerate forward into the Universal Mirror, and then I feel nothing. Just my own thoughts.

This is exactly how I felt when I first came to Starrs, but I'm a bit more at ease. I know what's coming to me now.

I'll be back in the garage…

If Aaron even has the equipment set up in the garage.

"I cannot permit your return."

The voice echoes around me, but I don't see its source. It's a man's voice.

"Why have you cursed me so?"

It sounds like my voice, but the words aren't mine. I see a shimmer of light, like cloth riding a soft breeze.

The other voice speaks again. "We need your help, Goddess."

The wave of light disappears and sucks away the voices with a ghostly reverb. I try to reach for them, strain myself to hear more.

Unlike their voices, mine has no presence here. "Are you not gonna let me leave?"

"Pesaeton!"

I gasp and turn my head toward the voice. Floating there is the image of the angel who greeted me when I first came here, but she's obscured—like I see her through a broken mirror.

"You must stop this," she continues.

I float between Saei and who I presume is Pesaeton. He's no different than the way he appears in the Universal Mirror. His back is to me, and he's veiled in a dark mist.

"Saei," he says. "Can you not see that this power is yours? This is your creation… Will you not destroy it as well?"

"If you are not careful, you will sever the bridges between the other worlds."

This time, the dark mist of Pesaeton devours Saei's light. It drains away into the core of his being, then he flows away like an encircling eel.

"Goddess. Goddess," he says, his voice becoming more distorted, beastly, and less human each time he repeats the word.

The last thing he says sounds like the howling wind.

"Goddess, what have you done to me?"

The snaking mist expands into the crude image of a wide jaw, diving at me faster than a train—

"Michelle."

Suddenly I feel the soft tulle hanging from my waist and a warm light shines through my eyelids. Goddess Saei.

"You have not yet fulfilled your duty as the Creator of Starrs," she continues. "Though you may leave Starrs and return to Tyme, it is not without risk. Your life and memories as you know them may be lost in this transfer between universes. If you return to Tyme now, the Cycle will take over and you will not even have a home to return to. It is, in fact, safer for you and the Cycle if you remain on Starrs to fulfill your duty."

It's hard to swallow. All the hope I had that I can live a normal life again, all the good-byes, and now this?

"So you're saying I can't go home?"

Saei nods. "That is correct."

"Why? Because this…*Cycle* says so? What *is* the Cycle, anyway?"

"The governor of life and death, of memories and incarnation." She lowers her head. "In Starrs, the Cycle of the Six Moons is Lord Pesaeton's punishment for that with which I cursed him. His trials must be halted at the Sixth Moon, and that is your responsibility."

Responsibility on top of more responsibility.

"I just want to go home." I sound pathetic.

"Then it was best for you to stay home. It is your decision now, Michelle. Return to Tyme, even though it will disappear within four months, or remain on Starrs and put an end to the Cycle."

Maybe this is the extra incentive I need. I've been telling myself I have to leave because I don't want to die here, but I've spent almost two months here and I'm still alive. Everyone believes in me, so surely I can last another four. And then can I go home?

Can I?

I don't want to think about it too much, but I can't let my home disappear. I can't allow everyone on Starrs to suffer the Cycle's wrath. It is my responsibility, isn't it? After all, I was the one who breached it.

I look right into Saei's eyes and tell her, "I'll stay."

Saei nods, and her curls of hair dissipate like smoke. The darkness around us lightens to the color of sky, and I hear the lingering echo of her voice: "Good luck."

It's just like last time. Gravity takes over, and I fall.

The sun is high in the sky. It's midday, only a few wispy clouds, and I see two moons in the sky. I haven't seen one of them before.

I'm back in Starrs. I don't even scream when I realize that this time, I'm not going to land in water.

Chapter Twenty-Nine
The Last Summer Failure

It's like lying in a lush meadow. Cool and breezy—the wind brushes atop the flowers and they're so sweet that I can taste them. The sun warms my cheeks, but flower petals protect my skin from burning.

A hand—firm but comforting, the very touch tingling like menthol running through my veins—grips into mine and pulls away a lingering ache from the core of my body.

When I open my eyes, I realize I'm not in a meadow after all. I see the leafy ceiling of my room in Arriscyal. My balcony doors are open, and the sheer fabric flutters over the head of my bed.

Sitting at my bedside, reaching over the blankets is Jayse, smiling and holding my hands. He looks as if he hasn't had a full night's rest for a while, but still—

"Have I told you how pretty your eyes are?"

He lets out a breathy laugh, then says, "How are you feeling?"

"Comfortable." Then I realize, "Hungry."

"Then we'll bring you whatever you want to eat!" He sighs. "I healed you as soon as I could. We found you near the southern

Highbridge. Madam Manasa was taking care of you, and she told us that you had decided to stay on Starrs."

I grunt in agreement. "I need to take care of the Cycle."

"It's the first of Hermise now." He chuckles. "I guess I won't get to see your super awesome Tyme."

I smile. "Now I feel stupid for saying bye to everyone."

He laughs. "But they're glad you're back!"

I stretch out my arms to hug him, and he has to flop onto the bed to reach me. Just as he wraps his arms around me, I hear squealing, and at once I know it's my maids.

"Isn't that just the sweetest?" Simmy says.

"Michelle, you're awake!" Mirra says.

"I totally didn't have to say bye to you guys!"

They line up on the other side of my bed and smile at me. Jayse stands, helps prop up the pillows behind me, and I push myself into a sitting position.

"You've healed quite well, Michelle," Mirra says.

I point at Jayse. "Thanks to my buddy here."

"Sir Gediyon was here as well," Canaria says, "but he left to fetch you flowers."

"Aw, that's nice."

Canaria continues, "His Majesty has also informed us that the Temple debris has fallen in Dissett."

"Wait a minute, the Temple debris?"

"The building shattered when you left," Jayse says. "No one was hurt badly—I healed them, of course. We thought the remains would've fallen into the ocean, but…"

"I've already asked for permission to help repair the city," Canaria says. "And then I might help with the Ceremony of Crescent Starrs!"

Jayse looks at me. "We should go, too! The priests there know more about the Cycle than even Gare. They can help you find a way to stop Pesaeton!"

I sigh. "Since I'm here to stay, I'm going to need all the help I can get."

I guess learning how to save the world beats US history, chemistry, or pre-calculus any day.

My summer vacation is officially over, but I'm still the Goddess of Starrs.

End of Book One

Acknowledgements

I'd first like to thank Mrs. McCarty for teaching me TOK for one year and English for two. I have such a different perspective on writing and life because of you. If it weren't for writer's club in high school and the support I found there, I'm not sure how far I would have continued with my writing. You're the best, and I'M SORRY I CAN'T CALL YOU LINDA.

A big thank you to my voice acting friends who brought my characters to life in the promotional shorts. Thank you Caleb Hyles for voicing Aaron, John Archer for voicing Gediyon, Patrick M. Seymour for voicing Mayor Rayel, Elissa Park for voicing Dreana, River Kanoff for voicing Wolf, and Steven Kelly for voicing Jayse. You guys are awesome and I'm ever so grateful and humbled that you had stepped forth to do such a little thing. I'd also like to thank all of my friends who took the time to audition and spread the word about the project.

Thanks to Brandon Lacey for making the amazing cover art. Check out more of his work and commission him at blue-paint-sea.deviantart.com!

Next, thanks to all of my cool, supportive friends. My college roomies, Jennifer and Sue. My PAHLS—Patdy, Angela, Lady, and Shana. Antonette for always being there whenever I need to vent.

And the most extroverted but possibly most supportive of all, Tadao.

To all the friends whose support never wavered, thank you so much for believing in me.

Thanks to my parents for giving me a place to rest and food to eat :P Thanks to my older sister for giving me character fuel without knowing it. Thanks to my baby sister for being the first one to sit down and listen to the entire story, because I kind of forced you into it. Love you ♥

About the Author

Adelle Yeung is a voice-over artist who can't go a day without a cup of tea. When she's not writing or recording, she enjoys sewing costumes, baking sweets, and escaping on video game adventures. She lives in California with a cat that dreams of eating the pet bird.

Visit Adelle's web page at **AdelleYeung.com**

Follow Adelle Yeung on Facebook.
Facebook.com/AdelleYeungBooks

The Cycle of the Six Moons Trilogy

✦ Book Two ✦
An Eclipsing Autumn

✦ Book Three ✦
The Last Winter Moon

Made in the USA
San Bernardino, CA
30 January 2018